ISBN 978-1-331-51572-2
PIBN 10200524

1 MONTH OF
FREE
READING

at

www.ForgottenBooks.com

By purchasing this book you are eligible for one month membership to ForgottenBooks.com, giving you unlimited access to our entire collection of over 700,000 titles via our web site and mobile apps.

To claim your free month visit:
www.forgottenbooks.com/free200524

English
Français
Deutsche
Italiano
Español
Português

www.forgottenbooks.com

Mythology Photography **Fiction**
Fishing Christianity **Art** Cooking
Essays Buddhism Freemasonry
Medicine **Biology** Music **Ancient
Egypt** Evolution Carpentry Physics
Dance Geology **Mathematics** Fitness
Shakespeare **Folklore** Yoga Marketing
Confidence Immortality Biographies
Poetry **Psychology** Witchcraft
Electronics Chemistry History **Law**
Accounting **Philosophy** Anthropology
Alchemy Drama Quantum Mechanics
Atheism Sexual Health **Ancient History**
Entrepreneurship Languages Sport
Paleontology Needlework Islam
Metaphysics Investment Archaeology
Parenting Statistics Criminology
Motivational

THE ATHENIAN SOCIETY'S
PUBLICATIONS
V

HELIODORUS

(THE AETHIOPICA)

LITERALLY AND COMPLETELY TRANSLATED
FROM THE GREEK, WITH INTRODUCTION
AND NOTES

ATHENS : PRIVATELY PRINTED FOR THE
ATHENIAN SOCIETY : MDCCCXCVII

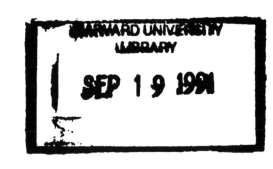

INTRODUCTION

It is not in the early literature of Greece and Rome that the romance of love and adventure must be looked for.[1] We can observe the remote origin of writings of this kind during the Attic period, we can follow its obscure development in the Alexandrine period, but it is not until the Roman period that its growth and perfection become perceptible.

We must not be surprised at the tardy recognition accorded by the ancients to a class of literature which is so popular amongst ourselves — distinguished from history by the admixture of fiction and the comparative unimportance of the events described; from poetry by the employment of prose and the representation of the manners of social life in place of the nearly always ideal picture of life in general. The fact is to be

[1] See Introduction to *Daphnis and Chloe.*

explained by the difference of manners and societies.

Amongst the peoples of modern times, the progress of the sciences and abstract studies has somewhat dried up the sources of poetical fables, and the political constitution of the great states of Europe, even of those where the greatest liberty is allowed to each citizen, does not allow public to absorb private life. In Greece and Rome, on the contrary, it was not until late that the imagination was sated with the marvellous as introduced in the epic fables ; and, as long as the turbulent freedom of the little Greek republics and the city of Rome occupied, in the Agora and in the *F*orum, the existence of nearly all the citizens, the picture of the ordinary circumstances of private life was capable of attracting, and at the same time, not strong enough, to retain its hold upon men's minds. Preference was given to the heroic spectacles of tragedy, and, in its first origin, even comedy itself only borrowed its interest from political passions. It was not until the time of Menander, that is to say, the period of the Macedonian conquest, that comedy became a picture of private life ; and

then it became possible for romance to make its appearance. No doubt the *Milesian Fables* may claim greater antiquity; but they were originally only simple oral recitals, like the *Phrygian Fables* or the Aesopian apologue, and they came into being in the midst of a society quite different from that of the other Greek populations — a society in which the enjoyments of private life caused the interests of public life to be forgotten.

In Greek society, before the Macedonian conquest, and in Roman society, before the Empire, everything concurred in retarding the development of these pictures of familiar life. In fact, in the young days of their republics, the Greeks and Romans had scarcely any time to devote to reading simply for the sake of amusement; their whole life was taken up by private and public affairs; literature itself was an active and, in a manner, a living literature, which addressed itself to hearers rather than readers, and filled the temples, the theatres, the festivals, the law courts, and the schools.

In proportion as the activity of public life died out in Greece and Rome,

the taste for pictures of manners was bound to spread. Already, in Euripides, we see tragedy departing from its heroic traditions and manifesting a taste for romantic pictures of *bourgeois* life; in the "*Flower*" of Agathon, tragedy is nothing but a romance. The New Comedy sprang up under the successors of Alexander. It must be observed that, in the works of Menander, Alexis, and Philemon, the family sanctuary is not yet open, and that these poets limit themselves to describing courtesans, young men and women, fathers, and slaves. We may believe that, at the same period, the *Milesian Fables* made their way from Ionia to Greece, the authors of which, more audacious, no doubt cast indiscreet glances upon the interior of the household; but these fables were only short stories, very different from the lengthy narratives to which the Roman period gave birth. It is not until then that writers such as Petronius, Lucian, Apuleius, Iamblichus, Heliodorus, and Achilles Tatius appeared. A new era had also commenced for the ancient world; with the Empire, an end was put to republican manners and public life;

excess of liberty had strangled liberty; there were no longer any citizens; private individuals had ample leisure, which they were able to occupy by frivolous reading, and the rhetoricians took advantage of the idleness of the wealthy classes to launch into their midst interminable romances of love and adventure.

The East is the true country of stories of this nature, because the East has been from all time the land of political slavery and private life. It is in the East that we find the oldest examples of compositions of this kind; it is in the Greek countries most exposed to contact with Oriental civilisation, that is to say, in Asia Minor, that the first attempts of romantic literature among the Greeks made their appearance, and it is there, above all, that later they find their development. Ionia has produced the *Milesian Fables;* Iamblichus, the author of the *Babylonica,* was born in Syria, as was Lucian, the author of *Lucius*[1] and the *True History;* Heliodorus came from Emesa in Phoenicia, Achilles Tatius from Alexandria. Cyprus, Antioch, and

[1] This is not universally admitted.

Ephesus have given birth to three romance-writers each named Xenophon.

It is impossible to deny that the influence of Oriental fancy has inclined certain imaginations to the marvellous and extraordinary, and in this manner favoured, in Greece, the development of romantic compositions ; but it seems less probable that the Greek Romance is the direct product of Oriental stories.[1] The character of the Oriental stories and the Greek Romances is not, in general, the same. In spite of a number of somewhat unnatural and improbable pictures, the whole colouring of the latter is Greek, even to the pictures of Eastern life. The marvellous, which holds a certain place in some of these fabulous narratives, never exhibits the breadth and simplicity of the marvellous which is so predominant in the Eastern stories. The taste for romance has passed from the East into Greece, but romance has become transformed. We know how readily the Greek race assimilated and stamped with the impress of its genius all that it borrowed from foreign civilisations. The

[1] As maintained by Huet, in his *Lettre à Segrais sur l'origine des romans.*

Greeks were naturally story-tellers; before fabulous narratives became, in the hands of the rhetoricians, a form of literature, they had told tales in abundance, in which the Eastern influence might have lost itself and disappeared. Such were the stories told by mothers and nurses to their children, by the idlers in the barbers' shops, by parasites and guests at banquets. Even in the highways of Athens there were to be found persons who made it their profession to relate stories for the amusement of the passers-by, like *Philepsius* in the *Plutus* of Aristophanes.

These oral tales were of various kinds. There were moral tales, after the style of the Aesopian apologue, and the *Libyan Fable*; humorous and satirical tales, to which the *Sybaritic Fables* had given rise. In their origin, these fables, which were sometimes called the *Sybaritic Apophthegms*, were not so much stories as witty anecdotes and sayings, like those which Aristophanes (in the *Wasps*) puts into the mouth of Philocleon.

But it is doubtful whether the *Sybaritic Fables* always preserved their primitive simplicity, and the close alliance between

Sybaris and Miletus seems in time to have confounded these stories with the *Milesian Fables*. We have mentioned the stories which had the greatest vogue amongst the ancients, both when they were still transmitted orally, and when, later, they were collected, altered, or imitated by various writers. But it was a far cry from these brief and fugitive stories to the long romances which were later composed by the rhetoricians.

Before we proceed to devote our attention to these romances, it is necessary to cast a rapid glance upon the stories which gave birth to them.

It was natural that the elegant and effeminate Ionia should be a centre of erotic tales. The very name of the Ionians recalls the people most happily gifted of all the Hellenes, the people in whose midst were very early developed poetry, philosophy, music, architecture— all the elegances and delicacies of civilisation, but also the people most inclined to the refinements of sensual pleasure.

Subject in turn to the rule of the Lydians and Persians, they had always been more anxious for comfort than for liberty, which in their opinion consisted

in the absence of all restraint in their pleasures. A Sybarite remarked, " In all my travels I have only found one free city, Miletus." Miletus, the birth-place of Aspasia and so many courtesans, as famous as those of Corinth, afforded, in fact, the model of the kind of inde-pendence which won for it the admiration of the inhabitants of Sybaris and estab-lished friendly relations between the two cities. Miletus, like Sybaris, gave birth to a host of agreeable, but mostly licen-tious stories, which spread throughout Greece, together with the renown of these two cities, the taste for their pleasures.

In vain was Miletus desolated by the Persian War; in vain was Sybaris de-stroyed; the *Milesian* and *Sybaritic Tales* succeeded to the prosperity of both. These tales formed the delight of degenerate Rome. After the defeat at Carrhae, a collection of stories of this kind was found amongst the baggage of a Roman officer, and the *Surena* read it to the Senate of Seleucia, to give them an idea of the manners of the arrogant people who claimed to be able to subjugate the Parthians.[1] Albinus (the rival of

[1] See *Plutarch*, Life of Crassus, ch. 32.

Septimius Severus), who was for some time Emperor, occupied the leisure which his ambition permitted him in reading Apuleius and composing Milesian Tales, which his courtiers considered excellent, but for which his historian professes only a moderate regard.[1]

The most famous of the *Milesian Tales* was that which was composed (it is not known when) by a certain Aristides of Miletus and translated into Latin by Lucius Cornelius Sisenna. It is twice mentioned by Ovid, who seems to say that the work was presented in the form of a history. The work probably contained, together with a short sketch of Milesian history, various anecdotes of Milesian life. These anecdotes were Milesian Tales. Similar works had already been composed by a certain Hegesippus and some other writers, whom Parthenius of Nicaea mentions without naming. In the love-stories written by this grammarian, we find several Milesian tales, for we must, no doubt, regard as such, not only those which Parthenius borrowed from Hegesippus or some writer

[1] See *Scriptores Historiae Augustae*, Vita Albini, by Julius Capitolinus, ch. 11-12.

of *Milesian Histories*, but also those of which the scene is laid at Miletus, and which have for their subject the incontinence of the women of this city. The memory of these tales lingers in all the erotic narratives of antiquity, especially the oldest. One of the interlocutors in Lucien's *Amores*, speaking of similar stories which he has just heard, calls them *Milesian Tales*. Apuleius merely strung together several stories of this kind, such as the history of the amorous step-mother, and the story of the " washing-tub," from which La Fontaine has borrowed.

It seems doubtful whether the fable of *Psyche* should be included, although purely imaginative fictions somewhat obliterate its originally allegorical character. The Milesian Tales gave more room to the senses than to sentiment. At most, there was intermingled some moral lesson, as in one of Parthenius's stories; or some satirical meaning, as in the *Ephesian Matron*. This last story, one of the incidental episodes of Petronius, no doubt also came to him from Ionia.

Perhaps Ephesus, like Miletus, had her erotic literature; in Xenophon she

produced her Aristides. At any rate, like Miletus, this city was famous for its fondness for pleasure, and it is in one of the two that the Greek romance writers, as a rule, place the scene of their stories.

The Milesian Tales exhibit the first form of the erotic tales of antiquity. They were slight and hasty sketches, like the *Fabliaux* of the Middle Ages (only in prose) and the *Nouvelles* of Boccacio's *Decameron*, or the *Heptameron* of Marguerite of Navarre. Intended solely to amuse and excite sensual imaginations, they at first had no literary pretensions, and, being more natural, were the more agreeable Perhaps, as a rule, they were not longer than the stories of the same kind which were extracted from various historians by Parthenius of Nicaea to furnish his friend Cornelius Gallus with subjects for elegy. We see from the work of Parthenius, from a similar collection of stories by Plutarch, from some of the *Narratives* of Conon, and the *Varia Historia* of Aelian, that the influence of the Milesian Tales made itself felt even in history, into which it introduced a number of erotic and, for the most part, imaginary episodes.

Such were the stories relating to Rhodopis the courtesan. According to some, she built one of the pyramids of Egypt by inviting each of her lovers to bring a stone ; according to others, she became queen of Egypt thanks to the loss of her slipper, like Cinderella. The name of Rhodopis is as dear to the Greek romance-writers as that of Helen is to the poets. In *Theagenes and Chariclea*, the seductions of another Rhodopis nearly triumphed over the austerity of a high priest of Memphis ; and in *Leucippe and Clitophon*, we meet with another Rhodopis, but this time so pure and virtuous as to provoke the wrath of the goddess of Love. Plutarch, in his *Moralia*, mentions, together with the Panthea of Xenophon, the Timoclea of Aristobulus and the Thebe of Theopompus. This list might be increased by the stories of this class which have been extracted from history by Conon, Parthenius, and Plutarch.

The Milesian Tale passed from history into the writings of philosophers. It has left its traces in the *Symposium* of Xenophon, the *Treatise upon Love* by Clearchus of Soli, some similar works

by Theophrastus, Ariston of Iulis, Spho-
drius the Cynic, Favorinus of Arles, and
some of the intermingled dialogues and
stories which Plutarch has left us. It
was not until considerably later (perhaps
shortly before the time of Petronius)
that the love-stories, so brief in the
Milesian *Fables*, so rapid when they
were intermingled with history and his-
torical or philosophical romances, under-
went extended developments. The an-
cient stories of the Milesian class were
sometimes preserved, in the form of
episodes, in the lengthy romances which
came into being during the Roman and
Byzantine periods; but, as a rule, they
were lost in fuller and more extended
narratives, which embraced a longer
period of time and surrounded the prin-
cipal incident and the chief characters
with a number of secondary incidents and
characters. The transition from the tale
to the romance did not take place with-
out an effort.

It is sufficient to compare the *Lucius*
and the *Metamorphoses* of Apuleius to see
how completely artificial was the method
which combined a number of episodic
tales with the fable of romance, and how
obvious the " soldering " was.

Few stories, in ancient times, met with as great success as the tale of Lucius transformed into an ass by a magic ointment, and afterwards restored to human form by eating roses. It was not only an erotic story, it was a tale of a fantastic character, which was highly popular in ancient days. While the poets fed the popular imagination with stories of the Olympian Gods and Goddesses, superstition continually multiplied tales of supernatural beings and marvellous occurrences. In order to make children good, they were told amusing fables, such as those of Æsop; in order to turn them from evil ways, they were frightened with terrible stories about Lamias, Gorgons, Ephialtes, Mormolyx, Empusa, and Manducus, the ogres and ogresses of antiquity. Then, as the empire of credulity is not limited to the days of childhood, people of all ages allowed themselves to be terrified by stories of evil spirits, spiteful genii by whom the air was peopled—phantoms and ghosts.

When, about the first century of the Christian era, the passion for magic took possession of the whole pagan world, this kind of marvellous story opened an un-

limited field to the fancy of the narrator.
We have already seen an indication of
this in the *Heroica* of Philostratus. Love
romances borrowed several of their episodes
from fantastic stories; there is not a single
one of them which dispenses with this
method of affording pleasure, a sure
means of gaining the approval of the
readers of their time. How can we be
astonished at this, when even history
itself did not dispense with it, as we may
see from the spirit which Plutarch intro-
duces as appearing to Brutus before the
battle of Philippi? The compilations of
Apollonius and Phlegon of Tralles, which
have been preserved to us under the
title of "Wonderful Histories," contain
several stories of this kind, with which,
in some cases, is intermingled the artifice
of an ingenious fiction. Lucian, in a
dialogue called "The Liar," gives us a
regular series of fantastic stories, which
were current in his time, one of which
has furnished Goethe with his story of
the "Sorcerer Pupil." But, if the philo-
sopher quizzed the superstitious beliefs
of his time, the wit did not disdain to
make use of them in his turn as the
subject for his refined badinage. He is

believed to be the author of *Lucius*, which
he wrote by way of diversion, just as his
contemporary, the Platonist Apuleius,
amused himself with the *Metamorphoses*.

Was the work which we possess under
the title of *Lucius* written by Lucian?[1]
Again, as there is no doubt that the
subject produced at least two distinct
works, one attributed to Lucius of Patras,
and the other to Lucian, did the latter
imitate the former? or has some forger
imitated him while bringing his work out
in the name of Lucius of Patras? These
are questions which have exercised the
minds of the critics. To us it seems
clear that the subject was handled several
times in Greek; it must be older than
the version which has come down to us
as the work of Lucian. One of the
strangest scenes in the romance, the
monstrous adventure of the ass with the
lady of Patras, had its prototype in the
stories of Pasiphae as told by the poets,
and the daughter of Hippomenes as told
by the historians. Photius, who had
before him two Greek versions of this
romance, one by Lucius, the other by
Lucian, draws a comparison between

[1] See *Introduction* to Lucian.

the two. He reproaches the pretended Lucius with having spoken of all these wonders and enchantments in the tone of a man who believes what he relates; he prefers the narrative of Lucian, which he considers a humorous attack upon pagan superstitions. Most assuredly the false Lucius did not believe in his own metamorphoses any more than the author of the Luciad; but there is this difference between the two works that, while the one related in a dull and uninteresting style anecdotes that were sufficiently insipid in themselves, the other gave charm to his extravagances by the liveliness of his narrative. It seems to us that those critics are wrong who refuse to admit Lucian as the author of this work; tradition has attributed it to him, and the style is not unworthy of him. What is there improbable in his having done for the stories of the marvellous what he has done in his *True History* for the stories of imaginary voyages?

One of the merits of *Lucius* is its brevity. On the other hand, diffuse prolixity is the chief fault of the Metamorphoses of Apuleius, a fault which is nowhere more appreciable than when

dealing with humorous subjects. It is not known which of the two works has been imitated by Apuleius — that attributed to Lucius, or Lucian; but the author himself tells us that he is relating a *Greek* story. He further tells us that he has patched together various tales of the nature of the Milesian *Fables*. He thereby reveals to us the secret of his method of composition, which consists in repeating all the stories of the *Luciad*, and supplementing them by a number of accessory circumstances and episodical narratives. One only of these narratives is more valuable than the rest of the work—the story of *Psyche*. This is not original; it evidently comes from a Greek source, and goes back to a remote origin. This graceful story contrasts strangely with the licentious and sometimes obscene stories which Apuleius borrows from the *Luciad* or adds to it, with numerous immoral pictures which betray an age when the amours of Pasiphae and Leda were represented in the open amphitheatre.

Like the *Luciad* and the *Metamorphoses*, the work of Petronius owes its origin to the Milesian Tales, and contains others

which, taken as a whole, are superior to those of the romance of Apuleius. Besides this, Petronius possesses the advantage of a purer style and a more probable story; but, as far as morality is concerned, the *Satyricon* is even more offensive in its outspokenness and more revolting in its cynicism than the *Luciad* and the *Metamorphoses*. In these works, vice is at least not flaunted complacently, and various immoralities (especially such as those of Encolpius and Giton) are at times vigorously lashed; whereas the *Satyricon* is a gallery of pictures which are worse than obscene. But, if we can manage to overcome the disgust with which such a picture inspires us, it is impossible to forget this description of the wandering and disorderly life led by some of the youths of Rome, those profligate scholars and professional poets, who delivered harangues upon virtue in houses of ill-fame, who plied the trade of parasites, and who were at once profligates and rascals. This work describes, in the liveliest colours, the vices which, in imperial Rome, had infected not only the citizens of the lower orders, but even members of the highest society. It

is not surprising that it should have been confounded with the " history of the debaucheries of Nero, containing the details of all his immoralities, and the names of the profligate men and abandoned women who took part in them," a work written by Petronius a few hours before his death, and sent by his order to the Emperor.

The *Satyricon* supplements the *Satires* of Juvenal as a picture of Roman depravity, the extravagances of luxury, and the shocking inequality between the different classes. How vigorously the author sketches the stupidity and insolence of the wealthy! What a portrait is that of Trimalchion, the Amphitryon so arrogant towards his guests, the ignorant man so proud of his ignorance, the rich man who does not know the amount of his wealth, and who, hearing a " poor man " spoken of, asks what the term means; the master so merciless to his slaves, who has one of them flogged for dropping a silver dish, and afterwards orders the dish to be thrown upon the dung-heap, to show at one and the same time that he is an inexorably strict master and superior to all considerations of economy!

If Roman literature had not supplied us with " The Banquet of Trimalchion," we should lack a characteristic feature of the picture of the Roman aristocracy, so senseless in its extravagances, whose most mad caprices were unable to exhaust their wealth. Cicero had shown its greed and brutality in the case of Verres ; it was left for Petronius to show its absurdity in the case of Trimalchion. Nor is Trimalchion a fancy portrait ; we can find traces of him here and there in the works of the period. The vast estates possessed by Trimalchion, to the number of which he is eager to add, so as to be able to go from Italy to Sicily over his own property, remind us of the immense estates (*latifundia*) which, according to Pliny, were the ruin of Italy. And the melancholy reflections mingled with the descriptions of debauchery, the idea of death which is introduced after the most disgraceful witticisms, the banquet finished by the making of a will, strikingly remind us of the whim of a certain Pacuvius mentioned by Seneca, who wished that he could have the pleasure of being present at his own funeral.

In decaying societies, there are never

wanting protests against the corruption of manners and aspirations to a better state of things. But, of all those who express indignation at the boldness of vice, how many are there who are free from the disgraceful vices which they deplore? The virulent satires of Horace, Petronius and Juvenal do not prove that they had not themselves paid tribute to the vices of their times; their unblushing language scarcely tallies with virtue. The pure-minded are less inclined to lash vices, because this renders it necessary to describe them, than to praise the good and celebrate its triumphs. This was done in the second century by the Christian Dion Chrysostom. This honest man, the most philosophical of all the rhetoricians, and the greatest rhetorician of all the philosophers, filled in a manner amongst the heathen the office of a preacher of morality. We owe to him one of the few "moral tales" of antiquity, the *Huntsman*, or *Euboean History*.

This is not the only composition of Dion Chrysostom in which the purpose of amusing by means of an ingenious story and the idea of instructing by

means of salutary moral lessons are found combined. In addition to his *Libyan Fable* and his dialogues intermingled with stories of Diogenes the Cynic, he had composed several pieces of the nature of panegyrics, in which narrative holds an important place, the details of which are so fictitious and the moral purpose so obvious, that we feel tempted to regard them as short moral stories. We are speaking of the *First Melancomas* and *Charidemus*. The *First Melancomas* commences with a story prepared with too obtrusive artifice. Dion meets a friend and speaks of an athlete who has recently been victorious ; his interlocutor mentions another athlete, Melancomas, whom he opposes to the first as a model of beauty, manly vigour, and virtue ; he praises this athlete highly, and leaves Dion delighted at what he has just heard. Melancomas is no doubt an imaginary personage, and Dion had been previously commissioned to sing his praises. But what a difference there is between the two works ! The one has a purely authentic character, the other is purely imaginary. We should be glad to believe the same of the *Charidemus*, which also sings the praises

of a virtuous athlete—praises also introduced by an ingenious story.

Whatever we may think of these compositions, there is no doubt that Dion's *Euboean History* is a moral tale, and a model of its kind. It precedes *Daphnis and Chloe*, and is certainly superior to the latter in truthfulness of description and purity of sentiment ; it exhibits features worthy of the author of *Paul and Virginia*. It is a charming pastoral, the scene of which is well drawn, and the characters interesting, because they are real. Dion has enlivened his picture of rustic manners by describing two huntsmen instead of the shepherds, ox herds, and goatherds so familiar in eclogues. Their solitary but nevertheless happy life, poor yet hospitable, forms a striking but not too exaggerated contrast to the noisy, restless, and selfish life of the wealthy inhabitants of cities. Sons of outlaws, deprived of their inheritance, thrown from their earliest years upon the desert shores of Euboea, these two men have grown up, living on the produce of the chase and the lands which their own hands have cultivated ; each has married his friend's sister and thus

founded a family; their knowledge of other men is limited to the shipwrecked mariners whom they have assisted, and they would never have known the city had not one of them been involuntarily led to it. While they were living thus, apart from the world, strangers to the burdens of society and the refinements of civilisation, without ever having reflected whether the land which they watered with the sweat of their brow legally belonged to them, an orator, eager to make a stir and greedy of popularity, denounced them as usurpers of the public domains, and one of them was dragged to the city to answer for himself before the magistrates. He was astounded at the sight of so many splendid houses, so many magnificent buildings, and the theatre filled by a crowd that was by turns noisy and silent; he appears without alarm before the multitude assembled to judge him for crimes which he does not even understand; he answers simply, and not without a shade of natural sarcasm, to the accusations of the demagogue whose aim is to destroy him; he repels with scorn the ridiculous charge of burying gold. One of those present, touched by

his evident unhappiness, undertakes his defence, and soon striking evidence is given in favour of the poor huntsman; one of the citizens recognises in him his benefactor, the man who had formerly received him into his hut after a ship-wreck. The story ends with a marriage; the author has supplemented his agreeable picture of pastoral life by a love episode, lightly handled, fresh and pure, which has nothing in common with the sensual pictures of *Daphnis and Chloe*. Perhaps Dion does not sufficiently conceal the moral idea which has inspired the story—the happiness of virtuous poverty. How-ever, taken as a whole, the *Euboean History* shows us in Dion Chrysostom a worthy predecessor of Marmontel.

Lucius himself, the witty but licentious historian of the misfortunes of Lucius of Patras, has left us something that re-sembles the moral tale, in the dialogue called *Toxaris*, which is a collection of tales of Hellenic and Oriental colouring. The former are related by a certain Mnesippus, the latter by the Scythian Toxaris; the subject of both is, generous actions inspired by friendship. Lucian is careful to inform us that these stories

are imaginary, but he does so in a round-about and piquant manner. Mnesippus, the first narrator, swears by the gods that he will say nothing that is not true; this somewhat embarrasses Toxaris, who says: "I could have wished that you had not taken this oath, for I should have been able to dispense with believing you." Toxaris did not know the value of a Greek oath. However, being somewhat of a Greek himself, he repays his interlocutor in the same coin. Mnesippus also, less polished than the Scythian, says at the end of one of his stories, "That is really tragic. I should think it was a fable, if it were not for the respect due to the cemetery, and the wind by which you have sworn. I think that, without much offence to you, one might dispense with believing you."

It is curious to notice the important part played by the Oriental tale in the *Toxaris*. We have already seen in Herodotus, Ctesias, and Diodorus Siculus, more than one trace of it; but it is especially after the Roman period that the Oriental imagination is freely developed in Greek literature: in the *Life of Apollonius of Tyana*, in the *Lives of Pythagoras*

and Plotinus, in the Romance of Antonius Diogenes, and in the apocryphal gospels; it is destined to flourish later in the more modern versions of the false Callisthenes, and in the *Life of Barlaam and Josaphat*. Lucian, through the mouth of his Scythian, takes the trouble to point out to us the difference between Greek and Oriental taste as exhibited in the *Toxaris*. " Do not expect," says Toxaris to Mnesippus, " incidents of friendship like those which you have recounted to me. What, in fact, did you say ? That, out of devotion to a friend, one man married a very ugly girl without a dowry, that another gave two talents to bring about the marriage of a friend's daughter, that a third caused himself to be put in prison with the certainty of being set free a few moments afterwards. For my part, I shall relate to you the story of numerous massacres, of death faced on behalf of friends, and you will see that your exhibitions of friendship are mere child's play compared with those of the Scythians." Toxaris keeps his word, and his narratives reproduce faithfully the fondness of Orientals for exaggerated language, for extraordinary and marvellous facts. It is this character,

combined with the sophistical genius of the Greeks, that is present in the majority of the romances of which we still have to speak, the authors of which all belong, by birth, to the East, by intellectual culture, to Greece.

One of the oldest of these works, in which the Oriental inspiration is most evident, is the romance of Iamblichus the Syrian. This author affords us the curious example of an Asiatic writing in Greek a story taken, as he himself tells us, from an Asiatic work. Photius, Suidas, and a marginal note in a manuscript of the *Bibliotheca* of Photius give us precise details in regard to this writer. He was a freedman, born at Babylon of Syrian parents. At first brought up in the language and manners of his countrymen, he was afterwards entrusted to the care of a Babylonian, who initiated him into the language, manners, and literature of Babylon. His master, who had been one of the king's secretaries, had been taken prisoner at the time of Trajan's entry into Babylon (A.D. 102) and sold to a Syrian. Later, Iamblichus learned the Greek language, which he spoke and wrote with ease and ele-

gance, as is proved by his *Babylonica*.
In this work he mentions the defeat of
Vologeses by Verus, which took place
about 162. He must, therefore, have been
born and brought up between these two
dates, 102 and 162, earlier rather than
later. Photius speaks of the *Babylonica*
in a complimentary manner which is not
justified by his analysis : " Iamblichus is
distinguished by beauty of style, the regu-
larity and arrangement of his narrative.
He should rather have employed all his
efforts and all his art upon serious sub-
jects, instead of wasting these qualities
over puerile fictions." In spite of the
praises of Photius, the *Babylonica*, of all
the romances up to the fifth century which
have come down to us, is the one which
contains the most improbable, the most
confused, and the most incoherent story.
It is not, however, the least curious, for it
is one of the oldest. We are surprised
to find in it the germ of these erotic meta-
physical discussions so much in fashion
during the Middle Ages. A youthful
coquette has given one of her lovers a
cup, another her garland of flowers, a
third a kiss. Which is the most favoured?
The case is tried, and, after a debate, the

decision of the judge, as may be imagined, is given in favour of the latter.

It is not easy to decide which romances belong to the Roman period, and which do not go beyond the Byzantine period. We have very few trustworthy details in regard to the authors; even their names seem to be, for the most part, fictitious. The date of their works can only be fixed by analogy and induction, which afford but slight evidence.

Two writers of the fifth century, Socrates and Sozomen, speak of *Heliodorus* and his *Theagenes and Chariclea*. The date of this work is thus assigned, by two authentic witnesses, to the fourth century. That is all we know for certain concerning this writer. The anecdote which shows us Heliodorus as obliged to choose between his bishopric and his romance, and re-nouncing the former, is only found in the monk Nicephorus Callistus, by no means a weighty authority. It is by no means proved that the author of the romance of *Theagenes and Chariclea*, who calls himself, at the end of his work, " a descendant of the race of the Sun," is identical with the Bishop of Tricca, who was famous

for the severity with which he enforced ecclesiastical discipline. Socrates does not affirm the identity, but relates it as a simple tradition. What supports the tradition is, the high moral tone which distinguishes the romance, and the fact that a great deal of attention is devoted to Thessalian manners and customs; and Tricca was in Thessaly.

The romance of Heliodorus enjoyed, in its own time and during the whole Byzantine period, a great reputation, which it has never entirely lost. Three high authorities have recommended it: Amyot, who translated it; Racine, whose favourite reading it was in his youth; and Boileau, who draws a comparison between it and *Fénélon's* Telemachus. The first thing that strikes the reader is, that the romance is an olio; and from what works? The epic and tragic poems of antiquity. On every page we find imitations of Homer and Euripides, his chief models; by no means a merit, for a prose writer ought not to seek his inspiration amongst the poets. Heliodorus writes in prose, but he borrows the style, sometimes even the language of the poets; his romance is one of the

earliest examples of *poetic-prose* works, which we cannot look upon favourably.

Theagenes and Chariclea is not only a romance in poetic prose; it is almost a prose epic poem, but a middle-class epic poem. Like the epic poets, and Herodotus their pupil, Heliodorus is careful to follow the order of the times; he flings us into the midst of the life of his characters; and it is only incidentally that he goes back to preceding events. His romance is conceived upon the plan of the Odyssey.

In like manner, the incidents are nearly all reminiscences of ancient Greek poetry. Heliodorus has not drawn largely on his own imagination; most of his episodes are taken from tragedies and epic poems. Although he has changed the names, multiplied details, and spread over his pictures his own effeminate and somewhat gloomy colouring, the episode of Cnemon and Demaeneta is the story of Phaedra and Hippolytus; Petosiris and Thyamis are the counterparts of Eteocles and Polynices; the incident of Hydaspis and Chariclea is the same as that of Agamemnon ready to sacrifice Iphigenia.

Not satisfied with borrowing from epic

poetry, Heliodorus borrows from the marvellous. The Gods intervene in the affairs of Theagenes and Chariclea. If the author really believed in such intervention, we might tolerate the fables of Heliodorus ; but this is not the case. Credulity and scepticism clash in this romance. We hear continually of oracles, dreams, apparitions, facts miraculously announced and accomplished ; and, amidst all these marvels, we find a priest of Egypt, who, although interested in the general belief in these prodigies, himself shows us how he imposes on simple minds by such artifices. Calasiris affects to believe in such oracles, dreams, and revelations, and amuses himself by deceiving, with the aid of superstitious practices, the ingenuousness of Chariclea, Nausicles, and even his colleague, Charicles, the high priest of Delphi.

The purely human events described by Heliodorus are not much more probable —a defect common to all the Greek romances of that period. Anxious to excite surprise rather than interest, the writers endeavour to arouse curiosity by stories of singular events, at variance with

real life; it seems as if improbability were one of the ruling principles of the Greek literature of the time. Desirous of striking the imagination of the readers, which was longing for something new, they abuse the picturesque, and scatter upon the path of their characters rocks, precipices, and, above all, caverns. There is not one of these romances in which there does not occur some adventure with brigands or pirates; but they are fancy brigands and pirates. The brigands of Heliodorus are the brigands of comic opera, who are quite capable of killing and robbing, but are not ignorant of the respect they owe to ladies. Chariclea twice finds herself in their power; she is at first a captive of Trachinus, who wishes to marry her, and gives her time to make up her mind; another time, she falls into the hands of Thyamis, who also wishes to marry her, but begins by calling his subjects, the pirates, to witness that he leaves her free to do as she pleases.

The greatest defect of the story is its somewhat excessive length. Heliodorus has merits; he has drawn his plot cleverly, and knows how to vary his

episodes and connect them with the chief action; his style, in spite of its patchiness, is pleasant and graceful; but his work is one which we do not care to read again. He has not known how to create interesting situations or living characters.

We cannot deny the romance one merit—its moral tone. We are conscious in it of the idea of the holiness of Christian marriage, which has inclined one of his editors to the belief that the author was at least a Christian. Certain moral developments are made the occasion of a homily; in general, however, the moral tone is more prominent in the narrative than in the reflections introduced. The author shows, with considerable art, the growth of faults from faults, and punishment brought about by the perversity of the guilty one. Thus, passion drives Demaeneta to the most cowardly vengeance, and Arsaces to the most atrocious cruelty, and remorse subsequently makes them both commit suicide. Taken altogether, the work of Heliodorus is the best of the Greek Romances later than the second century, with the exception of *Daphnis and Chloe.*

The merit of the latter does not con-

sist in its moral tone. The story of
Daphnis and Chloe is very simple, a
quality which we appreciate, when we
remember all the clumsily dramatic in-
cidents which are heaped together in the
other Greek Romances. Its style is any-
thing but simple; the author was a man
of elegant accomplishments, and pos-
sessed a fairly keen appreciation of nature,
but the work exhibits traces of decadence.
Nothing is known of the author, not even
his name. How could a Greek writer
bear the name of Longus? It has been
conjectured, not without probability, that
the Latin name is the result of an error
in the reading of the MSS.

Suidas has a brief notice of Achilles
Tatius, but it gives us few precise
details. We merely learn from it that,
after having composed the *Loves of Leu-
cippe and Clitophon*, Achilles Tatius em-
braced Christianity and became a bishop.
His romance is not so well put together
as *Theagenes and Chariclea*. It was an
unfortunate idea to put the story into
the mouth of the chief character, and to
give him for his auditor an unknown
person, who does not once interrupt the
story, because it does not interest him.

The affected style, the hankering after antithesis, the numerous digressions, the prolix analysis of passions and emotions, render it inferior to the romances of Longus and Heliodorus. Certainly, Tatius has the advantage of not being so diffuse as the latter; his faults are partly redeemed by the liveliness of the narrative, and a certain vivacity apparently borrowed from the Greek comedians.

The romance of *Abrocome and Anthia*, by Xenophon of Ephesus, is certainly inferior to the works we have mentioned. The story is unpleasant, and the incidents improbable. The style, however, is pure and natural, which has led to the belief that he was the earliest of the romance-writers. But this cannot be; the composition of the work is far too complicated for it to belong to a remote period, and the triviality of the style exhibits the decline of Greek literature. However, like *Leucippe and Clitophon* and *Daphnis and Chloe*, it can hardly be later than the fifth century of the Christian era. The colouring is too pagan for us to attribute these stories to a period when morals had been regenerated by Christianity. *F*ilthy subjects, of which

Achilles Tatius and Xenophon of Ephesus speak with indifference, disappear from the Byzantine period ; we find no trace of them in *Chaereas and Callirhoe*, by Chariton of Aphrodisias, in *Hysmine and Hysminias*, by Eumathius Macrembolites, or in the *History of Apollonius of Tyre*, who has the merit of describing an amour in which feeling plays a larger part than the senses. We do not mention the romances of Xenophon of Cyprus and Xenophon of Antioch, of which nothing but the names has come down to us, nor the verse romances of Theodorus Prodromus, Constantine Manasses, and Nicetas Eugenianus, which belong to the twelfth and thirteenth centuries.[1]

HELIODORUS, bishop and famous Greek romance-writer, born at Emesa in Syria, lived towards the end of the fifth century of the Christian era, under Theodosius and his sons. He was descended from a family of priests of the Sun. In his youth, and perhaps before his conversion to Christianity, he composed a romance called *Aethiopica*. The time and cir-

[1] From *l'Histoire du Roman dans l'antiquité*, by A. Chassang.

cumstances of his conversion are not
known ; but he is known to have become
Bishop of Tricca in Thessaly. According
to the ecclesiastical historian Socrates,
he established the rule that every priest
who did not separate from his wife after
his ordination should be deprived of his
office. Another ecclesiastical annalist,
Nicephorus, relates that, on a provincial
synod accusing the *Aethiopica* of being
injurious to young people, the author was
reduced to the alternative of agreeing to
the suppression of his book or of losing
his episcopal office. Heliodorus, if we
may believe the historian, preferred to
sacrifice his bishopric to his romance.
Valois, Petau, Huet, and other critics
have refuted this improbable story. Even
if he had wished it, Heliodorus could not
have suppressed his romance, and be-
sides, nothing in the work called for
measures so severe. The *Aethiopica* is
irreproachable on the score of morality.
As a literary production, it is the master-
piece of its kind amongst the Greeks.

The plot of Theagenes and Chariclea
being somewhat intricately set forth, the

following analysis, from *Dunlop's History of Fiction*,[1] may be of service:

"The action of the romance is supposed to take place previous to the age of Alexander the Great, while Egypt was tributary to the Persian monarchs. During that period a queen of Aethiopia, called Persina, having viewed at an amorous crisis a statue of Andromeda, gives birth to a daughter of fair complexion. Fearing that her husband might not think the cause proportioned to the effect, she commits the infant in charge to Sisimithres, an Aethiopian senator, and deposits in his hand a ring and some writings, explaining the circumstances of her birth. The child is named Chariclea, and remains for seven years with her reputed father. At the end of this period he becomes doubtful of her power to preserve her chastity any longer in her native country. He therefore determines to carry her along with him, on an embassy to which he had been appointed to Oroondates, satrap of Egypt. In that land he accidentally meets Charicles, priest of Delphi, who was travelling on account of domestic afflictions, and to

[1] Vol. I., p. 23.

him he transfers the care of Chariclea. Charicles brings her to Delphi, and destines her for the wife of his nephew Alcamenes. In order to reconcile her mind to this alliance, he delivers her over to Calasiris, an Egyptian priest, who at that period resided at Delphi, and undertook to prepossess her in favour of the young man. About the same time Theagenes, a Thessalian, and descendant of Achilles, comes to Delphi, for the purformance of some sacred rite; Theagenes and Chariclea having seen each other in the temple, become mutually enamoured.

"Calasiris, who had been engaged to influence the mind of Chariclea in favour of her intended husband, is warned in a vision by Apollo that he should return to his own country, and take Theagenes and Chariclea with him. Henceforth, his whole attention is directed to deceive Charicles, and effect his escape from Delphi. Having met with some Phoenician merchants, and having informed the lovers of his intention, he sets sail along with them for Sicily, to which country the Phoenician vessel was bound; but, soon after passing Zacynthus, the ship is attacked by pirates, who carry Cala-

siris and those under his protection to the coast of Egypt. On the banks of the Nile, Trachinus, the captain of the pirates, prepares a feast to solemnise his nuptials with Chariclea, but Calasiris, with considerable ingenuity, having persuaded Pelorus, the second in command, that Chariclea is enamoured of him, a contest naturally arises between him and Trachinus during the feast, and the other pirates, espousing different sides of the quarrel, are all slain except Pelorus, who is attacked and put to flight by Theagenes. The stratagem of Calasiris, however, is of little avail, except to himself, for, immediately after the contest, while Calasiris is sitting on a hill at some distance, Theagenes and Chariclea are seized by a band of Egyptian robbers, who conduct them to their haunt on an island on a remote lake. Thyamis, the captain of the banditti, becomes enamoured of Chariclea, and declares his intention of espousing her. Chariclea pretends that she is the sister of Theagenes, in order that the jealousy of the robber may not be excited, and the safety of her lover endangered. This deception is practised in other parts of the romance.

Chariclea is not, however, long compelled
to assume the character of the sister of
Theagenes. The colony of brigands
is speedily destroyed by the forces of
the satrap of Egypt, who was excited
to this act of authority by a com-
plaint from Nausicles, a Greek mer-
chant, that the banditti had carried off
his mistress. Thyamis, the captain of
the robbers, escapes by flight, and
Cnemon, a young Athenian, who had
been detained in the colony, and with
whom Theagenes had formed a friend-
ship during his confinement, sets out in
quest of him Theagenes and Chariclea
depart soon after on their way to a cer-
tain village, where they had agreed to
meet Cnemon, but are intercepted on the
road by the satrap's forces. Theagenes
is sent as a present to the King of Persia,
and Chariclea, being falsely claimed by
Nausicles as his mistress, is conducted
to his house. Here Calasiris had acci-
dently fixed his abode since his separa-
tion from Theagenes and Chariclea,
and was also doing the honours of
the house to Cnemon in the landlord's
absence. Chariclea being recognised by
Calasiris, Nausicles abandons the claim

d

to her which he had advanced, and sets sail with Cnemon for Greece, while Calasiris and Chariclea proceed in search of Theagenes. On arriving at Memphis, they find that, with his usual good luck, he had again fallen into the power of Thyamis, and was besieging that capital with the robber. A treaty of peace, however, is speedily concluded. Thyamis is discovered to be the son of Calasiris, and is elected high priest of Memphis. Arsace, who commanded in that city, in the absence of her husband, falls in love with Theagenes; but, as he perseveres in resisting all her advances, and in maintaining his fidelity to Chariclea, she orders him to be put to the torture; she also commands her nurse, who was the usual confidante of her amours, and instrument of her cruelty, to poison Chariclea; but, the cup-bearer having given the nurse the goblet intended for Chariclea, she expires in convulsions. This, however, serves as a pretext to condemn Chariclea as a poisoner, and she is accordingly condemned to be burnt. After she had ascended the pile, and the fire had been lighted, she is saved for that day by the miraculous effects of the stone Pantarbe, which she

wore on her finger, and which warded
off the flames from her person. During
the ensuing night, a messenger arrives
from Oroondates, the husband of Arsace,
who was at that time carrying on
a war against the Aethiopians; he had
been informed of the misconduct of his
wife, and had despatched one of his
officers to Memphis, with orders to bring
Theagenes and Chariclea to his camp.
Arsace hangs herself; but the lovers are
taken prisoners, on their way to Oroon-
dates, by the scouts of the Aethiopian
army, and are conducted to Hydaspes,
who was at that time besieging Oroon-
dates in Syene This city having been
taken, and Oroondates vanquished in a
great battle, Hydaspes returns to his
capital, Meroe, where, by advice of his
Gymnosophists, he proposes to sacrifice
Theagenes and Chariclea to the Sun
and Moon, the deities of Aethiopia. As
virgins alone were entitled to the privi-
lege of being accepted as victims, Chari-
clea is subjected to a trial of chastity.
Theagenes, while on the very brink of
sacrifice, performs many feats of strength
and dexterity. A bull, which was his
companion in misfortune, having broken
from the altar, Theagenes follows him on

horseback, subdues him, and returns on his back. At length, when the two lovers are about to be immolated, Chariclea, by means of the ring and fillet which had been attached to her at her birth, and had been carefully preserved, is discovered to be the daughter of Hydaspes, which is further proved by the testimony of Sisimithres, once her reputed father, and by the opportune arrival of Charicles, priest of Delphi, who was wandering through the world in search of Chariclea. After some demur on the part of the Gymnosophists, Chariclea obtains her own release and that of Theagenes, is united to him in marriage, and acknowledged as the heiress of the Aethiopian Empire."

In modern times, the *Aethiopica* was scarcely known till, at the sacking of Ofen, in 1526, a MS. of the work in the library of Mathias Corvinus, King of Hungary, attracted, by its rich binding, the attention of a soldier, who brought it into Germany, and at last it came into the hands of Vincentius Opsopaeus, who printed it at Basel, 1534. For information as to succeeding editions the reader is referred to the *Bibliography*.

THE AETHIOPICA

OF

HELIODORUS

ΗΛΙΟΔΩΡΟΥ

ΑΙΘΙΟΠΙΚΩΝ

ΒΙΒΛΙΑ ΔΕΚΑ

ΒΙΒΛΙΟΝ ΠΡΩΤΟΝ

Αʹ. Ἡμέρας ἄρτι διαγελώσης καὶ ἡλίου τὰς ἀκρωρείας καταυγάζοντος, ἄνδρες ἔνοπλοι λῃστρικοὶ ὄρους ὑπερκύψαντες, ὃ δὴ κατʼ ἐκβολὰς τοῦ Νείλου καὶ στόμα τὸ καλούμενον Ἡρακλεωτικὸν ὑπερτείνει, μικρὸν ἐπιστάντες, τὴν ὑποκειμένην θάλατταν ὀφθαλμοῖς ἐπήρχοντο· καὶ τῷ πελάγει τὸ πρῶτον τὰς ὄψεις ἐπαφέντες, ὡς οὐδὲν ἄγρας λῃστρικῆς ἐπηγγέλλετο μὴ πλεόμενον, ἐπὶ τὸν πλησίον αἰγιαλὸν τῇ θέᾳ κατήγοντο· καὶ ἦν τὰ ἐν αὐτῷ τοιάδε.

Ὁλκὰς ἀπὸ πρυμνησίων ὥρμει, τῶν μὲν ἐμπλεόντων χηρεύουσα, φόρτου δὲ πλήθουσα· καὶ τοῦτο γὰρ ἦν συμβαλεῖν καὶ τοῖς πόρρωθεν· τὸ γὰρ ἄχθος ἄχρι καὶ ἐπὶ τρίτου ζωστῆρος

THE AETHIOPICA

OF

HELIODORUS

I. THE light of day had just begun to smile and the rays of the sun to illumine the mountain ridges, when some armed men, whose attire proclaimed them brigands, showed themselves on the top of a promontory which overhangs the outlet of the Nile, which is called the Heracleotic mouth; there they halted for a while, carefully examining the expanse of sea that lay beneath them. Having first cast their eyes over the open and seeing no vessel that held out hopes of plunder, they turned their gaze towards the beach, where they beheld the following sight:

A vessel was lying at anchor; there was no one on board, but it carried a heavy cargo, as could be guessed even by those at a distance; for the weight of it caused

I—2

τῆς νεὼς τὸ ὕδωρ ἀνέθλιβεν. Ὁ δ' αἰγιαλὸς μεστὸς ἅπας σωμάτων νεοσφαγῶν τῶν μὲν ἄρδην ἀπολωλότων, τῶν δ' ἡμιθνήτων καὶ μέλεσι ἔτι σπαιρόντων, ἄρτι πεπαῦσθαι τὸν πόλεμον κατηγορούντων. Ἦν δ' οὐ πολέμου καθαροῦ τὰ φαινόμενα σύμβολα, ἀλλ' ἀναμέμικτο καὶ εὐωχίας οὐκ εὐτυχοῦς ἀλλ' εἰς τοῦτο ληξάσης ἐλεεινὰ λείψανα· τράπεζαι τῶν ἐδεσμάτων ἔτι πλήθουσαι καὶ ἄλλαι πρὸς τῇ γῇ τῶν κειμένων ἐν χερσὶν ἀνθ' ὅπλων ἐνίοις παρὰ τὴν μάχην γεγενημέναι, (ὁ γὰρ πόλεμος ἐσχεδίαστο), ἕτεραι δ' ἄλλους ἔκρυπτον, ὡς ᾤοντο, ὑπελθόντας· κρατῆρες ἀνατετραμμένοι καὶ χειρῶν ἔνιοι τῶν ἐσχηκότων ὑπορρέοντες, τῶν μὲν πιόντων, τῶν δ' ἀντὶ λίθων κεχρημένων. Τὸ γὰρ αἰφνίδιον τοῦ κακοῦ τὰς χρείας ἐκαινοτόμει καὶ βέλεσι κεχρῆσθαι τοῖς ἐκπώμασιν ἐδίδασκεν. Ἔκειντο δὲ, ὁ μὲν πελέκει τετρωμένος, ὁ δὲ κάχληκι βεβλημένος, αὐτόθεν ἀπὸ τῆς ῥαχίας πεπορισμένῳ, ἕτερος ξύλῳ κατε-

the ship to sink in the water as high as the third band. The whole beach was covered with bodies of men but lately massacred, some quite dead, others still alive, their limbs yet quivering, which proved that a fierce struggle had just ended. But the indications were not those of a regular battle; with the dead and dying were mingled the miserable remains of an ill-starred feast, which had had so disastrous an issue; tables still covered with viands, fragments of others still clutched in the hands of the dead, who had used them as weapons in the sudden outburst of the fray, while others again, to all appearance, had been used as hiding-places; drinking-cups lying on the ground, some of which had fallen from the hands of the banqueters who had been slain in the act of lifting them to their mouth, while others had been used as stones. The suddenness of the attack had invented new uses for them and taught the combatants to use cups in place of weapons. One lay wounded by an axe, another with his brains dashed out by stones picked up from the beach;

αγὼς, ὁ δὲ δαλῷ κατάφλεκτος, καὶ ἄλλος ἄλλως· οἱ δὲ πλεῖστοι βελῶν ἔργον καὶ τοξείας γεγενημένοι. Καὶ μυρίον εἶδος ὁ δαίμων ἐπὶ μικροῦ τοῦ χωρίου μετεσκεύασεν, οἶνον αἵματι μιάνας καὶ συμποσίοις πόλεμον ἐπιστήσας, πότους καὶ φόνους, σπονδὰς καὶ σφαγὰς ἐπισυνάψας καὶ τοιοῦτον θέατρον λῃσταῖς Αἰγυπτίοις ἐπιδείξας.

Οἱ γὰρ δὴ κατὰ τὸ ὄρος θεωροὺς ἑαυτοὺς τῶνδε καθιστάντες, οὐδὲ συνιέναι τὴν σκηνὴν ἐδύναντο, τοὺς μὲν ἑαλωκότας ἔχοντες, οὐδαμοῦ δὲ τοὺς κεκρατηκότας ὁρῶντες· καὶ τὴν μὲν νίκην λαμπρὰν, τὰ λάφυρα δ' ἀσκύλευτα, καὶ τὴν ναῦν μόνην ἀνδρῶν μὲν ἔρημον, τἄλλα δ' ἄσυλον, ὥσπερ ὑπὸ πολλῶν φρουρουμένην καὶ ὥσπερ ἐν εἰρήνῃ σαλεύουσαν. Ἀλλὰ καίπερ τὸ γεγονὸς ὅ τι ποτ' ἐστὶν ἀποροῦντες, εἰς τὸ κέρδος ἔβλεπον καὶ ἐπὶ τὴν λείαν, αὑτοὺς νικητὰς ἀποδείξαντες, ὥρμησαν.

one had been battered to pieces with a club, another scorched by the fire of a blazing torch; death had overtaken them in various ways, but most of them had been pierced with arrows. Fortune had gathered together in a small space a countless variety of objects, polluting wine with blood, uniting war and festivity, and mingling promiscuously drinking and death, libations and slaughter. Such was the sight she set before the eyes of the Egyptian brigands.

The latter, spectators from the top of the mountain, were unable to understand the scene; they beheld numbers overthrown, but could not see their conquerors; all the signs of a brilliant victory, but the spoils untouched; a vessel without a crew, but in other respects uninjured, as if it were strongly defended or were tossing quietly at anchor. Although they did not know what had happened, the greed of gain excited them, and, as if they had been themselves the conquerors, they proceeded to descend, in order to lay hands upon the plunder.

Β΄. Ἤδη δ᾽ αὐτοῖς κεκινηκόσιν ἄποθεν μικρὸν τῆς νεὼς καὶ τῶν κειμένων, θέαμα προσπίπτει τῶν προτέρων ἀπορώτερον. Κόρη καθῆστο ἐπὶ πέτρας, ἀμήχανόν τι κάλλος καὶ θεὸς εἶναι ἀναπείθουσα, τοῖς μὲν παροῦσι περιαλγοῦσα, φρονήματος δ᾽ εὐγενοῦς ἔτι πνέουσα· δάφνῃ τὴν κεφαλὴν ἔστεπτο καὶ φαρέτρα τῶν ὤμων ἐξῆπτο καὶ τῷ λαιῷ βραχίονι τὸ τόξον ὑπεστήρικτο, ἡ λοιπὴ δὲ χεὶρ ἀφροντίστως ἀπῃωρεῖτο· μηρῷ δὲ τῷ δεξιῷ τὸν ἀγκῶνα θατέρας χειρὸς ἐφεδράζουσα καὶ τοῖς δακτύλοις τὴν παρειὰν ἐπιτρέψασα, κάτω νεύουσα καί τινα προκείμενον ἔφηβον περισκοποῦσα, τὴν κεφαλὴν ἀνεῖχεν.

Ὁ δὲ τραύμασι μὲν κατήκιστο καὶ μικρὸν ἀναφέρων ὥσπερ ἐκ βαθέος ὕπνου τοῦ παρ᾽ ὀλίγον θανάτου κατεφαίνετο. Ἤνθει δὲ καὶ ἐν τούτοις ἀνδρείῳ τῷ κάλλει, καὶ ἡ παρειὰ καταρρέοντι τῷ αἵματι φοινιττομένη, λευκότητι πλέον ἀντέλαμπεν. Ὀφθαλμοὺς δ᾽ ἐκείνου οἱ

II. When they were only a short distance from the vessel and the bodies of the dead and dying, another sight, which perplexed them even more, arrested their attention. They saw a young girl, of wondrous beauty, sitting on a rock, whom they took to be a goddess; though smitten with grief at the scene, her mien and features displayed a dignified and noble spirit; her head was crowned with laurel, a quiver was slung over her shoulders, her left arm rested upon her bow, while the hand hung carelessly down; with her right elbow resting upon her thigh, she leaned her cheek upon her hand, with head bent, looking from time to time at a young man lying a little distance from her on the shore.

This young man, covered with cruel wounds, with difficulty managed to lift up his head from a deep sleep, that resembled the sleep of death. But, even in this plight, a manly beauty shone upon his face; the blood, trickling down his cheeks, enhanced the charm of his fair complexion. But pain and grief, in spite of all his efforts, drew down his eyelids,

μὲν πόνοι κατέσπων, ἡ δ' ὄψις τῆς κόρης ἐφ'
ἑαυτὴν ἀνεῖλκε καὶ τοῦτο ὁρᾶν αὐτοὺς ἠνάγ-
καζεν, ὅτι ἐκείνην ἑώρων. Ὡς δέ πνεῦμα συλ-
λεξάμενος καὶ βύθιόν τι ἀσθμήνας, λεπτὸν
ὑπεφθέγξατο, καὶ, Ὦ γλυκεῖα, ἔφη, σώζῃ μοι
ὡς ἀληθῶς, ἢ γέγονας καὶ αὐτὴ τοῦ πολέμου
πάρεργον, οὐκ ἀνέχῃ δ' ὅμως οὐδὲ μετὰ θάνατον
ἀποστατεῖν ἡμῶν, ἀλλὰ φάσμα τὸ σὸν καὶ
ψυχὴ τὰς ἐμὰς περιέπει τύχας; Ἐν σοὶ, ἔφη,
τὰ ἐμά, ἡ κόρη, σώζεσθαί τε καὶ μή. Τοῦτο
γοῦν ὁρᾷς, (δείξασα ἐπὶ τῶν γονάτων ξίφος)
εἰς δεῦρο ἤργησεν ὑπὸ τῆς σῆς ἀναπνοῆς ἐπεχό-
μενον. Καὶ ἅμα λέγουσα, ἡ μὲν τῆς πέτρας
ἀνέθορεν· οἱ δ' ἐπὶ τοῦ ὄρους, ὑπὸ θαύματος
ἅμα καὶ ἐκπλήξεως, ὥσπερ ὑπὸ πρηστῆρος
βληθέντες, ἄλλος ἄλλον ὑπεδύετο θάμνον·
μεῖζον γάρ τι καὶ θειότερον αὐτοῖς ὀρθωθεῖσα
ἔδοξε, τῶν μὲν βελῶν τῇ ἀθρόᾳ κινήσει κλαγ-
ξάντων, χρυσοϋφοῦς δὲ τῆς ἐσθῆτος πρὸς τὸν

while, on the other hand, the sight of the maiden attracted his gaze, and his eyes were constrained to look, because they saw her. At last he recovered himself, and, heaving a deep sigh, cried in a feeble voice: "My dearest, are you really preserved to me? or have you too been slain amongst the rest? has not even death been able to separate us, that your shade and spirit still accompany my fortunes?" "My destiny, my life or death, is bound up with yours," replied the young girl; "you see this (here she showed him a dagger on her knees); if it has hitherto remained idle, it has only been held back by the signs of life in you." With these words, she sprang up from the rock. The spectators on the mountain, smitten with wonder and amazement, as if they had been struck by lightning, ran to shelter themselves beneath the bushes; for, when she stood up, she appeared even taller and more divine. The arrows in her quiver, which her sudden movements caused to rattle on her shoulders, the dazzling brilliancy of her gold-bedecked

ἥλιον ἀνταυγαζούσης, καὶ τῆς κόμης ὑπὸ τῷ στεφάνῳ βακχεῖον σοβουμένης καὶ τοῖς νώτοις πλεῖστον ὅσον ὑποτρεχούσης. Τοὺς μὲν ταῦτ' ἐξεδειμάτου, καὶ πλέον τῶν ὁρωμένων ἡ τῶν γενομένων ἄγνοια.

Οἱ μὲν γὰρ θεόν τινα ἔλεγον, ἡ Ἄρτεμιν, ἡ τὴν ἐγχώριον Ἶσιν· οἱ δ' ἱέρειαν ὑπό του θεῶν ἐκμεμηνυῖαν καὶ τὸν ὁρώμενον πολὺν φόνον ἐργασαμένην. Καὶ οἱ μὲν ταῦτ' ἐγίγνωσκον· τὰ ὄντα δ' οὔπω ἐγίγνωσκον.

Ἡ δ' ἀθρόον κατενεχθεῖσα ἐπὶ τὸν νεανίαν καὶ πανταχόθεν αὐτῷ περιχυθεῖσα, ἐδάκρυεν, ἐφίλει, κατέματτεν, ἀνῴμωζεν, ἠπίστει κατέχουσα. Ταῦθ' ὁρῶντες οἱ Αἰγύπτιοι πρὸς ἑτέρας ἐννοίας τὴν γνώμην μετέβαλον, καὶ ποῦ ταῦτ' ἂν εἴη θεοῦ τὰ ἔργα, λέγοντες. ποῦ δ' ἂν νεκρὸν σῶμα φιλοίη δαίμων οὕτω περιπαθῶς; τολμᾶν ἀλλήλοις παρεκελεύοντο καὶ πορευ-

robe which glittered in the rays of the sun, her long hair which floated from beneath her crown like that of a Bacchante, hanging half-way down her back, and, more than what they saw, their ignorance of what had taken place — all this struck terror into their soul.

"She is a goddess," cried some, "either Artemis or Isis, the divine patroness of Egypt"; while others declared that she was some priestess inspired with divine frenzy, who had wrought such slaughter. Such was their opinion; but as yet they knew not the truth.

Meanwhile, the young girl hastened to the youth, flung her arms around him, wept and kissed him, wiped off the blood, uttered loud groans, and, although she held him in her grasp, seemed scarcely able to believe her eyes. When the Egyptians saw this, they altered their opinion. "How," said they, "can this be the act of a goddess? would she embrace a lifeless corpse so affectionately?" After this, they encouraged one another to take heart, and draw nearer

θέντες ἐγγύθεν, λαμβάνειν τὴν τῶν ἀληθῶν γνῶσιν. Ἀναλαβόντες οὖν ἑαυτοὺς καταθέουσι, καὶ τὴν κόρην ἔτι πρὸς τοῖς τραύμασιν οὖσαν τοῦ νεανίου καταλαμβάνουσι· καὶ ἐπιστάντες ὄπισθεν, εἶχον ἑαυτούς, οὔτε τι λέγειν, οὔτε τι πράττειν ἀποθαρροῦντες. Κτύπου δὲ περιηχήσαντος, καὶ τῆς αὐτῶν σκιᾶς τοῖς ὀφθαλμοῖς παρεμπεσούσης, ἀνένευσεν ἡ κόρη· καὶ ἰδοῦσα, αὖθις ἐπένευσε, πρὸς μὲν τὸ ἄηθες τῆς χροιᾶς καὶ τὸ ληστρικὸν τῆς ὄψεως ἐν ὅπλοις δεικνυμένης οὐδὲ κατὰ μικρὸν ἐκπλαγεῖσα, πρὸς δὲ τὴν θεραπείαν τοῦ κειμένου πᾶσαν αὐτὴν τρέπουσα. Οὕτως ἄρα πόθος ἀκριβὴς καὶ ἔρως ἀκραιφνὴς τῶν μὲν ἔξωθεν προσπιπτόντων ἀλγεινῶν τε καὶ ἡδέων πάντων ὑπερφρονεῖ, πρὸς ἓν δὲ τὸ φιλούμενον καὶ ὁρᾶν καὶ συννεύειν τὸ φρόνημα καταναγκάζει.

Γ΄. Ὡς δὲ παραμείψαντες οἱ λησταὶ κατὰ πρόσωπον ἔστησαν καί τι καὶ μέλλειν ἐπιχειρεῖν ἐῴκεσαν, αὖθις ἡ παῖς ἀνένευσε, καὶ μέλανας ἰδοῦσα τὴν χροιὰν καὶ τὴν ὄψιν αὐχμηρούς,

Εἰ μὲν εἴδωλα τῶν κειμένων ἐστέ, φησίν, οὐκ ἐν δίκῃ παρενοχλεῖτε ἡμῖν· οἱ μὲν γὰρ πλεῖσ-

and learn the truth. Their courage re-
vived, they descended, and found the
young girl still tending the other's
wounds; standing behind, they remained
motionless, venturing neither to speak
nor to act. The girl, hearing the noise
of their footsteps and seeing their shadows
on the ground, looked up; in no way
alarmed by their strange complexion, or
their arms, which proclaimed them brig-
ands, she lowered her eyes again, and
devoted her whole attention to the pros-
trate youth. Thus the keenness of regret
and the sincerity of love make us disregard
all external objects whether pleasant or
painful, and compel us to see nothing
but the one beloved object, and to de-
vote to it our whole attention.

III. When the brigands stopped in
front of her, apparently intending to lay
hands on her, she looked up again, and,
seeing their dark complexions and hideous
appearance, thus addressed them:

"If you are the shades of the dead that
are lying here, you do wrong to trouble
us; for most of you have died by your

τοι χερσὶ ταῖς ἀλλήλων ἀνήρησθε· ὅσοι δὲ
πρὸς ἡμῶν, ἀμύνης νόμῳ καὶ ἐκδικίας τῆς εἰς
σωφροσύνην ὕβρεως πεπόνθατε· εἰ δέ τινες
τῶν ζώντων ἐστέ, ληστρικὸς μὲν ὑμῖν, ὡς ἔοικεν,
ὁ βίος, εἰς καιρὸν δ᾽ ἥκετε, λύσατε τῶν περιεσ-
τηκότων ἀλγεινῶν, φόνῳ τῷ καθ᾽ ἡμῶν δρᾶμα
τὸ περὶ ἡμᾶς καταστρέψαντες.

Ἡ μὲν ταῦτ᾽ ἐπετραγῴδει, οἱ δὲ, οὐδὲν
συνιέναι τῶν λεγομένων ἔχοντες, τοὺς μὲν
αὐτοῦ καταλείπουσιν, ἰσχυρὰν αὐτοῖς φυλακὴν
τὴν ἀσθένειαν αὐτῶν ἐπιστήσαντες, ἐπὶ δὲ τὴν
ναῦν ὁρμήσαντες, τὸν φόρτον ἐξήντλουν, τῶν
μὲν ἄλλων ὑπερορῶντες, πολλῶν ὄντων καὶ
ποικίλων, χρυσοῦ δὲ καὶ ἀργύρου καὶ λίθων
πολυτίμων καὶ σηρικῆς ἐσθῆτος, ὅση δύναμις
ἑκάστοις, ἐκφοροῦντες. Ἐπεὶ δ᾽ ἅλις ἐδόκει
ἔχειν, καὶ τοσαῦτ᾽ ἦν ὡς καὶ ληστρικὴν κορέσαι
πλεονεξίαν, τὴν λείαν ἐπὶ τὸν αἰγιαλὸν κατα-
θέντες, εἰς φορτία καὶ μοίρας κατενέμοντο, οὐ
πρὸς τὴν ἑκάστου τῶν ληφθέντων ἀξίαν ἀλλὰ
πρὸς τὸ ἴσον βάρος τὴν νέμησιν ποιούμενοι.
Τὰ δὲ περὶ τὴν κόρην καὶ τὸν νεανίαν ἐν δευτέ-
ροις πράξειν ἔμελλον.

own hands; those who were slain by us
deserved their fate; we only exercised
the right of self-defence to protect our
honour. If you are living men, you
would seem to be brigands; then you
have arrived at a fitting moment to
deliver us from our present calamities,
and to end this scene of horror by our
death."

Such was the tragic plaint she uttered.
The others, unable to understand what
she said, left the unhappy pair, think-
ing their weakness a sufficient guard;
then, hurrying to the ship, they ran-
sacked the cargo, which was considerable
and consisted of various kinds of wares;
to some they paid no heed, but carried
off gold and silver, precious stones, and
silken stuffs, as much as they could carry.
When their greed was satisfied, they spread
the booty on the shore, and divided it
into equal portions, making the distribu-
tion not according to the value, but by
the weight of each article. They had
decided to defer the consideration of
what they should do with their prisoners.

Κἀν τούτῳ δὲ πλῆθος ἕτερον ἐφίσταται λῃστρικὸν, ἱππέων δύο τοῦ τάγματος ἡγουμένων· ὅπερ ὡς εἶδον οἱ πρότεροι, οὔτε χεῖρας ἀνταράμενοι, οὔτε τι τῶν σκύλων ἀπενεγκάμενοι, τοῦ μὴ ἐπιδιωχθῆναι ἕνεκεν, ὡς δρόμου εἶχον, ἔφευγον· αὐτοὶ μὲν ἐς δέκα τὸν ἀριθμὸν ὄντες, τρὶς δὲ τοσούτους τοὺς ἐπελθόντας θεασάμενοι. Καὶ οἱ μὲν ἀμφὶ τὴν κόρην δεύτερον ἤδη ἡλίσκοντο, οὐδέπω ληφθέντες, οἱ δὲ λῃσταὶ πρὸς τὴν διαρπαγὴν, καὶ ταῦτα σπεύδοντες, ὑπὸ τῆς τῶν ὁρωμένων ἀγνοίας ἅμα καὶ ἐκπλήξεως, τέως ἀνεστέλλοντο· τοὺς μὲν γὰρ πολλοὺς φόνους ὑπὸ τῶν προτέρων γεγενῆσθαι λῃστῶν εἴκαζον, τὴν κόρην δ' ὁρῶντες ἐν ξένῃ καὶ περιβλέπτῳ τῇ στολῇ καὶ τῶν μὲν προσπιπτόντων φοβερῶν ὡς ἂν μηδὲ γιγνομένων ὑπερορῶσαν, ὅλην δὲ τοῦ νεανίου πρὸς τοῖς τραύμασιν οὖσαν καὶ ὡς ἴδιον τὸ ἐκείνου πάθος ἀλγοῦσαν, τὴν μὲν τοῦ κάλλους καὶ τοῦ φρονήματος ἐθαύμαζον, τὸν δὲ καὶ τραυματίαν ἐξεπλήττοντο· τοιοῦτος τὴν μορφὴν

Meanwhile, another band of brigands came up, with two horsemen riding at their head. When the first band perceived them, without venturing to show fight or carry off any portion of the booty, for fear they might be pursued, they fled with all speed, being only ten in number, while those whom they saw coming were three times as many. Thus the young girl found herself captured a second time, although not actually a prisoner. The new arrivals, although intent on plunder, halted for a while, astounded at what they saw and ignorant of the cause. They imagined that those who had just fled had perpetrated the massacre, and seeing that the young girl, dressed in strange and magnificent attire, paid no attention to the dangers that threatened her, as if they had no existence, but devoted all her care to the young man's wounds, and seemed to feel his sufferings as if they were her own, they stood still, struck with admiration at her beauty and courageous spirit, while they were equally astonished at the form and stature of the

καὶ τοσοῦτος τὸ μέγεθος ἔκειτο, κατὰ μικρὸν
ἤδη πως ἀνειληφὼς ἑαυτὸν καὶ πρὸς τὸ σύνηθες
βλέμμα ἀποκαθιστάμενος.

Δ΄. Ὀψὲ δὴ οὖν πλησιάσας ὁ λήσταρχος
ἐπιβάλλει τε τῇ κόρῃ τὴν χεῖρα καὶ ἀνίστασθαί
τε καὶ ἔπεσθαι ἐκέλευεν. Ἡ δὲ τῶν μὲν λεγο-
μένων οὐδὲν συνιεῖσα, τὸ δὲ προσταττόμενον
συμβαλοῦσα, συνεφείλκετο τὸν νεανίσκον, οὐδ᾽
αὐτὸν μεθιέντα, καὶ τὸ ξίφος ἐπιφέρουσα τοῖς
στέρνοις, ἑαυτὴν ἀποσφάξειν ἠπείλει, εἰ μὴ
ἀμφοτέρους ἄγοιεν. Συνεὶς οὖν ὁ λήσταρχος
τὸ μέν τι τοῖς λεγομένοις, πλέον δὲ τοῖς νεύ-
μασι, καὶ ἅμα συνεργὸν ἕξειν εἰς τὰ μέγιστα
τὸν νεανίαν, εἰ περισωθείη, προσδοκήσας, κατα-
βιβάσας τόν θ᾽ ὑπασπιστὴν καὶ ἑαυτὸν τῶν
ἵππων, ἀνατίθεται τοὺς αἰχμαλώτους, τοὺς μὲν
ἄλλους τὰ λάφυρα συσκευασαμένους ἔπεσθαι
προστάξας, αὐτὸς δ᾽ ἐκ ποδὸς παραθέων καὶ
προσανέχων, εἴ ποί τις αὐτῶν περιτρέποιτο.
Καὶ ἦν δόξης οὐκ ἐκτὸς τὸ γιγνόμενον· δου-
λεύειν ὁ ἄρχων ἐφαίνετο καὶ ὑπηρετεῖσθαι ὁ
κρατῶν τοῖς ἑαλωκόσιν ᾑρεῖτο. Οὕτως εὐγενείας

wounded young man, who had gradually recovered, while his features resumed their ordinary expression.

IV. At length the captain of the band drew near, laid his hand upon the young girl, and commanded her to get up and follow him. Guessing what he meant (although she did not understand his words), she began to drag the young man along with her, who himself refused to part from her; then, pointing the dagger towards her breast, she threatened to kill herself, unless they took him as well. Her gestures, rather than her words, explained her meaning to the Captain, who, hoping that the young man, if he recovered, might be of great service to him, dismounted and ordered his esquire to do the same, and bade his prisoners mount in their places. Bidding his men collect the spoil and follow him, he himself walked on foot by the side of the captives, to hold them up in case they should be in danger of falling. Nor was their lot without its compensation; the master seemed to be the slave, and the captor the servant of the captured.

ἔμφασις καὶ κάλλους ὄψις καὶ λῃστρικὸν ἦθος
οἶδεν ὑποτάττειν καὶ κρατεῖν καὶ τῶν αὐχμηρο-
τέρων.

Ε΄. Παραμείψαντες οὖν ὅσον δύο στάδια
τὸν αἰγιαλὸν, ἐκτραπέντες, εὐθὺ τοῦ ὄρους πρὸς
τὰ ὄρθια ἐχώρουν, τὴν θάλατταν ἐν δεξιᾷ
ποιησάμενοι, καὶ ὑπερβάντες χαλεπῶς τὰς
ἀκρωρείας ἐπί τινα λίμνην κατὰ θατέραν τοῦ
ὄρους πλευρὰν ὑπερτείνουσαν ἠπείγοντο. Ἦν
δὲ τοιάδε τις. Βουκόλια μὲν σύμπας κέκληται
πρὸς Αἰγυπτίων ὁ τόπος· ἔστι δὲ κοιλὰς τῆς
αὐτόθι γῆς, τοῦ Νείλου ὑπερεκχύσεις τινὰς
ὑποδεχομένη καὶ λίμνη γιγνομένη, τὸ μὲν κατὰ
μέσον βάθος ἄπειρον, περὶ δὲ τὰς ἄκρας εἰς
ἕλος ἀποτελευτῶσα. Ὃ γὰρ ταῖς θαλάτταις
αἰγιαλοὶ, τοῦτο ταῖς λίμναις τὰ ἕλη γίγνεται.
Ἐν δὴ τούτοις, ὅσον Αἰγυπτίων λῃστρικὸν
πολιτεύεται, ὁ μὲν ἐπὶ γῆς ὀλίγης, εἴ πῄ
τις ὑπερέχει τοῦ ὕδατος, καλύβην πηξάμενος,
ὁ δ᾽ ἐπὶ σκάφους βιοτεύει, πορθμεῖον τὸ
αὐτὸ καὶ οἰκητήριον ἔχων. Ἐπ᾽ αὐτοῦ μὲν
αὐτοῖς αἱ γυναῖκες ἐριθεύουσιν, ἐπ᾽ αὐτοῦ δ᾽
ἀποτίκτουσιν. Εἰ δὲ γένοιτο παιδίον, τὰ μὲν
πρῶτα τῷ μητρῴῳ γάλακτι, τὰ δ᾽ ἀπὸ τούτου

So true is it that the appearance of nobility and the sight of beauty is able to subjugate even the hearts of brigands and to conquer the harshest natures.

V. After the brigands had followed the coast for a distance of about two stades, they left the sea on their right, and turned aside in the direction of a mountain, which they climbed with difficulty, and, descending the other side with all speed, arrived at a lake which lay below. The whole district is called Bucolia (Pasture) by the Egyptians. In it there is a valley, which receives the overflow of the Nile and becomes a lake, very deep in the middle, while its shores are shallow and marshy; for the waters of lakes, like those of the sea, diminish in depth the nearer they are to the land. This spot is as it were the republic of all the brigands of Egypt. Some dwell in huts which they have built upon rising ground above the level of the water, while others live in boats, which they use both for habitation and purposes of transport; it is here that their wives spin, and are brought to bed. Their children are first

τοῖς ἀπὸ τῆς λίμνης ἰχθύσι πρὸς ἥλιον ὀπτω-
μένοις ἐκτρέφει. Ἕρπειν δ᾽ ὀρεγόμενον εἰ
αἴσθοιτο, ἱμάντα τῶν σφυρῶν ἐξάψας, ὅσον
ἐπ᾽ ἄκρου τοῦ σκάφους ἤ τῆς καλιᾶς προβαίνειν
ἐπέτρεψε, καινόν τινα χειραγωγὸν αὐτῷ τὸν
δεσμὸν τοῦ ποδὸς ἐπιστήσας.

Ϛ΄. Καί πού τις βουκόλος ἀνὴρ ἐτέχθη τ᾽
ἐν τῇ λίμνῃ καὶ τροφὸν ἔσχε ταύτην καὶ πατρίδα
τὴν λίμνην ἐνόμισεν, ἱκανὴν δὲ, φρούριον ἰσχυρὸν
εἶναι λῃσταῖς· διὸ καὶ συρρεῖ ἐπ᾽ αὐτὴν ὁ
τοιοῦτος βίος, τῷ μὲν ὕδατι πάντες ὅσα τείχει
χρώμενοι, τὸν δὲ πολὺν κατὰ τὸ ἕλος κάλαμον,
ἀντὶ χαρακώματος προβεβλημένοι· σκολιὰς
γάρ τινας ἀτραποὺς τεμόμενοι καὶ πολλοῖς
ἐλιγμοῖς πεπλανημένας, καὶ σφίσι μὲν διὰ τὴν
γνῶσιν ῥᾴστας, τοῖς δ᾽ ἄλλοις ἀπόρους τοὺς
διέκπλους κατασκευάσαντες, μέγιστον ὀχύρωμα
πρὸς τὸ μὴ ἄν τι παθεῖν ἐξ ἐπιδρομῆς ἐμηχανή-
σαντο. Καὶ τὰ μὲν κατὰ τὴν λίμνην καὶ τοὺς
ἐνοικοῦντας ἐν αὐτῇ βουκόλους ὧδέ πως ἔχει.

Ζ΄ Ἤδη δ᾽ ἡλίου πρὸς δυσμὰς ἰόντος,
ἀφικνοῦνται πρὸς αὐτὴν οἱ ἀμφὶ τὸν λήσταρχον·
καὶ οἱ μὲν τῶν θ᾽ ἵππων ἀπεβίβαζον τοὺς νέους
καὶ τὴν λείαν ἐνετίθεντο τοῖς σκάφεσιν, ὁ δὲ
πολὺς τῶν κατὰ χώραν μεινάντων λῃστῶν
ὅμιλος, ἄλλος ἄλλοθεν τοῦ ἕλους ἐκδὺς, ἀνε-

brought up on their mothers' milk, after-
wards upon fish caught in the lake and
dried in the sun. As soon as a child can
crawl, a cord is tied to its ankles, and it is
allowed to go as far as the edge of the
boat or the door of the hut, the cord being
used as a guide.

VI. Thus those who are born on the
lake look upon it as their nurse and native
land, and regard it as a safe stronghold for
brigands like themselves, who flock thither
in large numbers. The water serves them
as a wall, and the reeds, which grow in
abundance, as a palisade. Amongst these
reeds they have cut several winding and
tortuous paths, easy for themselves to find
who know them, but which are difficult of
access to others and form a strong defence
against invasion. Such is this little republic,
and such the manners of its inhabitants.

VII. The sun was setting when the
captain and his followers reached the lake.
They made the prisoners dismount, and
put the booty on board the boats. Those
who had not taken part in the expedition
issued in large numbers from different sides

φαίνετο καὶ συνέθεον καὶ τὸν λήσταρχον οἱονεὶ
βασιλέα τινὰ ἑαυτῶν προσαπαντῶντες ὑπεδέ-
χοντο. Τῶν δὲ λαφύρων τὸ πλῆθος ὁρῶντες
καὶ τὸ κάλλος τῆς κόρης θεσπέσιόν τι χρῆμα
περισκοποῦντες, ἱερά τινα ἢ ναοὺς πολυχρύσους
ἀποσεσυλῆσθαι παρὰ τῶν ὁμοτέχνων ὑπε-
λάμβανον, προσαφῃρῆσθαι δὲ καὶ τὴν ἱέρειαν
αὐτὴν, ἢ καὶ αὐτὸ ἔμπνουν μετῆχθαι τὸ ἄγαλμα
διὰ τῆς κόρης, ὑπ᾽ ἀγροικίας εἴκαζον· καὶ πολλὰ
τὸν λήσταρχον τῆς ἀνδραγαθίας εὐφημοῦντες
ἐπὶ τὴν οἴκησιν αὐτοῦ παρέπεμπον. Ἡ δὲ
νησίδιον ἦν ἄποθεν τῶν ἄλλων, εἰς καταγώγιον
μόνῳ σὺν ὀλίγοις τοῖς περὶ αὐτὸν ἀπονενεμη-
μένον. Ἐνταῦθ᾽ ὡς κατήχθη, τοὺς μὲν πολ-
λοὺς οἴκαδε ἀπιέναι προσέταττεν, εἰς τὴν
ὑστεραίαν ἅπαντας ἥκειν ὡς αὐτὸν ἐπιστείλας,
αὐτὸς δὲ σὺν ὀλίγοις τοῖς εἰωθόσιν ὑπολειφθεὶς
καὶ δείπνου πρὸς βραχὺ τοῖς τ᾽ ἄλλοις μεταδοὺς
καὶ αὐτὸς μεταλαβών, τοὺς μὲν νέους Ἕλληνι
τινι παραδίδωσι νεανίσκῳ, οὐ πρὸ πολλοῦ παρ᾽
αὐτοῖς αἰχμαλώτῳ γεγονότι, τοῦ διαλέγεσθαι
ἕνεκεν καλύβης τῆς ἑαυτοῦ πλησίον ἀποκληρώ-
σας, τά τ᾽ ἄλλα ἐπιμεληθῆναι τοῦ νέου προσ-

of the marsh, and hurried to meet their chief, whom they received with as much reverence as if he had been a king. At the sight of the rich spoil and the divine beauty of the maiden, they imagined that some temple or shrine had been plundered by their companions, thinking, in their rustic simplicity, that they had carried off the priestess or the breathing image of some goddess. Then, with loud praises and congratulations, they escorted their chief in triumph to his abode.

This was a small island, apart from the rest, which he shared with a small number of intimate friends. As soon as he arrived there, he bade the multitude return home, after having ordered them all to assemble before him on the following day. He himself, with a few intimate friends, took a hasty supper, and then handed over the young couple to a young Greek, who had been taken prisoner by the brigands a short time before, that he might serve as interpreter; he lodged them in part of his own hut, and charged the Greek to pay careful attention to the young man, and, above

τάξας καὶ τὴν κόρην ἀνύβριστον ἀπὸ πάντων
διαφυλάττειν. Αὐτὸς δὲ καμάτῳ τε τῆς ὁδοι-
πορίας βαρούμενος καὶ φροντίδι τῶν παρόντων
συνεχόμενος πρὸς ὕπνον ἐτέτραπτο.

Η΄. Σιγῆς δὲ τὸ ἕλος κατεχούσης καὶ νυκτὸς
εἰς πρώτην φυλακὴν προελθούσης, τὴν ἐρημίαν
τῶν ὀχλησάντων εὐπορίαν εἰς θρήνους οἱ περὶ
τὴν κόρην ἐλάμβανον· ἀνακινούσης αὐτῆς, οἶμαι,
πλέον τὰ πάθη τῆς νυκτὸς, ἅτ᾽ οὐδεμιᾶς οὔτ᾽
ἀκοῆς οὔτ᾽ ὄψεως ἐφ᾽ ἑαυτὴν ἀντισπώσης ἀλλὰ
μόνῳ τῷ λυποῦντι σχολάζειν ἐπιτρεπούσης.
Πολλὰ δὴ οὖν ἀνοιμώξασα καθ᾽ ἑαυτὴν ἡ κόρη,
(κεχώριστο γὰρ τοῦτο προσταχθὲν ἐπί τινος
χαμεύνης κατακεκλιμένη,) καὶ ὅσον πλεῖστον
ἐπιδακρύσασα, Ἄπολλον, ἔφη, ὡς λίαν ἡμᾶς
καὶ πικρότερον ἀμύνῃ τῶν ἁμαρτημάτων. Οὐδ᾽
ἱκανά σοι πρὸς τιμωρίαν τὰ παρελθόντα; στέ-
ρησις τῶν οἰκείων, καὶ καταποντιστῶν ἅλωσις
καὶ θαλασσῶν μυρίος κίνδυνος καὶ λῃστῶν ἐπὶ
γῆς ἤδη δευτέρα σύλληψις καὶ πικρότερα τῶν
ἐν πείρᾳ τὰ προσδοκώμενα; καὶ ποῖ ταῦτα
στήσεις; εἰ μὲν εἰς θάνατον ἀνύβριστον, ἡδὺ

all, to see that no insult was offered to the young lady. He himself, exhausted by the fatigues of his journey, and overwhelmed with the anxieties of command, soon fell asleep.

VIII. When silence reigned throughout the marsh, about the first watch of the night, the maiden took advantage of the solitude and the absence of those who were likely to disturb her, to give vent to her sorrow; the quiet of the night only increased her grief, since nothing was to be seen or heard that could divert her painful thoughts. Separated from the rest by the captain's order, and lying upon a miserable couch, she sighed and shed bitter tears: "O Apollo, how cruel is the punishment you inflict upon us, far greater than our offences deserve! Is not your vengeance satisfied with the misfortunes which we have already suffered? Deprived of our parents, captured by pirates, exposed to perils without number on the sea, a second time fallen into the hands of brigands—can worse than this await us? when will you put an end to our miseries? Provided I

τὸ τέλος, εἰ δέ με γνώσεταί τις αἰσχρῶς, ἣν
μηδεπώποτε μηδὲ Θεαγένης, ἐγὼ μὲν ἀγχόνῃ
προλήψομαι τὴν ὕβριν, καθαρὰν ἐμαυτὴν ὥσπερ
φυλάττω καὶ μέχρι θανάτου φυλάξασα καὶ
καλὸν ἐντάφιον τὴν σωφροσύνην ἀπενεγκαμένη·
σοῦ δ' οὐδεὶς ἔσται δικαστὴς πικρότερος.

Καὶ ἔτι λέγουσαν ἐπεῖχεν ὁ Θεαγένης, Παῦε,
λέγων, ὦ φιλτάτη καὶ ψυχὴ ἐμὴ Χαρίκλεια·
θρηνεῖς μὲν εἰκότα παροξύνεις δὲ πλέον ἢ δοκεῖς
τὸ θεῖον. Οὐ γὰρ ὀνειδίζειν, ἀλλὰ παρακαλεῖν
χρεών. Εὐχαῖς, οὐκ αἰτίαις, ἐξιλεοῦται τὸ
κρεῖττον. Ἡ δὲ, Εὖ μὲν λέγεις, σὺ δέ μοι
πῶς ἔχεις, διηρώτα. Ῥᾷον, ἔφη, καὶ βέλτιον
ἀπὸ τῆς ἑσπέρας, ἐκ τῆς τοῦ μειρακίου θερα-
πείας ἢ τὰ φλεγμαίνοντά μοι τῶν τραυμάτων
ἐκούφισεν. Ἀλλὰ καὶ μᾶλλον εἰς ἕω κουφισ-
θήσῃ, ἔφη ὁ τὴν φρουρὰν αὐτῶν ἐπιτετραμ-
μένος· τοιαύτην σοι ποριοῦμαι βοτάνην ἣ διὰ

could die pure and without reproach, death would be welcome. But if anyone should dare to attempt to obtain by force the favours which even my Theagenes has never obtained, I would strangle myself and anticipate the insult; so would I keep myself pure and chaste, as I have hitherto done, even to the hour of death, and virtue itself should be my honourable shroud. No judge will ever be more pitiless than you, O Apollo!"

She would have proceeded, but Theagenes interrupted her: "Hush, my life, my dearest Chariclea! your laments are just, but they provoke the god more than you imagine. You must not reproach him, but invoke his aid. Prayers are more likely than accusations to appease the wrath of those who are mightier than ourselves." "You are right," she replied: "but, tell me, I beg you, how are you yourself?" "Better, since evening; this young man's attention has allayed the inflammation of my wounds." "You will find yourself much easier in the morning," rejoined their keeper: "I will apply a certain

τρίτης ἐνώσει τὰς πληγάς· ἔχω δ' αὐτῆς ἔργῳ
τὴν πεῖραν λαβών. Ἐξ οὗ γάρ με δεῦρο
αἰχμάλωτον οἵδε ἤγαγον, εἴ τίς ποτε τῶν
ὑπηκόων τῷδε τῷ ἄρχοντι συμβολῆς γενομένης
τραυματίας ἧκεν, οὐ πολλῶν ἐδεήθη πρὸς ἴασιν
ἡμερῶν, ταύτῃ τῇ βοτάνῃ χρησάμενος. Εἰ δέ
μοι μέλει τῶν ὑμετέρων οὐκ ἄξιον ὑμῖν θαυ-
μάζειν, τύχης τε γάρ μοι τῆς αὐτῆς ἐοίκατε
κοινωνεῖν καὶ ἅμα Ἕλληνας ὄντας οἰκτείρω καὶ
αὐτὸς Ἕλλην γεγονώς. Ἕλλην; ὦ θεοί, ἐπε-
βόησαν ὑφ' ἡδονῆς ἅμα οἱ ξένοι. Ἕλλην ὡς
ἀληθῶς καὶ τὸ γένος καὶ τὴν φωνήν. Τάχα τις
ἔσται τῶν κακῶι ἀνάπνευσις. Ἀλλὰ τίνα σε
χρὴ καλεῖν; ἔφη ὁ Θεαγένης. Ὁ δὲ, Κνήμωνα.
Πόθεν δὲ γνωρίζειν; Ἀθηναῖον. Τύχῃ τίνι
κεχρημένον; Παῦε, ἔφη. Τί ταῦτα κινεῖς καὶ
ἀναμοχλεύεις; τοῦτο δὴ τὸ τῶν τραγῳδῶν.
Οὐκ ἐν καιρῷ γένοιτ' ἂν ἐπεισόδιον ὑμῖν τῶν
ὑμετέρων τἀμὰ ἐπεισφέρειν κακά· καὶ ἅμα

herb to your wounds, which in three days will heal them. I know its valuable properties by experience. Since I have been a prisoner here, when any of the Captain's followers return wounded from an expedition, I apply this remedy, which soon restores them to health. Do not be surprised if I sympathize with you; your lot seems to resemble mine; besides, since I myself am a Greek, I cannot help pitying you who are Greeks."
"A Greek! Oh, heavens!" exclaimed the youthful pair, transported with joy. "Yes, most assuredly: a Greek both by birth and language." "Perhaps we shall obtain some alleviation of our sorrows. But by what name are we to call you?" "My name is Cnemon." "From what part of Greece do you come?" "From Athens." "What has been your history?" "Forbear," said Cnemon: "why do you attempt to revive the recollection of my sorrows? let us leave this to the tragedians; my story would be an unnecessary aggravation of your own misfortunes; besides, the rest of the

οὐδ' ἂν ἐπαρκέσειε τὸ λειπόμενον πρὸς τὸ διήγημα τῆς νυκτός, ὕπνου καὶ ταῦτα δεομένοις ὑμῖν ἀπὸ πολλῶν τῶν πόνων καὶ ἀναπαύσεως.

Θ. Ἐπεὶ δ' οὐκ ἀνίεσαν, ἀλλὰ παντοίως λέγειν ἱκέτευον, μεγίστην ἡγούμενοι παραψυχὴν τὴν τῶι ὁμοίων ἀκοὴν, ἄρχεται ὁ Κνήμων ἐντεῦθεν·

Ἦν μοι πατὴρ Ἀρίστιππος, τὸ μὲν γένος Ἀθηναῖος, βουλῆς δὲ τῆς ἄνω, τὴν περιουσίαν τῶν μέσων. Οὗτος, ἐπειδή μοι τὴν μητέρα τελευτῆσαι συνέβη, πρὸς δευτέρους ἀπεκλίνετο γάμους, ἐπὶ μόνῳ μοι παιδὶ σαλεύειν ἐπιμεμφόμενος καὶ τοῖς οἴκοις ἐπεισάγει γύναιον ἀστεῖον μὲν ἀλλ' ἀρχέκακον, ὄνομα Δημαινέτην. Ὡς γὰρ τάχιστα εἰσῆλθεν, ὅλον ὑπεποιεῖτο καὶ πράττειν ὅ τι βούλοιτο ἔπειθε τῇ θ' ὥρᾳ τὸν πρεσβύτην ἐπαγομένη καὶ τἆλλα ὑπερθεραπεύουσα· δεινὴ δὲ, εἴπερ τις γυναικῶν, ἐφ' ἑαυτὴν ἐκμῆναι καὶ τέχνην τὴν ἐπαγωγὸν ἐκτόπως ἠκριβωμένη, προόδοις τε τοὐμοῦ πατρὸς

night would not suffice to tell the tale, especially as you must need rest and sleep after all your fatigues."

IX. But, as they persisted and begged Cnemon to tell his story, thinking that it would be a great consolation to them to hear of misfortunes equal to their own, he began as follows:

I am the son of Aristippus, an Athenian by birth, a man of considerable means, and a member of the Areopagus. After my mother's death, he married again; I was his only son, and he did not wish to be dependent upon my care alone in his old age. He married a lady, named Demaeneta, a most charming woman, but the cause of all my misfortunes. As soon as she entered the house, she endeavoured to make herself absolute mistress, and easily persuaded the old man to do whatever she wanted, by the charm of her beauty and the obsequious attention which she bestowed upon him; more than any woman I have ever known, she possessed the art of inspiring passion, and a wonderful knack of seducing those of the opposite sex. When

3—2

ἐπιστένουσα καὶ εἰσόδοις προστρέχουσα καὶ
βραδύνοντι μεμφομένη καὶ ὡς ἀπώλετ' ἄν,
εἰ ὀλίγον ἐμέλλησε καὶ περιβάλλουσα ἐφ'
ἑκάστῳ ῥήματι καὶ ἐπιδακρύουσα τοῖς φιλή-
μασιν· οἷς ἅπασιν ὁ πατήρ μου σαγηνευθεὶς,
ὅλην ἐκείνην καὶ ἔπνει καὶ ἔβλεπεν.

Ἡ δὲ κἀμὲ τὰ πρῶτα ἶσα καὶ παῖδα ὁρᾶν
ἐπλάττετο, κἀν τούτῳ τὸν Ἀρίστιππον ὑπο-
ποιουμένη, καί ποτε καὶ ἐφίλησεν ἂν προσελ-
θοῦσα καὶ ὄνασθαί μου συνεχῶς ηὔξατο. Κἀγὼ
προσιέμην, τῶν μὲν ὄντων οὐδὲν ὑποπτεύων·
ὅτι δὲ μητρῴαν ἐνδείκνυται περὶ ἐμὲ θαυμά-
ζων διάθεσιν. Ἐπεὶ δ' ἰταμώτερον προσῄει
καὶ θερμότερα ἦν τὰ φιλήματα τοῦ πρέποντος
καὶ τὸ βλέμμα τοῦ σώφρονος ἐξιστάμενον,
πρὸς ὑπόνοιαν ἦγεν ἤδη τὰ πολλὰ καὶ ὑπέ-
φευγον καὶ πλησιάζουσαν ἀπωθούμην. Καὶ
τὰ μὲν ἄλλα τί δεῖ μηκύνοντα ἐνοχλεῖν; τὰς
πείρας ἃς καθῆκε, τὰς ὑποσχέσεις ἃς ἐπηγ-
γείλατο, νῦν μὲν παιδίον, νῦν δὲ γλυκύτατον
ὀνομάζουσα καὶ αὖθις κληρονόμον καὶ μετ'

my father went out, she wept; when he returned, she ran to meet him, complained of his long absence, and declared that, if he had delayed longer, it would have killed her; she embraced him after every word, and moistened her kisses with her tears. Ensnared by her artifices, my father saw no one but her, and lived for her alone.

At first she pretended to look upon me as her own son, thereby strengthening her hold upon my father. Sometimes she would kiss me, and desired that I would give her the pleasure of my company. I permitted her caresses, in no way suspecting the purpose she had in view; my only surprise was that she showed such motherly affection towards me. But when she grew more wanton, and her kisses became hotter than decency permitted, and her looks immodest—all this aroused my suspicions, and I began to avoid and repel her advances. I omit the rest, why need I weary you with recalling it? the different ways in which she tempted me, the promises which she made; calling me her little boy, her darling, her heir, her

ὀλίγον ψυχὴν ἑαυτῆς ἀποκαλοῦσα καὶ ἁπλῶς
τὰ καλὰ τῶν ὀνομάτων τοῖς ἐπαγωγοῖς παρα-
μιγνῦσα καὶ οἷστισι μᾶλλον προστρέχω περι-
σκοποῦσα· ὡς ἐν μὲν τοῖς σεμνοτέροις μητέρα
ἑαυτὴν ἀναπλάττουσα, ἐν δὲ τοῖς ἀτοπωτέροις
τοῦτ' ἐκεῖνο λαμπρῶς ἐρωμένην ὑποφαίνουσα.

Ι'. Τέλος δὲ γίγνεταί τι τοιοῦτον. Πανα-
θηναίων τῶν μεγάλων ἀγομένων, ὅτε τὴν ναῦν
Ἀθηναῖοι διὰ γῆς τῇ Ἀθηνᾷ πέμπουσιν,
(ἐτύγχανον μὲν ἐφηβεύων) ᾄσας δὲ τὸν εἰωθότα
παιᾶνα τῇ θεῷ καὶ τὰ νενομισμένα προπομ-
πεύσας ὡς εἶχον στολῆς, αὐτῇ χλαμύδι καὶ
αὐτοῖς στεφάνοις, ἔρχομαι οἴκαδε ὡς ἐμαυτόν.
Ἡ δὲ, ἐπειδὴ τὸ πρῶτον εἶδεν, ἐκτὸς ἑαυτῆς
γίγνεται, καὶ οὐδ' ἐσοφίστευεν ἔτι τὸν ἔρωτα
ἀλλ' ἀπὸ γυμνῆς τῆς ἐπιθυμίας προσέτρεχε
καὶ περιβαλοῦσα, ὁ νέος Ἱππόλυτος, ὁ Θησεὺς
ὁ ἐμὸς ἔλεγε. Τίνα με οἴεσθε γεγενῆσθαι, ὃς
καὶ νῦν ἐρυθριῶ διηγούμενος; ἀλλ' ἑσπέρας
γενομένης, ὁ μὲν πατὴρ εἰς τὸ πρυτανεῖον
ἐσιτεῖτο καὶ ὡς ἂν ἐν τοιαύτῃ πανηγύρει καὶ
πότῳ πανδήμῳ καὶ διανυκτερεύειν ἔμελλεν· ἡ

life and soul, mingling with the tenderest
names all that was most likely to win
my affections; in more serious matters she
played the part of a mother, but in dal-
liance clearly showed that she was in love.

X. At last, her passion declared itself.
During the celebration of the great
Panathenaic festival, the Athenians carry
a ship through the streets in honour of
Athena. I had just arrived at man's
estate, and, after I had sung the usual
hymn in honour of the goddess, and duly
led the customary procession, I returned
home, still wearing my ceremonial robes,
my head still crowned with garlands.
As soon as Demaeneta saw me, she lost
her reason, and, no longer able to dis-
guise her passion, ran towards me, calling
me "her young Hippolytus, her darling
Theseus." You can judge of my feelings
at the time, seeing that the mere recollec-
tion of it makes me blush. That evening,
my father supped in the Prytaneum; and,
as was usual on the occasion of such meet-
ings and public banquets, had arranged
to pass the night there. During the

δὲ ἐπιγίγνεταί μοι νυκτὸς καὶ ἐπειρᾶτό τινος τῶν ἀθεμίτων τυγχάνειν. Ὡς δὲ παντοίως ἀντεῖχον καὶ πρὸς πᾶσαν θεραπείαν καὶ ὑπό- σχεσιν καὶ ἀπειλὴν ἀπεμαχόμην, βαρύ τι καὶ βύθιον· στενάξασα, ἀπιοῦσα ᾤχετο· καὶ μόνην ἡ παλαμναία τὴν νύκτα ὑπερθεμένη, τῶν ἐπι- βουλῶν τῶν εἰς ἐμὲ κατήρχετο.

Καὶ πρῶτον μὲν οὐ διανέστη τότε τῆς εὐνῆς ἀλλ᾽ ἥκοντι τῷ πατρὶ καὶ τί τοῦτο πυνθανο- μένῳ, μαλακῶς τ᾽ ἔχειν ἐσκήπτετο καὶ οὐδὲν ἀπεκρίνατο τὴν πρώτην, ὡς δ᾽ ἐνέκειτο καὶ τί πεπόνθοι πολλάκις ἀνηρώτα, Ὁ θαυμαστὸς, φησὶ, νεανίας, ὁ κοινὸς ἡμῶν παῖς, ὃν ἐγὼ πλέον καὶ σοῦ ἠγάπησα (καὶ μάρτυρες οἱ θεοὶ) κύειν με πρός τινων αἰσθόμενος, ὃ δή σε τέως ἔκρυπτον, ἕως ἂν τὸ ἀσφαλὲς γνοίην, τὴν σὴν ἀπουσίαν ἐπιτηρήσας, ταῦτα δὴ τὰ εἰωθότα παραινοῦσαν καὶ σωφρονεῖν παρακελευομένην, μηδὲ πρὸς ἑταίραις ἔχειν τὸν νοῦν καὶ μέθαις, (οὐ γάρ με ἐλάνθανεν οὕτως ἔχων, σοὶ δ᾽ οὐκ

night, Demaeneta entered my room, and endeavoured to obtain the satisfaction of her unholy desires. When I firmly resisted all her caresses, promises, and threats, she sighed deeply and left me; and, when only one night had passed, the accursed woman plotted revenge.

At first, she kept her bed in the morning, and, when my father returned, and asked her what was the matter with her, she pretended that she was indisposed, and at first refused to answer him further; but at last, yielding to his pressing enquiries, she said: "That wonderful young man, that son of yours, whom I looked upon as my own, whom (as the gods can testify) I loved even more than you did, observing, from certain indications, that I was with child, (which I had concealed from you until I was certain of it) took advantage of your absence, while I was admonishing him, as I have always done, and exhorting him to be temperate, and avoid women and drinking (for I was aware of his irregularities, but I would not disclose

ἔφραζον, μή τινα λάβοιμι μητρυιᾶς ὑπόνοιαν), ταῦτα λέγουσαν μόνην πρὸς μόνον, τοῦ μὴ ἐρυθριᾶν αὐτὸν ἕνεκεν, τὰ μὲν ἄλλα ὅσα περὶ σέ τε κἀμὲ περιύβρισεν, αἰσχύνομαι λέγειν, λὰξ δὲ κατὰ τῆς γαστρὸς ἐναλλόμενος, οὕτως ἔχειν ὡς ὁρᾷς διέθηκε.

ΙΑ΄ Ταῦθ᾽ ὡς ἤκουσεν, οὐκ εἶπεν, οὐκ ἠρώτησεν, οὐκ ἀπολογίαν προὔθηκεν, ἀλλὰ πιστεύων μηδ᾽ ἂν ψεύσασθαι κατ᾽ ἐμοῦ τὴν οὕτω περὶ ἐμὲ διακειμένην, εὐθὺς ὡς εἶχε κατά τι μέρος τῆς οἰκίας περιτυχὼν, οὐδὲν εἰδότα, πὺξ ἔπαιε καὶ παῖδας προσκαλεσάμενος μάστιξιν ᾐκίζετο, μηδὲ τὸ κοινὸν δὴ τοῦτο διότι ξαινοίμην γιγνώσκοντα. Ὡς δ᾽ ἐμπέπληστο τῆς ὀργῆς, Ἀλλὰ νῦν γε, ἔφην, ὦ πάτερ, εἰ καὶ μὴ πρότερον, δίκαιος ἂν εἴην τὴν αἰτίαν τῶν πληγῶν μανθάνειν. Ὁ δὲ, μᾶλλον παροξυνθεὶς,

them to you, for fear you might suspect me as his stepmother)—while, I say, I was discussing these matters with him alone, to spare his blushes, he burst forth into such abuse of both of us, that I should be ashamed to repeat it; after which, he kicked me in the belly, and reduced me to the condition in which you now see me."

XI. On hearing these words, my father, without saying anything to me, without questioning me or giving me time to defend myself, came to the conclusion that one who had shown such affection for me could not have accused me falsely. Chancing to meet me in the house, he attacked me with his fists, called his slaves and ordered them to scourge me, although I knew not for what I was being punished, a privilege usually granted to the greatest criminals. At length, when he had satisfied his anger, I said to him: "Now at least, my father, you ought to let me know for what crime I have been scourged, although you refused to tell me before." These words only provoked him more. "Deceitful wretch!"

Ὧ τῆς εἰρωνείας, φησὶ, τὰς πράξεις αὐτοῦ τὰς
ἀνοσίας παρ' ἐμοῦ βούλεται μανθάνειν. Καὶ
ἀποστραφεὶς, πρὸς τὴν Δημαινέτην ἔσπευδεν.
Ἡ δὲ, οὔπω γὰρ κεκόρεστο, δευτέρας ἐπιβουλῆς
κατ' ἐμοῦ τοιᾶσδε ἥπτετο. Θίσβη παιδισκάριον
ἦν αὐτῇ, ψάλλειν τε πρὸς κιθάραν ἐπιστάμενον,
καὶ τὴν ὄψιν οὐκ ἄωρον. Τοῦτ' ἐπ' ἐμὲ καθίησιν,
ἐρᾶν μου δῆθεν προστάξασα· καὶ ἤρα παρα-
χρῆμα ἡ Θίσβη· καὶ ἡ πολλάκις πειρῶντά μ'
ἀπωσαμένη, τότε παντοίως ἐφείλκετο, βλέμ-
μασι, νεύμασι, συνθήμασιν. Ἐγὼ δ' ὁ μάταιος
ἀθρόον καλὸς γεγενῆσθαι ἐπεπείσμην· καὶ
τέλος ἐπὶ τὸν θάλαμον ἐλθοῦσαν νυκτὸς ὑπε-
δεχόμην. Ἡ δὲ καὶ αὖθις ἐπανῆκε καὶ πάλιν
καὶ τοῦ λοιποῦ συνεχῶς ἐφοίτα. Ἐπεὶ δέ ποτε
φυλάττεσθαι αὐτῇ τὰ πολλὰ παρῄνουν, μὴ
γνωσθείη παρὰ τῆς δεσποίνης, Ὦ Κνήμων, ἔφη,
ὡς λίαν ἀπλοϊκός τις εἶναί μοι δοκεῖς· εἰ γὰρ
ἐμὲ θεράπαιναν οὖσαν καὶ ἀργυρώνητον ἡγῇ
χαλεπὸν εἶναί σοι προσομιλοῦσαν ἁλῶναι,
τίνος ἂν ἀξίαν εἴποις εἶναι τιμωρίας ἐκείνην,
ἢ καὶ εὐγενὴς εἶναι φάσκουσα καὶ νόμῳ τὸν

he cried, "is it from me that you would learn your infamies?" Then, turning away from me, he hastened to Demaeneta, whose rage, not yet satisfied, had laid a second plot to destroy me.

She had a maid called Thisbe, a handsome girl, who played admirably upon the lute. Demaeneta sent her to me with instructions to gain my affections. Without delay, she made advances to me; and she, who had oftentimes before rejected my suit, endeavoured to attract me by looks, signs, and gestures. In my vanity, I believed that I had suddenly become an Adonis, and at last, one night, I admitted her to my arms; she visited me a second and a third time, and indeed, on several occasions. But, when I exhorted her to take care that she was not surprised by her mistress, she said: "Oh, Cnemon, how simple you are! Do you think there is any danger for a slave such as I am, bought for a price, even if I am caught with you? if so, what punishment do you think my mistress deserves, a woman who boasts of noble birth, to whom the laws

συνοικοῦντα ἔχουσα καὶ θάνατον τὸ τέλος τοῦ παρανομήματος γιγνώσκουσα, μοιχᾶται; Παῦε, ἔφην, οὐ γὰρ ἔχω σοι πιστεύειν. Ἡ δὲ, Καὶ μὴν, εἴ σοι δόξειεν, ἐπ᾽ αὐτοφώρῳ παραδώσω τὸν μοιχόν. Εἰ γὰρ οὕτω βουληθῇς, ἔφην. Καὶ μὴν βουλήσομαί γε, ἀπεκρίνατο, σοῦ θ᾽ ἕνεκεν οὕτως πρὸς αὐτῆς περιυβρισμένου, κἀμαυτῆς δ᾽ οὐκ ἔλαττον, ἢ πάσχω τὰ ἔσχατα ἐφ᾽ ἑκάστης, ζηλοτυπίαν ἐκείνης ἐπ᾽ ἐμὲ γυμναζούσης. Ἀλλ᾽ ὅπως ἀνὴρ ἔσῃ κατάλαβε.

ΙΒ'. Ἐπεὶ δ᾽ οὕτως ἕξειν ὑπεσχόμην, τότε μὲν ἀπιοῦσα ᾤχετο. Τρίτῃ δ᾽ ὕστερον νυκτὶ καθεύδοντά μ᾽ ἐξανίστησι καὶ τὸν μοιχὸν ἔνδον εἶναι κατεμήνυε· τὸν πατέρα μὲν εἰς ἀγρὸν αἰφνιδίου τινὸς χρείας καλούσης πεπορεῦσθαι λέγουσα· τὸν δὲ, οὕτω συγκείμενον αὐτῷ πρὸς τὴν Δημαινέτην, ἄρτι παρεισδεδυκέναι· προσήκειν δὲ καὶ πρὸς ἄμυναν εὐτρεπίζεσθαι καὶ ξιφήρη ποιεῖσθαι τὴν ἔφοδον τοῦ μὴ διαδρᾶναι τὸν ὑβριστήν.

have assigned a husband, and who, although she well knows that death is the punishment of conjugal infidelity, is not afraid to commit adultery?" "Do not say so," I answered, "I cannot believe you." "Well, if you like, I will let you see her in the act." "If it is your wish," I said. "It is," she answered: "I desire for your sake, you have been so cruelly outraged by her, as well as for my own, who suffer terribly every day at her hands—the result of the bitter jealousy she feels against me. Therefore be a man, and surprise her with her paramour."

XII. I promised, and she retired. Three nights afterwards, she came and woke me, telling me that Demaeneta was with her lover; that my father had been suddenly called into the country on business; and that the dishonourer of his bed had secretly, by appointment, entered his wife's room. She declared that it was my duty to prepare to avenge him and to arm myself with a sword, to prevent the villain's escape.

Ἐποίουν οὕτως· καὶ λαβὼν ἐγχειρίδιον, τῆς Θίσβης ἡγουμένης καὶ δᾷδας προαπτούσης, ἐπὶ τὸν θάλαμον ᾔειν. Ἐπεὶ δ' ἐπέστην, λύχνου τέ τινος ἔνδοθεν αὐγὴ διεξέπιπτε, [καὶ] τὰς θύρας ἐπικειμένας ὡς ὀργῆς εἶχον ἐκραγεὶς, ἀνοίγω, καὶ εἰσδραμὼν, Ποῦ ποθ' ὁ ἀλιτήριος, ἐβόων, ὁ λαμπρὸς τῆς πάντα σωφρονούσης ἐρώμενος; καὶ ἅμα λέγων, ἐπῄειν ὡς ἄμφω διαχειρισόμενος. Ἐκ δὲ τῆς εὐνῆς ὁ πατὴρ, ὦ θεοί, περιτραπεὶς προσπίπτει μου τοῖς γόνασι, καὶ, Ὦ τέκνον, ἐπίσχες μικρὸν, ἔλεγεν, οἴκτειρον τὸν γεννήσαντα, φεῖσαι πολιῶν, αἵ σε ἀνέθρεψαν. Ὕβρισα μέν σε, ἀλλ' οὐ μέχρι θανάτου τιμωρητέος. Μὴ γίγνου τῆς ὀργῆς ὅλος, μηδὲ φόνῳ πατρῴῳ χεῖρας μιάνῃς τὰς σάς. Ὁ μὲν ταῦτα καὶ ἕτερα πρὸς τούτοις ἐλεεινῶς ἱκέτευεν· ἐγὼ δὲ ὥσπερ τυφῶνι βληθεὶς, αὖος, ἀπόπληκτος εἱστήκειν, τὴν Θίσβην περιέβλεπον, οὐκ οἶδ' ὅπως ἑαυτὴν ὑποστείλασαν, τὴν κλίνην καὶ τὸν θάλαμον ἐν κύκλῳ περιεσκόπουν, εἰπεῖν τι διαπορῶν,

I did as she advised: I took a sword, and proceeded towards my father's room, while Thisbe carried a lighted torch in front. When I came to the door, I saw that there was a light burning inside; transported with rage, I broke upon the door, and rushed in, exclaiming, "Where is the wretch, the fine lover of this most virtuous woman?" With these words, I advanced, intending to run them both through with my sword. But, great heavens! my father leaped out of bed and fell on his knees before me, exclaiming: "Oh! my son, restrain yourself; pity your father; spare these grey hairs, that have brought you up. I have done you wrong, it is true; but death would be too cruel a vengeance. Do not abandon yourself to your rage, nor stain your hands with your father's blood."

Such were his piteous pleadings; for my part, as if smitten by a thunderbolt, I stood dumbfounded, unable to utter a word, looking for Thisbe, who had stealthily withdrawn. I gazed at the bed and round the room, not knowing what to say or do.

πρᾶξαι ἀμηχανῶν. Ἐκπίπτει μου καὶ τὸ ξίφος τῶν χειρῶν· καὶ τὸ μὲν ἡ Δημαινέτη προσδραμοῦσα σπουδαίως ἀνήρπασεν, ὁ δὲ πατὴρ ἐν τῷ ἀκινδύνῳ γεγονώς, ἐπιβάλλει τέ μοι τὰς χεῖρας καὶ δεσμεῖν ἐκέλευε, πολλὰ τῆς Δημαινέτης παροξυνούσης, καὶ 'Οὐ ταῦτ' ἦν ἃ προηγόρευον, βοώσης, ὡς φυλάττεσθαι προσήκει τὸ μειράκιον, ὡς ἐπιβουλεύσειε καιροῦ λαβόμενον; ἑώρων τὸ βλέμμα, συνίην τῆς διανοίας. Ὁ δὲ, Προηγόρευες, εἰπὼν, ἀλλ' ἠπίστουν, τότε μὲν ἐν δεσμοῖς εἶχε, λέγειν τι βουλομένῳ τῶν ὄντων καὶ φράζειν οὐκ ἐπιτρέψας.

ΙΓ'. Ἅμα δὲ τῇ ἔῳ λαβὼν οὕτως ὡς εἶχον δεσμῶν ἐπὶ τὸν δῆμον ἦγε καὶ τῆς κεφαλῆς κόνιν καταχεάμενος, Οὐκ ἐπὶ τοιαύταις μὲν ἐλπίσιν, ὦ Ἀθηναῖοι, τόνδε ἀνέτρεφον, ἔλεγεν, ἀλλὰ τοῦ γήρως τοὐμοῦ βακτηρίαν ἔσεσθαι προσδοκῶν, ἐπειδὴ τάχιστά μοι ἐγένετο, ἐλευθερίου τε τροφῆς μεταδούς, καὶ τὰ πρῶτα τῶν γραμμάτων διδαξάμενος, εἰς τοὺς φράτορας καὶ

The sword fell from my hand; Demaeneta jumped out of bed, and seized it. When my father saw that he was out of danger, he laid hands upon me, and gave orders that I should be bound. Demaeneta, meanwhile, continued to exasperate him. "Did I not warn you of this?" she exclaimed; "did I not tell you to be on your guard against the youth, since he would seize the first opportunity of attacking you? I read his purpose in his eyes." "It is true," replied my father; "you warned me, but I refused to believe you." He then ordered me to be kept in chains, and refused to allow me to speak, or to tell him the real truth of the matter.

XIII. As soon as it was day, he took and led me, bound as I was, before the people; then, having poured ashes over his head, he thus addressed them: "Oh Athenians, it was not in expectation of this that I brought up my son; hoping that he would prove the support of my old age, I gave him, from his earliest years, a liberal education; after I had taught him the elements of letters, I introduced

γεννητὰς εἰσαγαγὼν, εἰς ἐφήβους ἐγγράψας,
πολίτην ὑμέτερον καὶ τοῖς νόμοις ἀποφήνας,
πάντα τὸν βίον ἐπὶ τούτῳ τὸν ἐμὸν ἐσάλευον.
Ἐπεὶ δὲ, τούτων ἁπάντων λήθην λαβὼν, ἐμὲ
μὲν ὕβρισε τὰ πρῶτα καὶ πληγαῖς ταυτηνὶ τὴν
κατὰ νόμους συνοικοῦσάν μοι ᾐκίσατο· τέλος δὲ
καὶ ξιφήρης νύκτωρ ἐπῆλθε καὶ παρὰ τοσοῦτον
γέγονε πατραλοίας, παρ' ὅσον ἀντέσχεν ἡ
τύχη, ἀπροσδοκήτῳ φόβῳ τὸ ξίφος τῶν τούτου
χειρῶν ἐκπεσεῖν παρασκευάσασα, καταπέφευγα
τε πρὸς ὑμᾶς καὶ προσαγγέλλω τοῦτον,
αὐτόχειρ μὲν αὑτοῦ γενέσθαι κατὰ τοὺς νόμους
ἐξὸν, οὐ βουληθείς· ὑμῖν δὲ τὸ πᾶν καταλιπὼν,
νόμῳ βέλτιον ἡγούμενος ἢ φόνῳ παιδὸς τὴν
δίκην λαμβάνειν. Καὶ ἅμα ἐδάκρυεν· ἐπεκώκυε
δὲ καὶ ἡ Δημαινέτη καὶ περιαλγεῖν ἐπ' ἐμοὶ

him amongst the members of his clan and family, registered his name amongst those who had reached the age of manhood, and secured him the standing of a citizen of our country, in conformity with the laws; in a word, my life's hopes were centred in him. But he, forgetting all this, first abused me and assaulted my lawful wife; and at last, with a naked sword in his hand, entered my chamber by night; if he is not guilty of the murder of his own father, he has only to thank Fortune, which inspired him with sudden terror, and caused the sword to fall from his hands. I now, therefore, have recourse to you, and formally denounce him. For although, according to the law, I might have slain him with my own hand, I did not wish to do so; I am content to leave the decision in your hands, for I am convinced that it is better that my son should be punished by the verdict of the law, rather than by death before a verdict has been pronounced." With these words, he began to shed tears.

Demaeneta also wept and pretended to

δῆθεν ἐπεδείκνυτο, τὸν ἄθλιον ἀποκαλοῦσα, τὸν ἐν δίκῃ μὲν ἀλλὰ πρὸ ὥρας τεθνηξόμενον, τὸν ὑπὸ δαιμόνων ἀλαστόρων ἐπὶ τοὺς γεννήσαντας ἐλαθέντα· οὐ θρηνοῦσα μᾶλλον ἢ καταμαρτυροῦσα τοῖς θρήνοις καὶ ὡς ἀληθῆ τὴν κατηγορίαν βεβαιοῦσα τοῖς γόοις. Ἐπεὶ δὲ μεταδοῦναι κἀμοὶ λόγων ἠξίουν, ὁ γραμματεὺς προσελθὼν, ἠρώτα στενὸν ἐρώτημα, Εἰ τῷ πατρί ξιφήρης ἐπῆλθον; ἐμοῦ δὲ, Ἐπῆλθον μὲν, εἰπόντος, ἀλλ' ὅπως ἀκούσατε· ἀνεβόησαν ἅπαντες καὶ οὐδ' ἀπολογίας μοι μετεῖναι κρίναντες, οἱ μὲν λίθοις βάλλειν, οἱ δὲ τῷ δημίῳ παραδιδόναι καὶ ὠθεῖσθαι εἰς τὸ βάραθρον ἐδοκίμαζον. Ἐμοῦ δὲ παρὰ πάντα τὸν θόρυβον καὶ τὸν χρόνον, ὃν περὶ τῆς τιμωρίας διεχειροτόνουν, Ὦ μητρυιὰ, βοῶντος, διὰ μητρυιὰν ἀναιροῦμαι, μητρυιά με ἄκριτον ἀπόλλυσι,

be grieved at my sad lot. "Unhappy wretch!" she cried; "his death will be just, but premature; some avenging Deity has driven him to lift his hand against his parents." But her lamentations were not so much an indication of sorrow for me as a fresh evidence of the truth of the accusation.

In my turn, I asked permission to speak; but the clerk came forward and put the simple question to me: "Did you attack your father with a sword?" "I certainly did, but hear how that came to pass," I answered. Then all cried out that I had no right to ask to be heard in my defence. Some demanded that I should be stoned; others, that I should be handed over to the executioner; and others, that I should be thrust headlong into the Barathrum. As for myself, while all this disturbance was taking place and they were deciding what should be my punishment, I kept crying out: "Oh, stepmother! I am destroyed by a stepmother! a stepmother is taking away my life without a trial!" My words attracted the attention of some

προσέστη τοῖς πολλοῖς τὸ λεγόμενον καὶ εἰσῄει τῶν ὄντων ὑποψία. Καὶ ἠκούσθην μὲν οὐδὲ τότε, προκατείληπτο γὰρ ὁ δῆμος ἀκαταπαύστῳ θορύβῳ.

ΙΔ΄. Τῶν δὲ ψήφων διακρινομένων, οἱ μὲν τὸν θάνατον καταχειροτονήσαντες ἦσαν εἰς ἑπτακοσίους καὶ χιλίους, οἱ μὲν καταλεῦσαι, οἱ δ᾽ εἰς τὸ βάραθρον πέμψαι κρίναντες· οἱ λοιποὶ δ᾽ εἰς χιλίους, ὅσοι τι καὶ τῇ ὑπονοίᾳ τῇ κατὰ τῆς μητρυιᾶς δόντες, φυγῇ με ἐς τὸ διηνεκὲς ἐζημίωσαν Ἀλλ᾽ ὅμως ἡ τούτων ἐκράτει ψῆφος. Τῶν μὲν γὰρ ἄλλων ὁμοῦ πάντων ἦσαν ἐλάττους, ἐκείνων δὲ διάφορα ψηφισαμένων, εἰς τὸ μέρος οἱ χίλιοι πλείους ἐγένοντο. Κἀγὼ μὲν οὕτως ἐξηλαυνόμην ἑστίας τε πατρῴας καὶ τῆς ἐνεγκούσης. Οὐ μὴν ἀτιμώρητός γ᾽ ἡ θεοῖς ἐχθρὰ Δημαινέτη περιελείφθη. Τὸν δὲ τρόπον εἰσαῦθις ἀκούσεσθε, τὸ δὲ νῦν καὶ ὕπνου μεταληπτέον, τό τε γὰρ πολὺ προέβη τῆς νυκτός, καὶ ὑμῖν πολλῆς δεῖ

of the judges, and made them suspect the truth; yet even then they refused to listen to me; for the mind of the people was preoccupied by the incessant disturbance.

XIV. When the votes were counted, 1,700 were found to be in favour of putting me to death, some voting that I should be stoned; others, that I should be flung headlong into the Barathrum. The rest, to the number of 1,000—and that no doubt because their suspicions of my stepmother inclined them to mercy—were for condemning me to perpetual banishment. Their opinion gained the day; for, although the others, taken together, were in an actual majority, yet, as there had been a difference of opinion amongst them in regard to my punishment, the 1,000 votes formed a relative majority. Thus I was driven from my father's hearth and my native land. However, the gods did not suffer the wickedness of Demaeneta to go unpunished. I will tell you afterwards what happened to her. But now you must have some sleep; the

τῆς ἀναπαύσεως. Καὶ μὴν προσεπιτρίψεις γ' ἡμᾶς, ἔφη ὁ Θεαγένης, εἰ τὴν κακίστην ἀτιμώρητον ἐάσῃς ἐν τῷ λόγῳ Δημαινέτην. Οὐκοῦν ἀκούοιτ' ἀν, ἔφη ὁ Κνήμων, ἐπειδήπερ ὑμῖν οὕτω φίλον.

Ἐγὼ μὲν, ὡς εἶχον, μετὰ τὴν κρίσιν εἰς τὸν Πειραιᾶ κατέβην, καὶ νεὼς ἀναγομένης ἐπιτυχὼν, τὸν πλοῦν εἰς Αἴγιναν ἐποιούμην, ἀνεψιοὺς εἶναί μοι τῆς μητρὸς ἐνταῦθα πυνθανόμενος. Κατάρας δὲ καὶ τοὺς ἐπιζητουμένους ἀνευρὼν, οὐκ ἀηδῶς τὰ πρῶτα διῆγον. Εἰκοστῇ δ' ὕστερον ἡμέρᾳ συνήθως ἁλύων, ἐπὶ λιμένα κατῆλθον. Καὶ λέμβος ἄρτι κατεφέρετο. Μικρὸν οὖν ἐπιστὰς, ὁπόθεν τ' εἴη καὶ τίνας ἄγοι περιεσκόπουν. Οὔπω δὲ τῆς ἀποβάθρας ἀκριβῶς κειμένης, ἐξήλατό τις καί με προσδραμὼν περιέβαλεν, ἦν δ' ἄρα Χαρίας

night is far advanced and you need repose.

" By no means," said Theagenes; "you will only vex us still more, if you break off your story before telling us how this vilest of women was punished." " Listen, then," said Cnemon, " since such is your pleasure."

After the result of the trial I went down to the Piraeus, just as I was, and finding a ship there which was ready to set sail for Aegina, I embarked; for I remembered that some cousins of my mother lived there. On my arrival, I found those of whom I was in search, and at first I spent my time agreeably enough. About three weeks afterwards, in the course of my usual walk, I found myself down at the harbour; at the same moment, a bark was putting in to shore; and I waited a little to see where it hailed from, and who were on board. Almost before the ladder was properly let down, some one leaped on shore, hurried towards me, and embraced me. It turned out to be

τῶν ἐμῶν συνεφήβων, καὶ Ὦ Κνήμων, εὐαγγέ-
λιά σοι κομίζω, φησὶν· ἔχεις παρὰ τῆς πολεμίας
τὴν δίκην· Δημαινέτη τέθνηκεν. Ἀλλὰ σώζοιο
μὲν, ἔφην, ὦ Χαρία, τί δὲ παρατρέχεις τὸ
εὐαγγέλιον, ὥσπερ τι τῶν ἀτόπων ἀπαγ-
γέλλων; εἰπὲ δὲ καὶ τὸν τρόπον, ὡς σφόδρα
δέδοικα, μὴ τῷ κοινῷ κέχρηται θανάτῳ καὶ
διέδρα τὸν πρὸς ἀξίαν. Οὐ παντάπασιν, ἔφη ὁ
Χαρίας, ἐκλέλοιπεν ἡμᾶς ἡ δίκη καθ' Ἡσίοδον,
ἀλλὰ μικρὸν μὲν ἄν τι καὶ παρίδοι ποτὲ, τῷ
χρόνῳ τὴν ἄμυναν παρέλκουσα, τοῖς δ' οὕτως
ἀθέσμοις ὀξὺν ἐπιβάλλει τὸν ὀφθαλμόν· ὡς
δὴ καὶ τὴν ἀλιτήριον μετῆλθε Δημαινέτην.
Ἔλαθε δέ με τῶν γεγονότων ἢ λεχθέντων
οὐδὲν, τῆς Θίσβης, ὡς οἶσθα, κατὰ τὴν πρός
με συνήθειαν πάντα διηγουμένης. Τῆς γὰρ
ἀδίκου σοι φυγῆς ἐπιβληθείσης, ὁ μὲν ἄθλιός
σου πατὴρ ἐπὶ τοῖς πραχθεῖσι μεταμελούμενος
εἰς ἀγρόν τινα ἐσχατιὰν ἑαυτὸν ἀπῴκισε, κἀκεῖ
διῆγεν—ὃν θυμὸν κατέδων, τοῦτο δὴ τὸ τοῦ

Charias, one of the friends of my youth. "I have good news for you, Cnemon," said he; "you are revenged upon your enemy. Demaeneta is dead." "Welcome, Charias," I said; "but why hurry over this good news so rapidly, as if you were the bearer of evil tidings? Let me have further details; for I am very much afraid that she has died a natural death, and has thus escaped the punishment she deserved." "Justice, to use the words of Hesiod, has not entirely deserted us; although she sometimes appears to wink at men's crimes, and to put off the day of punishment, nevertheless she casts her avenging eye upon such criminals; and it is she who has just punished the infamous Demaeneta. I know all that was said and done; you are aware of my relations with Thisbe; she told me everything. After the unjust sentence of banishment had been pronounced upon you, your unhappy father, regretting what he had done, retired into a lonely villa in the country, far from the haunts of men, and there he passed his days, 'eating his

ἔπους· τὴν δ' εὐθὺς Ἐριννύες ἥλαυνον καὶ
μανικώτερον ἥρα σου μὴ παρόντος καὶ θρήνων
οὐκ ἐπαύετο, δῆθεν μὲν τῶν ἐπὶ σοὶ, τὸ δ'
ἀληθὲς, τῶν ἐφ' ἑαυτῇ καὶ Κνήμων ἐβόα νύκτα
τε καὶ μεθ' ἡμέραν, παιδίον γλυκύτατον, ψυχὴν
ἑαυτῆς ὀνομάζουσα, ὥστε καὶ αἱ γνώριμοι τῶν
γυναικῶν φοιτῶσαι παρ' αὐτὴν σφόδρα μὲν
ἐθαύμαζον καὶ ἐπῄνουν, εἰ μητρὸς ἢ μητρυιὰ
πάθος ἐπιδείκνυται, παραμυθεῖσθαί τε καὶ
ἐπιρρωννῦναι ἐπειρῶντο. Ἡ δὲ, ἀπαραμύθητον
εἶναι τὸ κακὸν καὶ οἷον ἐγκεῖσθαι τῇ καρδίᾳ
κέντρον ἀγνοεῖν τὰς ἄλλας ἔλεγεν.

ΙΕ'. Εἰ δέ ποτε γένοιτο καθ' ἑαυτὴν, πολλὰ
τὴν Θίσβην ἐμέμφετο, ὡς οὐ προσηκόντως
ὑπηρετησαμένην, Ἡ σπουδαία περὶ τὰ δεινὰ,
λέγουσα, ἡ πρὸς μὲν τὸν ἔρωτα μὴ συμπράξασα,
ἐπὶ δὲ τὸ στερηθῆναί με τοῦ φιλτάτου καὶ
λόγου ταχίων ἀποδειχθεῖσα, μηδὲ μεταβου-

heart out,' in the words of the poet. As for Demaeneta, the Furies immediately began to torment her; your absence had only inflamed her passion for you; she never ceased to weep, apparently for your misfortunes, but in reality for her own unhappy fate; night and day she cried, 'Oh, Cnemon, my dear, my darling boy, my well-beloved!' The ladies of her acquaintance, when they came to visit her, were astonished, and loudly praised her, because, although only a stepmother, she showed a mother's affection. They endeavoured to console her and restore her courage; but she answered that her sorrow was inconsolable, and that others did not know by what goads her heart was pierced.

XV. "Whenever she was alone, she bitterly reproached Thisbe for not having served her properly: 'How ready you were to do harm, how slow to assist me in my love! you hastened, almost before the words were uttered, to deprive me of all that I held most dear, without even leaving me time to reflect or change my

λεύσασθαί μοι συγχωρήσασα. Καὶ δήλη παν-
τοίως ἐγένετο κακόν τι διαθήσουσα τὴν Θίσβην.
Ἡ δὲ βαρυμηνιῶσαν ὁρῶσα καὶ πάντῃ λυπη-
θεῖσαν, ἐπιβουλεῦσαι πρόχειρον καὶ οὐχ ἥκιστα
τῷ τε θυμῷ καὶ ἔρωτι περιμανῆ τυγχάνουσαν,
ἔγνω προλαβεῖν καὶ φθῆναι, τῇ κατ' ἐκείνης
ἐπιβουλῇ σωτηρίαν ἑαυτῇ περιποιοῦσα· καὶ
προσελθοῦσα, Τί ταῦτα, ὦ δέσποινα, ἔλεγε, τί
μάτην ἔχεις ἐν αἰτίᾳ τὴν σὴν θεραπαινίδα; ἐγὼ
μέν σοι πρὸς τὸ βούλημα τὸ σὸν ἀεί τε καὶ
νῦν ὑπηρετησάμην. Εἰ δέ τι τῶν μὴ κατὰ
γνώμην ἐκβέβηκεν, ἐκεῖνα μὲν τῇ τύχῃ λογισ-
τέον, ἕτοιμος δ' εἰμὶ, εἰ κελεύεις, ἐπινοεῖν τινα
τῶν παρόντων λύσιν. Ἡ δὲ, Καὶ τίς ἂν
εὑρεθείη, φιλτάτη, ἔφη, τοῦ δυναμένου λῦσαι
τὰ νῦν ἐκποδὼν γεγονότος κἀμὲ τῆς παρ'
ἐλπίδας τῶν δικαζόντων φιλανθρωπίας ἀνελού-
σης; Εἰ γὰρ ἐβέβλητο τοῖς λίθοις, εἰ γὰρ
ἀνήρητο, πάντως ἂν κἀμοὶ συνετεθνήκει τὰ τοῦ
πάθους. Τὸ γὰρ ἀπελπισθὲν ἅπαξ, ἐξῄρηται

mind.' From these words, it was perfectly clear that she intended to do Thisbe a mischief.

"The latter, seeing how furiously indignant her mistress was, devoured by rage, and ready to plot against her, out of her mind, as she was, from anger and love, resolved to anticipate her, and, by laying a trap for her, to provide for her own safety. 'Why do you accuse your servant without cause, oh, my mistress?' said she; 'I have always, both now and in the past, studied your wishes; if anything has happened contrary to them, you must set it down to Fortune; I myself, even now, am ready, if you so desire it, to assist you in finding some remedy for your present distress.' 'But what remedy can be found, my dear girl?' she asked; 'he who alone might have comforted me is far away, and the unexpected clemency of the judges has destroyed me. If he had been stoned, if he had been killed, my desire would have ended with his life. For, when once all hope is lost, desire is extin-

τῆς ψυχῆς καὶ τὸ μηδαμόθεν ἔτι προσδοκώ-
μενον ἀπαλγεῖν παρασκευάζει τοὺς κάμνοντας.
Νῦν δ' ὁρᾶν φαντάζομαι, παρόντος ἀκούειν
ἀπατῶμαι, ὀνειδίζοντα τὴν ἄδικον ἐπιβουλὴν
αἰσχύνομαι συντεύξασθαι. Ποτὲ δ' ἐπελθόντι
καὶ ἀπολαύσειν, ἢ καὶ αὐτὴ παρ' ἐκεῖνον
φοιτήσειν, ὅπου ποτ' ἂν ᾖ γῆς, ὑποτίθεμαι.
Ταῦθ' ὑπεκκαίει, ταῦτ' ἐκμαίνει· δίκαια μὲν, ὦ
θεοὶ, πάσχω· τί γὰρ οὐ περιεῖπον ἀλλ' ἐπεβού-
λευον; τί δ' οὐχ ἱκέτευον ἀλλ' ἐδίωκον; ἠρνή-
σατο τὴν πρώτην; ἀλλὰ προσηκόντως. Ἀλλο-
τρίαν μὲν ἀλλ' οὖν γε πατρῴαν εὐνὴν ᾐσχύνετο.
Τυχὸν ἂν μετεπείσθη χρόνῳ πρὸς τὸ ἡμερώτερον
καὶ πειθοῖ μεταπλαττόμενος. Ἀλλ' ἡ θηριώδης
ἐγὼ καὶ ἀνήμερος, ὥσπερ οὐκ ἐρῶσά τινος ἀλλ'
ἄρχουσα, δεινὸν ὅτι μὴ ἐξ ἐπιτάγματος ὑπή-
κουσεν ἐποιησάμην, καὶ εἰ τῆς Δημαινέτης

guished in the soul; and the impossibility
of reckoning upon anything in the future
hardens the afflicted to sorrow. But now
I seem to see him by my side, to hear
his voice; he reproaches me with my
unjust perfidy, and I blush for very shame
to hear him. Sometimes I fancy that he
will come back, and that I shall possess
him; at other times I determine to go in
search of him, wheresoever he may be.
Such thoughts inflame my mind, they
drive me mad. Oh Gods! I deserve my
sufferings. Why, instead of trying to win
his affection by kindness, did I plot against
him? why, instead of supplicating him,
did I pursue him with my hatred? He
at first rejected my advances, as was
only natural. I belonged to another, and,
above all, he was ashamed to defile his
father's bed. Perhaps time would have
rendered him more tractable; persuasion
might have induced him to yield. But I,
cruel and savage beast that I was, treated
him more like a tyrant than a mistress,
and wrought a cruel deed against him,
because he did not obey my commands

ὑπερεῖδε πολὺ τὴν ὥραν αὐτῆς ὑπερβάλλων.
Ἀλλ' ὦ γλυκεῖα Θίσβη, τίνα λύσιν ὠνόμαζες
ῥαδίαν; Ὦ δέσποινα, ἔφη, τοῖς πολλοῖς μὲν ὁ
Κνήμων ὑπεξῆλθε τοῦ ἄστεος καὶ τῆς Ἀττικῆς
ἐξώρμησε τῇ κρίσει πειθόμενος, ἐμὲ δ' ἅπαντα
διά σε πραγματευομένηι οὐκ ἔλαθεν, αὐτοῦ
που πρὸ τοῦ ἄστεος παρακρυπτόμενος. Ἀρσι-
νόην ἀκούεις που πάντως τὴν αὐλητρίδα; ταύτῃ
ἐκέχρητο. Μετὰ δὲ τὴν δυστυχίαν, ὑποδέχεται
αὐτὸν ἡ μεῖραξ καὶ συναπαίρειν ἐπαγγελλομένη,
παρ' ἑαυτῇ κατέχει, κρυπτόμενον τέως, ἕως ἂν
συσκευάσηται. Καὶ ἡ Δημαινέτη, Μακαρία
μὲν Ἀρσινόη, φησὶ, τῆς τε πρότερον πρὸς
Κνήμωνα συνηθείας, καὶ τῆς σὺν αὐτῷ νυνὶ
προσδοκωμένης ἐκδημίας. Ἀλλὰ τί ταῦτ' ἂν
εἴη πρὸς ἡμᾶς; Μεγάλα, ἔφη, ὦ δέσποινα.
Ἐρᾶν μὲν ἐγὼ προσποιήσομαι τοῦ Κνήμωνος,
παρακαλέσω δὲ τὴν Ἀρσινόην, οὖσάν μοι πάλαι
γνώριμον ἀπὸ τῆς τέχνης, εἰσαγαγεῖν με ὡς

and spurned the advances of Demaeneta, whom he far surpassed in beauty. But, my dear Thisbe, what is this easy remedy of which you speak?' 'Mistress,' she replied, 'it is generally believed that Cnemon left the city and Attica, in obedience to the sentence of banishment pronounced upon him; but I, who have made the most careful enquiries in your interest, have discovered that he is concealed somewhere in the neighbourhood of the city. You have no doubt heard of the flute-player Arsinoe; he was on intimate terms with her. After his misfortune, she received him, and, having promised to share his exile, is now hiding him in her house until she has made the necessary preparations for the journey.' 'Happy Arsinoe,' cried Demaeneta; 'how I envy your former relations with him, and the exile into which you are now going to accompany him! But, what has all this to do with us?' 'Much, my mistress,' replied Thisbe; 'I will pretend that I am in love with Cnemon, and I will ask Arsinoe, with whom I have long had professional

αὐτὸν νύκτωρ ἀνθ᾽ αὑτῆς· ὅπερ εἰ γένοιτο, σὸν
ἂν εἴη τὸ ἐντεῦθεν Ἀρσινόην εἶναι δοκεῖν καὶ
φοιτᾶν παρ᾽ αὐτὸν ὡς ἐκείνην. Μελήσει δέ μοι
καὶ ὑποβεβρεγμένον αὐτὸν κατακλῖναι παρα-
σκευάσαι. Εἰ δὲ τύχοις, ὧν βούλει, μάλιστα
μὲν εἰκὸς σχολάσειν τὸν ἔρωτα, πολλαῖς γὰρ
κατὰ τὴν πρώτην πεῖραν ἐναπεσβέσθη τὰ τῆς
ἐπιθυμίας· κόρος γὰρ ἔρωτος τῶν ἔργων τὸ
τέλος. Εἰ δ᾽ ἐναπομείνειεν, ὃ μὴ γένοιτο,
δεύτερος ἔσται, φασὶ, πλοῦς καὶ ἑτέρα βουλή·
Τὸ παρὸν τέως θεραπεύωμεν.

ΙΕʹ. Ἐπῄνει ταῦθ᾽ ἡ Δημαινέτη καὶ προσ-
τιθέναι τάχος τοῖς δεδογμένοις ἱκέτευεν. Ἡ
δὲ μίαν ἡμέραν ἐνδοθῆναι αὐτῇ πρὸς τὸ διανῦσαι
ταῦτα παρὰ τῆς δεσποίνης αἰτήσασα, παρὰ
μὲν τὴν Ἀρσινόην ἐλθοῦσα, Τελέδημον οἶσθα,
ἔλεγε· τῆς δ᾽ ὁμολογούσης, Ὑπόδεξαι ἡμᾶς,
ἔφη, τὸ τήμερον· ὑπεσχόμην γὰρ αὐτῷ συγκα-

relations, to introduce me to him some night in her stead. If she consents, it will rest with you to represent that you are Arsinoe and to take her place by his side. I myself will take care that he does not go to bed until he has drunk pretty freely. If you obtain what you desire, in all probability your passion will be cured; for very frequently the first experience extinguishes the flame of desire; when we have once got what we want, love is sated. If, however, your passion continues (which heaven forfend l), we must set sail again, in the words of the proverb, and try some other scheme. Meanwhile, let us think about the present.'

XVI. "Demaeneta eagerly embraced the proposal, and begged Thisbe to put it into execution without delay. Having asked her mistress to allow her a day to make all necessary arrangements, she hurried to Arsinoe, and asked her if she knew Teledemus. When Arsinoe answered that she did, Thisbe said, ' Will you let us come to your house this evening, for I have promised to see him to-night ? He will

θευδήσειν· ήξει δὲ πρότερος, ἐγὼ δὲ, ὅταν κατακλίνω τὴν δέσποιναν. Πρὸς δὲ τὸν Ἀρίστιππον εἰς ἀγρὸν διαδραμοῦσα, Ὦ δέσποτα, ἔλεγεν, ἥκω σοι κατήγορος ἐμαυτῆς καὶ κέχρησο ὅ τι βούλει. Τὸν παῖδα δι' ἐμὲ τὸ μέρος ἀπολώλεκας οὐχ ἑκοῦσαν μὲν ἀλλ' ὅμως συναιτίαν γενομένην. Αἰσθομένη γὰρ τὴν δέσποιναν οὐκ ὀρθῶς βιοῦσαν ἀλλ' εὐνὴν τὴν σὴν ὑβρίζουσαν, αὐτή τε περὶ ἐμαυτῆς δείσασα μή ποτε κακὸν λάβοιμι, τὸ πρᾶγμα εἰ δι' ἄλλου φωραθείη καὶ ἐπί σοι περιαλγήσασα, εἰ οὕτω περιέπων τὴν συνοικοῦσαν τοιαῦτα ἀντιπάσχοις, αὐτὴ μέν σοι προσαγγεῖλαι κατώκνησα, φράζω δὲ τῷ νέῳ δεσπότῃ, νύκτωρ παρ' αὐτὸν ἐλθοῦσα, ὡς ἂν γνοίη μηδεὶς, καὶ ἔλεγον, ὡς μοιχὸς ἅμα τῇ δεσποίνῃ συγκαθεύδοι. Ὁ δὲ, (προυλελύπητο γὰρ, ὡς οἶσθα, πρὸς αὐτῆς) ἔνδον εἶναι τότε με λέγειν τὸν μοιχὸν νομίσας, ὀργῆς ἀκατασχέτου πληρωθεὶς, ἀνελόμενος τὸ ἐγχειρίδιον, ἐμοῦ πολλὰ κατέχειν πειρωμένης καὶ

come first, and I will follow, after I have put my mistress to bed.' Thisbe then hurried into the country to Aristippus, and said to him: 'Master I am come to accuse myself before you; punish me as you think fit; I helped to ruin your son, against my will indeed, but nevertheless I did so. Knowing that my mistress led a dissipated life and defiled your bed, I feared some misfortune for myself, in case anyone discovered what was going on; but, above all, I was grieved to see you so ill-rewarded for the affection which you bestowed upon your wife. Being afraid, however, of revealing the state of affairs to you, I told my young master; I went to him by night, that no one might know anything about it, and told him that my mistress was in the habit of sleeping with a lover. He, being (as you know) already embittered against her, thought that I meant that a lover was actually in her room, and, in a transport of ungovernable rage, he seized a sword, and ran madly towards your chamber. I did my utmost to hold him back, assuring him that there

ὡς οὐδὲν εἴη τοιοῦτον ἐπὶ τοῦ παρόντος λεγού-
σης, μικρὰ φροντίσας ἢ καὶ μεταβαλέσθαι
προσδοκήσας, ἐπὶ τὸν θάλαμον ἐμμανὴς ἵεται·
καὶ τὰ λοιπὰ γιγνώσκεις. Τὸ δὲ παρὸν ἔνεστί
σοι βουλομένῳ πρὸς τὸν παῖδα καὶ εἰ φεύγει
τὰ νῦν ἀπολογήσασθαι καὶ παρὰ τῆς ἀμφο-
τέρους ὑμᾶς ἀδικούσης τιμωρίαν λαβεῖν. Ἐπι-
δείξω γάρ σοι τήμερον ἅμα τῷ μοιχῷ τὴν
Δημαινέτην ἐν οἰκίᾳ καὶ ταῦτ' ἀλλοτρίᾳ ἐκτὸς
τοῦ ἄστεος κατακεκλιμένην. Εἰ γὰρ ταῦθ'
οὕτως ἐπιδείξειας, φησὶν ὁ Ἀρίστιππος, σοὶ
μὲν ἐλευθερίας μισθὸς ἀποκείσεται, ἐγὼ δὲ
τάχ' ἂν ἐπιβιῴην τὴν πολεμίαν ἀμυνόμενος.
Ὡς πάλαι γε σμύχομαι ἐμαυτῷ καὶ τὸ πρᾶγμα
δι' ὑποψίας ἔχων, ἀπορίᾳ τῶν ἐλέγχων ἡσύ-
χαζον. Ἀλλὰ τί δεῖ ποιεῖν; ἡ δέ, Τὸν κῆπον
οἶσθα, ἔλεγεν, ἔνθα τὸ μνῆμα τῶν Ἐπικουρείων;
ἐνταῦθ' εἰς ἑσπέραν ἐλθὼν περίμενε.

ΙΖ΄. Καὶ ἅμ' εἰποῦσα ἀπέτρεχε καὶ πρὸς
τὴν Δημαινέτην ἐλθοῦσα, Κόσμει, ἔφη, σαυτήν,

was no one in the room at that moment; he paid no heed to what I said, or perhaps he thought that I had repented and changed my mind. The rest you know. Now, if you wish, you can at least clear your son's character, although he is now in exile, and punish her who has done you so much injury. This very day I will show you Demaeneta in bed with her lover, and, what is worse, in a strange house, outside the city.' 'If you show me this,' said Aristippus, 'your freedom shall be your reward. Life will always be unendurable, until I have punished this enemy of my household. For a long time I have been tortured by anxiety; but, although I suspected her, I remained silent, for want of convincing proofs. But what must I do now?' 'You know the garden in which the Epicurean monument stands; go and wait for me there in the evening.'

XVII. "With these words, she returned to the house, and went to find Demaeneta. 'Come,' she said, 'dress yourself carefully; you must keep the

ἁβρότερον ἔχουσαν ἥκειν προσήκει· πάντα σοι τὰ ἐπηγγελμένα ηὐτρέπισται. Ἡ δὲ περιέβαλέ τε καὶ ἔπραττεν ὡς ἐκέλευσεν. Ἤδη δ᾽ ἑσπέρας οὔσης, ἀναλαβοῦσα ἦγεν, οὗ συνετέτακτο. Ἐπεὶ δ᾽ ἐπλησίαζον, τὴν μὲν ἐπιστῆναι μικρὸν ἐκέλευεν· αὐτὴ δὲ προλαβοῦσα παρεκάλει τὴν Ἀρσινόην εἰς ἕτερον μεταστῆναι δωμάτιον καὶ σχολὴν αὐτῇ παρασχεῖν. Ἐρυθριᾶν γὰρ, ἔφη, τὸ μειράκιον, ἄρτι τῶν Ἀφροδίτης μυούμενον. Τῆς δὲ πεισθείσης, ἐπανελθοῦσα παραλαμβάνει τὴν Δημαινέτην καὶ εἰσαγαγοῦσα κατακλίνει τε καὶ τὸν λύχνον ἀφαιρεῖ, τοῦ μὴ γνωρισθῆναι αὐτὴν παρά σου δῆθεν τοῦ ἐν Αἰγίνῃ διάγοντος καὶ σιωπῶσαν πληροῦν τὴν ἐπιθυμίαν παρεγγυήσασα, ἐγὼ δ᾽ ἐπὶ τὸν νεανίαν ἄπειμι, φησὶ, καὶ ἥξω σοι φέρουσα. Πίνει δ᾽ ἐνταῦθα ἐκ γειτόνων. Καὶ ὑπεξελθοῦσα, τὸν μὲν Ἀρίστιππον ἔνθα προεί-

appointment in an elegant attire. I have arranged everything as I promised you.' Demaeneta dressed herself according to Thisbe's instructions. When evening came, Thisbe took her to the place of assignation. When they were close to the house, she bade her wait a little; then she went on and asked Arsinoe to go into another room and leave her undisturbed, being desirous, as she said, of sparing the young man's blushes, since he had only recently been initiated into the mysteries of love. Having without difficulty persuaded Arsinoe, she went out, and fetched Demaeneta, took her into the house and put her to bed. Then she took away the light, in order, as she pretended, that she might not be recognised by you, (who were at the time in Aegina), and bade her satisfy her passion without saying anything. ' I myself,' she said, ' will now go and find the young man and bring him to you. He is drinking somewhere in the neighbourhood.' As soon as she was outside, she ran to find Aristippus at the place which had been agreed upon,

ρητο καταλαμβάνει καὶ δεσμεῖν ἐπιστάντα τὸν μοιχὸν ἤπειγεν. Ὁ δ' εἵπετο καὶ ἐπιστὰς εἰστρέχει τ' εἰς τὸ δωμάτιον καὶ τὴν κλίνην πρὸς μικρὰν τῆς σελήνης αὐγὴν χαλεπῶς ἀνευρών, Ἔχω σε, εἶπεν, ὦ θεοῖς ἐχθρά. Καὶ ἡ Θίσβη παραχρῆμα, ταῦτα λέγοντος, τάς τε θύρας ὡς ὅτι πλεῖστον ἐψόφησε καὶ Ὦ τῆς ἀτοπίας, διαδέδρακεν ἡμᾶς ὁ μοιχὸς, ἀνεβόησε· καὶ ὅρα, δέσποτα, μὴ καὶ τὰ δεύτερα σφαλῇς. Ὁ δὲ, Θάρσει, ἔφη· τὴν ἀλιτήριον καὶ ἣν μάλιστα ἐβουλόμην ἔχω. Καὶ συλλαβόμενος ἦγεν ὡς ἐπὶ τὴν πόλιν. Ἡ δ' ἅμα πάντα τὰ περιεστῶτα, ὡς εἰκὸς, ἐννοήσασα, τὴν ἀποτυχίαν τῶν προσδοκηθέντων, τὴν ἐπὶ τοῖς παροῦσιν ἀτιμίαν, τὴν ἐκ τῶν νόμων τιμωρίαν, ἀνιωμένη μὲν ἐφ' οἷς ἡλίσκετο, χαλεπαίνουσα δ' ἐφ' οἷς ἠπάτητο, ἐπειδὴ κατὰ τὸν βόθρον ἐγένετο τὸν ἐν Ἀκαδημίᾳ, (πάντως γιγνώσκεις ἔνθα τοῖς ἥρωσιν οἱ πολέμαρχοι τὸ πάτριον ἐναγίζουσιν,) ἐνταῦθ' ἀθρόον τοῦ πρεσβύτου

and urged him to go without delay, and
bind the adulterer fast. He followed her,
and, when he arrived at the house, rushed
into the room, found his way to the bed
as well as he could by the dim light of
the moon, and exclaimed, 'Now I have
caught you, oh ! accursed woman.' While
he was speaking, Thisbe rattled the doors
as loudly as she could, and cried out,
'What untoward misfortune ! her para-
mour has escaped. Mind you do not fail
a second time.' 'Make yourself easy,' he
answered, 'I have the abandoned woman
in my power; it was she whom I wanted
most.' With these words he seized her and
dragged her towards the city. Demaeneta,
reflecting, no doubt, upon her terrible situ-
ation, the disappointment of her hopes,
her present disgrace, and the punishment
which awaited her at the hands of the
law, enraged at having been surprised,
and furious at having been deceived, seized
the moment when she was passing by the
pit which is in the Academy (you know
the place where the generals offer sacrifice
to the shades of the heroes), suddenly

σπαράξασα τὰς χεῖρας ὦσεν ἑαυτὴν ἐπὶ κεφαλήν.

Καὶ ἡ μὲν ἔκειτο κακὴ κακῶς, ὁ δ' Ἀρίστιππος, ἔχω παρά σου καὶ πρὸ τῶν νόμων τὴν δίκην, εἰπὼν τότε, τῷ δήμῳ πάντα εἰς τὴν ἑξῆς ἀνεκοινοῦτο καὶ μόλις συγγνώμης τυχὼν, τοὺς φίλους περιενόστει καὶ γνωρίμους εἴ πή σοι κάθοδον λάβοι πρυτανευόμενος. Καὶ εἰ μέν τι πέπρακται τούτων οὐκ ἔχω λέγειν, ἔφθην γὰρ δεῦρο, ὡς ὁρᾷς, κατά τι χρέος ἐμὸν ἴδιον ἐκπλεύσας. Πλὴν ἀλλὰ χρή σε προσδοκᾶν, τήν τε κάθοδον ἐπινεύσειν τὸν δῆμον καὶ τὸν πατέρα σου κατὰ ζήτησιν ἥξειν· τοῦτο γὰρ ἐπηγγέλλετο.

ΙΗ'. Ταῦτά μοι ὁ Χαρίας ἀπήγγειλε. Τὰ δ' ἑξῆς καὶ ὅπως δεῦρο ἀφικόμην, καὶ τίσι ποτὲ κεχρημένος τύχαις, μακροτέρου δεῖται καὶ λόγου καὶ χρόνου. Καὶ ἅμα ἐδάκρυεν. Ἐδάκρυον δὲ

tore herself from the hands of the old man, and leaped headlong into the pit. Thus the miserable woman perished by a miserable death.

"Thereupon Aristippus exclaimed, 'I have obtained satisfaction from you, without having recourse to the law.' On the following day, he laid everything before the people, and having with difficulty obtained pardon, went round amongst his friends and acquaintances, to consult them as to the best means of securing your return. I cannot tell you whether anything has been done; for, as you see, being summoned here on private business, I set sail before anything had been decided. You may, however, feel sure that the people will agree to your return and that your father will come and fetch you; he has announced his intention of doing so."

XVIII. This was what Charias had to tell me. As for the rest of my story, how I came here, what I have gone through, it would take up too much time to tell.

With these words, he shed tears; the

καὶ οἱ ξένοι· τὰ μὲν ἐκείνου πρόφασιν, μνήμῃ δὲ τῶν ἰδίων ἕκαστος. Καὶ οὐδ' ἂν ἔληξαν θρηνοῦντες, ὑφ' ἡδονῆς τῶν γόων, εἰ μή τις ὕπνος ἐπιπτὰς ἔπαυσε τῶν δακρύων. Καὶ οἱ μὲν οὕτως ἐκάθευδον. Ὁ δὲ Θύαμις (τοῦτο γὰρ ἦν ὄνομα τῷ ληστάρχῳ) τῆς νυκτὸς τὸ πλεῖστον ἠρεμήσας, ὑπό τινων ὀνειράτων πεπλανημένων τεταραγμένος ἀθρόον τὸν ὕπνον ἀποσεσύλητο καὶ τὴν ἐπίλυσιν διαπορῶν ἐπηγρύπνει τοῖς φροντίσμασι. Καθ' ὃν γὰρ καιρὸν ἀλεκτρυόνες ᾄδουσιν, εἴτε (ὡς λόγος) αἰσθήσει φυσικῇ, τῆς τοῦ ἡλίου καθ' ἡμᾶς περιστροφῆς ἐπὶ τὴν τοῦ θεοῦ πρόσρησιν κινούμενοι, εἴθ' ὑπὸ θερμότητος ἅμα καὶ τῆς περὶ τὸ κινεῖσθαι καὶ σιτεῖσθαι θᾶττον ἐπιθυμίας, τοὺς συνοικοῦντας ἰδίῳ κηρύγματι ἐπὶ ἔργον ἐγείροντες, ὄναρ αὐτῷ θεῖον ἔρχεται τοιόνδε. Κατὰ τὴν Μέμφιν μὲν τὴν ἑαυτοῦ πόλιν, καὶ τὸν νεὼν τῆς Ἴσιδος ἐπερχόμενος

strangers did the same, apparently moved by the tale of his misfortunes, but really at the memory of their own. Their lamentations would never have ceased, had not sleep, induced by the luxury of their grief, suddenly come upon them and dried their tears. Thus, then, they went to sleep. In the meantime, Thyamis (this was the robber chieftain's name), who had rested quietly during the greater part of the night, was afterwards tormented by wandering visions; and, pondering what could be the meaning of the dream, he lay awake all night, plunged in meditation. It was the hour when the cocks begin to crow, either because a natural instinct warns them of the return of the sun to earth and they are moved to salute the god, or because a feeling of warmth and an eager desire to move and eat inclines them to rouse to work those who live in the same house. At this moment the gods sent Thyamis a vision.

He thought that he was in Memphis, his native country; he entered the temple

λαμπάδων πυρὶ τὸν ὅλον ἐδόκει καταλάμ-
πεσθαι· πεπλῆσθαι δὲ βωμοὺς μὲν καὶ ἐσχάρας
ζώων παντοίων αἵματι διαβρόχους, προπύλαια
δὲ καὶ περιδρόμους ἀνθρώπων κρότου καὶ
θορύβου συμμιγοῦς πάντα πληρούντων. Ἐπεὶ
δὲ καὶ αὐτῶν ἐντὸς ἥκειν τῶν ἀνακτόρων, τὴν
θεὸν ὑπαντῶσαν, ἐγχειρίζειν τε τὴν Χαρίκλειαν
καὶ λέγειν, ὦ Θύαμι, τήνδε σοι τὴν παρθένον
ἐγὼ παραδίδωμι, σὺ δ' ἔχων οὐχ ἕξεις, ἀλλ'
ἄδικος ἔσῃ καὶ φονεύσεις τὴν ξένην· ἡ δ' οὐ
φονευθήσεται. Ταῦθ' ὡς εἶδεν, ἀμηχάνως διῆγε,
τῇδε κἀκεῖσε τὸ δηλούμενον ὅ τι ποτ' ἐστὶν
ἀναστρέφων. Ἤδη δ' ἀπειρηκὼς, ἕλκει πρὸς
τὴν ἑαυτοῦ βούλησιν τὴν ἐπίλυσιν. Τὸ μὲν
γάρ, ἕξεις καὶ οὐχ ἕξεις, γυναῖκα καὶ οὐκ ἔτι
παρθένον ὑπετίθετο· τὸ δὲ, φονεύσεις, τὰς
παρθενίους τρώσεις εἴκαζεν, ὑφ' ὧν οὐκ ἀπο-
θανεῖσθαι τὴν Χαρίκλειαν. Καὶ τὸ μὲν ὄναρ
τοῦτον ἔφραζε τὸν τρόπον, οὕτως αὐτῷ τῆς
ἐπιθυμίας ἐξηγουμένης.

of Isis, which seemed to be one blaze of
lamps; the altars were full of all kinds of
victims, and dripping with blood; the
vestibule of the temple and its open spaces
were filled by a noisy and agitated crowd.
After he had entered the sanctuary, the
goddess came forward to meet him,
and presenting Chariclea to him, said:
"Thyamis, I intrust this maiden to your
care; you shall possess her without pos-
sessing her; you shall be guilty of a crime,
you shall cover the stranger with blood,
but she shall not die." This vision sorely
troubled him: after turning the words
over every way in his mind, in order to
discover their meaning, he at last gave
up the attempt, and interpreted them in
accordance with his own desires. "You
shall possess her without possessing her,"
he interpreted to mean that he should
have her as a wife, not as a virgin; by
the words "you shall cover her with blood,"
he understood the wounds inflicted upon
her virginity, wounds which would not
prove mortal. In this manner he explained
the vision, agreeably to the suggestions of
his passion.

ΙΘ'. Ἅμα δὲ τῇ ἔῳ, τούς τε πρώτους τῶν ὑφ' αὑτὸν ἥκειν ἐκέλευε καὶ λάφυρα, τὰ σκῦλα σεμνότερον ὀνομάζων, φέρειν εἰς μέσους ἐπέταττε. Καὶ τὸν Κνήμωνα ὡς αὑτὸν μετεπέμπετο, ἄγειν καὶ τοὺς φρουρουμένους ἐντειλάμενος. Ἐπεὶ δ' ἤγοντο, Τίς ἄρα τύχη διαδέξεται ἡμᾶς, ἐβόων καὶ πολλὰ τὸν Κνήμωνα ἱκέτευον εἴ τι δύναιτο συμπράττειν Ὁ δ' ἐπηγγέλλετο καὶ θυμὸν ἔχειν ἀγαθὸι προῦτρεπεν· οὐ παντάπασι βάρβαρον εἶναι τὰ ἤθη τὸν λήσταρχον ἐγγυώμενος ἀλλ' ἔχειν τι καὶ ἥμερον, γένος τ' ὄντα τῶν ἐπὶ δόξης καὶ πρὸς ἀνάγκης τὸν παρόντα βίον ἑλόμενον. Ἐπεὶ δ' ἤχθησαν, ἤθροιστο δὲ καὶ ὁ λοιπὸς ὅμιλος, ἐπί τινος ὑψηλοῦ προκαθίσας ἑαυτὸν ὁ Θύαμις καὶ τὴν νῆσον ἐκκλησίαν ἀποφήνας καὶ τὰ λεχθησόμενα φράζειν τὸν Κνήμωνα [καὶ] τοῖς αἰχμαλώτοις προστάξας, (συνίη γὰρ ἤδη τὰ Αἰγυπτίων, ὁ δὲ Θύαμις οὐκ ἠκρίβου τὰ Ἑλλήνων) Ἄνδρες, ἔλεγε, συσ-

XIX. As soon as it was day, he summoned his chief followers, and ordered them to bring the plunder, which he called by the high-sounding name of "spoils," into the midst; he also sent for Cnemon, with instructions to fetch the prisoners who had been intrusted to his care. While they were being conducted to the chief, they exclaimed, "What fate is reserved for us?" and begged Cnemon to assist them in any way he could. He promised to do so, and bade them be of good cheer, assuring them that the chief of the brigands was not an utter barbarian, but was of a kind and gentle disposition; that he belonged to an illustrious family, and had only adopted his present mode of life from necessity.

When they reached his presence, and the whole band had assembled, Thyamis took his seat upon an eminence in the island, the appointed meeting-place, and ordered Cnemon to translate what he said to the prisoners; for, while he had only an imperfect knowledge of Greek, Cnemon had now learned to speak Egyptian.

τρατιῶται, τὴν ἐμὴν ἐπίστασθε γνώμην οἵαν ἀεὶ κέχρημαι πρὸς ὑμᾶς. Ἐγὼ γὰρ, ὡς ἴστε, παῖς μὲν προφήτου τοῦ ἐν Μέμφει γεγονὼς, ἀποτυχὼν δὲ τῆς ἱερωσύνης μετὰ τὴν τοῦ πατρὸς ὑπαναχώρησιν, ἀδελφοῦ νεωτέρου ταύ-την παρελομένου, ἐφ' ὑμᾶς τε καταφυγὼν, ἐφ' ᾧ γε τιμωρίαν μὲν λαβεῖν, τὴν τιμὴν δ' ἀπολαβεῖν καὶ τοῦ ἄρχειν ὑμῶν παρ' ὑμῶν ἀξιωθεὶς, εἰς τὴν δεῦρο διήγαγον, οὐδὲν τῶν πολλῶι ἐμαυτῷ πλέον ἀπονέμων· ἀλλ' εἴτε χρημάτων νέμησις, ἰσομοιρίαν ἠγάπησα· εἴτ' αἰχμαλώτων διάπρασις, εἰς τὸ κοινὸν κατέθηκα, προσήκειν ἡγούμενος τὸν οὕτω δὴ καλῶς ἐξηγού-μενον τῶν μὲν ἔργων πλεῖστον μετέχειν τῶν δὲ ποριζομένων τὸ ἴσον· τῶν δ' ἁλισκομένων τοὺς μὲν ἄνδρας ὑμῖν αὐτοῖς ἐγκαταλέγων, ὅσοι τι ῥώμῃ σώματος ὠφελήσειν ἔμελλον, τοὺς δ' ἀσθενεστέρους ἀπεμπολῶν· γυναικῶν δ' ὕβρεως

Thyamis then addressed the meeting as follows: "Comrades, you know what my feelings towards you have always been. You are aware that, being the son of a priest of Memphis, deprived of my right of succession to the sacerdotal functions, of which a younger brother, after my father's death, had robbed me, in violation of the laws, I took refuge amongst you, in order to avenge myself and recover my dignity. You thought me worthy to be your leader; since then, I have lived with you, without ever claiming any special privileges for myself. When there was money to be distributed, I was content with the same share as each of yourselves; when prisoners were sold, I paid what they fetched into the common stock; for I considered it the duty of a good leader to take upon himself the greatest share of fatigue and to be content with an equal share of the spoils. As to the prisoners, I have enrolled amongst your band those who, from their bodily strength, were likely to be useful to us, and sold the weaker. I have never been

ἀπείρατος, τὰς μὲν εὖ γεγονυίας ἢ χρημάτων ἀφεὶς, ἢ τῆς τύχης μόνης οἰκτείρων, τὰς δ᾽ ἐλάττους καὶ ἃς δουλεύειν οὐχὶ αἰχμαλωσία μᾶλλον ἀλλὰ συνήθεια κατηνάγκαζε, θεραπαίνας ἑκάστοις διανέμων. Τὸ δὲ νῦν παρὸν, ἕν τι τῶν λαφύρων αἰτῶ παρ᾽ ὑμῶν, τὴν κόρην ταυτηνὶ τὴν ξένην· ἣν δυνατὸν ἐμαυτῷ με δοῦναι, βέλτιον παρὰ τοῦ κοινοῦ λαβεῖν ἡγοῦμαι. Καὶ γὰρ εὔηθες, τὴν αἰχμάλωτον βιασάμενον, ἀκόντων τι τῶν φίλων φαίνεσθαι διαπραττόμενον. Ἀλλὰ καὶ ταύτην αἰτῶ παρ᾽ ὑμῶν οὐ προῖκα τὴν χάριν ἀλλ᾽ ἀντιδοὺς τὸ μηδὲν αὐτὸς τῶν ἄλλων τῆς λείας μεταλαβεῖν. Ἐπειδὴ γὰρ τὴν πάνδημον Ἀφροδίτην τὸ προφητικὸν ἀτιμάζει γένος, οὐ τῆς καθ᾽ ἡδονὴν χρείας ἀλλὰ τῆς εἰς διαδοχὴν σπορᾶς, τήνδε ἐμαυτῷ γενέσθαι διεσκεψάμην.

Κ΄. Ἐγὼ δὲ καὶ τὰς αἰτίας ὑμῖν ἀπολογίσασθαι βούλομαι. Πρῶτον μὲν εὐγενὴς

guilty of violence towards the women; those of noble birth I have released either on payment of ransom, or out of pure compassion for their lot; those of lower rank, who were condemned to slavery by habit rather than the rights of war, I have distributed amongst you as servants. On the present occasion, I ask nothing from you out of all this booty, except this stranger maiden; although I might have claimed her by right, I yet think it better to receive her from you by common consent; for it would be foolish to seem to be acting against the wishes of my friends by appropriating a prisoner by force. However, I do not ask even her from you for nothing; in return, I resign all share in the rest of the booty. The priestly caste despises indiscriminate love; I have made up my mind to wed this maiden, not to satisfy my lust, but in order to propagate my family.

XX. " I will also tell you the reasons which have led me to act thus. In the first place, she appears to me to be well

εἶναί μοι δοκεῖ. Τεκμαίρομαι δὲ τῷ τ' ἀμφ'
αὐτὴν εὑρεθέντι πλούτῳ καὶ ὅτι πρὸς τὰς
παρούσας οὐκ ἐνέδωκε συμφορὰς ἀλλὰ τὸ
φρόνημα πρὸς τὴν ἐξ ἀρχῆς ἀναφέρει τύχην.
Ἔπειτα τὴν ψυχὴν ἀγαθήν τε καὶ σώφρονα
στοχάζομαι. Εἰ γὰρ εὐμορφίᾳ νικῶσα τὰς
πάσας, αἰδοῖ τοῦ βλέμματος καὶ τοὺς ὁρῶντας
καταστέλλει πρὸς τὸ σεμνότερον, πῶς οὐ τὴν
βελτίονα περὶ αὐτῆς εἰκότως παρίστησι φαν-
τασίαν; ὃ δὲ μέγιστόν ἐστι τῶν εἰρημένων,
ἱέρεια θεῶν τινος εἶναί μοι φαίνεται. Τὴν γοῦν
ἱερὰν στολὴν καὶ τὰ στέμματα μεθεῖναι καὶ
δυστυχοῦσα δεινὸν καὶ οὐ θεμιτὸν ἡγεῖται.

ΚΑ΄. Τίς οὖν γένοιτ' ἂν, ὦ παρόντες,
γάμος ἁρμοδιώτερος, τοῦ προφητικοῦ τὴν
ἱερωμένην λαμβάνοντος; Ἐπευφήμησαν ἅπαν-
τες καὶ γαμεῖν ἐπ' αἰσίοις ἐκέλευον. Ὁ δ'
ἀναλαβὼν τὸν λόγον, Ὑμῖν μὲν ἔχω τὴν χάριν,
ἔφη, εἰκότα δ' ἂν ποιοῖμεν, εἰ καὶ τὴν γνώμην,
ὅπως ἔχει πρὸς τοῦτο, τῆς κόρης μάθοιμεν.
Εἰ μὲν γὰρ ἔδει τῷ τῆς ἀρχῆς ἀποχρήσασθαι
νόμῳ, πάντως ἐξήρκει μοι τὸ βούλεσθαι·
βιάζεσθαι γὰρ οἷς ἐξὸν τὸ πυνθάνεσθαι περιτ-

born; this I conjecture from the money found upon her, and also because she is by no means overwhelmed by her misfortunes, but from the first has met them boldly. Next, I am convinced that she is of a good and virtuous disposition; for if, while she surpasses all in beauty, she yet imposes respect upon all who see her by her modest looks, how can we help thinking highly of her? An even still more weighty reason is, that she seems to me to be the priestess of some god, since, even in her misfortune, she considers it an offence against religion to put off her garlands and sacred vestments.

XXI. "Could any union be more fitting than that of a priest and priestess?" All applauded his words, and wished him a happy marriage, under favourable auspices. Then Thyamis continued: "I thank you, my friends; but we shall now do well to enquire what the maiden thinks about the matter. If I were disposed to make use of the right of authority, my wish alone would be sufficient; for those who can command obedience have no need to ask.

τόν. Εἰ δὲ γάμος, τὸ γιγνόμενον τὸ παρ' ἀμφοτέρων βούλημα συννεύειν ἀναγκαῖον. Καὶ ἀποστρέψας τὸν λόγον, Πῶς οὖν ἔχεις, ὦ κόρη, πρὸς τὸ συνοικεῖν ἡμῖν, διηρώτα. Καὶ ἅμα τίνες εἶεν καὶ ἐκ τίνων φράζειν ἐκέλευεν. Ἡ δὲ πολύν τινα χρόνον τῇ γῇ τὸ βλέμμα προσερείσασα καὶ πυκνὰ τὴν κεφαλὴν ἐπισείουσα λόγον τινὰ καὶ ἐννοίας ἀθροίζειν ἐῴκει καὶ δή ποτε πρὸς τὸν Θύαμιν ἀντωπήσασα καὶ πλέον ἢ πρότερον αὐτὸν τῷ κάλλει καταστράψασα, αἱ γὰρ πεφοίνικτο τὴν παρειὰν ὑπὸ τῶν ἐνθυμημάτων πλέον ἢ σύνηθες καὶ τὸ βλέμμα κεκίνητο πρὸς τὸ γοργότερον, ἑρμηνεύοντος τοῦ Κνήμωνος, Μᾶλλον, ἔφη, ὁ μὲν λόγος ἥρμοζεν ἀδελφῷ τῷ ἐμῷ Θεαγένει τούτῳ, πρέπειν γὰρ οἶμαι γυναικὶ μὲν σιγὴν ἀνδρὶ δ' ἀπόκρισιν ἐν ἀνδράσιν.

ΚΒ'. Ἐπειδὴ δὲ κἀμοὶ λόγου μετεδώκατε καὶ τοῦτο πρῶτον ἔνδειγμα φιλανθρωπίας παρέχεσθε, τὸ πειθοῖ μᾶλλον ἢ βίᾳ τῶν

But, in the case of lawful marriage, mutual consent is necessary." Then, addressing himself to Chariclea, he said: "What do you think of the proposal that we should marry? Tell me, who you two are, and who are your parents?" Chariclea remained for a long time with her eyes fixed upon the ground, shaking her head from time to time, as if she were collecting her thoughts before answering. When at length she lifted her eyes towards Thyamis, her beauty dazzled him even more than before; for her cheeks, animated by her thoughts, were ruddier than usual, and her kindling eyes were full of vehemence. Then, Cnemon acting as interpreter, she thus addressed Thyamis: "It would be more seemly that my brother Theagenes should answer; for I think that silence becomes a woman, and that it is a man's duty to answer amongst men.

XXII. "But, since you have invited me to speak, and have given us in this the first proof of your humanity, showing that you wish to obtain what you have a right to claim by persuasion rather than by force

δικαίων πειρᾶσθαι τυγχάνειν, ἄλλως τε διότι τὸ πᾶν εἰς ἐμὲ τείνει τῶν εἰρημένων, ἐκβαίνειν ἀναγκάζομαι τοὺς ἐμαυτῆς τε καὶ παρθένων νόμους καὶ πρὸς τὴν πεῦσιν τοῦ κρατοῦντος ἀποκρίνασθαι περὶ γάμου καὶ ταῦτ' ἐν ὁμίλῳ τοσούτων ἀνδρῶν. Ἔστι δὲ τὰ περὶ ἡμῶν τοιάδε. Γένος μὲν ἐσμὲν Ἴωνες, Ἐφεσίων δὲ τὰ πρῶτα γεγονότες καὶ ἀμφιθαλεῖς ὄντες, νόμου τοὺς τοιούτους καλοῦντος ἱερατεύειν, ἐγὼ μὲν Ἀρτέμιδος Ἀπόλλωνος δ' ὁ ἐμὸς ἀδελφὸς οὗτος ἐλάχομεν. Ἐπετείου δὲ τῆς τιμῆς οὔσης καὶ τοῦ χρόνου πληρουμένου, θεωρίαν εἰς Δῆλον ἤγομεν ἔνθα μουσικούς τε καὶ γυμνικοὺς ἀγῶνας διαθήσεσθαι καὶ τὴν ἱερωσύνην ἀποθήσεσθαι κατά τι πάτριον ἠμέλλομεν. Ὁλκὰς οὖν ἐπληροῦτο χρυσοῦ τε καὶ ἀργύρου καὶ ἐσθήτων καὶ τῶν ἄλλων ὅσα πρός τε τοὺς ἀγῶνας καὶ τὴν πάνδημον εὐωχίαν ἐπαρκέσειν ἤμελλε. Καὶ ἀνηγόμεθα τῶν μὲν πατέρων γήρᾳ τε προηκόντων καὶ δέει

(since everything that has been said concerns myself), I feel compelled to abandon my usual practice and that of my sex, and, even in the presence of so large an audience of men, to reply to the question put to me by him who is now my master. Listen, then, to the following account of us:

"We are Ionians: our family is one of the most illustrious in Ephesus. When we had attained to years of discretion, we were summoned by the law to undertake priestly functions; I was consecrated to Artemis, and my brother to Apollo. These functions last a year. When our term was over, we had to set out for Delos on the sacred embassy, to arrange the athletic sports and contests of music, and to lay down our priestly office in accordance with the established custom. For this purpose, a vessel was loaded with gold, silver, garments, and all that was necessary to invest with suitable dignity the public feast and entertainments. We set sail; our parents, already advanced in years, being afraid of the sea

τοῦ πλοῦ καὶ τῆς θαλάττης οἴκαδε καταμεινάν-
των, ἄλλων δὲ πολιτῶν εἰς πλῆθος τῶν μὲν
κατὰ τὴν αὐτὴν ὁλκάδα συνεισβάντων, τῶν δὲ
σκάφεσιν ἰδίοις χρωμένων. Ἐπεὶ δὲ τὸ πολὺ
τοῦ πλοῦ διήνυστο, κλυδώνιον ἀθρόον ἐμπεσὸν
καὶ ἄνεμος ἐξώστης καὶ λαίλαπες συμμιγεῖς καὶ
πρηστῆρες τὴν θάλατταν καταιγίζουσαι τὴν
ναῦν τοῦ εὐθέος παραφέρουσι, τοῦ κυβερνήτου
πρὸς τὸ ὑπερβάλλον κακὸν ἐνδόντος καὶ τῷ
βιαίῳ τῆς ὁλκάδος ἐκστάντος καὶ τῇ τύχῃ
κυβερνᾶν ἐπιτρέψαντος. Ἡγόμεθα οὖν ὑπὸ
τοῦ ἀεὶ πνέοντος ἡμέρας μὲν ἑπτὰ νύκτας δ᾽
ἴσας καὶ τέλος εἰς τὴν ἀκτὴν ἐξωκείλαμεν
ἔνθα πρὸς ὑμῶν ἑάλωμεν· οὗ καὶ τὸν πολὺν
ἑωράκατε φόνον, τῶν ναυτῶν ἡμῖν παρὰ τὴν
εὐωχίαν ἣν ἐπὶ σωτηρίοις ἤγομεν ἐπιθε-
μένων, ἀνελεῖν τε διὰ τὰ χρήματα βουλευ-
σαμένων, ἕως σὺν πολλῷ τῷ κακῷ καὶ
ὀλέθρῳ τῶν οἰκείων ὁμοῦ πάντων, αὐτῶν δ᾽
ἐκείνων ὀλλύντων τε καὶ ὀλλυμένων, ἐπεκρατή·
σαμεν ἐξ ἁπάντων, (ὡς μή ποτ᾽ ὤφελον) οἰκτρὸν

and the voyage, remained at home; but a large number of the citizens accompanied us, either on board our vessel, or upon others which they had fitted out themselves. When the voyage was nearly over, a storm suddenly arose; a violent hurricane, accompanied by thunder and lightning, lifted up the waves, and drove the ship out of its course; the pilot, obliged to yield to the fury of the storm, abandoned the helm, and allowed the vessel to drift haphazard. Seven days and seven nights we were borne along by the wind that never ceased, until at last we were cast upon the shore where we were found by you, and where you saw the traces of the great slaughter that had taken place. I must explain how it happened. The sailors conspired against us, while we were celebrating a feast in thanksgiving for our preservation, and resolved to kill us and seize our property. A terrible struggle ensued, in which all our companions perished, while the sailors themselves slew and were slain: we alone survived the disaster—and would to Heaven

περισωθέντες λείψανον, ἓν μόνον ἐν δυστυχή-
μασιν εὐπραγοῦντες ὅτι θεῶν τις εἰς χεῖρας τὰς
ὑμετέρας ἤγαγε καὶ οἱ περὶ θανάτου δεδιότες
περὶ γάμου σκοπεῖν ἐπετράπημεν· ὃν οὐ
βούλομαι κατ' οὐδένα τρόπον ἀρνήσασθαι. Τό
τε γὰρ αἰχμάλωτον οὖσαν τῆς τοῦ κρατοῦντος
εὐνῆς ἀξιοῦσθαι, πᾶσαν εὐδαίμονα τύχην ὑπερ-
βέβληκε. Τό τε θεοῖς ἀνακειμένην προφήτου
παιδὶ καὶ μετ' ὀλίγον θεοῦ νεύοντος καὶ προφήτῃ
συνοικεῖν οὐ παντάπασιν ἔοικεν εἶναι τῆς ἐκ τοῦ
θείου κηδεμονίας ἄμοιρον. Ἑν μόνον αἰτῶ, καὶ
δὸς, ὦ Θύαμι· συγχώρησον εἰς ἄστυ με πρό-
τερον ἐλθοῦσαν ἢ ἔνθα βωμὸς ἢ ναὸς 'Απόλλωνι
νενόμισται, τὴν ἱερωσύνην καὶ τὰ ταύτης ἀπο-
θέσθαι σύμβολα. Βέλτιον μὲν εἰς Μέμφιν
ὅταν καὶ τὴν τιμὴν ἀνακτήσῃ τῆς προφητείας·
οὕτω καὶ ὁ γάμος εὐθυμότερον ἂν ἄγοιτο,
νίκῃ συναπτόμενος καὶ ἐπὶ κατορθουμένοις τε-

we had not !—we alone remain, a miserable remnant. Our only consolation amidst our misfortunes is, that some god has brought us into your hands; and that we, who feared for our lives, have been granted permission to discuss the question of my marriage, which I certainly do not desire to decline. The idea that I, a captive, should be considered worthy of my master's bed, is indeed too great a happiness! and further, that a maiden, consecrated to the service of God, should be united to the son of a priest, who will soon, with Heaven's approval, be a priest himself, this is clearly the work of divine Providence. I only ask you, Thyamis, to grant me one favour: let me first go to the city, or wherever there is a temple or altar dedicated to Apollo, to lay aside my priest-hood and deposit there these badges of my office. The best thing would be to wait until you return to Memphis, when you receive the dignity of priesthood; in this manner, our marriage would be more joyful as being associated with victory and celebrated after success. However, I leave

λούμενος. Εἰ δὲ καὶ πρότερον, ἕν σοι κατα-
λείπω τὴν σκέψιν. Μόνον τελεσθείη μοι τὰ
πάτρια πρότερον· καὶ οἶδ' ὡς ἐπινεύσεις, ἱεροῖς τ'
ἐκ παίδων, ὡς φῂς, ἀνακείμενος, καὶ τὸ περὶ τοὺς
θεοὺς ὅσιον ἀποσεμνύνων.

ΚΓ΄. Καὶ ἡ μὲν ἐνταῦθα τῶν λόγων ἐπαύ-
σατο δακρύων δ' ἤρξατο. Τῶν δὲ παρόντων οἱ
μὲν ἄλλοι πάντες ἐπῄνουν καὶ πράττειν οὕτως
ἐκέλευόν τε καὶ ἑτοίμως ἔχειν ἐβόων. Ἐπῄνει
δὲ καὶ ὁ Θύαμις ἑκών τε τὸ μέρος καὶ ἄκων,
ὑπὸ μὲν τῆς περὶ τὴν Χαρίκλειαν ἐπιθυμίας
καὶ τὴν παροῦσαν ὥραν, ἀπέραντον χρόνου
μῆκος εἰς ὑπέρθεσιν ἡγούμενος, ὑπὸ δὲ τῶν
λόγων, ὥσπερ τινὸς σειρῆνος κεκηλημένος καὶ
πρὸς τὸ πείθεσθαι κατηναγκασμένος· ἅμα δέ
τι καὶ πρὸς τὸ ἐνύπνιον ἀναφέρων καὶ τὸν
γάμον κατὰ τὴν Μέμφιν ἔσεσθαι καταπιστεύων·
καὶ διαλύει μὲν τὸν σύλλογον, τὴν λείαν πρό-
τερον διανείμας, πολλὰ τῶν ἐξαιρέτων αὐτὸς
ἑκοντὶ παραχωρούντων κομισάμενος.

it to you to decide whether it shall take place sooner; let me only first perform the sacred rites enjoined by the custom of my country. I know that you will grant my request, since, as you say, you have been devoted to the service of the gods from your infancy, and you are full of respect for everything that concerns them."

XXIII. With these words she left off speaking, and began to weep.

All those who were present approved, and urged her to do as she proposed, and declared that they were ready to support her. Thyamis also approved, willing and yet unwilling. His passion for Chariclea caused him to look upon the delay of a single hour as an eternity. But, on the other hand, her words, like some siren's song, charmed him and compelled him to assent. Besides, he saw in this some connection with his dream, and believed that the wedding would be celebrated at Memphis. Having distributed the booty, he dismissed the assembly; he himself obtained some of the most valuable articles, a voluntary gift from his comrades.

ΚΔ΄. Ἐπιστέλλει δ᾽ εἰς δεκάτην ηὐτρεπισ-
μένους εἶναι, τὴν ὁρμὴν ὡς ἐπὶ τὴν Μέμφιν
ποιησομένους. Τοῖς δ᾽ Ἕλλησι τὴν προτέραν
ἀπεκλήρου σκηνήν. Συνεσκήνου δ᾽ αὐτοῖς καὶ
ὁ Κνήμων αὖθις ἐκ προστάγματος, οὐ φρουρὸς
ἔτι τὸ ἐντεῦθεν ἀλλὰ συνόμιλος ἀποδεδειγμένος·
καὶ δίαιτάν τε τὴν ἀβροτέραν τῆς οὔσης παρ-
εῖχεν ὁ Θύαμις, καί πῃ καὶ τὸν Θεαγένην εἰς
αἰδῶ τῆς ἀδελφῆς ὁμοδίαιτον ἐποιεῖτο. Αὐτὴν
δὲ τὴν Χαρίκλειαν οὐδὲ ὁρᾶν τὰ πολλὰ διε-
γνώκει, τοῦ μὴ τὴν θέαν ὑπέκκαυμα γίγνεσθαι
τοῦ ἐγκειμένου πόθου καὶ πρᾶξαί τι παρὰ τὰ
δόξαντα καὶ προδηλωθέντα καταναγκασθείη.
Καὶ ὁ μὲν Θύαμις ἐκ τούτων παρῃτεῖτο τὴν
ὄψιν τὴν κόρης, οὐ δυνατὸν βλέπειν θ᾽ ἅμα καὶ
σωφρονεῖν ἡγούμενος. Ὁ δὲ Κνήμων ἐπειδὴ
τάχιστα πάντες ἐκποδὼν ἦσαν ἄλλος κατ᾽ ἄλλο
τῆς λίμνης καταδύντες, ἣν τῷ Θεαγένει βοτάνην
ὑπέσχετο τῇ προτεραία μαστεύων ὀλίγον τῆς
λίμνης ἄποθεν ἐπορεύετο.

XXIV. They were ordered to hold themselves in readiness to proceed to Memphis in ten days' time. He assigned the same tent to the young Greeks as before, and ordered that Cnemon should attend them, no longer as their custodian, but as their friend and companion. He also gave them more luxurious food than he ate himself, and sometimes invited Theagenes to his table, out of regard for his sister. He had resolved to see Chariclea only rarely and at intervals, for fear the sight of her might still more inflame his violent passion and drive him to do something contrary to the agreement that had been entered into. For these reasons Thyamis avoided her presence, thinking that, if he saw her, he would find it impossible to restrain himself.

As soon as the meeting had broken up, and all had dispersed to their several quarters in the marsh, Cnemon went some little distance from the lake, to look for the herb which he had promised Theagenes the day before.

ΚΕ΄. Κἂν τούτῳ σχολῆς ἐπιλαβόμενος ὁ Θεαγένης ἐδάκρυέ τε καὶ ἀνώμωξε, πρὸς μὲν τὴν Χαρίκλειαν οὐδ' ὁτιοῦν διαλεγόμενος, θεοὺς δὲ συνεχῶς ἐπικαλούμενος μάρτυρας. Τῆς δὲ, εἰ τὰ συνήθη καὶ κοινὰ ταῦτα θρηνεῖ, πυνθανομένης, ἢ εἰ μή τι πεπόνθοι καινότερον· Καὶ τί δ' ἂν γένοιτο, ὁ Θεαγένης ἔφη, καινότερον, ἢ τί ἀθεμιστότερον ἢ ὅρκων μὲν καὶ σπονδῶν παραβαινομένων, Χαρικλείας δὲ λήθην ἐμοῦ λαβούσης, καὶ πρὸς ἄλλων γάμους ἐπινευούσης; Εὐφήμησον, ἔφη ἡ κόρη, μηδέ μοι γίγνου τῶν συμφορῶν βαρύτερος, μηδὲ τοσαύτην ἔχων ἐκ τῶν παρελθόντων τὴν κατ' ἐμοῦ διὰ τῶν ἔργων δοκιμασίαν, ἐκ λόγων ἐπικαίρων καὶ πρός τι χρειῶδες εἰρημένων, ἄγε δι' ὑποψίας· εἰ δὲ μὴ γίγνεται τοὐναντίον καὶ μᾶλλον αὐτὸς μεταβάλλεσθαι δόξεις ἢ μεταβαλλομένην εὑρήσεις. Ἐγὼ γὰρ δυστυχεῖν μὲν οὐκ ἀρνοῦμαι, μὴ σωφρονεῖν δὲ, οὐδὲν οὕτω βίαιον ὥστε με μεταπεισθῆναι. Ἓν μόνον οἶδα μὴ σωφρονοῦσα

XXV. Meanwhile Theagenes, taking advantage of the freedom afforded him, began to weep and sob; he did not address a word to Chariclea, but called upon the gods without ceasing. Thereupon the maiden asked him whether he was only lamenting their common misfortunes, or whether anything fresh had happened. "What fresh misfortune could be worse?" replied Theagenes; "what greater infidelity, what greater violation of vows and promises could there be than that Chariclea should forget me, and consent to another union?" "Hush!" said the maiden; "be not more cruel to me than my misfortunes; do not, after so many proofs of my fidelity in the past, suspect me in consequence of words uttered under stress of circumstances, and adapted to the necessities of the moment. Otherwise, you will show that you are changed yourself rather than that you have found any change in me. I am ready to endure unhappiness; but no force in the world will ever persuade me to do anything that virtue forbids. I know that

τὸν ἐξ ἀρχῆς ἐπί σοι πόθον ἀλλὰ καὶ τοῦτον
ἔννομον. Οὐ γὰρ ὡς ἐραστῇ πειθομένη, ἀλλ'
ὡς ἀνδρὶ συνθεμένη τότε πρῶτον ἐμαυτὴν ἐπέ-
δωκα καὶ εἰς δεῦρο διετέλεσα καθαρὰν ἐμαυτὴν
καὶ ἀπὸ σῆς ὁμιλίας φυλάττουσα, πολλάκις
μὲν ἐπιχειροῦντα διωσαμένη, τὸν δ' ἐξ ἀρχῆς
ἡμῖν συγκείμενόν τε καὶ ἐνώμοτον ἐπὶ πᾶσι
γάμον, ἔνθεσμον, εἴ πῃ γένοιτο, περισκοποῦσα.
Πῶς οὖν οὐκ ἂν εἴης ἄτοπος, εἰ τὸν βάρβαρόν
με τοῦ Ἕλληνος, τὸν λῃστὴν τοῦ ἐρωμένου
πιστεύοις ἐπίπροσθεν ἄγειν; Τί οὖν ἐβούλετό
σοι τὰ τῆς καλῆς δημηγορίας ἐκείνης; ἔφη ὁ
Θεαγένης. Τὸ μὲν γὰρ ἀδελφόν με σαυτῆς
ἀναπλάττειν, σοφὸν εἰς ὑπερβολὴν καὶ πόρρω
τὸν Θύαμιν τῆς ζηλοτυπίας τῆς ἐφ' ἡμῖν ἀπάγον
καὶ συνεῖναι ἡμᾶς ἀλλήλοις ἀδεῶς παρασκευάζον.
Συνίην καὶ τῆς Ἰωνίας καὶ τῆς κατὰ τὴν Δῆλον

in one thing alone I am immoderate—my passion for you; but this is lawful and honourable. I did not yield to you as a lover; I abandoned myself entirely to you from the first, as a husband with whom I had made a solemn compact; hitherto, I have kept myself pure from all illegitimate intercourse with you; I have frequently repelled your advances, waiting for the opportunity of legitimately consecrating that union to which we have been pledged from the commencement, and which has been confirmed by most solemn oaths. Besides, you could not be so foolish as to think that I should prefer a barbarian to a Greek, a brigand to one whom I love ! "

" What, then, was the meaning of your fine speech ? " asked Theagenes; " your idea of calling me your brother was a very wise precaution, which prevented Thyamis from being jealous of our affection for each other, and allowed us to associate freely and without fear. I understood that all you said about Ionia and our wanderings in the neighbourhood of Delos were so

πλάνης, ὅτι τῶν ὄντων ἦν καὶ ἀληθῶν ἐπικαλύμματα καὶ πλάνην τῷ ὄντι τοῖς ἀκούουσιν ἐπάγοντα.

ΚϚ'. Τὸ δ' ἑτοίμως οὕτω ἐπινεύειν τὸν γάμον, καὶ συντίθεσθαι διαρρήδην καὶ καιρὸν ὁρίζειν ταῦτα συμβάλλειν οὔτ' ἐδυνάμην οὔτ' ἐβουλόμην. Εὐχόμην δὲ καταδῦναι μᾶλλον ἢ τοιαύτην ἐπιδεῖν τῶν ἐπί σοι πόνων τε καὶ ἐλπίδων τὴν τελευτήν.

Καὶ ἡ Χαρίκλεια περιβαλοῦσα τὸν Θεαγένην καὶ μυρία φιλήσασα καὶ διάβροχον ποιήσασα τοῖς δάκρυσιν, Ὡς ἥδιστα, ἔφη, δέχομαί σου τοὺς ἐπ' ἐμοὶ τούτους τοὺς φόβους. Εὔδηλος γὰρ εἶ κἀκ τούτων, μὴ ὀκλάσας τὸν ἐπ' ἐμοὶ πόθον ὑπὸ τῶν πολλῶν συμφορῶν. Ἀλλ' εὖ ἴσθι, Θεάγενες, οὐδ' ἂν τὸ παρὸν τοῦτ' ἀλλήλοις διελεγόμεθα, μὴ τούτων οὕτως ἐπηγγελμένων. Ὁρμὴν γὰρ, ὡς οἶσθα, κρατούσης ἐπιθυμίας μάχη μὲν ἀντίτυπος ἐπιτείνει, λόγος δ' εἴκων καὶ πρὸς τὸ βούλημα συντρέχων τὴν πρώτην καὶ ζέουσαν φορὰν ἔστειλε καὶ τὸ κάτοξυ τῆς ὀρέξεως τῷ ἡδεῖ τῆς ἐπαγγελίας κατεύνασε. Πρώτην γὰρ, ὡς οἶμαι, πεῖραν οἱ ἀγριώτερον

many fictions to disguise the truth and to mislead your hearers.

XXVI. " But, when you showed yourself so ready to agree to the proposal of Thyamis, definitely promised to marry him, and even fixed the day, I neither could nor would understand what it meant ; rather, I wished that the earth had opened and swallowed me up before I had lived to see such a result of my hopes and labours on your behalf." At these words Chariclea embraced Theagenes, covered him with kisses, and watered his face with her tears. " How delightful to me are your fears on my account! They prove that your love for me is not shaken, in spite of our calamities. Be assured, Theagenes, that had I not made this promise, we should not be conversing together at the present moment. Resistance, as you are aware, only aggravates a violent passion ; whereas yielding words, calculated to humour the will, soothe its first outbursts, and blunt the edge of desire by the delights of which they hold out promise in the future. Those who love most fiercely consider a

ἐρῶντες τὴν ὑπόσχεσιν νομίζουσι καὶ κρατεῖν ἀπὸ τῆς ἐπαγγελίας ἡγούμενοι, ῥᾴτερον διάγουσιν ἐπὶ τῶν ἐλπίδων σαλεύοντες. Ἃ δὴ καὶ αὐτὴ προμηθουμένη τοῖς λόγοις ἐμαυτὴν ἐξεδόμην, θεοῖς τὰ ἑξῆς ἐπιτρέψασα καὶ δαίμονι τῷ τὴν ἀρχὴν λαχόντι τὸν ἡμέτερον ἐπιτροπεύειν ἔρωτα. Πολλὰ μία ἡμέρα καὶ δύο πολλάκις ἔδοσαν τῶν εἰς σωτηρίαν καὶ τύχαι παρέσχον ἃ βουλαῖς ἄνθρωποι μυρίαις οὐκ ἐξεῦρον. Τοῦτό τοι καὶ αὐτὴ τὸ παρὸν ἐπινοίαις ὑπερεθέμην, τὰ πρόδηλα τοῖς ἀδήλοις διακρουσαμένη. Φυλακτέον οὖν, ὦ γλυκύτατε, καθάπερ πάλαισμα τὸ πλάσμα καὶ σιγητέον οὐ πρὸς τοὺς ἄλλους μόνον ἀλλὰ καὶ πρὸς αὐτὸν τὸν Κνήμωνα. Φιλάνθρωπος μὲν γάρ ἐστι περὶ ἡμᾶς καὶ Ἕλλην ἀλλ' αἰχμάλωτος καὶ τῷ κρατοῦντι πλέον, ἂν οὕτω τύχῃ, χαριούμενος. Οὔτε γὰρ φιλίας χρόνος, οὔτ' ἀγχιστείας θεσμός, ἐνέχυρον ὑμῖν ἀκριβὲς τῆς πίστεως αὐτοῦ τῆς περὶ ἡμᾶς δίδωσι. Διὸ κἂν ἔκ τινος ὑπονοίας ἐπιψαύσῃ ποτὲ τῶν

first attempt implies consent, and, thinking that possession will follow, grow calmer, resting on their hopes. This consideration made me yield to Thyamis in words, leaving the future issue to the gods and the Genius who, from the beginning, has taken our love under his protection. An interval of a day or two is often most salutary, and Fortune brings means of safety which no human wisdom can devise. Wherefore I have deferred the present by my inventiveness, putting off the certainties of the present by the uncertainties of the future. Wherefore, my dearest, we must use this fiction as a wrestler's trick and conceal it not only from the rest, but even from Cnemon. For, although he is kindly disposed to us, and is a Greek, he is, like ourselves, a prisoner, and therefore more likely to try and gain his master's favour, should the opportunity occur. Neither the time our acquaintance has lasted nor the ties of kindred race are sufficiently sure pledges of his fidelity to us ; wherefore, should he at any time touch upon the truth, you

ἡμετέρων, ἀρνητέον τὴν πρώτην. Καλὸν γάρ ποτε καὶ τὸ ψεῦδος ὅταν ὠφελοῦν τοὺς λέγοντας μηδὲν καταβλάπτῃ τοὺς ἀκούοντας.

ΚΖ΄. Ταῦτα τῆς Χαρικλείας καὶ τοιαῦτα πρὸς τὸ βέλτιστον ὑποτιθεμένης, ὁ Κνήμων εἰστρέχει λίαν ἐσπουδασμένος καὶ πολὺν ἐκ τῶν ὄψεων θόρυβον ἐπαγγελλόμενος, καὶ, Ὦ Θεάγενες, τὴν μὲν πόαν ἥκω σοι φέρων, ἔλεγε, καὶ θεράπευε τὰς πληγὰς ἐπιθέμενος, χρὴ δὲ πρὸς ἕτερα τραύματα καὶ φόνους ἴσους εἶναι παρεσκευασμένους. Τοῦ δὲ σαφέστερον ὅ τι λέγοι δηλοῦν ἱκετεύοντος, Οὐ καιρὸς, ἔφη, τὸ παρὸν ἀκούειν, δέος γὰρ προληφθῆναι τοὺς λόγους ὑπὸ τῶν ἔργων· ἀλλ᾽ ἕπου τὴν ταχίστην, συνεπέσθω δὲ καὶ ἡ Χαρίκλεια. Καὶ παραλαβὼν ἄμφω παρὰ τὸν Θύαμιν ἦγε, καὶ κράνος διασμῶντα καὶ παλτὸν θήγοντα καταλαβὼν, Εἰς καιρὸν, ἔφη, πρὸς ὅπλοις τυγχάνεις. Ἀλλ᾽ αὐτός γ᾽ ἔνδυνε καὶ τοὺς ἄλλους κέλευε· πλῆθος γὰρ πολεμίων ὅσον οὐδέπω περὶ ἡμᾶς καὶ

must flatly deny it. For a lie is some-times permissible, even praiseworthy, when it benefits those who tell it and does no harm to those who hear it."

XXVII. While Chariclea was thus sug-gesting to Theagenes the best course to take, Cnemon entered in great haste, with agitation depicted in his looks. "Oh, Theagenes!" said he, "here is the herb which I promised you; take and apply it to your wounds. But we must be prepared for other wounds, and another massacre such as that you have already witnessed." Theagenes begged him to explain himself more clearly "It is not the time to tell you now," he answered; "there is reason to fear that words might be anticipated by deeds. But follow me without delay, both you and Chariclea." He then conducted them both to Thyamis, whom they found polishing his helmet and sharpening his spear, and said to him: "Your employment is opportune; gird on your arms and order your comrades to do the like. We are threatened by foes more numerous than we have yet encountered;

τοσοῦτον ἀπολειπόμενον ὅσον τοῦ λόφου τοῦ πλησίον ὑπερκύπτοντας προϊδὼν ἥκω δρομαῖος τὴν ἔφοδον προμηνύων, οὐδὲν τάχους ἀνιεὶς ἀλλὰ καὶ ὅσους ἐδυνάμην ἐν τῷ διέκπλῳ τῷ μέχρι δεῦρο παρασκευάζεσθαι διαγγείλας.

ΚΗ΄. Ἀνῆλατο πρὸς ταῦθ᾽ ὁ Θύαμις καὶ ποῦ Χαρίκλεια διηρώτα καθάπερ περὶ ἐκείνης πλέον ἢ περὶ αὑτοῦ δεδιώς. Ἐπεὶ δ᾽ ἐπὶ τῇ φλιᾷ τῇ πλησίον ὑπεσταλμένην ἔδειξεν ὁ Κνήμων, Σὺ μὲν λαβὼν ταύτην ἄγε εἰς τὸ σπήλαιον, πρὸς μόνον ἔλεγεν, οὗ καὶ τὰ κει- μήλια ἡμῖν ἐν ἀσφαλεῖ τεθησαύρισται, καὶ καθεὶς, ὦ φίλος, καὶ τῷ στομίῳ τὸ πῶμα, ὡς ἔθος, ἐπαγαγών, ἧκε τὴν ταχίστην ὡς ἡμᾶς· ὁ δὲ πόλεμος ἡμῖν μελήσει. Τὸν δ᾽ ὑπασπιστὴν ἱερεῖον ἄγειν προσέταττεν, ὡς ἂν θεοῖς ἐγχω- ρίοις ἐναγίσαντες οὕτω τῆς μάχης ἄρχοιεν. Καὶ ὁ μὲν Κνήμων τὸ προστεταγμένον ἔπραττε καὶ πολλὰ τὴν Χαρίκλειαν ὀδυρομένην καὶ θαμὰ πρὸς τὸν Θεαγένην ἐπιστρέφουσαν ἦγέ τε καὶ ἐς τὸ ἄντρον ἐνέβαλε. Τὸ δ᾽ ἦν οὐ φύσεως

they are close upon us; I descried them advancing over the top of the hill, and have hastened with all speed to announce their approach. I have also warned all those whom I met to get ready for battle."

XXVIII. At these words, Thyamis started up, and asked where Chariclea was, as if he feared more for her than for himself. When Cnemon showed her trembling at the entrance of the tent, Thyamis whispered in his ear: "Take her into the cave where all our treasures are stored; and when you have taken her down, close the entrance in the usual way, and come back to me with all speed; we must make arrangements for the fight." At the same time he ordered his armour-bearer to bring him a victim, that he might offer sacrifice to the gods of the place, before beginning battle.

Obedient to orders, Cnemon led away Chariclea, who sighed and lamented and kept looking back at Theagenes, and shut her down in the cave. This cave was not the work of nature, like many others

ἔργον οἷα πολλὰ περὶ γῆν τε καὶ ὑπὸ γῆν αὐτόματα σηραγγοῦται, ἀλλὰ τέχνης λῃστρικῆς τὴν φύσιν μιμησαμένης καὶ χειρῶν Αἰγυπτίων ὄρυγμα πρὸς σκύλων φυλακὴν περιέργως κοιλαινόμενον.

ΚΘ΄. Εἴργαστο δ᾽ ὧδέ πως. Στόμιον ἦν αὐτῷ στενόπορόν τε καὶ ζοφῶδες οἰκήματος κρυφίου θύραις ὑποκείμενον, ὡς τὸν οὐδὸν θύραν ἄλλην τῇ καθόδῳ γίγνεσθαι, ὡς πρὸς τὴν χρείαν ἐνέπιπτέ τ᾽ αὐτῇ ῥᾳδίως καὶ ἀνεπτύσσετο· τὸ δ᾽ αὐτόθεν εἰς αὐλῶνας σκολιοὺς ἀτάκτως σχιζόμενον. Οἱ γὰρ ἐπὶ τοὺς μυχοὺς πόροι καὶ αὔλακες πῇ μὲν ἕκαστος ἰδίᾳ τεχνικῶς πλανώμενοι, πῇ δ᾽ ἀλλήλοις ἐμπίπτοντες καὶ ῥιζηδὸν πλεκόμενοι, πρὸς μίαν εὐρυχωρίαν τὴν ἐπὶ τὸν πυθμένα συρρέοντες ἀνεστομοῦντο, καθ᾽ ὃ καὶ φέγγος ἀμυδρὸν ἔκ τινος διατρήσεως πρὸς ἄκροις τῆς λίμνης ἐνέπιπτεν. Ἐνταῦθ᾽ ὡς καθῆκε τὴν Χαρίκλειαν ὁ Κνήμων καὶ πρὸς τὸ ἔσχατον τοῦ ἄντρου διεβίβασε τῇ πείρᾳ χειραγωγήσας, πολλὰ καὶ ἐπιθαρσύνας καὶ ὡς εἰς

that are hollowed out on the surface and in the interior of the earth. The art of the brigands had imitated nature, and had cleverly hollowed it out as a receptacle for their spoils.

XXIX. It was constructed in the following manner : Its entrance was narrow and dark, made beneath the door of a secret chamber, the threshold of which was another door, which easily shut and opened upon the entrance, and afforded a passage for descent, whenever necessary ; within were a number of winding paths, cut at haphazard. These paths or galleries, sometimes separate and winding alone, sometimes purposely connected and intertwined like roots of trees, all converged into an open space at the bottom, which was dimly lighted through an opening in the lower part of the marsh. Here Cnemon made Chariclea descend; he led her by the hand to the inmost recesses of the cave, along the winding passages with which he was familiar, encouraging her in every way he could, and promising to return for her in

ἑσπέραν ἅμα τῷ Θεαγένει φοιτήσει κατεπαγ-
γειλάμενος, οὐ γὰρ ἐπιτρέψειν αὐτῷ συμ-
πλακῆναι τοῖς πολεμίοις ἀλλὰ διαδρᾶναι [σοι]
τὴν μάχην, οὐδὲν φθεγξαμένην, ἀλλ' ὥσπερ
θανάτῳ τῷ κακῷ βεβλημένην καὶ ὥσπερ ψυχῆς
τοῦ Θεαγένους ἀφῃρημένην, ἄπνουν καὶ σιγῶσαν
ἀπολιπὼν, ἀνεδύετο τοῦ σπηλαίου καὶ τὸν οὐδὸν
ἐπαγαγὼν καί τι καὶ ἐπιδακρύσας αὐτόν τε
τῆς ἀνάγκης κἀκείνην τῆς τύχης, ὅτι μονονουχὶ
ζῶσαν εἴη καταθάψας καὶ τὸ φαιδρότατον τῶν
ἐν ἀνθρώποις Χαρίκλειαν νυκτὶ καὶ ζόφῳ παρα-
δεδωκὼς, ἀπέτρεχεν ὡς τὸν Θύαμιν καὶ κατα-
λαμβάνει ζέοντα πρὸς τὴν μάχην καὶ αὐτόν θ'
ἅμα τῷ Θεαγένει λαμπρῶς ἐξωπλισμένον καὶ
τοὺς ἤδη παρ' αὐτὸν συνειλεγμένους πρὸς τὸ
μανικώτερον τῷ λόγῳ παρασκευάζοντα. Στὰς
γὰρ εἰς μέσους ἔλεγε, Συστρατιῶται, προ-
τρέπειν μὲν ὑμᾶς, οὐκ οἶδ' ὅτι δεῖ διὰ πλειόνων,
αὐτούς θ' ὑπομνήσεως οὐδὲν δεομένους ἀλλὰ
βίον ἀεὶ τὸν πόλεμον ἡγουμένους καὶ ἄλλως
τῆς ἀπροσδοκήτου τῶν ἐναντίων ἐφόδου τὸ
παρέλκον τῶν λόγων ὑποτεμνομένης. Ὧν

the evening with Theagenes, whom he said he would not permit to take part in the coming engagement, but would keep him out of the way. Chariclea did not utter a word; she appeared stricken to death, deprived of Theagenes, her life and soul. He left her scarcely breathing and silent, and came up from the cave. Then he shut down the door, shedding tears over her lot and the necessity which compelled him to bury her alive, and to deliver over to darkness and obscurity the most beautiful of human beings. After this, he hastened back to Thyamis, whom he found burning with eagerness for the fray, and splendidly armed, with Theagenes by his side. In order to arouse to frenzy the warlike spirit of his comrades who surrounded him, he stood up in the midst, and thus addressed them:

"Comrades, I know that I need not exhort you at length; you want no encouragement, for you have always looked upon war as the breath of life. Besides, the sudden approach of the enemy cuts short all lengthy discourse. Those who,

γὰρ ἐν ἔργοις οἱ πολέμιοι, τούτους μὴ διὰ
τῶν ὁμοίων σὺν τάχει τὴν ἄμυναν ἐπάγειν,
παντάπασίν ἐστι τοῦ προσήκοντος ὑστερούν-
των. Εἰδότες οὖν ὡς οὐχ ὑπὲρ γυναικῶν ἐστι
καὶ παίδων λόγος, ὃ δὴ πολλοῖς εἰς τὸ παρο-
ξῦναι καὶ μόνον πρὸς μάχην ἤρκεσε, ταῦτα γὰρ
ἡμῖν ἐλάττονος λόγου καὶ τοσαῦτα ἔχειν
ἐξέσται, ὅσα καὶ νικᾶν περιγίγνεται, ἀλλ' ὑπὲρ
αὐτοῦ τοῦ εἶναι καὶ ψυχῶν τῶν ἡμετέρων· οὐ
γὰρ ἐπὶ ῥητοῖς ποτε ληστρικὸς ἔληξε πόλεμος
οὐδ' ἐν σπονδαῖς ἔσχε τὴν τελευτὴν, ἀλλ' ἢ
περιεῖναι κρατοῦντας, ἢ τεθνάναι τοὺς ἁλόντας
ἀναγκαῖον, οὕτω τοῖς ἐχθίστοις, ψυχήν θ' ἅμα
καὶ σῶμα τεθηγμένοι συμπίπτωμεν.

Λ. Ταῦτ' εἰπὼν τὸν ὑπασπιστὴν περιε-
σκόπει καὶ ὀνομαστὶ Θέρμουθιν ἐκάλει πολ-
λάκις· ὡς δ' ἦν οὐδαμοῦ, πολλὰ διατειλήσας
ἐπὶ τὴν πορθμίδα δρομαῖος ἔσπευδεν· ὁ γὰρ
πόλεμος ἤδη συνερράγη καὶ παρῆν ὁρᾶν καὶ
πόρρωθεν τοὺς τὰ ἔσχατα κατὰ τὰς εἰσβολὰς

when the enemy attacks them, do not promptly prepare to repulse them by the same means, show themselves utterly ignorant of their duty. Know, then, that it is not a question of defending your wives and children, which alone in the case of many would be sufficient to rouse their spirits to battle; for these and other like advantages to which we attach less importance, together with those that victory brings, will remain ours if we overcome our foes. But it is a question of our very existence, of our life; no quarter is given, a truce is unknown in wars between pirates; life is the reward of victory, defeat is death. Let us therefore fall upon our hated foes with fury of mind and body."

XXX. Having said this, he looked round for his squire, Thermuthis, and called him several times by name. When he did not appear, he burst out into violent threats against him, and hastened to the ferry. For the battle had already begun, and he was able to see from a distance the inhabitants of the extremity and approaches of the marsh in the hands

τῆς λίμνης οἰκοῦντας ἁλισκομένους. Οἱ γὰρ
ἐπελθόντες τῶν ὑποπιπτόντων ἢ καὶ φυγῇ
χρωμένων τὰ σκάφη καὶ τὰς καλύβας ἐνεπίμ-
πρασαν· ὑφ' ὧν τῆς φλογὸς ἐπὶ τὸ πλησίον
ἕλος διαρριπιζομένης καὶ τὸν πολὺν κατ' αὐτὸ
κάλαμον σωρηδὸν νεμομένης ἄφραστόν τι καὶ
ἀφόρητον ἐπὶ τοὺς ὀφθαλμοὺς σέλας ἔμπυρον,
ἐπὶ δὲ τὴν ἀκοὴν ἠχὴ κατάκροτος ἐπεφέρετο.
Καὶ πολέμου πᾶν εἶδος καὶ ἐνηργεῖτο καὶ
ἐξηκούετο· τῶν μὲν ἐγχωρίων προθυμίᾳ καὶ
ῥώμῃ πάσῃ τὴν μάχην ὑφισταμένων, τῶν δὲ τῷ
πλήθει καὶ τῆς ἐφόδου τῷ ἀπροσδοκήτῳ πλεῖ-
στον ὑπερφερόντων καὶ τοὺς μὲν ἐπὶ γῆς
ἀναιρούντων, τοὺς δ' εἰς τὴν λίμνην αὐτοῖς
σκάφεσι καὶ αὐτοῖς οἰκήμασι βαπτιζόντων.
Ὑφ' ὧν ἁπάντων δοῦπός τις πρὸς τὸν ἀέρα
συμμιγὴς ἤρετο, πεζομαχούντων ὁμοῦ καὶ
ναυμαχούντων, ὀλλύντων τε καὶ ὀλλυμένων,
αἵματι τὴν λίμνην φοινιττόντων, πυρὶ δὲ καὶ
ὕδατι συμπλεκομένων. Ἅπερ ὡς εἶδέ τε καὶ

of the enemy, who had set fire to the
boats and huts of those who had fallen
or sought safety in flight. The flames
spread to the neighbouring morass, and
consumed the reeds which grew there
in great abundance ; the conflagration
shed around a mighty and intolerable
blaze, that dazzled the eyes, while the
ears were stunned with the sharp crack-
ling and roaring of the flames.

War, in every form and shape, was
seen and heard ; the inhabitants sus-
tained the combat with all possible
courage and vigour ; but the enemy,
who possessed the advantage of superior
numbers and the suddenness of their
attack, slaughtered some upon land, and
overwhelmed others in the marsh with
their boats and huts. In the midst of the
tumult, a dull and confused sound rose in
the air, as if the engagement were going
on both on land and water ; the com-
batants slew and were slain ; the waters
of the lake were stained with blood, and
all were confusedly mingled with fire and
water. Thyamis, at this sight and the

ἤκουσεν ὁ Θύαμις, ἐνθύμιον αὐτῷ τὸ ὄναρ γίγνεται, καθὸ τὴν Ἶσιν ἑώρα καὶ τὸν νεὼν ἅπαντα λαμπάδων καὶ θυσιῶν ἀνάμεστον· καὶ ταῦτ᾽ ἐκεῖνα εἶναι τὰ νῦν ὁρώμενα. Καὶ πρὸς τἀναντία τῶν προτέρων τὴν ὄψιν συνέβαλεν, ὡς ἔχων οὐχ ἕξει τὴν Χαρίκλειαν, ὑπὸ τοῦ πολέμου ταύτης ἀφαιρεθείσης· καὶ ὡς φονεύσει καὶ οὐ τρώσει, ξίφει καὶ οὐκ Ἀφροδίτης νόμῳ. Καὶ πολλὰ τὴν θεὰν ὡς δολερὰν ὀνειδίσας, καὶ δεινὸν ἡγησάμενος εἴ τις ἄλλος ἐγκρατὴς ἔσται Χαρικλείας, μικρὸν ἐπισχεῖν τοὺς σὺν αὐτῷ κελεύσας καὶ ὡς κατὰ τόπον μένοντας ποιεῖσθαι δεήσει τὴν μάχην φράσας, κλοπεύοντας περὶ τὸ νησίδιον καὶ διὰ τῶν πέριξ ἑλῶν κρυφίους τὰς ἐμβολὰς ποιουμένους, ἀγαπητῶς γὰρ ἂν καὶ οὕτως ἀντισχεῖν πρὸς τὸ πλῆθος τῶν πολεμίων· αὐτὸς δῆθεν ὡς Θέρμουθιν ἐπιζητήσων καὶ τοῖς

terrible noise, suddenly remembered the vision, in which he had seen Isis and her temple, resplendent with lamps and full of victims for sacrifice; he saw in it the representation of what he now beheld, and, putting quite a different interpretation upon it from his earlier one, he thought that the words " you shall possess her, and yet shall not possess her," signified that Chariclea would be carried off from him by war, and that the words " you shall slay her and not merely wound her " referred to the sword, and not to the contest of love. He heaped abuse upon the goddess for having deceived him; and, exasperated at the thought that another should possess Chariclea, he bade his comrades halt, and, if they were obliged to fight, to carry on a war of ambuscade where they stood, and make secret sallies into the marshes around them, although even thus they would find it difficult to resist the enemy's superior numbers.

He himself, under pretence of going to look for Thermuthis, and offering up prayers

ἑστίοις θεοῖς κατευξόμενος ἕπεσθαί τε μηδενὶ
συγχωρήσας ἐπὶ τὸ δωμάτιον ἐμμανὴς ἀνέσ-
τρεφε. Δυσανάκλητον δὲ, πρὸς ὅπερ ἂν ὁρμήσῃ,
τὸ βάρβαρον ἦθος· κἂν ἀπογνῷ τὴν ἑαυτοῦ
σωτηρίαν, προαναιρεῖν ἅπαν τὸ φίλον εἴωθεν,
ἤτοι συνέσεσθαι αὐτοῖς καὶ μετὰ θάνατον
ἀπατώμενον, ἢ χειρὸς πολεμίας καὶ ὕβρεως
ἐξαιρούμενον. Ὑφ' ὧν καὶ ὁ Θύαμις τῶν μὲν
ἐν χερσὶ πάντων ἀμνημονήσας καὶ ταῦθ' ὥσπερ
ἄρκυσι τοῖς πολεμίοις κεκυκλωμένος, ἔρωτι δὲ
καὶ ζηλοτυπίᾳ καὶ θυμῷ κάτοχος, ἐπὶ τὸ σπή-
λαιον ἐλθὼν ὡς εἶχε δρόμου καθαλλόμενος,
ἐμβοῶν τε μέγα καὶ πολλὰ αἰγυπτιάζων, αὐτοῦ
που περὶ τὸ στόμιον ἐντυχών τινι Ἑλληνίδι
τῇ γλώττῃ προσφθεγγομένῃ, ἀπὸ τῆς φωνῆς
ἐπ' αὐτὴν χειραγωγηθεὶς, ἐπιβάλλει τε τῇ
κεφαλῇ τὴν λαιὰν χεῖρα καὶ διὰ τῶν στέρνων
παρὰ τὸν μαζὸν ἐλαύνει τὸ ξίφος.

ΛΔ'. Καὶ ἡ μὲν ἔκειτο πικρῶς, ἐλεεινόν θ'
ἅμα καὶ ἔσχατον κωκύσασα, ὁ δ' ἀναδραμὼν

to his household gods, gave orders that no one should follow him, and returned, almost beside himself, to his tent. It is in the nature of barbarians not to allow themselves to be turned aside from the object they have in view; when they despair of their own safety, they begin by slaying all those whom they hold most dear, either in the false belief that they will be with them again after death, or that, in so doing, they are delivering them from the violence and insults of the enemy. Thus Thyamis, forgetting all the dangers by which he was threatened, at the very moment when the enemy surrounded him like a net, raging with anger, love, and jealousy, hurried with all speed to the cave, and leaped down, crying out with all his might in the Egyptian language. At the entrance he found a woman who addressed him in Greek; her voice guided him to her person; he seized her hair with his left hand, and plunged his sword into her bosom.

XXXI. The unhappy woman uttered a piteous groan, and fell lifeless on the

καὶ τὸν οὐδὸν ἐπαγαγὼν καὶ χοῦν ὀλίγον ἐπι-
φορήσας καὶ, Ταῦτά σοι τὰ παρ' ἡμῶν νυμφικὰ
δῶρα σὺν δάκρυσιν εἰπὼν, ἐπί τε τὰ σκάφη
παραγενόμενος τούς τ' ἄλλους καταλαμβάνει
δρασμὸν ἤδη βουλεύοντας, τῶν πολεμίων
ἐγγύθεν ὁρωμένων, τόν τε Θέρμουθιν ἤκοντα
καὶ τὸ ἱερεῖον μεταχειριζόμενον· καὶ τὸν μὲν
λοιδορησάμενος, εἰπών τε, ὡς ἔφθη τὸ κάλλιστον
ἱερουργήσας θυμάτων ἐπιβαίνει τέ του σκάφους
αὐτὸς καὶ ὁ Θέρμουθις καὶ τρίτος ὁ ἐρέτης. Οὐ
γὰρ πλείονας οἷά τε φέρειν τὰ λιμναῖα σκάφη
ἀπὸ μόνου ξύλου καὶ πρέμνου παχέος ἑνὸς
ἀγροικότερον κοιλαινόμενα. Συναπαίρει δὲ καὶ
ὁ Θεαγένης ἅμα τῷ Κνήμωνι καθ' ἕτερον σκάφος
καὶ ἄλλος κατ' ἄλλο πορθμεῖον καὶ οὕτως
ἄπαντες. Ἐπεὶ δὲ τῆς νήσου μικρὸν ἄποθεν
ἄραντες καὶ περιπλεύσαντες μᾶλλον ἢ ἀποπλεύ-
σαντες, ἐπέσχον τὴν ἐρεσίαν καὶ τὰ σκάφη
διέταττον ἐπὶ μέτωπον, ὡς ἐναντίοι τοὺς πολε-
μίους δεξόμενοι, πλησιάσαντας μόνον, [καὶ]
μηδὲ τὸ ῥόθιον ὑπενεγκόντες οἱ μὲν ἄλλοι

ground. Thyamis hastened up, closed the entrance, and flung a few handfuls of earth upon it, saying: "Let this be my wedding present!" He then made his way to the boats, where he found his companions preparing to take to flight, since the enemy could be seen close at hand; at the same time, Thermuthis arrived with a victim for the sacrifice. Thyamis reviled him, told him that he had anticipated him by offering the most beautiful of victims, and got into a boat, accompanied by Thermuthis and a rower, these boats, consisting of a single piece of wood and rudely hollowed out of the trunk of a tree, being unable to hold more than three. Accordingly, Theagenes and Cnemon got into another boat, and the rest did the same. When all had embarked, they retired to a little distance from the island, and at first rowed round it instead of going out into the open sea; soon they even ceased rowing, and drew up their boats in line, ready to meet the attack of the enemy. But, at the mere approach of the latter, as soon as they saw them, the

πάντες ὁμοῦ τ' εἶδον καὶ ἔφευγον, οὐδὲ τὸν
ἐννάλιον ἔνιοι κέλαδον ἀνασχόμενοι· ὑπεχώρουν
δὲ Θεαγένης τε καὶ ὁ Κνήμων, οὐ πρὸς τὸν
φόβον τὸ πλέον ἐνδόντες. Μόνος δὲ ὁ Θύαμις
τὸ μέν τι τὴν φυγὴν ἴσως αἰσχυνόμενος, τάχα
δέ που καὶ εἶναι μετὰ Χαρίκλειαν οὐκ ἀνεχό-
μενος, ἐνέβαλεν ἑαυτὸν τοῖς πολεμίοις.

ΛΒ'. Ἤδη δ' εἰς χεῖρας ἰόντων, ἀνεβόησέ
τις, Οὗτος ἐκεῖνος ὁ Θύαμις· φυλάττου πᾶς.
Καὶ παραχρῆμα τὰ σκάφη πρὸς κύκλον ἐπι-
στρέψαντες, εἶχον ἐν μέσῳ. Τοῦ δ' ἀμυνομένου
καὶ τῷ δόρατι τοὺς μὲν τρώσαντος τοὺς δ'
ἀνελόντος, θαύματος ἦν ἐπέκεινα τὸ γιγνόμενον.
Εἷς γὰρ οὐδεὶς ξίφος οὔτ' ἔβαλλεν, οὔτ' ἔφερεν,
ἀλλ' ἅπασαν ἕκαστος εἰσεφέρετο σπουδὴν ζῶντα
λαβεῖν. Ὁ δ' ἀντεῖχεν ἐπιπλεῖστον, ἕως ἀφαι-
ρεῖται μὲν τοῦ δόρατος πλειόνων ἅμα ἐπιλα-
βομένων, ἀποβάλλει δὲ καὶ τὸν ὑπασπιστὴν
λαμπρῶς μὲν συναγωνισάμενον τραυματίαν δ'

brigands took to flight, frightened at the violence of the waves alone[1] and thrown into confusion by the sound of their war cry. Cnemon and Theagenes also retreated, but not from fear. Thyamis alone, either because he thought it would be disgraceful to flee, or because he could not endure the idea of surviving Chariclea, rushed into the midst of his enemies.

XXXII. Already he was engaged with them, when some one cried out, "It is Thyamis; do not lose sight of him." Then immediately the boats surrounded and shut him in on all sides. He fought stoutly, wounding some and killing others; but the most astonishing thing was what happened afterwards; in spite of their numbers, not one of the enemy lifted up the sword, or hurled a javelin against him; their only object seemed to be to capture him alive. For a long time Thyamis resisted with all his might; but at last, a body of men rushed upon him, and tore his spear from his hands. He also lost his armour-bearer, who had bravely assisted him, but at length, believing

[1] The word ῥόθιον might also mean "the shouts (of the enemy)."

ὥσπερ ἐδόκει καιρίως γεγενημένον καὶ πρὸς τὸ ἀνέλπιστον ἐνδόντα, ἔς τε τὴν λίμνην ἑαυτὸν καθέντα καὶ βολῆς ἐκτὸς ἐμπειρίᾳ τοῦ νεῖν ἀναδύντα, χαλεπῶς τε πρὸς τὸ ἕλος ἀπονηξάμενον καὶ ταῦτ' οὐδενὸς τὴν ἐπιδίωξιν φροντίσαντος. Ἤδη γὰρ τὸν Θύαμιν ᾑρήκεσαν καὶ νίκην ὁλόκληρον τὴν ἑνὸς ἀνδρὸς ἅλωσιν ἡγοῦντο. Καὶ τοσούτοις τοῖς φιλίοις ἐλάττους γεγονότες πλέον ἔχαιρον τὸν αὐτόχειρα ζῶντα περιέποντες ἢ τοὺς οἰκείους ᾤκτειρον ἀποβεβληκότες. Οὕτως ἄρα λῃσταῖς καὶ ψυχῶν αὐτῶν ἐστι χρήματα προτιμότερα καὶ τὸ φιλίας ὄνομα καὶ συγγενείας πρὸς ἓν τὸ κέρδος ὁρίζεται. Ὡς δὴ καὶ τούτοις συνέβαινεν. Ἐτύγχανον μὲν γὰρ ὄντες τῶν τὸν Θύαμιν καὶ τοὺς σὺν αὐτῷ κατὰ τὰς Ἡρακλεωτικὰς ἐκβολὰς ἀποδράντων.

ΛΓ' Ἀγανακτήσαντες δ' ὅτι τῶν ἀλλοτρίων ἐστέρηντο καὶ τὴν ἀφαίρεσιν τῶν σκύλων, ὡς ἰδίων περιαλγήσαντες, τούς θ' ὑπολειφθέντας αὐτῶν οἴκοι συλλεξάμενοι καὶ τὰς πέριξ ὁμοίως κώμας ἐπικαλεσάμενοι, ἐπὶ ὁμοίᾳ καὶ ἴσῃ τῶν

himself mortally wounded, and despairing
of his life, flung himself into the lake,
swam out of reach, and, although with
considerable difficulty, safely gained the
land, since the enemy did not think it
worth while to pursue him; for, as they
had already captured Thyamis, they re-
garded this as a complete victory. The
loss of a great number of their comrades
grieved them less than the capture alive of
the man who had been chiefly responsible
for it. So true is it that all brigands hold
money dearer than life itself, and the rights
of friendship and kinship are sacrificed to
greed alone. It was so in this case; for
the victors were the very same who had
formerly taken to flight before Thyamis
and his comrades at the Heracleotic
mouth of the Nile.

XXXIII. Indignant at being deprived
of that which was not really theirs, and as
furious at the loss of the spoils as if they
had been their own property, they gathered
together their comrades who had remained
at home and called upon the neighbouring
villages for assistance, and, offering them

ληφθησομένων διανομῇ, τῆς μὲν ἐφόδου κατέσ-
τησαν ἡγεμόνες, τὸν δὲ Θύαμιν ἐζώγρουν κατὰ
τοιάνδε τινὰ αἰτίαν. Πετόσιρις ἀδελφὸς ἦν
αὐτῷ κατὰ τὴν Μέμφιν. Οὗτος ἐπιβουλῇ τὴν
ἱερωσύνην τῆς προφητείας παρὰ τὸ πάτριον
τὸν Θύαμιν παρελόμενος, νεώτερος αὐτὸς ὤν,
τὸν προγενέστερον ἐξάρχειν ληστρικοῦ πυν-
θανόμενος, δεδιὼς μὴ καιροῦ λαβόμενος ἐπέλθῃ
ποτὲ, ἢ καὶ χρόνος τὴν ἐπιβουλὴν φωράσειεν,
ἅμα δὲ καὶ δι' ὑποψίας εἶναι παρὰ τοῖς πολλοῖς
αἰσθανόμενος, ὡς ἀνῃρηκὼς τὸν Θύαμιν, οὐ
φαινόμενον, χρήματα πάμπολλα καὶ βοσκή-
ματα τοῖς ζῶντα προσκομίσασιν εἰς τὰς κώμας
τὰς ληστρικὰς διαπέμπων ἐπεκήρυξεν. Ὑφ'
ὧν ἁλόντες οἱ λησταὶ καὶ μηδὲ παρὰ τὸ ζέον
τῆς μάχης τῆς μνήμης τὸ κέρδος ἀποβαλόντες,
ἐπειδή τις ἐγνώρισε, πολλῶν θανάτων ἐζώγρη-

an equal share of any spoils that might be taken, put themselves at the head of the expedition. The following was the reason why they took Thyamis alive. He had a brother named Petosiris living at Memphis, who had by intrigue dispossessed him of the dignity of chief priest, contrary to the custom of the country (for he was the younger brother). This Petosiris, having heard that his elder brother had become the captain of a band of brigands, and being afraid that, if he found an opportunity, he might return to Memphis, or that time might reveal his treachery; and, in addition, seeing that he was suspected of having made away with his brother, who had disappeared, he sent messengers into the villages inhabited by the brigands, offering a large sum of money and a large number of cattle to any who should capture Thyamis alive and bring him to him. The brigands, seduced by these offers, even in the heat of battle did not forget the hope of gain held out to them; and, as soon as Thyamis was recognised, did not hesitate to sacrifice a number of their comrades,

σαν, καὶ τὸν μὲν δέσμιον ἐπὶ τὴν γῆν παρα-
πέμπουσι, τὴν ἡμίσειαν αὐτῷ μοῖραν εἰς τὴν
φυλακὴν ἀποκληρώσαντες καὶ πολλὰ τῆς
δοκούσης φιλανθρωπίας ἐπιμεμφόμενον καὶ τὸν
δεσμὸν ἀγανακτοῦντα μᾶλλον ἢ θάνατον. Οἱ
δ' ὑπόλοιποι πρὸς τὴν νῆσον ἐτράπησαν, ὡς
τὰ ἐπιζητούμενα κειμήλια καὶ σκῦλα κατ'
αὐτὴν εὑρήσοντες. Ὡς δὲ πᾶσαν ἐπιδραμόντες
καὶ μέρος οὐδὲν ἀζήτητον ἀπολιπόντες, οὐδενὶ
τῶν ἐλπισθέντων ἢ μικροῖς ἐπετύγχανον, εἴ τι
καὶ περιλέλειπτο κατὰ τὸ σπήλαιον ὑπὸ τῇ
γῇ μὴ κρυπτόμενον, πῦρ ἐπὶ τὰς σκηνὰς
ἐμβαλόντες, ἑσπέρας ἤδη προσιούσης καὶ φόβον
ἐγκαταμεῖναι τῇ νήσῳ παρεχούσης, δέει τοῦ
μὴ λοχηθῆναι πρὸς τῶν διαδράντων, ἐπὶ τοὺς
οἰκείους ἀπεχώρησαν.

in order to take him alive. When they had captured him, they put him in irons and rowed him to land, half of their number being deputed to guard him, while he reproached them bitterly for their apparent humanity and expressed greater indignation at his imprisonment than if it had been death itself. The others, meanwhile, returned to the island, in the hope of finding the treasures and booty of which they were in search, and scoured it thoroughly, leaving no part unexplored. But, finding nothing of all that they had set their hearts upon, with the exception of a few articles of trifling value, which the owners had forgotten to hide in the underground cave, they set fire to the tents. Then, since night was approaching, being afraid to remain longer in the island, lest they should fall into the hands of those who had escaped from the battle, they returned to their comrades.

END OF BOOK I

ΛΟΓΟΣ ΔΕΥΤΕΡΟΣ

Α΄. Ἡ μὲν δὴ νῆσος ὧδ᾽ ἐπυρπολεῖτο, τοὺς δ᾽ ἀμφὶ τὸν Θεαγένην καὶ τὸν Κνήμωνα, ἕως μὲν ἥλιος ἦν ὑπὲρ γῆν, τὸ κακὸν ἐλάνθανεν. Ἡ γὰρ πυρὸς ὄψις ἀμαυροῦται δι᾽ ἡμέρας ὑπὸ τῶν ἀκτίνων τοῦ θεοῦ καταυγαζομένη. Ἐπειδὴ δ᾽ ἔδυ καὶ νύκτα ἐπήγαγεν, ἥ τε φλὸξ ἀπρόσμαχον τὴν αὐγὴν ἀπολαβοῦσα καὶ πορρωτάτω διεφαίνετο, αὐτοί τε τοῦ ἕλους τῇ νυκτὶ θαρροῦντες προὔκυψαν καὶ λαμπρῶς ἤδη τὴν νῆσον ὑπὸ τοῦ πυρὸς ἐχομένην ὁρῶσι. Καὶ ὁ μὲν Θεαγένης παίων τὴν κεφαλὴν καὶ τίλλων τὰς τρίχας, Ἐρρίφθω, φησὶν, ὁ βίος εἰς τὴν τήμερον· ἠνύσθω, λελύσθω πάντα, φόβοι, κίνδυνοι, φροντίδες, ἐλπίδες, ἔρωτες. Οἴχεται Χαρίκλεια, Θεαγένης ἀπόλωλε. Μάτην ὁ δυστυχὴς δειλὸς ἐγενόμην καὶ δρασμὸν ὑπέστην ἄνανδρον, σοὶ, γλυκεῖα, περισώζων ἐμαυτόν.

I. THUS the island was ravaged by fire;
but Theagenes and Cnemon did not per-
ceive the mischief as long as the sun was
above the earth. For the appearance of
fire is effaced by day, being illumined by
the beams of the god. But, when the sun
set and brought back the night, the flames,
recovering their irresistible brilliancy, were
clearly seen from afar. At the same time,
Theagenes and Cnemon, trusting to the
darkness of night, left the marsh, and be-
held the whole island in a blaze. Then
Theagenes beat his head, tore his hair, and
cried aloud: "Farewell to life this day!
fears, dangers, anxieties, hope, and love—
all are ended; Chariclea is dead, Theagenes
is undone. My cowardice has been of no
avail to me; in vain did I flee from the
battlefield in flight unworthy of a man,
to save myself for you, my dearest love!

Οὐ μὴν ἔτι σωθήσομαί σου, φιλτάτη, κειμένης, οὐδὲ τῷ κοινῷ τῆς φύσεως νόμῳ, (τὸ χαλεπώτατον) οὐδ' ἐν χερσὶν ἀπολιπούσης τὸν βίον αἷς ἠβουλήθης. 'Αλλὰ πυρὸς, οἴμοι, γέγονας ἀνάλωμα, τοιαύτας ἐπί σοι λαμπάδας ἀντὶ τῶν νυμφικῶν τοῦ δαίμονος ἄψαντος· καὶ δεδαπάνηται τὸ ἐξ ἀνθρώπων κάλλος, ὡς μηδὲ λείψανον τῆς ἀψευδοῦς ὡραιότητος διὰ νεκροῦ γοῦν ὑπολελεῖφθαι τοῦ σώματος. Ὦ τῆς ὠμότητος καὶ τῆς ἀρρήτου τοῦ δαίμονος βασκανίας· προσαφῄρηταί με καὶ τὰ τελευταῖα περιβαλεῖν. Ἐσχάτων καὶ ἀψύχων φιλημάτων ἀπεστερήθην.

Β. Καὶ ταῦτα λέγοντος καὶ τὸ ξίφος περισκοποῦντος, ὁ Κνήμων ἀθρόον τῆς χειρὸς ἀπεκρούσατο, καὶ Τί ταῦτα; ἔλεγεν, ὦ Θεάγενες, τί τὴν οὖσαν θρηνεῖς; Ἔστι Χαρίκλεια καὶ σώζεται· θάρσει. Τοῦδε, Πρὸς ἄφρονας ταῦτα καὶ παῖδας, ὦ Κνήμων, εἰπόντος, ἀπολώλεκάς με τὸν ἥδιστον ἀφελόμενος θάνατον· ἐπώμνυεν ὁ Κνήμων καὶ ἅπαντα ἔλεγε, τὸ πρόσταγμα τοῦ Θυάμιδος, τὸ σπήλαιον,

No longer will I survive you, now that you are lying dead, not (which is hardest of all) in accordance with the common law of nature, nor having breathed your last in your lover's arms. Alas! you have been consumed by fire; some cruel god has substituted these flames for the bridal torches. Your beauty has perished from amongst men; your dead body does not even preserve the remains of your unadulterated charms. Oh, unutterable cruelty! Oh, most bitter spite of fortune! I have been denied the favour of a last embrace, of a last and lifeless kiss."

II. With these words, he would have grasped his sword, when Cnemon suddenly caught hold of him and thrust back his hand, crying out: "What is the meaning of this, Theagenes? why lament for her who is still alive? Chariclea is safe; take heart." "This tale is only fit for fools and children," replied Theagenes; "you have crowned my woes, by depriving me of a most delightful death." Thereupon Cnemon swore that his words were true and told the whole story; the instructions that Thyamis had given him, how he had

ὡς καθῆκεν αὐτός, ὡς ἔχει φύσεως τὸ ἄντρον, ὡς οὐδὲν δέος εἰς τὸ βάθος διϊκνεῖσθαι τὸ πῦρ, ὑπὸ τῶν ἀπείρων ἑλιγμῶν ἀνακοπτόμενον. Ἀνέπνει πρὸς ταῦθ' ὁ Θεαγένης καὶ πρὸς τὴν νῆσον ἔσπευδε καὶ τὴν οὐ παροῦσαν τῷ νῷ περιέβλεπε καὶ θάλαμον αὑτῷ τὸ σπήλαιον ἀνέπλαττε, τοὺς ἐσομένους αὐτῷ κατ' αὐτὸ θρήνους ἀγνοῶν. Ἀνήγοντο οὖν ἐσπουδασμένως, αὐτερέται τὸν πλοῦν ἀνύοντες. Ὁ γὰρ δὴ πορθμεύων αὐτοῖς κατὰ τὴν πρώτην συμβολὴν καθάπερ ἀπὸ ὕσπληγος τῆς βοῆς ἀπεσφενδόνητο. Τῇδε οὖν κἀκεῖσε παρεφέροντο τοῦ εὐθέος, οἷα δὴ ἀπειρίᾳ τε τὴν ἐρεσίαν οὐχ ὁμοζυγοῦντες καί τι καὶ ἀνέμου πρὸς ἐναντίον ἐμπίπτοντος ἀλλ' ἐνίκα τὴν ἀτεχνίαν τῆς γνώμης τὸ πρόθυμον.

Γ'. Χαλεπῶς δὲ καὶ σὺν ἱδρῶτι πολλῷ τῇ νήσῳ προσορμίσαντες, ὡς εἶχον τάχους, ἐπὶ τὰς σκηνὰς ἀνέτρεχον. Καὶ τὰς μὲν καταλαμβάνουσιν ἤδη κατηθαλωμένας καὶ τῷ τόπῳ

let Chariclea down into the cave, and the formation of the same, which prevented all danger of the fire reaching the bottom, since it would be checked by the countless windings and turnings. At these words, Theagenes breathed again and hastened to the island, in his mind already seeing Chariclea and representing to himself the cave as his nuptial chamber, ignorant what sorrow awaited him there.

They advanced in all haste, being obliged to row themselves; for their boatman, at the beginning of the engagement, struck by the first shouts of the enemy, as if by a swine-goad,[1] had fallen overboard. Being little skilled in handling their oars and rowing together, they were carried backwards and forwards out of the straight course, while they also had to contend against an adverse wind. Nevertheless, their eagerness overcame their want of skill.

III. When, therefore, with great difficulty and effort they had at last reached the island, they hastened with all speed to the huts, which they found already con-

[1] The meaning of ὕσπληξ in this passage is very doubtful.

μόνῳ γνωριζομένας, τὸν λίθον δὲ τὸν οὐδὸν τοῦ
σπηλαίου τὸ κάλυμμα διαφαινόμενον. Ὁ γὰρ
ἄνεμος ἐπίφορος ταῖς καλύβαις ἐμπνεύσας καὶ
οἷα δὴ λεπτοῖς καλάμοις καὶ τούτοις ἐλείοις
διαπλόκοις τῇ ῥιπῇ κατὰ πάροδον καταφλέξας,
μικροῦ ἰσόπεδον ἐπεδείκνυ τὸ ὑποκείμενον, τῆς
μὲν φλογὸς ὀξέως μαρανθείσης καὶ εἰς τέφραν
ἀναλυθείσης, τῆς δὲ σποδιᾶς τῆς μὲν πολλῆς
τῷ ῥοίζῳ παρενεχθείσης, ὀλίγης δὲ τῆς ὑπολει-
πομένης, πρὸς τὸ πνέον ἀπάσης σχεδὸν ἀποσ-
βεσθείσης καὶ πρὸς τὸ βάσιμον ἀποψυγείσης.
Δᾷδας οὖν ἡμιφλέκτους ἀνευρόντες καὶ λείψανα
καλάμων ἐξάψαντες καὶ τὸ στόμιον ἀνοίξαντες
κατέθεον ἡγουμένου τοῦ Κνήμωνος. Ἐπεὶ δ᾽
ὀλίγον ὑπέβησαν, ἀθρόον ὁ Κνήμων ἀνέκραγεν·
Ὦ Ζεῦ, τί τοῦτο; ἀπολώλαμεν. Δῄρηται
Χαρίκλεια. Καὶ τό τε λαμπάδιον εἰς τὴν
γῆν καταβαλὼν ἀπέσβεσε καὶ τὸ χεῖρε τοῖς
ὀφθαλμοῖς ἐπαγαγὼν, εἰς γόνυ τ᾽ ὀκλάσας,

sumed by the fire, and only recognisable by the site which they had once occupied. The stone, however, which had formed the entrance to the cave was clearly to be seen; for a violent wind blowing upon the huts, that were only made of thin reeds and sedge intertwined, had fanned the flames in passing, and caused their total conflagration, exposing an almost level plain beneath. The flame, when it was extinguished, had left nothing but a heap of ashes, most of which had been carried away by the violence of the wind, while the few that remained, although still smouldering, had cooled sufficiently to allow anyone to pass over. Having found some half-lighted torches and kindled some fragments of reeds, they opened the mouth of the cave and hastened down, Cnemon going first. But, after they had proceeded a little way, he suddenly cried out: "O Jove! what means this? We are lost; Chariclea is no more!" With these words, he let the torch fall from his hands, and it went out; he himself, clasping his hands before his eyes, sank on his knees, weeping bitterly.

ἐθρήνει. Ὁ δὲ Θεαγένης ὥσπερ τινὸς πρὸς βίαν ὤσαντος ἐπὶ τὸ σῶμα τῆς κειμένης κατενεχθεὶς, ὁ μὲν ἐπὶ πλεῖστον ἀπρὶξ εἴχετο καὶ προσεπεφύκει πανταχόθεν ἐναγκαλιζόμενος. Ὁ δὲ Κνήμων ὅλον ὄντα πρὸς τῷ πάθει καταμαθὼν καὶ τῇ συμφορᾷ βεβαπτισμένον, δεδιώς τε μή τι κακὸν αὐτῷ ἐργάσηται, τὸ ξίφος ὑφαιρεῖ λάθρα τῆς θήκης ὑπὸ τὴν πλευρὰν αἰωρουμένης καὶ μόνον καταλιπὼν ἀνέδραμεν ὡς τὰς δᾷδας ἀναψόμενος.

Δ'. Κἂν τούτῳ τραγικόν τι καὶ γοερὸν ὁ Θεαγένης βρυχώμενος, Ὦ πάθους ἀτλήτου, φησὶν, ὦ συμφορᾶς θεηλάτου· τίς οὕτως ἀκόρεστος Ἐρινὺς τοῖς ἡμετέροις κακοῖς ἐνεβάκχευσε, φυγὴν τῆς ἐνεγκούσης ἐπιβαλοῦσα, κινδύνοις θαλασσῶν, κινδύνοις πειρατηρίων ὑποβαλοῦσα, λῃσταῖς παραδοῦσα πολλάκις, τῶν ὄντων ἀλλοτριώσασα; Ἓν μόνον ἀντὶ πάντων ὑπελείπετο, καὶ τοῦτ' ἀνήρπασται. Κεῖται Χαρίκλεια καὶ πολεμίας χειρὸς ἔργον ἡ φιλτάτη γεγένηται· δῆλον μὲν ὡς σωφροσύνης ἀντεχο-

But Theagenes, as if urged forward by some irresistible force, fell upon the body of the woman lying on the ground, and for a long time, motionless, held it clasped in a close embrace. Cnemon, seeing that he was utterly overwhelmed with grief and bathed in sorrow, was afraid that he might make an attempt upon his life. Secretly drawing his sword, which hung by his side, from its scabbard, he left him to himself, and ran out to light his torch again.

IV. In the meanwhile, Theagenes filled the cavern with his loud and mournful wailing: " Oh, grief unbearable ! oh, calamity sent upon me from heaven ! what insatiable fury rages for our destruction, and has driven us from our country, exposed us to dangers on sea and the attacks of pirates, often delivered us into the hands of brigands, and robbed us of all our possessions ? One comfort alone remained to me ; now, even this has been taken from me. Chariclea lies dead, and she who was dearer than all to me has been destroyed by the hand of the enemy, doubtless in defence of her

μένη, κἀμοὶ δῆθεν αὐτὴν φυλάττουσα. Κεῖται δ᾿ οὖν ὅμως ἡ δυστυχὴς, οὐδὲν μὲν αὐτὴ τῆς ὥρας ἀποναμένη, εἰς οὐδὲν δ᾿ ὄφελος ἐμοὶ γενομένη. ᾿Αλλ᾿, ὦ γλυκεῖα, πρόσφθεγξαι τὰ τελευταῖα καὶ εἰωθότα· ἐπίσκηψον, εἴ τι καὶ κατὰ μικρὸν ἐμπνεῖς. Οἴμοι, σιωπᾷς καὶ τὸ μαντικὸν ἐκεῖνο καὶ θεηγόρον στόμα σιγὴ κατέχει καὶ ζόφος τὴν πυρφόρον καὶ χάος τὴν ἐκ τῶν ἀνακτόρων κατείληφεν. ᾿Οφθαλμοὶ δ᾿ ἀφεγγεῖς, οἱ πάντας τῷ κάλλει καταστράψαντες, οὓς οὐκ εἶδεν ὁ φονεύσας, οἶδ᾿ ἀκριβῶς. ᾿Αλλ᾿ ὦ τί ἄν σέ τις ὀνομάσειε; νύμφην; ἀλλ᾿ ἀνύμφευτος· γαμετήν; ἀλλ᾿ ἀπείρατος. Τίνα οὖν ἀνακαλέσω; τίνα προσφθέγξομαι λοιπὸν, ἢ ἄρα τὸ πάντων ὀνομάτων ἥδιστον, Χαρίκλεια; ἀλλ᾿ ὦ Χαρίκλεια, θάρσει, πιστὸν ἔχεις τὸν ἐρώμενον· ἀπολήψῃ με μικρὸν ὕστερον. ᾿Ιδοὺ γάρ σοι χοὰς ἐπάξω τὰς ἐμαυτοῦ σφαγὰς καὶ σπείσυμαι τὸ σοὶ φίλον αἷμα τοὐμόν. Ἕξει

chastity, to preserve it for me. Now the unhappy woman lies dead, having reaped no benefit from her beauty, without my having enjoyed it myself. Oh, my dearest, bid me a last farewell; give me your last commands, if the breath of life is still in you. Alas! you are silent. Those heavenly and prophetic lips are hushed in silence; the shades of darkness have enveloped the bearer of the torch and chaos the priestess of the gods. Those eyes which charmed all with their beauty are closed for ever. I am convinced your murderer never saw them. But by what name am I to call you? my betrothed? But you have never been betrothed. My wife? But you never knew the meaning of the word. What, then, am I to call you? How shall I address you for the last time? By the sweetest name of all — Chariclea? Oh, Chariclea, be of good cheer; you have a faithful lover; soon you shall see me again. I will celebrate your obsequies by my own death and offer to you a libation of my own blood that is so dear to you. This

δ' ἡμᾶς αὐτοσχέδιον μνῆμα τόδε τὸ σπήλαιον. Ἐξέσται πάντως ἀλλήλοις συνεῖναι μετὰ γοῦν θάνατον εἰ καὶ ζῶσιν ὁ δαίμων οὐκ ἐπέτρεψε.

Ε΄. Καὶ ἅμα λέγων, ἐπέβαλε τὴν χεῖρα ὡς τὸ ξίφος σπασόμενος. Ὡς δ' οὐχ εὕρισκεν, Ὦ Κνήμων, ἐβόησεν, ὡς σύ με ἀπολώλεκας. Προσηδίκησας δὲ καὶ Χαρίκλειαν, τῆς ἡδίστης αὐτὴν κοινωνίας ἤδη δεύτερον ἀποστερήσας. Καὶ ταῦτα διεξιόντος, ἐκ μυχῶν τοῦ σπηλαίου φωνῆς τις ἦχος ἐξηκούετο, Θεάγενες, καλούσης. Ὁ δ' οὐδὲν ταραχθεὶς, ὑπήκουσέ τε καὶ ἤξω φιλτάτη ψυχὴ ἔλεγεν. Εὔδηλος εἶ περὶ γῆν ἔτι φερομένη· τὸ μέν τι τοιούτου σώματος οὐ πρὸς βίαν ἐξηλάθης ἀποστατεῖν οὐ φέρουσα, τὸ δὲ διὰ τὸ ἄταφον ἴσως ὑπὸ νερτερίων εἰδώλων εἰργομένη. Κἂν τούτῳ τοῦ Κνήμωνος ἅμα δᾳσὶν ἡμμέναις ἐπιστάντος, αὖθις ὁ αὐτὸς ἦχος ἐξηκούετο, καὶ ἦν τὸ λεγόμενον, Θεάγενες. Ὁ δὲ Κνήμων ἀναβοήσας, Ὦ θεοὶ, ἔφη, οὐ

cave shall be our impromptu tomb. In it we shall at least be united after death, although, during our lifetime, this has been denied us."

V. With these words, he stretched out his hand to draw his sword; but not finding it, he exclaimed: "Oh, Cnemon, you have destroyed me, and again wronged Chariclea, having a second time deprived her of the company of him who was her greatest delight."

While he was thus speaking, the sound of a voice came from the inmost recesses of the cave, crying out, "Theagenes." In no wise troubled, he heard and answered: "My dearest, I will come. It is evident that your shade still wanders upon earth; me-thinks you cannot endure to quit that body from which you were driven by force, or, being yet unburied, are perhaps refused admittance to the company of the shades below." In the meantime, Cnemon had returned with his torch relighted, when the same voice was heard again, calling "Theagenes." "Good heavens!" ex-claimed Cnemon, "is that not the voice

Χαρικλείας ἐστὶν ἡ φωνή; σώζεσθαί μοι δοκεῖ,
Θεάγενες· ἀπὸ γὰρ τῶν ἐσχάτων καὶ καθ᾽ ὃ
μέρος αὐτὴν οἶδα τοῦ ἄντρου καταλιπὼν, ἡ
φωνή μοι βάλλει τὴν ἀκοήν. Οὐ παύσῃ, ἔφη
ὁ Θεαγένης, ἀπατῶι με πολλάκις; Καὶ μὴν
ἀπατῶ σε καὶ ἀπατῶμαι τὸ μέρος, εἶπεν ὁ
Κνήμων, εἰ Χαρίκλειαν οὖσαν ταυτηνὶ τὴν κει-
μένην εὕροιμεν. Καὶ ἅμα λέγων ἀνέστρεφεν
ἐπ᾽ ὄψιν τὴν κειμένην καὶ ἰδὼν Τί τοῦτο;
ἀνέκραγεν, ὦ δαίμονες τεράστιοι, Θίσβης ἡ
ὄψις. Ὑπέβη δ᾽ εἰς τοὐπίσω καὶ τρόμῳ
συσχεθεὶς ἀχανὴς εἱστήκει.

5. Ὁ δὲ Θεαγένης, ἔμπνους ἐκ τῶνδε
γενόμενος καὶ πρὸς τὸ εὔελπι τὴν γνώμην
ἐπιστρέφων, ἀνεκαλεῖτό τε λειποψυχοῦντα
τὸν Κνήμωνα καὶ παρὰ τὴν Χαρίκλειαν ὡς
ὅτι τάχιστα ποδηγεῖν ἱκέτευε. Μικρὸν οὖν
διαλιπὼν εἰς αὑτόν τε γενόμενος ὁ Κνήμων,
τὴν κειμένην αὖθις ἐπεσκοπεῖτο. Ἡ δ᾽ ἦν
ἀληθῶς ἡ Θίσβη· καὶ ξίφος τὸ πλησίον ἐκ-
πεπτωκὸς ἐγνώριζεν ἀπὸ τῆς λαβῆς, ὃ παρὰ
τὸν φόνον ὁ Θύαμις ὑπὸ θυμοῦ καὶ σπουδῆς
τῇ σφαγῇ ἐναπέλιπε. Καὶ δέλτον τινὰ τῶν
στέρνων ὑπὸ τῇ μασχάλῃ προκύπτουσαν ἀνελό-

of Chariclea that I hear? I believe she is still alive, Theagenes; for the voice that has just struck my ear proceeds from the inmost recesses of the cave, where I remember that I left her." "Oh, Cnemon," said Theagenes, "will you never cease to deceive me?" "Well, if I deceive you, I am myself deceived; let us see whether this corpse be really Chariclea." With these words, he turned the body on its back, and, looking at it attentively, exclaimed: "Oh, ye gods! what prodigy is this? This is the face of Thisbe!" Then he stepped back, and stood trembling and motionless, like one dumbfounded.

VI. But Theagenes, who now began to breathe again, with hope revived, called upon Cnemon, who seemed ready to faint, and begged him to lead him with all speed to Chariclea. After a little time, Cnemon recovered, and again examined the corpse, and saw that it was really Thisbe; by her side lay a sword, which he recognised by its hilt as belonging to Thyamis, who, in his mad frenzy, had left it in the wound. Seeing a letter in Thisbe's bosom, he took it

μενος, ἐπειρᾶτό τι τῶν ἐγγεγραμμένων ἐπιέναι.
Ἀλλ' ὁ Θεαγένης οὐκ εἴα λιπαρῶς ἐγκείμενος
καὶ τὴν φιλτάτην, λέγων, κομιζώμεθα πρό-
τερον, εἰ μή τις ἡμᾶς παίζει καὶ νυνὶ δαίμων·
ταῦτα δ' ἐξέσται καὶ μετὰ ταῦτα γιγνώσκειν.
Ἐπείθετο ὁ Κνήμων καὶ τήν τε δέλτον ἐπι-
κομιζόμενοι καὶ τὸ ξίφος ἀνελόμενοι παρὰ τὴν
Χαρίκλειαν ἔσπευδον. Ἡ δὲ χερσί θ' ἅμα καὶ
ποσὶν ἐπὶ τὴν αὐγὴν ἀνερπύσασα, προσδρα-
μοῦσά τε τῷ Θεαγένει, τοῦ αὐχένος ἐξήρτητο.
Καὶ ἡ μὲν, ἔχω σε, Θεάγενες; ὁ δὲ, ζῇς μοι,
Χαρίκλεια, πολλάκις ἔλεγον· καὶ τέλος ἐς
τοὔδαφος ἀθρόον καταφέρονται, καὶ εἴχοντο
ἀλλήλων ἄναυδοι μὲν ἀλλ' ὥσπερ ἡνωμένοι, καὶ
μικροῦ ἔδει ἀποθνήσκειν αὐτούς. Οὕτως ἄρα
καὶ τὸ χαρᾶς ὑπερβάλλον εἰς ἀλγεινὸν περι-
έστη πολλάκις καὶ τῆς ἡδονῆς τὸ ἄμετρον
ἐπίσπαστον λύπην ἐγέννησεν. Ὡς δὴ κἀκεῖνοι
παρ' ἐλπίδα σωθέντες ἐκινδύνευον, ἕως ὁ
Κνήμων πίδακά τινα διαμώμενος καὶ τὴν συρ-
ρυεῖσαν καταβραχὺ νοτίδα κοίλαις ταῖς χερσὶν

out, and would have read it, but Theagenes would not permit him to do so, and earnestly pressed him, saying: " Let us first recover our dear Chariclea; who knows whether some god is even now mocking us; we shall be able to read the letter afterwards." Cnemon consenting, they took up the letter and the sword, and hastened to Chariclea, who, dragging herself on her hands and knees in the direction of the light, threw her arms round her lover's neck. "Oh, Theagenes, do I really hold you in my arms?" "Oh, Chariclea, are you still preserved to me?" This they kept repeating, until, at last, they suddenly fell upon the ground, clinging to each other, fast entangled in their embraces, and unable to utter a word. It seemed as if death had overtaken them; for oftentimes excess of joy ends in sorrow, and immoderate pleasure begets pain, which we have brought upon ourselves. Thus these two lovers, preserved beyond their hopes, seemed at death's door, until Cnemon, by scraping the rock, discovered a tiny stream of running water, under which he held his hands, caught some of

ὑδρευσάμενος, τὸ πρόσωπόν τ' αὐτῶν ἐπέρρανε καὶ θαμὰ τῶν ῥινῶν ἐπαφώμενος ἐπὶ τὸ φρονεῖν ἐπανήγαγεν.

Ζ'. Οἱ δὲ, ἑτέρως μὲν ἀλλήλοις ἐντυχόντες, κειμένους δ' αὐτοὺς καταλαβόντες, ὀρθωθέντες ἀθρόον, ἠρυθρίων τὸν Κνήμωνα (καὶ πλέον ἡ Χαρίκλεια) θεωρὸν τῶνδε γεγενημένον καὶ νέμειν συγγνώμην ἱκέτευον. Ὁ δ' ἐπιμειδιάσας καὶ πρὸς τὸ φαιδρότερον αὐτοὺς ἀνιεὶς, Ταῦτα μὲν, ἔφη, καὶ ἐπαίνων ἄξια κατ' ἐμὲ κριτὴν καὶ ἄλλον ὅστις ἔρωτι προσπαλαίσας ἡττήθη τε τὴν μάχην ἡδέως καὶ τἀκείνου σωφρόνως ἔγνωκεν ἀπαραίτητα πτώματα. Ἀλλ' ἐκεῖνα, ὦ Θεάγενες, οὔτ' ἐπαινεῖν εἶχον ὑπερῃσχυνόμην θ' ὁρῶν, ὡς ἀληθῶς, ὅτε τὴν ξένην καὶ προσήκουσαν οὐδαμόθεν γυναῖκα περιπεσὼν ἐθρήνεις ἀγεννῶς καὶ ταῦτα περιεῖναι καὶ ζῆν σοι τὴν φιλτάτην ἐμοῦ διατεινομένου. Καὶ ὁ Θεαγένης, Παῦε, φησὶν, ὦ Κνήμων, διαβάλλων με πρὸς

the slowly falling drops, and, dashing them in their faces and moistening their nostrils from time to time, gradually revived them.

VII. Theagenes and Chariclea, finding themselves in each other's arms, started up blushing (especially Chariclea) at the thought that they had thus abandoned themselves to their extravagant transports in the presence of Cnemon, and besought him to pardon their excesses. Cnemon, gently smiling, restored their cheerfulness. "Nay, your behaviour deserves praise in my opinion, and in the opinion of every man who has entered the lists with love, has felt the pleasure of being vanquished by him, and made acquaintance, but in moderation, with his inevitable accidents. But there are other things, of which I can by no means approve, Theagenes; I was really ashamed to see you embrace a strange woman who was in no way known to you, and weeping over the body of a slave, especially when I protested to you that the object of your affections was still alive." "Oh, Cnemon," replied Theagenes, "cease to slander me to

Χαρίκλειαν, ἣν ἐθρήνουν ἐν ἀλλοτρίῳ σώματι ταύτην εἶναι τὴν κειμένην ἡγούμενος. Ἐπεὶ δ᾽ ἀπάτην ἐκεῖνα θεῶν τις εὖ γε ποιῶν ἔδειξεν, ὥρα σοὶ σαυτὸν ὑπομνῆσαι τῆς ἄγαν ἀνδρείας, ὑφ᾽ ἧς ἐθρήνεις μὲν ἐμοῦ τἀμὰ πρότερος, τὴν δ᾽ ἀπροσδόκητον τῆς κειμένης ἐπίγνωσιν, ὥσπερ ἐπὶ σκηνῆς δαίμονας, ἀπεδίδρασκες, ἔνοπλος καὶ ξιφήρης γυναῖκα καὶ ταύτην νεκρὰν ὑποφεύγων, ὁ γενναῖος καὶ Ἀττικὸς πεζομάχος.

Η′. Ἐγέλασαν πρὸς ταῦτα βραχύ τι καὶ βεβιασμένον οὐδὲ τοῦτ᾽ ἀδάκρυτον, ἀλλ᾽ ὡς ἂν ἐν τοσαύτῃ συμφορᾷ πλέον τῷ θρήνῳ κεκερασμένον. Μικρὸν οὖν ἡ Χαρίκλεια διαλιποῦσα καὶ τὴν παρειὰν ὑπὸ τὸ οὖς ἐπικνῶσα, Μακαρίζω μὲν, ἔφη, τὴν θρηνηθεῖσαν ὑπὸ Θεαγένους ἢ καὶ φιληθεῖσαν, ὡς φησὶ Κνήμων, ἥτις ποτὲ καί ἐστιν. Ἀλλ᾽ εἰ μή τί με δακνομένην ἔρωτι ὑπονοεῖν μέλλετε, τίς ἄρ᾽ ἦν ἡ εὐδαίμων ἐκείνη καὶ δακρύων ἀξιωθεῖσα Θεαγενείων καὶ τίνα

Chariclea; it was she whom I was lamenting in the person of another; it was her body that I thought I was watering with my tears. But, since some kindly Deity has opened my eyes and shown me my mistake, it is time for you to remember the great bravery which led you first to deplore my misfortunes, and, when you suddenly came upon the dead body, made you, a brave Athenian warrior, armed from head to foot, with your drawn sword in your hand, run away from a woman—and a dead woman, too—like the actors from the devils on the stage."

VIII. At this they smiled slightly, but a forced smile, and not without tears, which were rather tears of grief, caused by the magnitude of their calamity. After a brief interval, Chariclea, gently passing her hand over her cheek, as if in thought, said : " I esteem her happy, whoever she may be, whom Theagenes lamented and even kissed ! Do not think me jealous, if I ask you to tell me who was the happy woman, who was honoured by the tears of Theagenes, and how you came

11

τρόπον τὴν ἄγνωστον ὡς ἐμὲ φιλεῖν ἐξηπατήθης, ἐβουλόμην εἴ πῃ γιγνώσκεις μανθάνειν. Καὶ δς, Θαυμάσεις μὲν, ἔφη. Θίσβην δ᾽ οὖν εἶναι Κνήμων ὅδε φησὶ τὴν Ἀθηναίαν ἐκείνην, τὴν ψάλτριαν, τὴν τῶν εἰς αὐτὸν ἐπιβουλῶν καὶ Δημαινέτην ποιήτριαν. Τῆς δὲ Χαρικλείας ἐκπεπληγμένης καὶ Πῶς ἦν εἰκὸς, ὦ Κνήμων, εἰπούσης, τὴν ἐκ μέσης τῆς Ἑλλάδος ἐπ᾽ ἐσχάτης γῆς Αἰγύπτου, καθάπερ ἐκ μηχανῆς ἀναπεμφθῆναι; πῶς δὲ καὶ ἐλάνθανεν ἡμᾶς δεῦρο κατιόντας; Ταῦτα μὲν οὐκ ἔχω λέγειν, ἀπεκρίνατο πρὸς αὐτὴν ὁ Κνήμων, ἃ δ᾽ οὖν ἔχω γιγνώσκειν ἀμφ᾽ αὐτῆς τοιάδ᾽ ἐστίν. Ἐπειδὴ γὰρ ἡ Δημαινέτη μετὰ τὴν ἀπάτην εἰς τὸν βόθρον αὐτὴν ἀπεκρήμνισεν, ὁ δὲ πατὴρ ἐξήγγειλε τῷ δήμῳ τὸ γεγενημένον, παρὰ μὲν τὴν πρώτην ἐτύγχανε συγγνώμης καὶ αὐτὸς μὲν ὅπως ἂν κάθοδον ἐμοί τε λάβοι παρὰ τοῦ δήμου καὶ κατὰ ζήτησιν ἐκπλεύσειε τὴν ἐμὴν διετίθετο, ἡ δὲ Θίσβη τὴν ἀσχολίαν τὴν ἐκείνου, σχολὴν αὐτῆς ἐποιεῖτο καὶ τοῖς συμποσίοις ἀδεῶς αὐτήν τε καὶ τὴν τέχνην ἐξεμίσθου. Καί

to be so deceived as to kiss her as if she had been myself: if you know, I wish you would tell me." "You will be surprised," replied Theagenes; "Cnemon here declares that it is Thisbe, the Athenian lute-player, who contrived the plots against Demaeneta and himself." Chariclea, astounded at what she heard, said: "But how could she have been transported, as if by enchantment, from the midst of Greece to the furthest bounds of Egypt? and how was it that we did not see her when we came hither?" "That I cannot tell you," answered Cnemon; "all I know is this. When Demaeneta, finding herself tricked, flung herself into the pit, my father informed the people of what had happened, and was immediately acquitted; after which he endeavoured to secure my recall from banishment, and made preparations to set sail in search of me. In the meantime Thisbe, taking advantage of the leisure which her master's occupation afforded her, frequented all the festivals, at which she shamelessly prostituted her art and person.

ποτε καὶ παρευδοκιμήσασα τὴν Ἀρσινόην ἀναβεβλημένον αὐλοῦσαν, ἐπίτροχον αὐτὴ ψάλλουσα καὶ γλαφυρὸν τῇ κιθάρᾳ προσᾴδουσα, ἔλαθεν ἑταιρικὴν ζηλοτυπίαν σὺν πολλῷ καθ' αὑτῆς κινήσασα τῷ φθόνῳ καὶ πλέον, ὅτε τις αὐτὴν Ναυκρατίτης ἔμπορος ὑπόχρυσος ὄνομα Ναυσικλῆς ἐνηγκαλίζετο, τὴν Ἀρσινόην καὶ ταῦτα πρότερον γιγνωσκομένην αὐτῷ παραγκωνισάμενος, ἐπειδὴ κυρτουμένην αὐτῇ τὴν παρειὰν ἐν τοῖς αὐλήμασιν εἶδε καὶ πρὸς τὸ βίαιον τῶν φυσημάτων ἀπρεπέστερον ἐπὶ τὰς ῥῖνας ἀνισταμένην, τό τ' ὄμμα πιμπράμενον καὶ τῆς οἰκείας ἕδρας ἐξωθούμενον.

Θ'. Ὑφ' ὧν οἰδουμένη τῷ χόλῳ καὶ ζήλῳ πυρακτουμένη, τοῖς οἰκείοις τῆς Δημαινέτης προσιοῦσα τὴν κατ' αὐτῆς ἐπιβουλὴν ὑπὸ τῆς Θίσβης ἐξηγόρευσε· τὰ μὲν αὐτὴ καθ' αὑτὴν ὑποτοπήσασα, τὰ δὲ καὶ τῆς Θίσβης αὐτῇ παρὰ τὴν ἑταιρίαν ἐξειπούσης. Συστάντες οὖν ἐπὶ τὸν πατέρα τὸν ἐμὸν οἱ κατὰ γένος τῇ Δημαινέτῃ προσήκοντες καὶ τοὺς δεινοτάτους τῶν ῥητόρων πρὸς τὴν κατηγορίαν ἐπὶ πολλοῖς χρήμασιν ἀναβιβασάμενοι ἄκριτον καὶ ἀνέλεγκ-

One day, having outdone Arsinoe, who had sung somewhat slowly and loosely, whereas she swept the strings rapidly and sang a delightful air, she drew upon herself, without knowing it, all the jealousy and hatred of which a courtesan is capable. This jealousy was increased when a wealthy merchant from Naucratis, by name Nausicles, embraced Thisbe, spurning Arsinoe, who had formerly been his mistress, because, while she was playing, he saw her cheeks puffed out, and, in consequence of her violent blowing, protruding most unbecomingly as far as her nose, while her flaming eyes seemed ready to start out of her head.

IX. "Arsinoe, swelling with rage and inflamed with jealousy, went and informed Demaeneta's relatives of Thisbe's intrigues against her mistress, some of which she had herself suspected, and had learnt the rest from Thisbe while they had been intimate. Demaeneta's relatives accordingly conspired against my father, and bribed the most famous orators to accuse him. They asserted that Demaeneta had

τον ἀνῃρῆσθαι τὴν Δημαινέτην ἐβόων καὶ τὴν
μοιχείαν προκάλυμμα τοῦ φόνου συγκεῖσθαι
διεξῄεσαν καὶ ἐπιδεικνύναι τὸν μοιχὸν ἢ ζῶντα,
ἢ τεθνηκότα ἠξίουν ἢ καὶ τοὔνομα φράζειν
μόνον ἐκέλευον· καὶ τέλος τὴν Θίσβην εἰς
βασάνους ἐξῄτουν. Ὡς δ' ὑποσχόμενος ὁ
πατὴρ οὐκ εἶχε παραδιδόναι, προϊδομένης ταῦτ'
ἐκείνης, ἔτι τῆς δίκης συνισταμένης καὶ (οὕτω
συγκείμενον αὐτῇ πρὸς τὸν ἔμπορον) δρασμῷ
χρησαμένης, ὁ δῆμος ἀγανακτήσας φονέα μὲν
οὐκ ἔκρινεν, ἅπανθ' ὡς ἔσχεν ὑποθέμενον, ὡς δὲ
συναίτιον τῆς τ' εἰς Δημαινέτην ἐπιβουλῆς καὶ
τῆς ἐμῆς ἀδίκου φυγῆς τοῦ τ' ἄστεος ἐδίωξε
καὶ δημεύσει τῶν ὄντων ἐζημίωσε, τοιαύτης τῶν
δευτέρων γάμων τῆς πείρας ἀπονάμενον. Οὕτω
μὲν ἡ κακίστη Θίσβη καὶ δίκας ὑπ' ὄψεσι νυνὶ
ταῖς ἐμαῖς ὑποσχοῦσα τῶν Ἀθηνῶν ἐξέπλευσε.

perished without having been judged or condemned; that the charge of adultery was only a pretext invented to excuse her murder; and they demanded that the supposed adulterer should be produced, alive or dead, or that, at least, his name should be given; lastly, they claimed that Thisbe should be handed over to them, that she might be put to the torture. My father promised, but was unable to produce her; for Thisbe, foreseeing what would happen, even before the process was drawn up, had taken flight with the merchant, by previous arrangement. The people, although highly indignant, did not indeed judge my father to be the murderer of his wife, for he had told them all that had taken place, but expelled him from the city as an accessory to the plot against Demaeneta and to the unjust sentence of banishment against myself, and confiscated his property. Such were the fruits of his second marriage; and this was how Thisbe, that vilest of women, came to leave Athens, and, as we see, paid the penalty of her crimes.

Καὶ ταῦτα μόνον ἔχω γιγνώσκειν, Ἀντι-
κλέους τινὸς κατὰ τὴν Αἴγιναν ἐξαγγείλαντος,
ᾧ καὶ δεύτερον εἰς τὴν Αἴγυπτον συνέπλευσα,
εἴ πῃ κατὰ τὴν Ναυκρατίαν εὕροιμι τὴν Θίσβην
καὶ εἰς τὰς Ἀθήνας ἐπαναγαγὼν λύσαιμι μὲν
τὰς κατὰ τοῦ πατρὸς ὑπονοίας τε καὶ αἰτίας,
ἀπαιτήσαιμι δὲ τῶν εἰς πάντας ἡμᾶς ἐπιβουλῶν
τὰς δίκας. Ἐνθάδε νυνὶ καὶ σὺν ὑμῖν ἐξετάζομαι.
Τὴν δ' αἰτίαν καὶ ὅπως καὶ ὅσα τοὺς μεταξὺ
χρόνους ὑποστάς, εἰσαῦθις ἀκούσεσθε. Τὸ δ'
ὅπως ἡ Θίσβη κατὰ τὸ ἄντρον καὶ πρὸς τίνων
ἀνῄρηται, θεοῦ τινος ἂν ἴσως δεήσει φράζοντος.

Ι'. Ἀλλ', εἰ δοκεῖ, τὴν δέλτον ἣν πρὸς τοῖς
στέρνοις αὐτῆς εὑρήκαμεν ἐπισκοπῶμεν· εἰκός
τι πλέον ἐντεῦθεν ἡμᾶς ἐκμαθεῖν. Ἐδόκει
ταῦτα. Καὶ διανοίξας ἐπήρχετο· καὶ ἦν τὰ
ἐγγεγραμμένα τοιάδε·

ΚΝΗΜΩΝΙ ΤΩι ΔΕΣΠΟΤΗι Ἡ ΠΟΛΕΜΙΑ
ΚΑΙ Ἐπαμυνασα ΘΙΣΒΗ.

Πρῶτα μὲν εὐαγγελίζομαί σοι τὴν Δημαι-
νέτης τελευτήν, δι' ἐμοῦ μὲν ὑπὲρ σοῦ γενο-
μένην, τὸ δ' ὅπως, εἴ με προσδέξαιο, παροῦσα

"Such are the facts which I heard from
one Anticles in Aegina, with whom I set
sail again for Egypt, to see whether I could
find Thisbe in Naucratia, take her back to
Athens, and so dispel the suspicions and
accusations directed against my father, and
at the same time exact vengeance from this
woman for her treachery against us all.
But now I am here with you. Another
time you shall learn the cause and manner
of my captivity, and my misfortunes during
the interval. But how Thisbe came into
this cave and by whom she was slain, we
shall need some god to tell us.

X. "But let us now examine the letter
which we found in her bosom; it is probable
that it will afford us further information."
His suggestion being approved of, he
opened the note, and read as follows:

"TO MY MASTER CNEMON, FROM HIS ENEMY
AND AVENGER, THISBE.

"First, let me announce to you the
welcome news of Demaeneta's death; it
is I who have avenged you. If you will
receive me, I will tell you the circumstances

διηγήσομαι. Έπειτα φράζω, κατὰ τήνδε με νυνὶ εἶναι τὴν νῆσον δεκάτην ἤδη ταύτην ἡμέραν, πρός τινος τῶν τῇδε λῃστῶν ἁλοῦσαν, ὃς καὶ ὑπασπιστὴς εἶναι τοῦ λῃστάρχου θρύπτεται, κἀμὲ κατακλείσας ἔχει, μηδ' ὅσον προκύψαι τῶν θυρῶν ἐπιτρέπων, ὡς μὲν αὐτός φησι διὰ φιλίαν τὴν περὶ ἐμέ, ταύτην ἐπιθεὶς τὴν τιμωρίαν, ὡς δ' ἔχω συμβαλεῖν, ἀφαιρεθῆναί με πρός τινος δεδιώς. Ἀλλ' ἐγώ σε θεῶν τινος ἐνδόντος καὶ εἶδον, ὦ δέσποτα, παριόντα καὶ ἐγνώρισα καὶ τήνδε σοι τὴν δέλτον διὰ τῆς συνοίκου πρεσβύτιδος λάθρα διεπεμψάμην, τῷ καλῷ Ἕλληνι καὶ φίλῳ τοῦ ἄρχοντος ἐγχειρίζειν φράσασα. Ἐξελοῦ δή με χειρῶν λῃστρικῶν καὶ ὑπόδεξαι τὴν σαυτοῦ θεραπαινίδα. Καί, εἰ μὲν βούλει, σῶζε, μαθὼν ὡς ἃ μὲν ἀδικεῖν ἔδοξα βιασθεῖσα, ἃ δὲ τετιμώρημαι τὴν σοὶ πολεμίαν ἑκοῦσα διεπραξάμην. Εἰ δ' ἔχει σέ τις ἀμετάβλητος ὀργή, κέχρησο ταύτῃ κατ' ἐμοῦ πρὸς ὃ βούλει· μόνον ὑπὸ σοὶ γενοίμην, καὶ εἰ τεθνάναι δέοι. Βέλτιον γὰρ ὑπὸ χειρῶν

of her death in person. In the next place, I have been for ten days in this island, taken prisoner by one of the brigands, who boasts that he is the captain's armour-bearer, and keeps me shut up, not even permitting me to peep out of the door; he declares that he acts thus from his friendship for me; but I myself suspect he is afraid that I may be carried off by some one else. But, by the mercy of some god, oh, my master! I saw you passing by and recognised you; and now I am secretly sending you this letter by an old woman who lives with me, having charged her to give it into the hands of the handsome Greek, the captain's friend. Rescue me, I beg you, from the brigand's hands, and receive your handmaid. If you will, save my life; remember that, when I seemed to wrong you, I was compelled to do so; but that, when I avenged you, I acted on my own impulse. But, if your resentment is so violent that it cannot be appeased, employ it against me as you please. I am ready even for death, if only I may die yours. For I consider it far better to die by your hands and to ob-

ἀνηρῆσθαι τῶν σῶν καὶ κηδείας μεταλαβεῖν
Ἑλληνικῆς ἢ θανάτου βαρυτέραν ζωὴν καὶ
φίλτρον βαρβαρικὸν ἔχθρας ἀνιαρώτερον
Ἀττικῆς ἀνέχεσθαι.

ΙΑ΄. Τοιαῦτα μὲν ἡ Θίσβη καὶ ἡ δέλτος
ἔφραζεν, ὁ δὲ Κνήμων, Ὦ Θίσβη, ἔφη, σὺ μὲν
καλῶς ποιοῦσα τέθνηκας καὶ γέγονας ἡμῖν
αὐτάγγελος τῶν σαυτῆς συμφορῶν ἐξ αὐτῶν
ἐγχειρίσασα τῶν σῶν σφαγῶν τὴν διήγησιν.
Οὕτως ἄρα τιμωρὸς Ἐρινὺς γῆν ἐπὶ πᾶσαν,
ὡς ἔοικεν, ἐλαύνουσά σε, οὐ πρότερον ἔστησε
τὴν ἔνδικον μάστιγα, πρὶν καὶ ἐν Αἰγύπτῳ με
τυγχάνοντα τὸν ἠδικημένον, θεατὴν ἐπιστῆσαι
τῆς κατὰ σοῦ ποινῆς. Ἀλλὰ τί ἦν ἄρα, ὃ καὶ
πάλαι σε κατ᾿ ἐμοῦ τεχναζομένην καὶ σοφισ-
τεύουσαν διὰ τοῦ γράμματος, ἡ δίκη προ-
αφείλετο τῶν ἐγχειρημάτων; ὡς κἀγώ σε καὶ
κειμένην ἔχω δι᾿ ὑποψίας καὶ σφόδρα δέδοικα
μὴ καὶ πλάσμα ἐστὶν ἡ Δημαινέτης τελευτὴ
κἀμὲ μὲν ἠπάτησαν οἱ ἐξαγγείλαντες, σὺ δὲ
καὶ διαπόντιος ἥκεις, ἑτέραν καθ᾿ ἡμῶν σκηνὴν

tain the rights of burial according to the custom of Greece, than to endure a life more terrible even than death, and the love of a barbarian more odious to me than the hatred of an Athenian."

XI. Such was the contents of Thisbe's letter. Then said Cnemon: " Oh Thisbe! you did well to die; and now you yourself are the messenger of your misfortunes, delivering into our hands after death this letter that tells the story of them. It seems that some avenging fury, driving you from one country to another, never stayed the lash of justice until she brought me, your injured master, although I was in Egypt, to be the spectator of your punishment. But what new stratagem were you plotting against me by this letter, when fortune cut you off before the attempt? Even in death I cannot help suspecting you, and I greatly fear that even Demaeneta's death may be a fiction, and that those who told me news of it may have deceived me. How do I know that you did not come across the sea to play upon the stage of Egypt a tragedy

'Αττικὴν καὶ ἐν Αἰγύπτῳ τραγῳδήσουσα.
Οὐ παύσῃ, ἔφη ὁ Θεαγένης, ἄγαν ἀνδριζόμενος,
εἴδωλά τε καὶ σκιὰς εὐλαβούμενος· οὐ γὰρ δὴ
κἀμέ τε καὶ τὴν ἐμὴν ὄψιν εἴποις ἂν ὡς ἐγοή-
τευσεν, οὐδὲν κοινωνοῦντα τοῦ δράματος. 'Αλλ'
ἡ μὲν κεῖται σῶμα νεκρὸν ὡς ἀληθῶς καὶ τούτου
γ' ἕνεκα θάρσει παντοίως, ὦ Κνήμων, τίς δ' ἄρα
ποτ' ἐστὶν ὁ σὸς εὐεργέτης, ὁ ταύτην ἀνῃρηκώς·
καὶ πῶς δεῦρο καθειμένην, καὶ πότε, σφόδρα
διαπορῶν ἐκπέπληγμαι. Τὰ μὲν ἄλλ' οὐκ ἔχω
λέγειν, ἔφη ὁ Κνήμων, ὁ δ' ἀνῃρηκὼς ὡς ἐπίπαν
ἐστὶ Θύαμις, εἰ δεῖ τῷ ξίφει τεκμαίρεσθαι ὃ
παρὰ τὴν σφαγὴν εὑρήκαμεν, ἐκείνου γὰρ εἶναι
γνωρίζω καὶ τὸ ἐπίσημον τουτὶ τῆς λαβῆς
ἐλέφας εἰς ἀετὸν ἐκτετόρευται. Ἆρ' οὖν εἴποις
ἂν, φησὶν ὁ Θεαγένης καὶ ὅπως καὶ πότε καὶ δι'
ἣν αἰτίαν ἔδρα τὸν φόνον; Καὶ πῶς ταῦτ' ἂν
εἰδείην; ἀπεκρίνατο. Οὐ γὰρ δὴ μαντικόν με
τόδε τὸ σπήλαιον ἀνέδειξε, καθάπερ τὸ ἄδυτον
τὸ Πυθοῖ καὶ ἐν Τροφωνίου λόγος θεοφωνεῖν
τοὺς ὑπελθόντας. 'Ανῴμωξαν ἀθρόον ὁ Θεα-

similar to that which you played in Athens ? " " What ! " said Theagenes, " still so brave and bold ? are you still afraid of ghosts and shadows ? I have nothing to do with the drama that has ended thus ; you cannot say that she has bewitched me and my eyesight. Believe me, Thisbe is really dead ; you have nothing more to fear from her. But, who has done you this kindness, whose hand has slain her, how and when she came here, this perplexes and astonishes me." " I am as ignorant as yourself," said Cnemon ; " but it was Thyamis who killed her, if we may conjecture from the sword, which we found lying by the victim's side ; I recognise it as his by the ivory eagle carved upon the hilt." " But can you say when, how, and why he committed this crime ? " " How should I know? This cave has not bestowed upon me the gift of divination, like the Delphic shrine or the cave of Trophonius, which are said to inspire with prophetic frenzy those who enter them." At these words, Theagenes and Chariclea suddenly began

γοης καὶ ἡ Χαρίκλεια, καὶ ὦ Πυθοῖ καὶ Δελφοὶ
θρηνοῦντες ἐβόων· ὁ δὲ Κνήμων ἐκπέπληκτο
καὶ ὅ τι πεπόνθοιεν πρὸς τοὔνομα τῆς Πυθοῦς
οὐκ εἶχε συμβαλεῖν.

ΙΒ'· Καὶ οἱ μὲν ἐν τούτοις ἦσαν, ὁ δὲ
Θέρμουθις ὁ τοῦ Θυάμιδος ὑπασπιστὴς, ἐπειδὴ
κατὰ τὴν μάχην τρωθεὶς ἀπενήξατο πρὸς τὴν
γῆν, νυκτὸς ἐπιγενομένης, πορθμείῳ φερομένῳ
κατὰ τὸ ἕλος ἐκ τῶν ναυαγίων ἐπιτυχὼν, αὑτόν
τ' ἐνθέμενος, ἐπὶ τὴν νῆσον καὶ παρὰ τὴν
Θίσβην ἔσπευδε· ταύτην ὀλίγων πρόσθεν
ἡμερῶν ἀγομένην ὑπὸ τοῦ ἐμπόρου τοῦ Ναυ-
σικλέους, κατά τινα στενὴν τῆς ὑπωρείας ὁδὸν
λοχήσας ὁ Θέρμουθις ἀφήρητο· παρὰ δὲ τὸν
τοῦ πολέμου θόρυβον καὶ τὴν τῶν ἐναντίων
ἔφοδον, ὅτ' αὐτὸν οἴσοντα τὸ ἱερεῖον ἀπέ-
στειλεν ὁ Θύαμις, ἔξω βελῶν ποιούμενος καὶ
περισώζειν αὐτῷ βουλόμενος, ἔλαθεν εἰς τὸ
σπήλαιον καθεὶς καὶ παρὰ τὸν τάραχον καὶ
τὴν σπουδὴν αὐτοῦ που περὶ τὸ στόμιον κατα-

to weep and wail, crying out, "Oh Pytho! Oh Delphi!" This amazed Cnemon, who could not imagine why the name of Pytho should have thus affected them.

XII. Such were the fortunes of Cnemon, Theagenes, and Chariclea. While they were thus engaged, Thermuthis, Thyamis's armour-bearer, who had been wounded in the engagement, had managed to swim ashore. When night came on, having found one of the shipwrecked barks drifting about the marsh, he got into it and directed his course towards the island in search of Thisbe; for it was he who, a few days before, had carried her off by a sudden attack, when she was being conducted by Nausicles, the merchant, through a narrow pass at the foot of the mountain. In the midst of the disturbance caused by the approach of the enemy, he had taken advantage of the instructions given him by Thyamis to go in search of a victim, to put Thisbe under shelter, in order to keep her unhurt for himself. But, while letting her down into the cavern, in his hurry and confusion he had unawares left her at the

λιπών. Ἐνθ' ὡς ἐνεβλήθη κατὰ τὴν πρώτην ἐγκαταμείνασαν δέει τε τῶν παρόντων φόβων καὶ ἀγνοίᾳ τῶν πρὸς τὰ βάθη φερουσῶν ἀτραπῶν, ἐντυχὼν ὁ Θύαμις, ὡς Χαρίκλειαν ἀνήρει τὴν Θίσβην. Παρὰ δὴ ταύτην, ὡς διαδράσας τὸν ἐκ τοῦ πολέμου κίνδυνον, ὁ Θέρμουθις ἐπειγόμενος, ἐπειδὴ τῇ νήσῳ προσέσχεν, ὡς εἶχε τάχους, ἐπὶ τὰς σκηνὰς ἀνέτρεχε. Καὶ αἱ μὲν ἦσαν οὐδὲν ἔτι πλὴν ὅτι τέφρα, τὸ δὲ στόμιον ἀπὸ τοῦ λίθου χαλεπῶς ἀνευρὼν, καλάμους, εἴ πῇ τινες ἔτι σμυχόμενοι περιελείφθησαν, ἀψάμενος κατέθεεν, ὡς εἶχε σπουδῆς· ὀνομαστί τε Θίσβην ἐκάλει, μέχρι τοῦ ὀνόματος ἑλληνίζων. Ὡς δ' εἶδε κειμένην, ἐπὶ πολὺ μὲν ἀχανὴς εἱστήκει, τέλος δὲ θροῦν τινα καὶ βόμβον αἰσθόμενος ἐκ τῶν κοίλων τοῦ σπηλαίου φερόμενον, διελέγοντο γὰρ ἔτι πρὸς αὐτοὺς Θεαγένης τε καὶ Κνήμων, τούτους ἐκείνους εἶναι τοὺς σφαγέας τῆς Θίσβης εἴκαζε καὶ ἀμηχάνως εἶχε ὅ τι καὶ δράσειεν, ὑπὸ μὲν θυμοῦ ληστρικοῦ καὶ βαρβαρικῆς ὀργῆς, πλέον

entrance. Fright, the imminence of danger, want of familiarity with the winding passages which led to the bottom, kept her fixed to the spot where he had left her, so that Thyamis, finding her there, slew her in mistake for Chariclea. It was in search of her that Thermuthis was hurrying, thinking that he had escaped the dangers of war. As soon as he reached the island, he hastened towards the huts, which he found in ashes. Having with difficulty recognised the entrance to the cave by the stone that formed its covering, he lighted a handful of reeds which were left, and hastened down, calling Thisbe by her name in Greek. When he saw her stretched upon the ground, he stood for a long time dazed, unable to speak. At last, he heard sounds and a kind of murmur proceeding from the recesses of the cave ; for Theagenes and Cnemon were still talking together. He had no doubt that they were Thisbe's murderers ; but his perplexity was great, and he did not know what to make up his mind to do; the ferocity natural to brigands and the rage of a barbarian, aggravated

τότε δι' ἐρωτικὴν ἀποτυχίαν ἐπιτεινομένης, ὁμόσε χωρεῖν αὐτόθι τοῖς νομιζομένοις αἰτίοις ἐπειγόμενος, ἀπορίᾳ δ' ὅπλων καὶ ξίφους ἄκων πρὸς ἐγκράτειαν καταστελλόμενος.

ΙΓ'. Ἐδόκει δὴ αὐτῷ βέλτιστον εἶναι, μὴ ὡς πολέμιον ἐντυγχάνειν τὴν πρώτην· εἰ δ' εὐπορήσειεν ἀμυντηρίου, μετιέναι τοὺς πολεμίους. Καὶ οὕτω κρίνας, ἐφίσταται τοῖς ἀμφὶ τὸν Θεαγένην ἄγριόν τε καὶ τραχὺ περισκοπῶν καὶ τὸ κρυπτόμενον βούλημα τῆς ψυχῆς τῷ βλέμματι καταμηνύων. Οἱ δὲ, ὡς εἶδον ἄνδρα γυμνὸν, ἀπροσδόκητον, τραυματίαν, φονῶντα τὴν ὄψιν, ἡ μὲν Χαρίκλεια [καὶ] πρὸς τὰ κοιλότερα τοῦ σπηλαίου κατεδύετο, τάχα μέν τι εὐλαβηθεῖσα, πλέον δ' ἄρα καταισχυνθεῖσα τὴν γυμνὴν καὶ οὐκ εὐσχήμονα τοῦ φανέντος ὄψιν. Ὁ δὲ Κνήμων ἠρέμα καὶ ὑπεδίδρασκε, γνωρίζων μὲν τὸν Θέρμουθιν, ὁρῶν δὲ παρ' ἐλπίδα καί τι τῶν ἀτοπωτέρων αὐτὸν ἐγχει-

at the moment by the disappointment of his desires, urged him to rush headlong upon those whom he believed to be the authors of the murder; but, on the other hand, the want of a sword or other arms obliged him to restrain himself, though much against his will.

XIII. It seemed to him that the best plan would be to go to meet them, without at first showing signs of any hostile intent; and then, if he could by any means procure arms, to attack them as enemies. Having resolved upon this, he directed his steps towards Theagenes, throwing round him wild and savage glances, and revealing in his looks the hidden purpose of his soul. At the sudden appearance of this stranger, naked and wounded, with his face covered with blood, Chariclea withdrew into the interior of the cave, partly in alarm, but partly also from a feeling of modesty at the hideous sight of this naked stranger. Cnemon also quietly drew back a little; he had recognised Thermuthis, but was surprised at his sudden appearance, and was afraid that he might do something

ρήσειν προσδοκῶν. Ἀλλὰ τὸν Θεαγένην οὐ κατέπληττεν ἡ θέα μᾶλλον ἢ παρώξυνε καὶ τό τε ξίφος ἐπανετείνετο ὡς πατάξων εἴ τι παράλογον ἐγχειροίη καὶ, Στῆθι, ἔλεγεν, οὗτος, ἢ βεβλήσῃ. Βέβλησαι δ᾽ οὐδέπω διότι σε κατὰ μικρὸν ἐγνώρισα καὶ τέως ἀμφίβολος ἥκεις τὴν γνώμην. Ἐδεῖτο ὑποπεσὼν ὁ Θέρμουθις, ἱκέτης ἐκ τοῦ καιροῦ μᾶλλον ἢ τοῦ τρόπου γιγνόμενος καὶ τὸν Κνήμωνα πρὸς ἐπικουρίαν ἐπεκαλεῖτο καὶ σώζεσθαι δίκαιος εἶναι πρὸς αὐτοῦ ἔλεγεν, ἀδικῶν τ᾽ οὐδὲν καὶ τῶν φιλίων εἰς τὴν παρελθοῦσαν ἡμέραν γεγενῆσθαι καὶ παρὰ φίλους ἥκειν διατεινόμενος.

ΙΔ΄. Ἐπεκλᾶτο πρὸς ταῦθ᾽ ὁ Κνήμων καὶ προσελθὼν, ἀνέστησέ τε τῶν γονάτων ἐχόμενον τοῦ Θεαγένους καὶ ποῦ Θύαμις ἐπυνθάνετο συνεχῶς. Ὁ δὲ πάντ᾽ ἔλεγεν· ὡς συνέρρηξε τοῖς πολεμίοις, ὡς ἐμβαλὼν εἰς μέσους ἐμάχετο, οὔτ᾽ ἐκείνων οὔθ᾽ αὑτοῦ φειδόμενος, ὡς ἀνῄρει

desperate. Theagenes, on the other hand, irritated rather than alarmed, pointed his sword at him, as if he intended to stab him at the first indication of hostility. "Stop," he cried, "or you will suffer for it; if I have spared you, it is because I recognised you, and I am not yet sure with what purpose you are come." Then Thermuthis, forced by necessity rather than his natural inclinations to become a suppliant, fell at his feet and asked for pardon. At the same time, he called upon Cnemon to help him, saying that he deserved succour from him; that he had never done him any injury, that he had fought by his side on the previous day, and that he now came to them as to friends.

XIV. Cnemon was touched by his entreaties; he went up to Thermuthis, who was still clasping the knees of Theagenes, lifted him up, and asked him eagerly where Thyamis was. Thermuthis told him all he knew about him; how he had attacked the enemy, how he had plunged into the thickest of the fight, without thought of their lives or his own; how he had slain all who

μὲν ἀεὶ τὸν ὑπὸ χεῖρας γιγνόμενον, ἐδορυφο-
ρεῖτο δ' αὐτὸς ἀπὸ κηρύγματος, πάντα τινὰ
Θυάμιδος φείδεσθαι παρεγγυῶντος· καὶ τέλος
ὡς ἐκεῖνος μὲν ὅ τι καὶ γέγονεν, οὐκ ἔχοι λέγειν·
αὐτὸς δὲ τραυματίας ἀπενήξατο πρὸς τὴν γῆν
καὶ τὸ παρὸν κατὰ ζήτησιν ἧκε τῆς Θίσβης ἐπὶ
τὸ σπήλαιον. Οἱ δὲ, τί διαφέρουσαν αὐτῷ καὶ
πόθεν γενομένην ἐπιζητοίη Θίσβην ἡρώτων.
Ἔλεγε καὶ ταῦθ' ὁ Θέρμουθις καὶ διηγεῖτο ὡς
ἐμπόρων ἀφέλοιτο, ὡς ἡράσθη μανικῶς καὶ τὸν
μὲν ἄλλον ἔκρυπτεν ἔχων χρόνον, παρὰ δὲ τὴν
ἔφοδον τῶν πολεμίων καθῆκεν εἰς τὸ σπήλαιον
καὶ νῦν εὑρίσκει πρός τινων ἀνῃρημένην, οὓς οὐκ
ἔχοι μὲν γιγνώσκειν, μαθεῖν δ' ἂν ἡδέως, ὑπὲρ
τοῦ γνῶναι καὶ τὴν αἰτίαν. Καὶ ὁ Κνήμων
ἄγαν ἐσπουδασμένος, Θύαμίς ἐστιν ὁ σφαγεὺς,
ἔλεγεν, ἀπολύσασθαι τῆς ὑποψίας αὐτὸν ἐπει-
γόμενος καὶ μαρτύριον ἐπεδείκνυ τὸ ξίφος ὃ
παρὰ τὴν σφαγὴν εὑρήκεσαν. Ὡς δ' εἶδεν ὁ
Θέρμουθις ἔτι τοῦ αἵματος ἀποστάζον καὶ τὸι
πρὸ ὀλίγου φόνον θερμὸν ἔτι τὸν σίδηροι

came in his way, being himself protected
by the general order that he was to be
taken alive. He declared that he did not
know what had been Thyamis's fate; for,
having been wounded himself, he had swum
to land, and was now come in search of
Thisbe. When they asked him what
interest he could have in Thisbe, why he
sought her, and how she had come into
his possession, he told them the whole
story; how he had taken her away from
the merchants, how he had fallen violently
in love with her, how he had kept her
hidden in his tent, and, on the approach
of the enemy, had let her down into the
cave, where he had just found her lying
dead, slain by an unknown hand; he added
that he was very eager to find out who had
committed the murder, and what had been
their motives. Cnemon, being exceedingly
anxious to free himself from all suspicion,
told him that Thyamis was the murderer,
in proof of which he showed him the sword
that had been found near the dead body.
When Thermuthis saw it, still dripping
with blood, the blade still warm from the

ἀποπτύοντα, ἐγνώρισέ τ᾽ εἶναι Θυάμιδος, βαθύ
τι καὶ βύθιον στενάξας καὶ τὸ γεγονὸς ὅπως
εἶχεν ἀμηχανῶν, ἀχλύϊ καὶ σιγῇ κάτοχος, ἐπὶ
τὸ στόμιον ἀνεδύετο τοῦ σπηλαίου καὶ παρὰ
τὸ σῶμα τῆς κειμένης ἥκων, ἐπιθείς τε τοῖς
στέρνοις τὴν κεφαλὴν, ᾿Ω Θίσβη, ἔλεγε, καὶ
τοῦτο πολλάκις καὶ πλέον οὐδέν· ἕως τοὔνομα
κατὰ μέρος ἀποτέμνων καὶ κατὰ μικρὸν ἐκλεί-
πων, ἔλαθεν εἰς ὕπνον ἐμπεσών.

ΙΕ΄. Τῷ δὲ Θεαγένει καὶ τῇ Χαρικλείᾳ
συνάμα τῷ Κνήμωνι πάντων ἔννοια τῶν καθ᾽
ἑαυτοὺς ἀθρόον ἐπεισῄει καὶ σκοπεῖν μέν τι
βουλομένοις ἐῴκεσαν, τῶν δὲ παρελθόντων
ἀλγεινῶν τὸ πλῆθος καὶ τῶν παρουσῶν συμφο-
ρῶν τὸ ἄπορον καὶ τῶν προσδοκωμένων τὸ
ἄδηλον, ἐζόφου τῆς ψυχῆς τὸ λογιζόμενον.
Εἰς ἀλλήλους δὲ ἐπὶ πλεῖστον ἑώρων καὶ ἕκαστος
τὸν ἕτερον εἰπεῖν τι προσδοκῶν, εἶτ᾽ ἀποτυγ-
χάνων εἰς γῆν τὸ βλέμμα ἐπέστρεφε καὶ
ἀνανεύσας αὖθις ἀνέπνευσε, στεναγμῷ τὸ πάθος
ἐπικουφίσας. Καὶ τέλος, κλίνει μὲν αὐτὸν εἰς
τὴν γῆν ὁ Κνήμων, ὀκλάζει δ᾽ ἐπὶ πέτραν ὁ

recently-inflicted wound, and recognised it as the property of Thyamis, he uttered a deep sigh, and, not knowing how to account for what had taken place, in a state of gloomy stupor made his way back to the entrance to the cave. When he came to the body of Thisbe, he placed his head upon her breast, and, continually repeating nothing but the name of Thisbe, at first the name in full, then, more slowly, syllable by syllable, at last he fell asleep.

XV. Theagenes, Chariclea and Cnemon, reflecting upon all that had taken place, began to deliberate what was best for them to do; but the multitude of their past calamities, their present sufferings and embarrassments, and the uncertainty of the future, obscured their reasoning powers. At every moment, they looked at each other, each of them waiting for the other to propose something; then, being disappointed, they bent their eyes upon the ground, lifted them up again, took breath, and lightened their grief by deep-drawn sighs. At length, Cnemon threw himself upon the ground. Theagenes

Θεαγένης, ῥίπτει δ' ἐπὶ τοῦτον αὐτὴν ἡ Χαρίκλεια καὶ τὸν ὕπνον ἐπιπολὺ μὲν ἐπιφερόμενον διωθοῦντο, βουλήν τινα στήσασθαι τῶν παρόντων ἐπιθυμοῦντες, λειποθυμίᾳ δὲ καὶ πόνοις ἐνδόντες, φύσεως νόμῳ καὶ ἄκοντες ἐπείθοντο καὶ πρὸς ἡδὺ κῶμα διὰ τὸ ὑπερβάλλον τῆς λύπης ὠλίσθησαν. Οὕτως ἄρα ποτὲ σώματος πάθει καὶ τὸ νοερὸν τῆς ψυχῆς συνομολογεῖν ἠνέσχετο.

ΙΕ΄. Ἐπεὶ δὲ μικρὸν ἐπάσαντο ὕπνου καὶ τοσοῦτον ὅσον τὰ ἄκρα τῶν βλεφάρων ἐπιλεᾶναι, τῇ Χαρικλείᾳ τῇδε ξυγκειμένῃ ὄναρ ἐφοίτησεν. Ἀνὴρ τὴν κόμην αὐχμηρὸς καὶ ὑποκαθειμένος τὸ βλέμμα καὶ τὴν χεῖρα ἔναιμος, ἐμβαλὼν τὸ ξίφος, τῶν ὀφθαλμῶν αὐτῇ τὸν δεξιὸν ἐξῄρητο· ἡ δ' ἀνέκραγέ τ' αὐτίκα καὶ οἱ τὸν ὀφθαλμὸν ἀνηρπάσθαι λέγουσα τὸν Θεαγένην ἐκάλει. Καὶ ὁ μὲν παρῆν αὐτίκα πρὸς τὴν κλῆσιν καὶ τὸ πάθο ὑπερήλγει καθάπερ καὶ τῶν ἐνυπνίων συναισ-

flung himself upon a rock, and Chariclea reclined upon his breast. For some time they struggled against the attacks of sleep, being anxious, if they could, to devise some plan; but at length, overcome by fatigue and exhaustion, they submitted, although against their will, to the call of nature, and fell into a refreshing slumber from very excess of sorrow. Thus the intelligent part of the soul is sometimes obliged to sympathise with and yield to the fatigues of the body.

XVI. But, almost as soon as they had closed their eyelids and snatched a few moments of sleep, Chariclea, lying upon Theagenes's bosom, had a dream. A man with dishevelled hair, a gloomy and savage look, and bloody hands, seemed to thrust out her right eye with a sword. She immediately cried out, declaring that her eye had been pulled out, and called upon Theagenes for help. When he heard her call, he immediately hastened up to her, being deeply affected himself, as if, while he was asleep, a kind of sympathy had made him share her suffering. She had

θανόμενος, ἡ δὲ τῷ τε προσώπῳ τὴν χεῖρα ἐπέβαλε καὶ τὸ μέρος ὃ κατὰ τὸ ὄναρ ἀπώλεσεν ἐπαφωμένη, πάντοθεν ἐπεξήτει. Ὡς δ' ὄναρ ἦν, Ὄναρ ἦν, ἔλεγεν, ἔχω τὸν ὀφθαλμόν. Θάρσει, Θεάγενες. Ἀνέπνευσε πρὸς τὴν ἀκοὴν ὁ Θεαγένης καὶ, Εὖ μὲν ποιοῦσα, ἔφη, τὰς ἡλιακὰς ἀκτῖνας ἀποσώζεις, τί δ' ἦν ὅ μοι πέπονθας; καὶ τίς ἡ περί σε πτοία γέγονεν; Ἀνὴρ ὑβριστὴς, ἔφη, καὶ ἀτάσθαλος καὶ οὐδὲ τὴν σὴν ἄμαχον καταδείσας ῥώμην, κειμένῃ μοι πρὸς τοῖς σοῖς γόνασιν ἐπεκώμαζε ξιφήρης καὶ τὸν ὀφθαλμὸν, ὡς ᾤμην, ἐξεῖλε τὸν δεξιὸν καὶ εἴθε γ' ὕπαρ ἦν καὶ μὴ ὄναρ, ὦ Θεάγενες, τὸ φανέν. Τοῦ δὲ, Εὐφήμησον, εἰπόντος, καὶ διότι τοῦτο λέγοι πυνθανομένου· Διότι με βέλτιον ἦν, ἔφη, θατέρου τῶν ὀφθαλμῶν ἐλαττωθῆναι ἤπερ ἐπί σοι φροντίζειν. Ὡς σφόδρα δέδοικα μὴ εἴς σε τείνοι τὸ ἐνύπνιον, ὃν ὀφθαλμὸν ἐγὼ καὶ ψυχὴν καὶ πάντα ἐμαυτῆς πεποίημαι. Παῦσαι, ἔλεγεν ὁ Κνήμων, (ἐπηκροᾶτο γὰρ ἁπάντων πρὸς τὴν ἐξαρχῆς βοὴν τῆς Χαρικλείας ἀφυπνισμένος), ἐμοὶ γὰρ ἄλλῃ πῃ φράζεσθαι τὸ ὄναρ καταφαίνεται, καὶ εἴγε σοι πατέρες

lifted her hand to her face, as if feeling everywhere for the part which she had lost in her vision; then, understanding that it was only a dream, she exclaimed: " I was dreaming; my eye is safe; fear nothing, Theagenes." At these words, he breathed again: " It is well that no harm has befallen those bright rays of the sun; but, tell me what has happened, what caused your sudden alarm?" " A fierce and savage man, not even fearing your invincible might, attacked me with a sword as I lay at your feet, and, as it seemed to me, struck out my right eye; and would to Heaven that it had been a reality rather than a dream." " Heaven forbid! " said Theagenes; "why do you wish that?" " It would be better for me to lose one of my eyes than to be anxious about you. I am greatly afraid that this dream has reference to you—you whom I look upon as my eyes, my life, my all." " Do not say that," interrupted Cnemon, who had heard everything, having been awakened by Chariclea's cries: " I can give another interpretation to the dream; tell me, are

εἰσὶν ἀπόκριναι. Τῆς δ' ὁμολογούσης καὶ εἴποτ'
ἦσαν, εἰπούσης, Οὐκοῦν τὸν πατέρα σοι τεθνη-
κέναι νόμιζε, ἔλεγε. Τοῦτο δ' ὧδε συμβάλλω.
Τοῦ προελθεῖν εἰς τὸν τῇδε βίον καὶ τοῦδε τοῦ
φωτὸς μεταλαβεῖν τοὺς φύντας ἴσμεν αἰτίους.
Ὥστ' εἰκότως ἐπὶ πατέρα καὶ μητέρα τὴν
ὀμμάτων συζυγίαν, ὡς ἂν φωτεινὴν αἴσθησιν καὶ
ὁρατῶν ὑπουργὸν οἱ ὄνειροι σοφίζονται. Βαρὺ
μὲν, ἔφη, καὶ τοῦτο, ἡ Χαρίκλεια, πλὴν ἀλλ'
ἔστω γ' ἀληθὲς μᾶλλον ἢ τὸ ἕτερον καὶ νικήσειεν
ὁ παρὰ σοὶ τρίπους, ἐγὼ δὲ ψευδόμαντις ἀπο-
φανθείην. Ταῦτα μὲν οὕτως ἔσται καὶ χρὴ
πιστεύειν, ἔλεγεν ὁ Κνήμων, ἡμεῖς δ' ὀνειρώττειν
ὡς ἀληθῶς ἐοίκαμεν, ἐνύπνια μὲν καὶ φαντασίας
ἐξετάζοντες, τῶν δὲ καθ' αὑτοὺς περίσκεψιν
οὐδ' ἡντινοῦν προτιθέντες καὶ ταῦτα μὲν ἕως
ἔξεστι, τοῦ Αἰγυπτίου τούτου (ἔλεγε δὲ τὸν
Θέρμουθιν) ἀπολειπομένου καὶ νεκροὺς ἔρωτας
ἀναπλάττοντος καὶ θρηνοῦντος.

your parents living ? " " Yes," she replied,
" and if they were——" " Then believe
that your father lives no longer; this I
conjecture for the following reason. We
know that our parents are the authors of
our life, and that it is owing to them that
we see the light of the day : therefore, the
comparison of our father and mother to
our two eyes, as being the sense capable of
light, and the means whereby we discern
things visible, seems to me a natural
one." "A grievous misfortune is this you
announce," said Chariclea ; " but may this
interpretation prove true rather than the
other; may your oracle be verified, and
may I be shown a false prophet." " The
event will show the truth of my predic-
tion," said Cnemon, "and you must rest
content. But methinks we are really
dreaming, while we trouble ourselves
about dreams and vain imaginations, in-
stead of taking advantage of the oppor-
tunity to consider what is best for us to
do, while this Egyptian (meaning Ther-
muthis) has left us, to mourn for his dead
mistress ? "

13

ΙΖʹ. Ὑπολαβὼν οὖν ὁ Θεαγένης, Ἀλλ᾽, ὦ Κνήμων, ἔφη, ἐπειδή σε θεῶν τις ἡμῖν συνῆψε καὶ συνέμπορον τῶν δυστυχημάτων ἐποίησεν, ἄρχε βουλῆς. Τόπων τε γὰρ τῶν τῇδε καὶ φωνῶν ἔμπειρος καὶ ἄλλως ἡμεῖς νωθέστεροι συνεῖναι τὸ δέον, πλείονι κλύδωνι κακῶν βεβυθισμένοι. Μικρὸν οὖν ἐπιστήσας ὁ Κνήμων, τοιάδ᾽ ἔφη. Κακῶν μὲν, ὦ Θεάγενες, ἄδηλον ὅστις πλεονεκτεῖ, ἀφθόνως γὰρ κἀμοὶ τῶν συμφορῶν ὁ δαίμων ἐπήντλησεν, ἐπειδὴ δὲ τὰ παριστάμενα ὡς προγενεστέρῳ κελεύετε λέγειν, ἡ μὲν νῆσος ἥδε, ὡς ὁρᾶτε, ἔρημος καὶ πλέον ἡμῶν οὐδέν· καὶ χρυσοῦ μὲν καὶ ἀργύρου καὶ ἐσθῆτος ἀφθονία, (πολλὰ γὰρ τάδ᾽ ἃ κατὰ τὸ σπήλαιον ὑμῶν τ᾽ ἀφελόμενοι, ἄλλων τ᾽ ἀποσυλήσαντες, ὁ Θύαμις καὶ οἱ σὺν αὐτῷ κατέθεντο), σίτου δὲ καὶ ἐπιτηδείων ἄλλων, οὐδ᾽ ὄνομα περιλέλειπται. Δέος δὲ διαφθαρῆναι μὲν καταμείναντας λιμῷ, διαφθαρῆναι δ᾽ ἐφόδῳ τινῶν, ἤτοι τῶν ἐναντίων πάλιν ἐλθόντων, ἢ καὶ τῶν σὺν ἡμῖν γεγονότων, εἰ καθ᾽ ἕνα

XVII. Theagenes, taking him up, said:
" Oh, Cnemon ! since some god has united
you to us and made you the partner of all
our misfortunes, do you give your advice
first. You know the neighbourhood and
understand the language of the country.
Overwhelmed with greater calamities than
you, we are less in a condition to under-
stand what is best to do." After a few
moments' silence, Cnemon spoke as follows:
" We do not know which of us is the most
unfortunate; Heaven has laid upon me
also a heavy burden of woes; yet, since
you desire that I, as being the eldest,
should give my advice first, I will do as
you wish. This island, as you see, is
deserted, and we are its only inhabitants.
It contains abundance of gold, silver, and
stuffs; for in this cave are stored the
treasures which Thyamis has taken from
you and many others; but it is absolutely
destitute of corn and all the necessaries
of life. If we stay here longer, we run
the risk of perishing from hunger, or at
the hands of the enemy, should they return,
or even of our own comrades, should they

ποτὲ συλλεγέντες καὶ τὸν ἐνθάδε θησαυρον οὐκ ἀγνοοῦντες, ἐπέλθοιεν διὰ τὰ χρήματα. Τότ' οὐκ ἂν φθάνοιμεν παραπολλύμενοι ἢ ταῖς ὕβρεσι ταῖς ἐκείνων, τὸ φιλανθρωπότερον, ἐκκείμενοι. "Αλλως τε γὰρ ἄπιστον τὸ βουκόλων γένος, καὶ νῦν πλέον, ὅτε τοῦ καταστέλλοντος τὴν γνώμην πρὸς τὸ σωφρονέστερον ἄρχοντος ἀμοιροῦσιν. 'Απολειπτέον οὖν ἡμῖν καὶ φευκτέον ὡς ἄρκυς τινὰς καὶ δεσμωτήριον τὴν νῆσον, ἀποπέμψαντας πρότερον τὸν Θέρμουθιν, πρόφασιν ὡς πευσόμενον καὶ πολυπραγμονήσοντα, εἴ τι περὶ τοῦ Θυάμιδος ἔχοι μανθάνειν. 'Ρᾷόν τε γὰρ ἐφ' αὑτῶν ἂν σκοποῖμεν καὶ ἐπιχειροῖμεν τὰ πρακτέα καὶ ἄλλως ἄνδρα ἐκποδὼν ποιήσασθαι καλὸν, φύσει τ' ἀβέβαιον καὶ ληστρικὸν καὶ δύσεριν τὸ ἦθος, πρὸς δὲ καὶ ὑποψίας τι φέροντα εἰς ἡμᾶς τῆς Θίσβης ἕνεκα καὶ οὐκ ἂν παυσόμενον εἰ μὴ ἐπιβουλεύσειεν, εἰ καιροῦ λάβοιτο.

ΙΗ΄ 'Επῃνέθη ταῦτα καὶ ἐδόκει γίγνεσθαι·

rally and come back for the sake of the treasures, of the existence and whereabouts of which they cannot be ignorant. Then we should be unable to escape death; or, even should they treat us more leniently, we should be exposed to insults and outrages at their hands. These men[1] are rarely to be trusted, and especially when they have no leader to restrain them and check their violence. We must therefore leave this island, and shun it as if it were a prison or a net; but we must first get rid of Thermuthis, under pretence of sending him to try if he can find out what has become of Thyamis. We shall be able to deliberate more at our ease if we are alone; and shall more readily carry into execution what we decide to do. Besides, it is better in any case to get this man out of the way; for he is by nature quarrelsome and savage, and not to be depended upon; he also suspects us of being Thisbe's murderers, and will not rest until he has made an attempt upon our lives, should he ever have the opportunity."

XVIII. The others approved of Cne-

[1] *Literally*, "cowherds."

καὶ ὁρμήσαντες ἐπὶ τὸ στόμιον τοῦ σπηλαίου,
(καὶ γάρ τι καὶ ἡμέρας ἤδη ξυνίεσαν) διανέστησάν
τε τὸν Θέρμουθιν ὁλοσχερῶς τῷ ὕπνῳ κατε-
σχημένον καὶ ὅσ᾽ εἰκὸς ἦν τῶν βουλευθέντων
φράσαντες καὶ ῥαδίως ὑπόκουφον ἄνδρα πείσαν-
τες, τό τε σῶμα τῆς Θίσβης εἴς τι κοῖλον
ἐνθέντες καὶ τὴν τέφραν τὴν ἐκ τῶν σκηνῶν ὅσα
γ᾽ ἦν ἐπιφορήσαντες καὶ τὰ εἰωθότα διὰ τὴν
ὁσίαν ἐξ ὧν ὁ καιρὸς ἐδίδου πληρώσαντες καὶ
δάκρυα καὶ θρήνους ἀντὶ πάντων τῶν νομιζομένων
ἐναγίσαντες, ἐξέπεμπον ἐφ᾽ ἣν ἔδοξε βουλὴν
τὸν Θέρμουθιν. Ὁ δὲ βραχὺ προελθὼν, ἀνέ-
στρεφέ τε καὶ οὐκ ἂν ἔφη μόνος πορεύεσθαι,
οὐδ᾽ ἀναρρίψειν τοσοῦτον κίνδυνον κατασκοπῆς,
εἰ μὴ καὶ Κνήμων ἐθέλοι κοινωνεῖν τῆς πράξεως.
Ἀποδειλιῶντα δὴ πρὸς ταῦτα τὸν Κνήμωνα
θεασάμενος ὁ Θεαγένης, (καὶ γὰρ φράζων τὰ
λεχθέντα πρὸς τοῦ Αἰγυπτίου δῆλος ἦν ὑπερ-
αγωνιῶν) Σὺ δὲ, ἔφη, τὴν μὲν γνώμην ἐρρωμένος

mon's advice and resolved to follow it.
Perceiving that it was day, they hastened
to the mouth of the cave, and woke Ther-
muthis, who was in a deep sleep; they
informed him of their resolution, but only
told him so much as it was absolutely
necessary for him to know; and he, being
of a credulous disposition, readily believed
what they said. They then dug a pit, in
which they deposited the body of Thisbe,
covered it with the ashes, the sole remains
of the huts that had been burnt, and
rendered the last rites to it, as well as
they were able and as far as time per-
mitted, watering the grave with tears in
place of libations; after which, they de-
spatched Thermuthis on the errand agreed
upon. But he had only gone a few steps,
when he turned back, declaring that he
would not go alone, that he would not under-
take so dangerous a search by himself, unless
Cnemon would consent to accompany him.
Theagenes, when he saw that Cnemon
was afraid (for, when Thermuthis's request
was explained to him, he was evidently
greatly alarmed), said: "What, Cnemon!

τις ἄρα ἦσθα, τὸ λῆμα δ᾽ ἀσθενέστερος· γνωρίζω
δ᾽ ἄλλοις τε καὶ οὐχ ἥκιστα τοῖς νῦν. Ἀλλὰ
θῆγε τὸ φρόνημα καὶ πρὸς τὸ ἀνδρειότερον
ὄρθου τὴν γνώμην. Τὸ μὲν γὰρ παρὸν ἀναγ-
καῖον δοκεῖ οὕτω συντίθεσθαι, τοῦ μή τινα τοῦ
δρασμοῦ λαβεῖν αὐτὸν ὑπόνοιαν καὶ συμπο-
ρεύεσθαι τὴν πρώτην, (δέος δὲ δήπουθεν οὐδὲν
ἀνόπλῳ τὴν χεῖρα ξυνιέναι ξιφήρη καὶ πεφραγ-
μένον αὐτὸν), καιροῦ δὲ λαβόμενον ἐγκατα-
λεῖψαι διαλαθόντα καὶ ἥκειν παρ᾽ ἡμᾶς, οὗπερ
ἂν συνθώμεθα. Συνθώμεθα δὲ, εἰ δοκεῖ, κώμην
τινὰ πλησίον, εἴ πῃ γιγνώσκεις ἥμερον. Εὖ
λέγειν ἔδοξε τῷ Κνήμωνι, καὶ Χέμμιν τινὰ
κώμην οὕτω καλουμένην ἔφραξεν εὐδαίμονά τε
καὶ πολυάνθρωπον καὶ ταῖς ὄχθαις τοῦ Νείλου
πρὸς ἐπιτειχισμὸν τῶν βουκόλων ἐπὶ λόφου
παρῳκισμένην· ἀπέχειν δὲ περαιωθεῖσι τὴν
λίμνην, στάδια οὐ πολλῷ λειπόμενα τῶν ἑκατόν·
δεῖν δ᾽ εὐθὺς πρὸς μεσημβρίας ὁρῶντας ἰέναι.

ΙΘ΄. Χαλεπῶς μὲν, ἀπεκρίνατο ὁ Θεαγένης,
Χαρικλείας γε ταύτης ἕνεκα, τοῦ βαδίζειν
μακρότερον ἀήθως ἐχούσης, ἐλευσόμεθα δ᾽ οὖ
ὅμως, εἰς πτωχοὺς καὶ τοὺς διὰ τροφὴν ἀγύρτας

so strong in counsel, and so weak in execution! Your present behaviour confirms my previous opinion of you. Come, recall your courage, pluck up your spirits. You must consent and accompany him at first, lest your refusal should make him suspect our design of flight. You are armed and carry a sword; what have you to fear from one who is unarmed? At the first favourable opportunity you can steal away from him and rejoin us at a place we will settle upon; let this be some neighbouring village, the inhabitants of which are kindly disposed." Cnemon approved of this suggestion, and mentioned a town called Chemmis, flourishing and populous, situated near the banks of the Nile, upon a hill, to defend it against the incursions of robbers. This town, after crossing the lake, is distant about a hundred stades, due south.

XIX. "That is a difficult matter," replied Theagenes, "at least for Chariclea, who is not accustomed to long journeys; however, we will go, and pretend that we are beggars, some of those jugglers who

αὐτοὺς μεταπλάσαντες. Νὴ Δία, εἶπεν ὁ Κνή-
μων, καὶ γὰρ τῶν ὄψεων σφόδρα διεστραμμένως
ἔχετε, (ἡ δὲ Χαρίκλεια καὶ πλέον ἅτε καὶ τὸν
ὀφθαλμὸν ἀρτίως ἐκκεκομμένη), κἀμοὶ δοκεῖτε
τοιοίδε ὄντες, οὐκ ἀκόλους ἀλλ' ἄοράς τε καὶ
λέβητας[1] αἰτήσειν. Πρὸς ταῦτ' ἐμειδίασεν
ὀλίγον καὶ βεβιασμένον καὶ μόνοις τοῖς χείλεσιν
ἐπιτρέχον. Ὅρκοις δὲ πιστωσάμενοι τὰ δόξ-
αντα καὶ μή ποτ' ἀπολείψειν ἀλλήλους ἑκόντες
ἐπιμαρτυρόμενοι τοὺς θεούς, ἔπραττον ὡς
ἐβούλετο ἡ σκέψις. Ὁ μὲν δὴ Κνήμων καὶ ὁ
Θέρμουθις ἅμ' ἡλίῳ τὴν λίμνην περαιωθέντες,
ἐχώρουν δι' ὕλης τινὸς βαθείας καὶ τὸ λάσιον
δυσδιέξοδον παρεχομένης. Ἡγεῖτο δ' ὁ Θέρ-
μουθις, τοῦτο τοῦ Κνήμωνος καὶ εἰπόντος καὶ
βουληθέντος, πρόφασιν μὲν αὐτῷ τὴν ἐμπειρίαν
τῆς δυσχωρίας ἀναθέντος καὶ ἡγεμονεύειν τὴν
ὁδὸν ἐπιτρέψαντος, πλέον δὲ τἀσφαλὲς αὐτῷ
περιποιοῦντος καὶ καιρὸν τοῦ διαδρᾶναι προε-
τοιμάζοντος. Ἐπεὶ δὲ προϊόντες ἐνέτυχον

[1] From Homer, *Odyssey*, xvii. 222. The words
are variously interpreted, although the general
sense is clear.

get their living from what the public bestow upon them." "Very good, by Hercules!" said Cnemon; "you are sufficiently ugly and deformed, especially Chariclea, who has just had her eye knocked out; from your present appearance, however, you seem to me to be candidates not for 'the crumbs, but for the knives and plates.'" At these words, he smiled slightly, but with a forced smile, which did not go beyond the lips. Having confirmed their agreement by an oath, they called the gods to witness that they would never desert one another, and commenced to put their plan into execution. Cnemon and Thermuthis, having crossed the lake early in the morning, made their way with difficulty through a dense wood. Thermuthis led the way, at the suggestion of Cnemon, on the pretence that, as the road was difficult and Thermuthis was more familiar with it, it would be better for him to act as guide; in reality he was thinking of his own safety and was looking for an opportunity of running away. As they went on, they fell in with some flocks, whose keepers fled at

ποίμναις οἱ δὲ νομεύοντες ἀπέδρασαν καὶ πρὸς
τὸ πυκνότερον τῆς ὕλης κατέδυσαν, κριόν τινα
τῶν ἡγουμένων καταθύσαντες, ἐπί τε τοῦ πυρὸς
ὃ προητοίμαστο τοῖς νομεῦσιν ἀφανῆναντες
ἐνεφοροῦντο τῶν κρεῶν, οὐδὲ τὴν ἀποχρῶσαν
ὄπτησιν ἀναμείναντες, ἐπειγομένης ὑπὸ τοῦ
λιμοῦ τῆς γαστρός. Οἷον οὖν λύκοι τινὲς ἢ
θῶες ἐλάφυσσον τὰ οὕτω ἀεὶ τετμημένα καὶ
πρὸς ὀλίγον τῷ πυρὶ μεμολυσμένα· τὰ δ᾽
ἡμίοπτα ταῖς παρειαῖς ἐν τῇ βρώσει τοῦ
αἵματος ἀπέσταξεν. Ὡς δ᾽ ἐνεφορήθησαν
γάλακτος ἐμπιόντες ὁδοῦ τῆς προκειμένης
εἴχοντο. Καὶ ἦν μὲν ὥρα περὶ βουλυτὸν ἤδη,
ἐπεὶ δὲ λόφον τιν᾽ ἀνιόντων, ὑπὸ τοῦτον εἶναι
τὴν κώμην ἔφραξεν ὁ Θέρμουθις, οὗπερ τὸν
Θύαμιν συνειλημμένον ἢ κατέχεσθαι ἢ ἀνῃρῆ-
σθαι εἴκαξεν, διεφθορέναι οἱ τὴν γαστέρα πρὸς
τῆς ἀδδηφαγίας ᾐτιᾶτο καὶ ῥυΐσκεσθαι χαλεπῶς
ἐκ τοῦ γάλακτος ἔλεγεν ὁ Κνήμων, προφθάνειν
τε τὸν Θέρμουθιν παρεκελεύετο, αὐτὸς δ᾽
ἐπικαταλήψεσθαι. Τοῦτο ποιῶν ἅπαξ μὲν καὶ

their approach, and concealed themselves in the thickest part of the forest. They seized one of the choicest rams, cut its throat, broiled it over a fire which the shepherds had lighted, and, being violently hungry, eagerly devoured the flesh, without waiting until it was properly cooked. Like wolves and jackals, they tore off and swallowed large pieces, hardly warmed through; the blood of the half-cooked flesh trickled down their mouths as they gorged themselves with it. After they had satisfied their hunger, they quenched their thirst with milk, and resumed their journey. In the evening, while they were ascending a hill, Thermuthis declared that there was a village at the foot of it, where it was probable that Thyamis was being kept prisoner, if indeed he had not been killed. Then Cnemon began to complain of pains in his stomach; he said that he had eaten too heartily, and that the milk had given him violent diarrhœa. He begged Thermuthis to go on ahead, saying that he would catch him up. He did the same two or three times, but his

δὶς καὶ τρίτον ἐπαληθεύσας ὤφθη καὶ κατα-
λαμβάνειν χαλεπῶς ἔλεγεν.

Κ'. Ὡς δ' εἰς ἔθος τὸν Αἰγύπτιον ἐνεβίβασεν,
ἔλαθε τὸ τελευταῖον ἐναπομείνας καὶ πρὸς τὰ
χαλεπώτερα τοῦ δάσους κατὰ τοῦ πρανοῦς
αὐτὸν ὡς εἶχε τάχους ἐπαφεὶς διεδίδρασκε. Καὶ
ὁ μὲν, ἐπειδὴ πρὸς ταῖς ἀκρωρείαις ἐγένετο τοῦ
ὄρους ἀνέπαυεν αὐτὸν ἐπί τινος πέτρας, ἑσπέραν
τε καὶ νύκτα ἀναμένων, καθ' ἣν συνέκειτο αὐτοῖς
ἥκουσιν εἰς τὴν κώμην τὰ περὶ τὸν Θύαμιν
πολυπραγμονεῖν καὶ ἅμα καὶ τὸν Κνήμωνα
περισκοπῶν, εἴ πή ποτ' ἐπέλθοι βουλὴν εἰς
αὐτὸν ποιούμενος ἀτοπωτέραν· οὐ γὰρ ἀνίει
τῆς γνώμης τὸ εἰς αὐτὸν ὕποπτον ὡς ἀνελόντα
τὴν Θίσβην καὶ ὅπως ἂν [οἱ] ποτε διαχρήσαιτο
ἐνενόει, ἐπιθέσθαι τε μετὰ τοῦτον καὶ τοῖς περὶ
τὸν Θεαγένην ἐλύττα. Ὡς δ' ὁ Κνήμων ἐφαίνε-
το οὐδαμοῦ, τῆς δὲ νυκτὸς ἐγίγνετο ἀωρὶ, πρὸς
ὕπνον τραπεὶς ὁ Θέρμουθις, χάλκεόν τινα καὶ
πύματον ὕπνον εἵλκυσεν, ἀσπίδος δήγματι,
μοιρῶν τάχα βουλήσει, πρὸς οὐκ ἀνάρμοστον

companion suspected nothing, and believed that he really had great difficulty in keeping up with him.

XX. When he had accustomed the Egyptian to his staying behind, he at last waited a considerable time; and then, plunging into the thickest part of the forest, ran downhill as fast as he could. When Thermuthis had reached the top of the hill, he sat down upon a rock, waiting for the approach of night; for it had been agreed between them that they should wait until it was .dark, before they entered the town to make enquiries about Thyamis. At the same time, he looked about to see whether there were any signs of Cnemon, against whom he had evil designs; for, as he still suspected that it was he who had killed Thisbe, he was thinking how he might treat him in like manner; in his furious rage, he even had an idea of killing Theagenes afterwards. However, finding that Cnemon did not appear, as the night was now far advanced, Thermuthis fell asleep—a deadly and last sleep for him; for an asp, no doubt guided by the will

τοῦ τρόπου τὸ τέλος καταστρέψας. Ὁ δὲ
Κνήμων, ἐπειδὴ τὴν ἀρχὴν κατέλιπε τὸν Θέρ-
μουθιν, οὐ πρότερον ἀνέπαυσε τὴν φυγὴν, ἕως
τὸ νυκτὸς ἐπελθὸν κνέφας ἐπέδησεν αὐτοῦ τὴν
ὁρμήν· αὐτοῦ θ' οὗ κατείληπτο αὐτὸν ἐγκρύψας
καὶ τῆς φυλλάδος ὅσον πλεῖστον ἠδύνατο ἐφ'
αὑτὸν ἐπαμήσας. Ὑφ' ᾗ κείμενος τὰ πολλὰ
μὲν ἄϋπνος ἐταλαιπωρεῖτο, πάντα καὶ κτύπον
καὶ ἀνέμου ῥιπὴν καὶ φύλλου κίνησιν Θέρμου-
θιν ἡγούμενος. Εἰ δέ που καὶ κατὰ μικρὸν
ἐκνικηθείη πρὸς ὕπνον, φεύγειν ἐδόκει καὶ θαμὰ
πρὸς τὰ κατόπιν ὑπέστρεφε καὶ περιεσκόπει
τὸν οὐδαμοῦ διώκοντα καὶ βουλόμενος καθεύδειν
ἀπηύχετο τοῦθ' ὃ ἐβούλετο, χαλεπωτέροις
ὀνείροις τῆς ἀληθείας ἐντυγχάνων. Πρός τε
τὴν νύκτα καὶ χαλεπαίνειν ἐῴκει μακροτέραν
τῶν ἄλλων ὑποτιθέμενος. Ὡς δὲ καὶ ἡμέραν
ἄσμενος εἶδε, πρῶτα μὲν ἀποτέμνει τῆς κόμης

of Fate, bit him and put a fitting end to his life.

Cnemon, from the moment he had left Thermuthis, continued his flight without taking breath, until night and darkness compelled him to halt. He hid himself in the place where night had surprised him, gathered together as many leaves as he could, and covered himself with them. But he scarcely slept, being a prey to mortal dread. At the slightest noise, at the least breath of wind, at the rustling of the leaves, he fancied that he heard Thermuthis. If sleep sometimes overcame him for a moment, he thought that he was fleeing; that he was turning round every instant to look behind and discover an enemy who had no existence. Although he wanted to sleep, he resisted its approach, in order to escape from the dreams which were more terrible than even the reality itself. At last, he vented his irritation upon the night, which appeared to him longer than usual. At length, to his great joy, daylight appeared. At first, being afraid of frightening those whom he might meet, or

τὸ περιττότερον καὶ ὅσον αὐτῆς εἰς τὸ ληστρι-
κώτερον εἶδος παρὰ τοῖς βουκόλοις ἤσκητο,
τοῦ μὴ ἀποτρόπαιος ἢ ὕποπτος εἶναι τοῖς ἐν-
τυγχάνουσι. Ἄλλα τε γὰρ βουκόλοι πρὸς
τὸ φοβερώτερον φαίνεσθαι καὶ δὴ καὶ τὴν
κόμην εἰς ὀφρὺν ἕλκουσι καὶ σοβοῦσι τῶν ὤμων
ἐπιβαίνουσαν, εὖ τοῦτ᾿ εἰδότες, ὡς κόμη τοὺς
μὲν ἐρωτικοὺς ἱλαρωτέρους τοὺς δὲ ληστρικοὺς
φοβερωτέρους ἀποδείκνυσιν.

ΚΑ΄. Ἀποτεμὼν οὖν ὁ Κνήμων ὅσον εἰκὸς
ἦν ἔλαττον κομᾶν τοῦ ληστρικοῦ τὸν ἁβρότε-
ρον, ἐπὶ τὴν Χέμμιν τὴν κώμην οὗ τῷ Θεαγένει
συνετέτακτο ἔσπευδεν. Ἤδη δ᾿ αὐτῷ πλησιά-
ζοντι τῷ Νείλῳ καὶ πρὸς τὴν Χέμμιν περαιοῦ-
σθαι μέλλοντι πρεσβύτης τις ἀνὴρ ἐναλύων ταῖς
ὄχθαις ἐφάνη καὶ δόλιχόν τινα τῷ ῥείθρῳ
πολλάκις ἄνω καὶ κάτω παραθέων καὶ ὥσπερ
τῷ ποταμῷ φροντίδων τινῶν κοινούμενος. Ἡ
κόμη πρὸς τὸ ἱερώτερον καθεῖτο καὶ ἀκριβῶς
ἦν λευκή, τὸ γένειον λάσιον καὶ σεμνότερον
βαθυνόμενον, στολὴ καὶ ἐσθὴς ἡ ἄλλη πρὸς τὸ
ἑλληνικώτερον βλέπουσα. Μικρὸν οὖν αὐτὸν

of arousing their suspicions, he cut his hair, which he had allowed to grow while he was with the shepherds, in order to give himself the appearance of a brigand. For these people, amongst other devices for making themselves look as terrible as possible, comb their hair down over their eyebrows and let it grow down over their shoulders; for they know well that, while a flowing head of hair adds grace to the lover, it makes the brigand look more terrible.

XXI. When he had cut his hair after the fashion of ordinary individuals, he hastened towards Chemmis, the meeting-place agreed upon with Theagenes. When he reached the Nile and was about to cross over to Chemmis, he saw an old man wandering upon the banks, hastily walking up and down, as if he were holding communication with the river. His hair, which he wore long like the priests, was as white as snow; his long, thick beard gave him a venerable aspect; his cloak and the rest of his garments resembled those of the Greeks. Cnemon stopped

14—2

ἐπιστήσας ὁ Κνήμων, ὡς ἀντιπαρέθει πολλάκις ὁ πρεσβύτης οὐδ' εἴ τις αὐτῷ πάρεστιν αἰσθάνεσθαι δοκῶν, (οὕτως ἄρ' ὅλος τῶν φροντισμάτων ἦν καὶ πρὸς μόνην τὴν σκέψιν ὁ νοῦς ἐσχόλαζε) κατὰ πρόσωπον ὑπαντιάσας, πρῶτα μὲν χαίρειν ἐκέλευε. Τοῦ δ' οὐ δύνασθαι φήσαντος ἐπειδὴ μὴ οὕτω συμβαίνειν αὐτῷ παρὰ τῆς τύχης, θαυμάσας ὁ Κνήμων, Ἕλλην, εἶπεν, ἢ ξένος ἢ πόθεν; ὁ δὲ, Οὔτ' Ἕλλην οὔτε ξένος ἀλλ' ἐντεῦθεν Αἰγύπτιος. Πόθεν οὖν ἑλληνίζεις τὴν στολήν; Δυστυχήματα, ἔφη, τὸ λαμπρόν με τοῦτο σχῆμα μετημφίασε. Τοῦ δὲ Κνήμωνος, εἰ φαιδρύνεταί τις ἐπὶ συμφοραῖς θαυμάζοντος καὶ ταῦτα μαθεῖν ἀξιοῦντος, Ἰλιόθεν με φέρεις, ἀπεκρίνατο ὁ πρεσβύτης καὶ σμῆνος κακῶν καὶ τὸν ἐκ τούτων βόμβον ἄπειρον ἐπὶ σαυτὸν κινεῖς. Ἀλλὰ ποῖ δὴ πορεύῃ καὶ πόθεν, ὦ νεανία; πῶς δὲ τὴν φωνὴν

for a moment; the old man kept passing
backwards and forwards in front of him,
as if he did not notice that there was any-
one there, so entirely absorbed was he
in his thoughts and wrapt in meditation.
Cnemon then accosted him with the
words: "Hail! be of good cheer." "There
is no more joy for me," replied the old
man, "my fortune forbids it." Cnemon,
in surprise, asked: "Are you a Greek
or a foreigner, or what is your native
country?" "I am neither a Greek nor
a foreigner, but an Egyptian, a native
of this country." "Why, then, do you
wear this Greek dress?" "It is my
misfortune that has clothed me in these
splendid garments." Cnemon, being unable
to understand how misfortune could im-
prove a man's attire, seemed desirous of
hearing his story. "You are carrying me
out of Ilium," said the old man, "and
are stirring up a swarm of evils, which
will assail you with perpetual buzzing.
But whence come you, young man, and
whither are you going? How comes it
that you, in Egypt, speak the Greek

Ἕλλην ἐν Αἰγύπτῳ; Γελοῖόν γ', ἔφη ὁ Κνή-
μων, τῶν γὰρ κατὰ σαυτὸν οὐδὲν ἐκδιδάξας
πρότερος καὶ ταῦτα ἐρωτηθεὶς, τῶν ἐμῶν
γνῶσιν ἐπιζητεῖς. Οὐκοῦν, ἦ δ' ὃς, ἐπειδὴ
Ἕλληνι ἔοικας ἀνδρὶ καὶ σέ τις ὡς ἔοικε
μετασχηματίζει τύχη καὶ πάντως τὰ ἡμέτερα
ποθεῖς ἀκούειν, (ὠδίνω δὲ καὶ αὐτὸς πρός τινα
ἐξειπεῖν, εἶπον ἂν τάχα καί τοῖσδε τοῖς καλάμοις
κατὰ τὸν μῦθον, εἰ μή σοι προσέτυχον), ὄχθας
μὲν Νείλου τάσδε καὶ Νεῖλον ἀπολίπωμεν· οὐ
γὰρ ἡδὺ μακροτέρων διηγημάτων ἀκροατήριον
τόπος ἡλίου μεσημβρίᾳ φλεγόμενος, πρὸς δὲ
τὴν κώμην, ἣν ὁρᾷς ἀντικρὺ κειμένην, ἴωμεν, εἰ
μή τί σε προὐργιαίτερον ἀπασχολεῖ. Ξενιῶ
δέ σε οὐκ ἐν ἐμαυτοῦ ἀλλ' ἐν ἀνδρὸς ἀγαθοῦ
κἀμὲ ὡς ἱκέτην ὑποδεξαμένου παρ' ᾧ γνώσῃ τε
τἀμὰ βουλόμενος, ἀναθήσει δ' ἐν μέρει τὰ κατὰ
σαυτόν. Ἴωμεν, ἔφη ὁ Κνήμων, καὶ γάρ μοι

language?" "Your request is unreasonable," said Cnemon; "you have told me nothing about yourself, although I asked you first, and now you want to know my story." "Very well, then," replied the old man, "I will not refuse; for you seem to me to be a Greek, in spite of the disguise which some caprice of Fortune has imposed upon you. Besides, if you are so eager to learn my history, I myself am terribly anxious to recount it; probably I should have told it to these reeds, like Midas in the fable, if I had not met you. But let us leave the Nile and its banks; a spot that is scorched by the noonday sun is by no means suitable for hearing a long story. Let us go to the town which you see on the other side, right opposite here, unless more important business prevents you. I can offer you hospitality, not at my own house, but at that of a worthy man who has received me as a suppliant; there, you shall hear the story of my misfortunes, if you so desire, and shall confide to me your own in return." "Let us go," said Cnemon; "in fact, I myself am going

καὶ ἄλλως ἡ πρὸς τὴν κώμην ὁδὸς σπουδάζεται ἀναμεῖναί τινας ἐν ταύτῃ τῶν ἐπιτηδείων συντεταγμένῳ.

ΚΒ'. Σκάφους οὖν ἐπιβάντες, (πολλὰ δὲ περὶ τὴν ὄχθην ἐσάλευον εἰς χρείαν τοῦ διαπορθμεύειν ἐπὶ μισθῷ παρεσκευασμένα) περαιοῦνται πρὸς τὴν κώμην, εἴς τε τὴν καταγωγὴν ἀφικνοῦνται, οὗ κατέλυεν ὁ πρεσβύτης· καὶ τὸν μὲν τοῦ οἴκου δεσπότην οὐ καταλαμβάνουσιν, ὑποδέχονται δ' αὐτοὺς προθυμότατα θυγάτηρ τε τοῦ ἑστιάτορος ἤδη γάμου ὡραία, θεραπαινίδες θ' ὅσαι κατὰ τὴν οἰκίαν, αἳ τὸν ξένον ἴσα καὶ πατέρα ἦγον, οὕτως, οἶμαι, πρὸς τοῦ κεκτημένου διατεταγμένον. Καὶ ἡ μέν τις ἀπένιζε τὼ πόδε, καὶ τῆς κόνεως ἠλευθέρου τὰ ὑπὸ κνήμην, ἡ δ' ἐφρόντιζε τῆς εὐνῆς καὶ μαλακὴν ηὐτρέπιζε τὴν κατάκλισιν· ἑτέρα κάλπην ἔφερε καὶ πῦρ ἀνέκαιε καὶ ἄλλη τράπεζαν εἰσεφέρετο ἄρτου τε πυρίνου καὶ ὡραίων παντοίων βρίθουσαν. Ὁ δὲ Κνήμων θαυμάσας, Ἀλλ' ἢ Ξενίου Διός, ὡς ἔοικεν, εἰς αὐλὰς ἥκομεν, ὦ πάτερ, οὕτως ἀπροφάσιστος ἡ θεραπεία καὶ πολὺ τὸ εὐνοοῦν τῆς γνώμης ἐμφαίνουσα. Οὐκ

to this very town, to wait for some friends, with whom I have an appointment."

XXII. They got into one of the numerous boats that were lying off the bank, ready to take passengers across for a fee, and directed their course towards the town. When they reached the house where the old man had found shelter, the master of the house was absent; but his daughter, a tall, well-grown girl, together with the servants of the household, gave them a cordial welcome. They treated the old man as if he had been their father, having probably been bidden to do so by their master. One washed his feet, and wiped off the dust which covered his legs; another looked after his bed, and strewed it with soft coverlets. One brought water and lighted a fire; another set bread and all fruits of the season upon the table.

Cnemon, astonished at all this, exclaimed · "It seems to me, father, that we have entered the abode of Jove the God of Hospitality, so unhesitating is the attention and so remarkable the kindness with which we have been received." "It

εἰς Διὸς, ἔφη, ἀλλ' εἰς ἀνδρὸς Δία τὸν Ξένιον
καὶ Ἱκέσιον ἀκριβοῦντος. Βίος γὰρ, ὦ παῖ,
κἀκείνῳ πλάνος καὶ ἔμπορος καὶ πολλαὶ μὲν
πόλεις, πολλῶν δ' ἀνθρώπων ἤθη τε καὶ νοῦς
εἰς πεῖραν ἤκουσιν· ὅθεν, ὡς τὸ εἰκὸς, ἄλλους
τε κἀμὲ οὐ πρὸ πολλῶν τῶνδ' ἡμερῶν ἀλύοντα
καὶ πλανώμενον, ὁμορόφιον ἐποιήσατο. Καὶ
τίς ἦν ἡ πλάνη, ὦ πάτερ, ἣν λέγεις; Παίδων,
ἔφη, πρὸς λῃστῶν ἀφαιρεθεὶς καὶ τοὺς μὲν
ἀδικοῦντας γιγνώσκων, ἐπαμῦναι δ' οὐκ ἔχων,
εἰλοῦμαι περὶ τὸν τόπον καὶ θρήνοις παρα-
πέμπω τὸ πάθος, ὥσπερ, οἶμαι, τὶς ὄρνις ὄφεως
αὐτῇ τὴν καλιὰν πορθοῦντος, ἐν ὀφθαλμοῖς τε
τὴν γονὴν θοινομένου, προελθεῖν μὲν ὀκνεῖ
φεύγειν δ' οὐ φέρει, πόθος γὰρ ἐν αὐτῇ καὶ
πάθος ἀνταγωνίζεται· τετριγυῖα δὲ περιπο-
τᾶται τὴν πολιορκίαν, εἰς ὦτα ἀνήμερα καὶ οἷς
ἔλεον οὐκ ἐγνώρισεν ἡ φύσις, ἀνήνυτον ἱκετηρίαν

is not the house of Jove," he replied, "but that of a man who reveres Jove the God of Hospitality, the protector of suppliants. He also, my son, leads a wandering life; he is a merchant, and with his own eyes has made acquaintance with many cities, and with the manners and the minds of many men. This is doubtless the reason why he has received under his roof so many other unfortunates like myself, who but a few days ago was a homeless vagabond." "And how, then, came you to be a wanderer?" "The brigands have taken away my children; I know those who have carried them off, but I am unable to punish them. This is why I roam about this spot, pursuing my misfortune with my grief. In like manner a bird, when a serpent attacks its nest, and devours its little ones before its eyes, fears to approach, and yet cannot resign itself to flight; love and fear struggle for mastery; it circles with mournful cries round the nest which is in the enemy's possession, and pours its maternal wailings and useless supplications into barbarous ears which

τὸν μητρῷον εἰσάγουσα θρῆνον. Ἆρ' οὖν ἄν
ἐθέλοις, ἔφη ὁ Κνήμων, καὶ ὅπως καὶ πότε
τὸν βαρὺν τοῦτον ὑπέστης πόλεμον, ἐξειπεῖν.
Εἰσαῦθις, ἔφη· νῦν δ' ὥρα καὶ τὴν γαστέρα
θεραπεύειν. Καὶ ἐς τάδ' ἀποσκοπῶν Ὅμηρος,
[καὶ] ὡς πάντα δεύτερα αὐτῆς ποιεῖται, θαυ-
μασίως οὐλομένην ὠνόμασεν. Ἀλλὰ πρῶτον
ἡμῖν, ὡς νόμος Αἰγυπτίων σοφοῖς, ἐσπείσθω τὰ
πρὸς τοὺς θεούς. Οὐ γὰρ δή με καὶ τοῦτο
ὑπερβῆναι πείσει, μὴ οὕτω ποτὲ πάθος ἰσχύ-
σειεν, ὡς μνήμην τὴν εἰς τὸ θεῖον ἐκπλῆξαι.

ΚΓ΄ Καὶ ταῦτ' εἰπὼν ἀπέχει τῆς φιάλης
ἄκρατον τὸ ὕδωρ (τοῦτο γὰρ ἔπινε), καὶ,
σπένδωμεν, ἔλεγε, θεοῖς ἐγχωρίοις τε καὶ Ἑλ-
ληνίοις καὶ αὐτῷ γ' Ἀπόλλωνι Πυθίῳ, καὶ
προσέτι Θεαγένει καὶ Χαρικλείᾳ, τοῖς καλοῖς
τε καὶ ἀγαθοῖς, ἐπειδὴ καὶ τούτους εἰς θεοὺς
ἀναγράφω. Καὶ ἅμ' ἐδάκρυσεν, ὥσπερ ἑτέραν
αὐτοῖς σπονδὴν ἐπιφέρων τοὺς θρήνους. Ἐ-
πλάγη πρὸς τὴν ἀκοὴν τῶν ὀνομάτων ὁ Κνήμων

nature has made deaf to all feelings of pity." "Tell me, then," said Cnemon, "how and when you have had to undergo this painful struggle." "I will do so later; in the meantime, we must look after our stomachs; it was a wonderfully happy expression on Homer's part, to call the belly 'destructive,' since it puts itself before everything else. And first, according to the custom of the Egyptian sages, let us pour libations to the gods. Nothing will ever make me neglect to do this; no misfortune, however great, will ever have power to make me forget what I owe to the gods."

XXIII. With these words, he poured pure water (this was his only drink) out of the cup, saying: "I pour this libation to the gods of the country and to those of Greece; also to you, oh Pythian Apollo, and to you, Theagenes and Chariclea, good and virtuous children; for you also I reckon amongst the number of the gods." At the same time he shed tears, as it were by way of a second libation. Cnemon, when he heard these names, was struck

ἄνω τε καὶ κάτω τὸν πρεσβύτην ἐπιθεωρήσας,
Τί λέγεις, ἔφη, παῖδές εἰσί σοι τῷ ὄντι Θεαγένης
καὶ Χαρίκλεια; Παῖδες, εἶπεν, ὦ ξένε, ἀμήτορες
ἐμοὶ γεγονότες· τύχῃ γάρ μου θεοὶ τούτους
ἀνέδειξαν καὶ ἀπέτεκον αἱ ψυχῆς ὠδῖνες καὶ
φύσις ἡ διάθεσις ἐπ᾽ αὐτοῖς ἐνομίσθη καὶ
πατέρα με ἀπὸ ταύτης ἐκεῖνοι καὶ ἐνόμισαν
καὶ ὠνόμασαν. Ἀλλὰ σὺ δὴ πόθεν, εἰπέ μοι,
τούτους ἐγνώρισας; Οὐκ ἐγνώρισα μόνον, ἔφη
ὁ Κνήμων, ἀλλὰ καὶ σώζεσθαί σοι αὐτοὺς
εὐαγγελίζομαι. Ἄπολλον, ἔφη ἀναβοήσας,
καὶ θεοὶ, καὶ ποῦ γῆς οὗτοι δείκνυε· σωτῆρά
σε καὶ θεοῖς ἰσοστάσιον ἡγήσομαι. Μισθὸς δέ
μοι τίς ἔσται; ἔφη. Τὸ μὲν παρὸν, ἦδ᾽ ὃς,
εὐχαριστία. Ξενίων δ᾽ οἶμαι τὸ κάλλιστον
ἀνδρὶ νοῦν ἔχοντι. Καὶ οἶδα πολλοὺς ὡς
θησαυρὸν τῇ ψυχῇ παραθεμένους τὸ δῶρον.
Εἰ δὲ καὶ τῆς ἐνεγκούσης ἐπιβαίημεν, (ἔσεσθαι

with astonishment, and looked at the old man from head to foot: "What do you say?" he exclaimed; "are Theagenes and Chariclea your children?" "They are my children, oh stranger, although they were not given to me by a mother; Fortune and the will of the gods have made them mine; the travail of my soul has brought them forth; my affection for them has taken the place of the ties of kinship; thanks to this affection, they look upon me as their father, and call me by that name. But, tell me, how do you come to know them?" "I not only know them," replied Cnemon, "but I tell you the good news that they are alive." "Oh Apollo, and all ye other gods!" exclaimed the old man; "where are they? Speak, and I will look upon you as my preserver and the equal of the gods." "And what shall be my reward?" "For the moment, my gratitude, the best of all rewards in the eyes of a man who is wise; I know many who have laid up this as a treasure in their hearts. Afterwards, when we have returned to my country—

δέ μοι τοῦτ' οὐκ εἰς μακρὰν οἱ θεοὶ προσημαί-
νουσιν), ἀρύσῃ πλοῦτον ὅσον ἂν δύναιο πλεῖσ-
τον. Μέλλοντα, εἶπε, καὶ ἄδηλα κατεγγυᾷς,
ἐξὸν ἐκ τῶν παρόντων ἀμείβεσθαι. ΞΕΝ.
Ἀπάγγελλε, εἴ τι παρὸν ὁρᾷς, ὡς ἕτοιμος ἐγὼ
καὶ μέρος τι προέσθαι τοῦ σώματος. ΚΝΗΜ.
Οὐδὲν δεῖ μέλος ἀκρωτηριάζειν ἀλλ' ἅπαν ἔχειν
ἡγήσομαι, εἰ τούτοις ὁπόθεν εἰσὶν καὶ ἐκ τίνων
φύντες καὶ πῶς δεῦρο ἀφιγμένοι καὶ ποίαις
κεχρημένοι τύχαις βουληθείης ἐξαγορεῦσαι.
Ἕξεις, ἀπεκρίνατο, τὸν μισθὸν μέγαν τινὰ καὶ
οὐχ οἷον ἄλλον, οὐδ' εἰ τὰ ἐξ ἀνθρώπων
χρήματα αἰτῶν ἐτύγχανες. Ἀλλὰ τὸ παρὸν
τροφῆς ὀλίγον ἀπογενώμεθα, μακροτέρας γὰρ
δεήσει σοί τε τῆς ἀκροάσεως, ἐμοί τε τῆς
ἀφηγήσεως. Ἐντραγόντες οὖν τῶν τε καρύων
καὶ σύκων, ἀρτιδρεπῶν τε φοινίκων καὶ ἄλλων
δὴ τοιούτων, ἀφ' ὧν ἐξ ἔθους ὁ πρεσβύτης
ἐσιτεῖτο, (ψυχῆς γὰρ διὰ βρῶσιν οὐδὲ ἐν ἀφῃ-
ρεῖτο) ἐπερρόφουν ὁ μὲν τοῦ ὕδατος, ὁ δὲ καὶ
οἶνον ὁ Κνήμων, ὅς γε καὶ μικρὸν διαλιπὼν,
Ὁ Διόνυσος εἶπεν, οἶσθα, ὦ πάτερ, ὡς χαίρει

and this, so the gods foretell, will not be long—you shall draw as much wealth as you please from my store." "These are vague and uncertain promises; you have it in your power to reward me on the spot." "Speak, if you see anything that I can offer you now; I would willingly sacrifice even one of my limbs." "There is no need of so great a sacrifice; I shall consider myself fully repaid, if you tell me whence they come, who were their parents, how they came here, and what their fortunes have been." "You shall have a reward second to none, even though you should ask for all the wealth of the universe. But, first of all, let us take some food; for you will have a long tale to listen to, and I shall have much to say." They then ate a few nuts, figs, fresh dates, and other fruits of this kind, which formed the old man's usual food; for he never deprived any animal of its life to provide food for himself; his drink was water, while Cnemon took some wine. After a brief interval of silence, Cnemon said: "You know, father, that Bacchus delights

μύθοις καὶ κωμῳδίας φιλεῖ. Κἀμὲ δὴ οὖν τὰ νῦν εἰσῳκισμένος, ἀνίησι πρὸς τὴν ἀκρόασιν, τόν τ' ἐπηγγελμένον πρὸς σοῦ μισθὸν ἀπαιτεῖν ἐπείγει καὶ ὥρα σοι τὸ δρᾶμα καθάπερ ἐπὶ σκηνῆς τῷ λόγῳ διασκευάζειν. Ἀκούοις ἂν, ἔφη. Ἀλλ' εἴθε γε καὶ τὸν χρηστὸν Ναυσικλέα παρεῖναι ἡμῖν συνέβαινεν, ὃν πολλάκις γε δι' ὄχλου γιγνόμενον μυηθῆναι τὴν ἀφήγησιν ἄλλως ἄλλοτε διεκρουσάμην.

ΚΔ'. Ποῦ δ' ἂν εἴη τὰ νῦν; ἠρώτα ὁ Κνήμων, ὡς τοὔνομα τοῦ Ναυσικλέους ἐπέγνω. Ἐπ' ἄγραν, ἔφη, πεπόρευται. Τοῦ δὲ ὁποίαν, πάλιν ἐρομένου, Θηρίων, ἔφη, τῶν χαλεπωτάτων, οἳ καλοῦνται μὲν ἄνθρωποι καὶ βουκόλοι, λησταὶ δ' εἰσὶ τὸν βίον καὶ δυσάλωτοι παντάπασιν, ὅσα φωλεοῖς καὶ σήραγξι τῷ ἕλει χρώμενοι. Ἐγκαλεῖ δ' αὐτοῖς τίνα αἰτίαν; Ἀττικῆς, ἔφη, ἐρωμένης ἁρπαγὴν, ἣν Θίσβην ἐκεῖνος ὠνόμαζε. Φεῦ, εἶπεν ὁ Κνήμων καὶ ἀθρόον ἐσιώπησεν,

in convivial tales and songs. He has this day claimed my hospitality; he has aroused in me a desire to listen to you, and urges me to claim my promised reward; it is time for you to put your piece upon the stage, as the saying is." "Listen then," said the old man; "and would to Heaven that the worthy Nausicles were here, for he has often entreated me to tell him this story, but has always been put off under some pretext or another."

XXIV. "And where may he be now?" asked Cnemon, as soon as he heard the name of Nausicles mentioned. "He is gone hunting," replied the old man. "After what kind of game?" "Wild beasts, the most savage in existence; they are called men and shepherds; in reality, they are brigands by profession, and are most difficult to catch; for they live in a marsh instead of lairs and caves." "And what injury have they done him?" "They have carried off from him an Athenian maiden whom he loved, who was called Thisbe." "Good heavens!" cried Cnemon, and then immediately

15—2

ὥσπερ αὐτοῦ λαβόμενος. Τοῦ δὲ πρεσβύτου,
Τί πέπονθεν; ἐρομένου, πρὸς ἄλλα ὁ Κνήμων
ἀπάγων, Θαυμάζω, ἔφη, πῶς ἢ τίνι χειρὶ πεποι-
θὼς ἐνεθυμήθη τὴν ἔφοδον. Καὶ ὃς, Βασιλεῖ,
ἔφη, ξένε, τῷ μεγάλῳ σατραπεύει τὴν Αἴγυπτον
Ὀροονδάτης, οὗ κατὰ πρόσταγμα φρούραρχος
Μιτράνης τήνδε κεκλήρωται τὴν κώμην. Τοῦτον
δὴ ὁ Ναυσικλῆς ἐπὶ χρήμασι μεγάλοις ἄγει
σὺν ἵππῳ καὶ ἀσπίδι πολλῇ. Χαλεπαίνει δὲ
τὴν ἀφαίρεσιν τῆς Ἀττικῆς κόρης οὐχ ὡς ἐρω-
μένης μόνον καὶ μουσουργίαν ἀρίστης, ἀλλ'
ὅτι αὐτὴν καὶ βασιλεῖ τῶν Αἰθιόπων ἀπάξειν
ἔμελλεν, ὡς αὐτὸς ἔφασκε, γαμετῇ τῇ ἐκείνου
συμπαίστριαν καὶ συνόμιλον τὰ Ἑλλήνων
ἐσομένην. Ὡς οὖν μεγάλων καὶ πολλῶν τῶν
ἐπ' αὐτῇ προσδοκωμένων χρημάτων ἐστερη-
μένος πᾶσαν ἐγείρει καὶ κινεῖ μηχανήν. Ἐπέρ-
ρωσά τε καὶ αὐτὸς πρὸς τὴν πρᾶξιν, εἴ πῃ ἄρα

stopped as if to check himself. When the old man asked what was the matter with him, Cnemon, in order to put him off the scent, replied that he was greatly surprised, and wondered with what forces he intended to attack them. " The satrap of the great king in Egypt is Oroondates, under whose orders Mitranes is in command of the garrison of this town. Nausicles, by means of a large sum of money, has persuaded the latter to assist him with a large number of soldiers, foot and horse. He is especially annoyed at the loss of this Greek girl, not only because he really loved her and she was a clever musician, but also because he was going to take her with him to the King of Aethiopia, to be companion of the queen's amusements, and her associate according to the usage of the Greeks. Finding himself thus disappointed of the considerable profit which he expected to make by her, he is doing his very utmost to get her back again. I myself have encouraged him in the undertaking, in the idea that he might perhaps meet my

καὶ τοὺς παῖδάς μοι περισώσειεν, ἐνθυμούμενος.
Ὑπολαβὼν οὖν ὁ Κνήμων, Ἅλις, ἔφη, βουκόλων
καὶ σατραπῶν καὶ βασιλέων αὐτῶν, ἔλαθες γάρ
με μικρὸν καὶ εἰς πέρας τῷ λόγῳ διαβιβάζων.
Ἐπεισόδιον δὴ τοῦτο, οὐδὲν, φασὶ, πρὸς τὸν
Διόνυσον ἐπεισκυκλήσας· ὥστ᾽ ἐπάναγε τὸν
λόγον πρὸς τὴν ὑπόσχεσιν. Εὕρηκα γάρ σε
κατὰ τὸν Πρωτέα τὸν Φάριον, οὐκ αὐτὸν
τρεπόμενον εἰς ψευδομένην καὶ ῥέουσαν ὄψιν
ἀλλ᾽ ἐμὲ παραφέρειν πειρώμενον. Μανθάνοις
ἂν, ἔφη ὁ πρεσβύτης. Διηγήσομαι δέ σοι
τἀμαυτοῦ πρότερον ἐπιτεμὼν, οὐ σοφιστεύων,
ὡς αὐτὸς οἴει, τὴν ἀφήγησιν, ἀλλ᾽ εὔτακτόν
σοι καὶ προσεχῆ τῶν ἑξῆς παρασκευάζων τὴν
ἀκρόασιν. Ἐμοὶ πόλις Μέμφις, πατὴρ δὲ καὶ
ὄνομα Καλάσιρις, βίος δὲ νῦν μὲν ἀλήτης,
πρότερον δ᾽ οὐ πάλαι προφήτης. Ἐγένετό
μοι καὶ γυνὴ νόμῳ τῆς πόλεως καὶ ἀπεγένετο
θεσμῷ τῆς φύσεως. Ταύτης εἰς τὴν ἑτέραν

children somewhere and restore them to me." "Enough of shepherds, satraps, and kings," said Cnemon; "you have wandered from the point, and nearly transported me at the very outset to the end of the story. This episode is brought in rather unnaturally, and has nothing to do with Bacchus, as the phrase goes; you are like Proteus of Pharos, with the difference that, instead of changing yourself into false and fleeting shapes, you are trying to lead me away from the subject." "Well, then, you shall hear all," replied the old man; "but I will first give you a rapid account of myself, not in order, as you imagine, to throw dust in your eyes, but in order to prepare you for a connected and well-arranged narrative of later events. I was born at Memphis; my father's name, like my own, was Calasiris. Although I now lead a wandering life, a short time ago I filled the office of high priest. I took a wife, according to the custom of the country; I lost her, according to the law of nature. When, released from the trammels of this life, she had entered

λῆξιν ἀναλυθείσης, χρόνον μὲν τινα διῆγον
ἀπαθὴς κακῶν, ἐπὶ παισὶ δύο τοῖς ἐξ αὐτῆς
ἀβρυνόμενος. Οὐ πολλοῖς δ᾽ ὕστερον ἔτεσιν,
οὐρανία φωστήρων εἱμαρμένη περίοδος τρέπει
τὰ καθ᾽ ἡμᾶς καὶ ὄμμα Κρόνιον εἰς τὸν οἶκον
ἐνέσκηψε, τὴν ἐπὶ τὸ χεῖρον ἐπάγον μεταβολὴν,
ἣν ἐμοὶ σοφία προΰφηνε μὲν, διαδρᾶναι δ᾽ οὐκ
ἔδωκε. Τοὺς γὰρ μοιρῶν ἀτρέπτους ὅρους
προϊδεῖν μὲν δυνατὸν, ἐκφεύγειν δ᾽ οὐκ ἐφικτόν.
Κέρδος δ᾽ ὡς ἐν τοῖς τοιούτοις ἡ πρόγνωσις,
ἀμβλύνουσα τοῦ δεινοῦ τὸ φλεγμαῖνον. Συμ-
φορᾶς γὰρ, ὦ παῖ, τὸ μὲν ἀπροσδόκητον
ἀφόρητον, τὸ δὲ προεγνωσμένον οἰστότερον.
Τὸ μὲν γὰρ ἡ διάνοια φόβῳ προληφθεῖσα
κατέπτηξε, τὸ δ᾽ ἡ συνήθεια τῷ λογισμῷ
διῄτησε.

ΚΕʹ. Γέγονε δὲ περὶ ἐμὲ τοιόνδε. Γύναιον
Θρᾳκικὸν τὴν ὥραν ἀκμαῖον καὶ τὸ κάλλος
δεύτερον μετὰ Χαρίκλειαν [ἔχουσα], ὄνομα
Ῥόδωπις, οὐκ οἶδ᾽ ὁπόθεν ἢ ὅπως κακῇ μοίρᾳ

the repose of another world, for some time I remained free from the blows of misfortune, delighting myself in the society of the two sons whom she had left me. But, a few years later, the fatal course of the celestial bodies upset my destiny; the eye of Saturn struck my house, and changed its fortunes for the worse. Wisdom revealed these ills to me, but without showing me the means of escaping them. For, although it is possible to foresee the immutable decrees of the Fates, it is useless to endeavour to avoid them. And yet foreknowledge is an advantage, at least relatively, since it blunts the edge of adversity. An unforeseen misfortune, my son, is intolerable; those which we know in advance are easier to bear; in the first case, the mind, seized with fear, is cast down; in the second, reflection familiarises it with the idea of them.

XXV. "The following is what happened to me: A Thracian woman, named Rhodopis, in the prime of life, as beautiful even as Chariclea, came to the country (I know not whence or how), to the ruin

τῶν ἐγνωκότων ὁρμηθὲν, ἐπεπόλαξε τὴν Αἴγυπ-
τον καὶ ἤδη καὶ εἰς τὴν Μέμφιν ἐκώμαξε, πολλῇ
μὲν θεραπείᾳ, πολλῷ δὲ πλούτῳ δορυφορου-
μένη, πᾶσι δ᾽ ἀφροδισίοις θηράτροις ἐξησκημένη.
Οὐ γὰρ ἦν ἐντυχόντα μὴ ἡλωκέναι· οὕτως
ἄφυκτόν τινα καὶ ἀπρόσμαχον ἑταιρίας σαγήνην
ἐκ τῶν ὀφθαλμῶν ἐπεσύρετο. Ἐφοίτα δὴ
θαμὰ καὶ εἰς τὸν νεὼν τῆς Ἴσιδος· ἧς προεφή-
τευον, καὶ τὴν θεὸν συνεχῶς ἐθεράπευε θυσίαις
τε καὶ ἀναθήμασι πολυταλάντοις. Αἰσχύνομαι
λέγειν, ἀλλ᾽ εἰρήσεται· γίγνεται δὴ κἀμοῦ
κρείττων ὀφθεῖσα πολλάκις. Ἐνίκα τὴν διὰ
βίου μοι μελετηθεῖσαν ἐγκράτειαν. Ἐπὶ πολύ
τε τοῖς σώματος ὀφθαλμοῖς τοὺς ψυχῆς ἀντι-
στήσας, ἀπῆλθον τὸ τελευταῖον ἡττηθεὶς καὶ
πάθος ἐρωτικὸν ἐπιφορτισάμενος. Ἀρχὴν δὴ
τῶν ἐσομένων καὶ προαγορευθέντων μοι πρὸς
τοῦ θείου δυσχερῶν τὴν γυναῖκα φωράσας καὶ
συνεὶς ὡς τῶν πεπρωμένων ἐστὶν ὑπόκρισις καὶ

of those who became acquainted with her. After travelling through Egypt, she settled at Memphis. Her numerous suite, the magnificence she displayed, her charms, her cleverness in setting the snares of Venus—all this made it impossible for anyone to look upon her without being hopelessly bewitched. Never was there a courtesan who knew better how to attract a man with her irresistible fascinations. From time to time she visited the temple of Isis, of which I was priest, frequently consecrating to the goddess victims and sumptuous offerings. I must tell the truth, although it makes me blush; the frequent sight of her overcame me; she gained the victory over the self-restraint which I had practised all my life. After I had for a long time resisted the eyes of the body with those of the mind, I at length succumbed, I fell overwhelmed by the weight of the burden of love. I saw in this woman the commencement of the misfortunes reserved for me by the gods, and which they had predicted; I foresaw in her the person of Destiny, and I under-

ὡς ὁ τότ' εἰληχὼς δαίμων οἰονεὶ προσωπεῖον
αὐτὴν ὑπῆλθε, τὴν μὲν ἐκ παίδων μοι σύντροφον
ἱερωσύνην ἔγνων μὴ καταισχῦναι καὶ ἀντισχεῖν,
μήδ' ἱερὰ καὶ τεμένη θεῶν βεβηλῶσαι. Τῶν
δ' ἡμαρτημένων οὐκ ἔργῳ (μὴ γένοιτο) ἀλλ'
ἐφέσει μόνῃ, τὴν ἁρμόζουσαν ἐπιβαλὼν ζημίαν,
δικαστὴν ἐμαυτῷ τὸν λογισμὸν ἀναδείξας, φυγῇ
κολάζω τὴν ἐπιθυμίαν καὶ τῆς ἐνεγκούσης ὁ
βαρυδαίμων ἐξῄειν, ὁμοῦ μὲν εἴκων ταῖς μοιρῶν
ἀνάγκαις καὶ πράττειν ὅ τι καὶ βούλοιντο τὰ
καθ' ἡμᾶς ἐπιτρέπων, ὁμοῦ δὲ τὴν ἀποτρόπαιον
Ῥόδωπιν ἀποφεύγων Ἐδεδίειν γὰρ, ὦ ξένε,
μὴ τοῦ τότε ἐπικρατοῦντος ἀστέρος ἐπιβρίσαν-
τος καὶ πρὸς τὸ αἰσχρότερον τῶν ἔργων ἐκνικη-
θείην. Ὁ δέ με πρὸ πάντων καὶ ἐπὶ πᾶσιν
ἐξήλαυνεν, οἱ παῖδες ἦσαν, οὓς ἡ ἄρρητός μοι
πολλάκις ἐκ θεῶν σοφία, ξιφήρεις ἀλλήλοις
συμπεσεῖσθαι προηγόρευε. Περιγράφων οὖν
τῶν ὀφθαλμῶν τὴν οὕτως ἀπηνῆ θέαν, (ἣν
ἐκτραπήσεσθαι καὶ τὸν ἥλιον εἰκάζω νέφος τῆς

stood that she was the mask beneath which the evil Genius, in whose power I then was, lay concealed. Fearing to disgrace my sacred office, in which I had been brought up from infancy, I determined to avoid profaning the temple and sanctuary of the gods. I appointed reason my judge, and, punishing as it deserved the fault which I had committed—not in very deed, in truth, indeed (Heaven forbid !), but in desire—I imposed upon myself the penalty of exile. Unhappy that I was, I left my native land; I yielded to the irresistible power of the Fates, and gave myself up to them to deal with me as they pleased. I also wanted to escape from the accursed Rhodopis; for I was afraid that, still under the influence of my baleful star, I might be dragged into more disgraceful acts. But what, above all, made me decide to flee, was the fact that my skill in divination had several . times foretold to me that my sons were destined to draw the sword against each other. I wished to tear my eyes away from so frightful a sight, in the presence of which even the sun would veil himself

ἀκτῖνος προκαλυψάμενον) καὶ πατρῴαις ὄψεσι
τὸν παίδων φόνον ἀθέατον χαριζόμενος, ἐξῴκιζον
ἐμαυτὸν γῆς τε καὶ οἰκίας πατρῴας, τὴν μὲν
ὁρμὴν οὐδενὶ φράσας, πρόφασιν δὲ ὡς εἰς Θήβας
τὰς μεγάλας ἀνακομίζομαι ποιησάμενος, ὡς ἂν
θάτερον τῶν παίδων τὸν πρεσβύτερον θεασαί-
μην, ἐκεῖ παρὰ τῷ μητροπάτορι τότε διάγοντα.
Θύαμις δ' ἦν ὄνομα αὐτῷ, ὦ ξένε. Συνεστάλη
πάλιν ὁ Κνήμων, ὥσπερ τῷ ὀνόματι τοῦ
Θυάμιδος βληθεὶς τὴν ἀκοήν, καὶ ὁ μὲν ἐκαρ-
τέρησε σιωπῆσαι τῶν ἑξῆς ἕνεκεν, ὁ δ' ἐπέραινε
τὸν λόγον ὧδε. Παραλείπω τὴν ἐν μέσῳ
πλάνην, ὦ νεανία, συντελεῖ γὰρ οὐδὲν εἰς τὴν
παρὰ σοῦ ζήτησιν.

ΚΣ'. Πυνθανόμενος δ' εἶναί τινα Δελφοὺς
Ἑλληνίδα πόλιν, ἱερὰν μὲν Ἀπόλλωνος, θεῶν
δὲ τῶν ἄλλων τέμενος, ἀνδρῶν δὲ σοφῶν ἐργα-
στήριον, θορύβου δὲ δημώδους ἐκτὸς ἀνῳκισ-
μένην, ἔστελλον εἰς ταύτην ἐμαυτόν, ἁρμόδιον
τῷ προφητικῷ καταγώγιον, τὴν ἱεροῖς καὶ

in a cloud to avoid being a witness of it. I spared the eyes of a father the sight of the murder of his children; I exiled myself from my country, from my father's house, without communicating my design to any-one. I had pretended that I was going to Egyptian Thebes, to see my eldest son, who was staying there on a visit to his grandfather. His name, oh stranger, was Thyamis." Cnemon started again, as if the name of Thyamis had struck him; but he restrained himself and kept silence to hear the continuation of the story. Calasiris proceeded: "I pass over in silence the intermediate part of my journey, which has nothing to do with what you want to know.

XXVI. "Having heard that there was a city in Greece, named Delphi, conse-crated to Apollo, and also that it was a sanctuary for all the other gods, and for the wise man a place of retirement[1] far removed from popular disturbances, I directed my course thither; for it appeared to me that no place of refuge could be better suited for a priest than a city

[1] Literally, "workshop."

τελεταῖς ἀνακειμένην ὁριζόμενος. Διά τε τοῦ Κρισσαίου κόλπου τῇ Κίρρᾳ προσορμισθεὶς, ἐκ νεὼς ἐπὶ τὴν πόλιν ἀνέθεον. Ἐπεὶ δ' ἐπέστην, ὀμφή με ὡς ἀληθῶς θεία προσέβαλεν αὐτόθεν. Καὶ τά τ' ἄλλα ἡ πόλις διαίτημα κρειττόνων ἔδοξε καὶ οὐχ ἥκιστα τῇ φύσει τῆς περιοχῆς. Οἷον γὰρ φρούριον ἀτεχνῶς καὶ αὐτοσχέδιος ἀκρόπολις ὁ Παρνασσὸς ἀπαιωρεῖται, πρὸ ποδῶν λαγόσι τὴν πόλιν ἐγκολπισάμενος. Ἄριστα, ἔφη, λέγεις, ὁ Κνήμων, καὶ ὡς ἄν τις ἐπιπνοίας ὡς ἀληθῶς Πυθικῆς ἐπῃσθημένος. Τῇδε γάρ πῃ καὶ ὁ πατήρ μοι θέσεως ἔχειν τοὺς Δελφοὺς ἔφραξεν, ὅτ' αὐτὸν ἱερομνήμονα ἡ πόλις Ἀθηναίων ἔστειλεν. Ἀθηναῖος ἆρ' ἦσθα, ὦ παῖ; Ναὶ, ἔφη. Ὄνομα δὲ τίς; Κνήμων, ἀπεκρίνατο, [Τύχῃ τίνι κεχρημένος;] τὰ δ' ἄλλα εἰσαῦθις [ἔφη] ἀκούσῃ, νῦν δ' ἔχου τῶν ἑξῆς. Ἕξομαι, ἔφη. Καὶ ἐπανήειν πρὸς τὴν πόλιν. Ἐπαινέσας οὖν τῶν τε δρόμων καὶ

entirely devoted to religion and sacrifice. Having crossed the Gulf of Crissa, I landed at Cirrha, and, on disembarking, hastened up to the city. When I drew near to it, a voice, evidently divine, sounded in my ears; the city appeared to me in every respect, but especially from its natural situation, an abode worthy of no ordinary mortals. Parnassus, like a natural fortress, with a citadel which owes nothing to art, rises aloft, and throws out on one side and the other its spurs, which embrace as in its bosom the city lying at its feet." "Your description is most accurate," said Cnemon; "it seems to have been made by one who was really under the influence of the Pythian god; it tallies with that given me by my father, when he was sent as the deputy[1] of the Athenian people to the Amphictyonic assembly." "So then you are an Athenian, my son?" "Yes." "What is your name?" "Cnemon." "What is your history?" "You shall hear it later; meanwhile, continue." "I will. I went up to the city, and, after having admired the race-courses,[2] the

[1] The *Hieromnēmon* was the secretary sent by each of the twelve Amphictyonic states to their council together with the *Pylagoras* (the actual deputy or minister).

ἀγορῶν καὶ κρηνῶν τὸ ἄστυ καὶ Κασταλίαι
αὐτὴν, ἣν δὴ καὶ περιρραντήριον ἐποιησάμην,
ἐπὶ τὸν νεὼν ἔσπευδον, καὶ γάρ με καὶ θροῦς
τῶν πολλῶν ἀνεπτέρωσεν, ὥραν εἶναι κινεῖσθαι
τὴν θεοπρόπον λέγοντες. Ἐπεὶ δ᾽ εἰσελθὼν
προσεκύνουν καί τι καὶ κατ᾽ ἐμαυτὸν ηὐχόμην,
ἀνεφθέγξατο ἡ Πυθία τοιάδε.

Ἴχνος ἀειράμενος ἀπ᾽ εὐστάχυος παρὰ Νείλου,
 Φεύγεις μοιράων νήματ᾽ ἐρισθενέων.
Τέτλαθι, σοὶ γὰρ ἐγὼ κυαναύλακος Αἰγύπτοιο
 Αἶψα πέδον δώσω. Νῦν δ᾽ ἐμὸς ἔσσο φίλος.

ΚΖ΄. Ταῦθ᾽ ὡς ἐθέσπισεν, ἐγὼ μὲν ἐμαυτὸν
ἐπὶ πρόσωπον τοῖς βωμοῖς ἐπιβαλὼν, ἵλεων
εἶναι τὰ πάντα ἱκέτευον. Ὁ δὲ πολὺς τῶν
περιεστώτων ὅμιλος ἀνευφήμησαν τὸν θεὸν
τῆς ἐπ᾽ ἐμοὶ παρὰ τὴν πρώτην ἔντευξιν προ-
φητείας. Ἐμὲ δ᾽ ἐμακάριζον καὶ περιείποντο
ἐντεῦθεν παντοίως, φίλον ἥκειν με τῷ θεῷ μετὰ
Λυκοῦργόν τινα Σπαρτιάτην λέγοντες, καὶ

market-places, and fountains (especially Castalia, with whose water I sprinkled myself), I hastened my steps towards the temple. The murmurs which announced that it was the hour when the priestess would be under the influence of the god, excited me greatly. Having entered the temple, I flung myself on the ground and uttered a silent prayer, and received the following oracle: ' Thou comest from the district of the fruitful Nile; thou fleest from the threads of the mighty Fates. Take heart; soon I will give thee the plains of Egypt with its dark furrows; meanwhile, be my friend.'

XXVII. "As soon as I heard these prophetic words, I fell upon my face at the foot of the altar, and besought the god to be propitious to me in everything. The whole multitude of the bystanders glorified Apollo for the oracle which he had vouchsafed to me on the occasion of my first visit to the temple; they congratulated me, and treated me with particular respect, saying that I was the only man, with the exception of Lycurgus of

16—2

ἐνοικεῖν τε βουλόμενον τῷ τεμένει τοῦ νεὼ
συνεχώρουν καὶ σιτηρέσιον ἐκ τοῦ δημοσίου
παρέχειν ἐψηφίσαντο, καὶ συνελόντι λέγειν
ἀγαθῶν ἀπέλιπεν οὐδέν. Ἢ γὰρ πρὸς ἱεροῖς
ἦν, ἢ πρὸς θυσίαις ἐξηταζόμην, ἃς πολλὰς καὶ
παντοίας ἀνὰ πᾶσαν ἡμέραν ξένος τε καὶ
ἐγχώριος λεὼς τῷ θεῷ χαριζόμενοι δρῶσιν, ἢ
φιλοσοφοῦσι διελεγόμην. Οὐκ ὀλίγος δ' ὁ
τοιοῦτος βίος συρρεῖ περὶ τὸν νεὼν τοῦ Πυθίου,
καὶ μουσεῖόν ἐστιν ἀτεχνῶς ἡ πόλις ὑπὸ μου-
σηγέτῃ θεῷ φοιβαζομένη. Τὸν μὲν δὴ πρότερον
χρόνον ἄλλοτε περὶ ἄλλων ἡμῖν αἱ ζητήσεις
ἀνεκινοῦντο· καὶ ὁ μέν τις ὅπως τοὺς ἐγχωρίους
οἱ Αἰγύπτιοι σέβομεν θεοὺς ἀνηρώτα, ὁ δὲ δι'
ἣν αἰτίαν ἄλλα παρ' ἄλλοις τῶν ζῴων ἐκθειά-
ζεται καὶ τίς ὁ περὶ ἑκάστου λόγος ἐπυνθάνετο·
ἄλλος πυραμίδων κατασκευὴν, ἕτερος σύριγγων

Sparta, upon whom the god had bestowed the title of friend. They granted me permission to inhabit the precincts of the temple, at my request, and it was decreed that I should be maintained at the public expense. In short, my situation left nothing to be desired; I took part in the sacred ceremonies; I studied the numerous sacrifices of various kinds performed daily by strangers as well as natives, in honour of the god; I joined in the conversations of the philosophers who flocked in great numbers to the temple of the Pythian Apollo; for the city is really a sanctuary of the Muses, under the inspiration of the God whom the Muses recognise as their head. At the beginning, questions were put to me upon different subjects: one asked me in what manner we worshipped our gods in Egypt; another enquired why certain animals were worshipped in different places, and wanted an account of each; while others, again, put questions to me concerning the construction of the Pyramids and the underground burial-vaults of the

πλάνην, καὶ συνελόντι τῶν κατ᾽ Αἴγυπτον ἐν οὐδὲν ἀπελίμπανον ἱστοροῦντες. Αἰγύπτιον γὰρ ἄκουσμα καὶ διήγημα πᾶν Ἑλληνικῆς ἀκοῆς ἐπαγωγότατον.

ΚΗ΄. Τέλος δέ ποτε καὶ περὶ τοῦ Νείλου καὶ τίνες μὲν αὐτῷ πηγαί, τίς δ᾽ ἡ παρὰ τοὺς ἄλλους ποταμοὺς ἰδιάζουσα φύσις καὶ ὁπόθεν τὴν θερινὴν ὥραν μόνος τῶν πάντων πλημμυρεῖ, πεῦσίν τις ἐμοὶ προσῆγε τῶν ἀστειοτέρων. Ἐμοῦ δ᾽ ἅπερ ἐγίγνωσκον εἰπόντος καὶ ὅσα περὶ τοῦ ποταμοῦ τούτου βίβλοις ἱεραῖς ἐγγεγραμμένα μόνοις τοῖς προφητικοῖς καὶ γιγνώσκειν καὶ ἀναγιγνώσκειν ἔξεστι· καὶ διελθόντος ὡς τὰς μὲν ἀρχὰς ἐκ τῶν μὲν ἄκρων τῆς Αἰθιοπίας ἐσχάτων δὲ τῆς Λιβύης λαμβάνει, καθ᾽ ὃ μέρος τὸ κλίμα τὸ ἀνατολικὸν ἀπολῆγον ἀρχὴν τῇ μεσημβρίᾳ δίδωσιν, αὔξεται δὲ κατὰ τὴν θερινὴν ὥραν, οὐχ ὡς τινες ᾠήθησαν πρὸς τῶν ἐτησίων ἀντικρὺ πνεόντων ἀνακοπτόμενος, ἀλλ᾽ αὐτῶν δὴ τούτων τῶν ἀνέμων κατὰ τροπὴν τὴν θερινὴν ἀπὸ τῶν ἀρκτῴων ἐπὶ τὴν μεσημβρίαν πᾶν νέφος ἐλαυνόντων τε καὶ ὠθούντων, ἕως ἐπὶ τὴν διακεκαυμένην ζώνην συνάξωσι, καθ᾽ ἣν τῆς πρόσω φορᾶς ἀνακόπτονται δι᾽ ὑπερβολὴν τοῦ περὶ τὰ μέρη πυρώ-

kings; in a word, none of the curiosities of Egypt were forgotten, for everything relating to that country has a special charm for the Greeks.

XXVIII. " At length, one of the most learned amongst them asked me about the Nile, its source, the special characteristics by which it is distinguished from other rivers, and why it is that it is the only river that overflows in summer. I told them what I knew on the subject, what I had gathered from the sacred books which the priests alone may read and consult. I told them that it rises in the mountains of Aethiopia, on the furthest confines of Libya, where the east ends and the south begins. The reason of its overflowing in summer is not, as is sometimes asserted, that its waters are driven back by the Etesian winds, which blow in an opposite direction; but rather, these winds, at the period of the summer solstice, drive the clouds before them from north to south, until they collect beneath the torrid zone, where they are arrested in their course by the excessive heat of these regions; all the vapours previously accumulated gradually

δους πάσης τῆς πρότερον καὶ κατὰ μικρὸν ἀθροισθείσης καὶ παχυνθείσης νοτίδος ἐξατμιζομένης, κἀκ τούτου λάβρων ὑετῶν ῥηγνυμένων, ὀργᾷ θ' ὁ Νεῖλος καὶ ποταμὸς εἶναι οὐκ ἀνέχεται ἀλλὰ καὶ ἐξανίσταται τῆς ὄχθης καὶ θαλασσώσας τὴν Αἴγυπτον τῇ παρόδῳ γεωργεῖ τὰς ἀρούρας. Διὸ πιεῖν τ' ἐστὶ γλυκύτατος, ἅτ' ἐξ ὄμβρων οὐρανίων χορηγούμενος καὶ θιγεῖν προσηνέστατος, οὐκ ἔτι μὲν θερμὸς ὡς ὅθεν ἤρξατο, ἔτι δὲ χλιαρὸς ὡς ἐκεῖθεν ἀρξάμενος. Δι' ἣν αἰτίαν καὶ μόνος ποταμῶν αὔρας οὐκ ἀναδίδωσι, πάντως ἂν, ὡς τὸ εἰκὸς, ἀναδοὺς, εἰ, καθώς τινες ἐβουλήθησαν, ὡς πυνθάνομαι, τῶν παρ' Ἕλλησιν εὐδοκίμων, χιόνος τηκομένης τὸ πλήρωμα ἐλάμβανε.

ΚΘ'. Ταῦτά μου καὶ τοιαῦτα διεξιόντος, ὁ ἱερεὺς τοῦ Πυθίου γνώριμος ἐμοὶ γεγονὼς ἐς τὰ μάλιστα, Χαρικλῆς ὄνομα ἦν αὐτῷ, Θαυμασίως, ἔφη, λέγεις· καὶ ταύτῃ τῇ γνώμῃ προστίθεμαι καὶ αὐτὸς, οὕτω καὶ παρὰ τῶν ἐν Καταδούποις ἱερέων τοῦ Νείλου πυθόμενος. Κἀγὼ πρὸς αὐτὸν, ὦ Χαρίκλεις, ἔφην, ἦλθες γὰρ κἀκεῖσε; Ἦλθον, εἶπε, ὦ σοφὲ Καλάσιρι. Τί

condense, are resolved into water, and fall in torrents of rain. The Nile swells, and, disdainfully overflowing its banks, is no longer a river, but a sea, which spreads over Egypt, and fertilises the plains over which it flows. This is the reason why its waters are so pleasant to drink, since they are composed of the rain from heaven, and are soft to the touch; although they are not so hot as they are at its source, they are nevertheless tepid. This explains why the Nile is the only river which exhales no vapours; whereas it would certainly do so, if it were true, as some learned men amongst the Greeks have asserted, that its rise is owing to the melting of the snows.

XXIX. "While I was giving these explanations, the priest of Apollo, whose name was Charicles, and an intimate friend of mine, said to me: 'What you say is perfectly correct, and I am inclined to share your opinion, according to what I have heard from the priests of the Nile at the cataracts.' 'What!' said I to him, 'have you been there?' 'Yes,' he replied. 'And

what necessity drove you thither?' 'A domestic misfortune, which turned out the cause of my happiness.' When I expressed my astonishment, he said: 'You will not be astonished when you hear how it happened; and you shall hear whenever you please.' 'You may speak at once,' I answered; 'I am ready to hear you.' 'Listen, then,' said Charicles, after he had dismissed the crowd; 'for I have long desired to confide to you the story of my adventures, and that from an interested motive.

"'After my marriage I remained for a long time without children. At last, when I was advanced in years, the God, who had long been wearied by my supplications, permitted me to become the father of a girl, but at the same time predicted that I should have no reason to rejoice that she had been born. When she was old enough to be married, I gave her to the one of her numerous suitors whom I thought most worthy of her; but, the very night of her wedding, when she was in bed with her husband, the unhappy woman was burnt either by fire from heaven

θαλάμοις ἐμπεσόντος. Καὶ τὸν ὑμέναιον ᾀδόμενον ἔτι διεδέχετο θρῆνος καὶ ἀπὸ τῶν παστάδων ἐπὶ τὸ μνῆμα παρεπέμπετο καὶ δᾷδες αἱ τὸ γαμήλιον ἐκλάμψασαι φῶς αὗται καὶ τὴν ἐπικήδειον πυρκαϊὰν ἐξῆπτον. Ἐπετραγῴδει τούτῳ τῷ δράματι καὶ ἕτερον πάθος ὁ δαίμων καὶ τὴν μητέρα μοι τῆς παιδὸς ἀφαιρεῖται τοῖς θρήνοις ἐγκαρτερήσασαν, τὸ δὲ θεήλατον τοῦ κακοῦ μὴ φέρων, ἐμαυτὸν μὲν οὐκ ἐξάγω τοῦ βίου, τοῖς θεολογοῦσιν ὡς ἀθέμιτον τὸ πρᾶγμα πειθόμενος, ὑπεξάγω δὲ τῆς ἐνεγκούσης καὶ τὴν ἐρημίαν τῆς οἰκίας ἀποδιδράσκω. Μέγα γὰρ εἰς λήθην κακῶν ἡ δι' ὀφθαλμῶν τῆς ψυχῆς ὑπόμνησις ἀμαυρουμένη. Καὶ πολλοῖς ἐμπλανηθεὶς τόποις, ἦλθον δὴ καὶ εἰς τὴν σὴν Αἴγυπτον καὶ Καταδούπους αὐτούς, καθ' ἱστορίαν τῶν καταρρακτῶν τοῦ Νείλου.

Λ'. Τῆς μὲν οὖν ἀφίξεως τῆς ἐκεῖσε ἔχεις τὸν ἀπολογισμόν, ὦ φίλος, ἣν δέ σε βούλομαι παρενθήκην γνῶναι τοῦ διηγήματος, μᾶλλον δ'

or by accident. The marriage-song, the strains of which had not yet ceased, was succeeded by lamentation; she passed from the marriage-chamber to the tomb, and the torches which had illuminated the wedding procession lighted up the funeral pile. To this tragic event the gods added a fresh misfortune; my wife succumbed to her grief. Incapable of resisting the misfortunes with which the Deity thus overwhelmed me, I would not, however, lay violent hands upon myself, so as not to disobey the interpreters of the divine law, who teach us that this is forbidden. I left my native land, and fled from the loneliness and desolation of my house. For nothing is better calculated to make us forget our misfortunes than to leave those objects the sight of which reawakens the sorrows of the soul. After having wandered through many countries, I also came to your Egypt and Catadupa,[1] to visit the cataracts of the Nile.

XXX. "'Now that I have explained to you the reasons for my journey to Egypt, I must now enter upon a digression,

[1] The name of the district of the Cataracts, as well as of the Cataracts themselves.

ἀληθέστερον εἰπεῖν, αὐτὸ δὴ τὸ κεφάλαιον,
ἀλύοντί μοι κατὰ τὴν πόλιν καὶ διατιθεμένῳ
σχολὴν, καί τινα τῶν παρ' Ἕλλησι σπανίων
ὠνουμένῳ, (ἤδη γάρ μοι τῆς λίαν ἀλγηδόνος
τῷ χρόνῳ πεττομένης ἡ πρὸς τὴν ἐνεγκοῦσαν
ἐπάνοδος ἐσπουδάζετο,) ἀνήρ τις πρόσεισι τὰ
μὲν ἄλλα σεμνὸς ἰδεῖν καὶ ἀγχίνοιαν ἀπὸ τοῦ
βλέμματος ἐμφανίζων, ἄρτι μὲν τὸν ἔφηβον
παραλλάξας, τὴν χροιὰν δ' ἀκριβῶς μέλας, καὶ
με ἠσπάζετο καὶ τι βούλεσθαι διαφράζειν
ἔλεγεν, Ἑλληνίζων οὐ βεβαίως. Ἐμοῦ δ' ἑτοί-
μως ὑπακούσαντος, εἴς τινα νεὼν παρακείμενον
εἰσαγαγὼν, Φύλλα τινά σε καὶ ρίζας, ἔφη, τῶν
Ἰνδικῶν καὶ Αἰθιοπικῶν καὶ Αἰγυπτίων ὠνού-
μενον ἑώρακα. Εἰ δὴ οὖν ἀκραιφνῶς ταῦτα
καὶ δόλου παντὸς ἐκτὸς ὠνεῖσθαι βουληθείης,
ἕτοιμος παρέχειν. Βούλομαι, ἔφην, καὶ δείκνυε.
Ὁ δὲ, Ὄψει μὲν, εἶπεν, ὅπως δὲ μὴ μικρολόγος
ἔσῃ περὶ τὴν ἀγοράν. Σαυτὸν παρεγγύα,
ἔφην, μὴ βαρύτερον εἶναι περὶ τὴν διάπρασιν.

although in reality it is my chief reason for telling my story. I was walking one day in the city, to occupy my time and buy some things which could not be procured in Greece (for time had by this time alleviated my excessive grief, and I was anxious to return to my own country), when I was accosted by a man of grave demeanour, whose look betokened shrewdness; his skin was perfectly black, and he had only just reached man's estate. He saluted me, and made me understand, in spite of the difficulty he found in expressing himself in Greek, that he had something to say to me. I willingly agreed to his request, and went with him into a temple in the neighbourhood. He then said to me: "I have seen you buying Indian, Aethiopian, and Egyptian roots and herbs; if you would like to buy some from me, at a fair price, without any cheating, I shall be happy to supply you." "Well," said I, "let me see them." "You are sure to be satisfied, but do not be too hard upon me in regard to the price." "Then you must not be too exorbitant in your de-

Καὶ ὃς ὑπὸ μάλης τι θαλαττίδιον ἔχων, προκο
μίσας ἐπεδείκνυ λίθων πολυτίμων ὑπερφυές τι
χρῆμα· μαργαρίδες τε γὰρ ἐνῆσαν εἰς καρύου
μικροῦ μέγεθος, εἰς κύκλον τ᾽ ἀκριβῶς ἀπαρτι
ζόμεναι, καὶ λευκότητι πλεῖστον ἀγλαϊζόμεναι
σμάραγδοί τε καὶ ὑάκινθοι, αἱ μὲν οἷα λήϊον
ἠρινὸν χλοάζουσαι, ἐλαιώδους αὐτὰς ποιὸς
λειότητος ὑπαυγαζούσης, αἱ δ᾽ ἀπεμιμοῦντο
χροιὰν ἀκτῆς θαλαττίας ὑπ᾽ ἀγχιβαθεῖ σκο
πέλῳ μικρὸν ὑποφριττούσης καὶ τὸ ὑποκεί
μενον ἰαζούσης· καὶ ἁπλῶς συμμιγής τις ἐν
πᾶσιν καὶ ποικίλη μαρμαρυγὴ τὸν ὀφθαλμὸν
εὐφραίνουσα. Ἅπερ ὡς εἶδον, Ἄλλους, ἔφην,
ὥρα σοι, ξένε, τῶνδε ἐπιζητεῖν ὠνητάς, ὡς
ἔγωγε καὶ ἡ κατ᾽ ἐμὲ περιουσία, σχολῇ γοῦν
καὶ ἑνὸς εἴη τῶν ὁρωμένων ἰσοστάσιος. Ἀλλ᾽
εἰ καὶ μὴ πρίασθαι δυνατός, εἶπε, δῶρόν γε
λαμβάνειν οὐκ ἀδύνατος. Ἐγὼ μὲν οὐκ
ἀνίκανος, ἔφην, δῶρόν γε λαμβάνειν, σὺ δ᾽ οὐκ
οἶδ᾽ ὅ τι βουλόμενος παίζεις ἡμᾶς. Οὐ παίζω,
εἶπεν, ἀλλὰ καὶ σφόδρα σπουδάζω καὶ ἐπό
μνυμί γε τὸν ἱδρυμένον ἐνθάδε θεόν, ἅπαντα

mands." He then pulled out a small bag from under his arm, and showed me a quantity of precious stones of very great value. There were some diamonds as big as nuts, quite round, cut with most perfect skill, pure and sparkling ; emeralds and sapphires,[1] the one as green as the corn in spring, with the brilliant lustre of the olive, the other imitating the tints of the sea when it ruffles its surface slightly under shelter of an overhanging rock, and tinges with purple the objects beneath it. In a word, the stones were of varied brilliancy, and enchanted the eye. When I saw them, I said: "You had better find other purchasers for these; as for me, all that I possess would scarcely be sufficient to pay for one of them." " But, if it is not possible for you to buy them, you can at least receive them as a present." " Certainly ; I am perfectly ready to receive them as a present, but I cannot understand why you are jesting with me." " I am not jesting," he replied; " I am in earnest; I swear by the god who presides over this temple that I will give all these stones,

[1] The identity of these stones is a matter of discussion.

δώσειν, εἰ πρὸς τούτοις καὶ ἕτερον δῶρον ὑποδέξασθαι βουληθείης, πολὺ τούτων ἐριτι- μότερον. Ἐγέλων πρὸς ταῦτα. Τοῦ δὲ τὴν αἰτίαν πυνθανομένου· Ὅτι γελοῖον, ἔφην, εἰ τηλικαῦτα δῶρα καθυπισχνούμενος προσέτι καὶ μισθὸν ἐπαγγέλλῃ, πολὺ τῶν δώρων αὐτῶν ὑπερφέροντα. Πίστευε, εἶπεν, ἀλλ᾽ ἐπόμνυε καὶ αὐτὸς ἦ μὴν ἄριστα χρήσεσθαι τῷ δώρῳ καὶ ὡς ἂν αὐτὸς ὑφηγήσωμαι. Ἐθαύμαζον μὲν, ἀπορῶν, ἐπώμνυον δὲ, τηλικαῦτα ἐλπίζων. Ἐπειδὴ δέ μοι ὀμώμοστο, ὡς ἐκεῖνος ἐπέσκηπ- τεν, ἄγει με παρ᾽ αὐτὸν καὶ δείκνυσι κόρην ἀμήχανόν τι καὶ δαιμόνιον κάλλος, ἣν αὐτὸς μὲν ἑπταέτιν γεγονέναι ἔλεγεν, ἐμοὶ δὲ καὶ ὥρᾳ γάμου πλησιάζειν ἐῴκει. Οὕτως ἄρα κάλλους ὑπερβολὴ καὶ εἰς μεγέθους ἔμφασιν φέρει προσθήκην. Κἀγὼ μὲν ἀχανὴς εἱστήκειν ἀγνοίᾳ τε τῶν γιγνομένων καὶ ἀκορέστῳ θέα τῶν ὁρωμένων.

ΛΑ΄. Ὁ δ᾽ ἄρχεται λόγων τοιῶνδε· Ταύτην, ἣν ὁρᾷς, ξένε, φησὶν ἡ μὲν τεκοῦσα δι᾽ αἰτίαν

if you will agree to accept in addition an even still more valuable present." At these words I began to laugh, and, when he asked me the reason, I replied : " It seems to me absurd that, in order to make me accept these valuable gifts, you should offer me, as an inducement, a present of even greater value." " You may take my word," he said; " only you must swear, on your part, that you will make the best use of this gift, and will follow my instructions." In my astonishment, I hardly knew what to do; but at last I took an oath to him, allured by the hope of such vast wealth. When I had taken the oath, he led me to his house, and showed me a young girl of divine and incomparable beauty. He told me that she was only seven years of age, although she seemed to me old enough to marry, so much did her rare beauty seem to add to her stature. I stood mute with astonishment, unable to understand what it all meant, and enchanted by what I saw.

XXXI. " ' Then my friend addressed me as follows: " This young girl whom you see, O stranger, was exposed in her

17—2

ἣν γνώσῃ μικρὸν ὕστερον ἐν σπαργάνοις ἐξέθετο,
τύχης ἀμφιβολίᾳ τὰ κατ᾽ αὐτὴν ἐπιτρέψασα,
ἐγὼ δὲ προστυχὼν ἀνειλόμην· οὐδὲ γὰρ ἦν μοι
θεμιτὸν ἐν κινδύνῳ ψυχὴν ἅπαξ ἐνανθρωπήσα-
σαν περιιδεῖν. Ἓν γὰρ καὶ τοῦτο παράγγελμα
τῶν γυμνῶν παρ᾽ ἡμῖν σοφῶν, ὧν ἀκουστὴς εἶναι
ὀλίγῳ πρόσθεν ἠξίωμαι. Καὶ ἄλλως καὶ τὸ
παιδίον αὐτόθεν μέγα τι καὶ θεῖον τῶν ὀφθαλ-
μῶν ἐξέλαμπεν· οὕτω μοι περισκοποῦντι, γορ-
γόν τε καὶ ἐπαγωγὸν ἐνεῖδε. Συνεξέκειτο δ᾽
αὐτῷ καὶ λίθων ὅρμος, ὃν ἀρτίως ἐπεδείκνυον
καὶ ταινία τις ἀπὸ σηρικοῦ νήματος ἐξυφασμένη,
γράμμασιν ἐγχωρίοις καὶ διηγήματι τῶν κατὰ
τὴν παῖδα κατάστικτος, τῆς μητρὸς, οἶμαι,
σύμβολα ταῦτα καὶ γνωρίσματα τῇ κόρῃ
προμηθευσαμένης. Ἅπερ ὡς ἀνέγνων, πόθεν
τ᾽ ἐστὶ καὶ τίνος ἔγνων, εἰς ἀγρόν τε κομίζω
πόρρω τῆς πόλεως ἀπῳκισμένον καὶ ποιμέσιν
ἐμαυτοῦ τρέφειν παραδοὺς, μηδενί τε φράζειν
ἐπαπειλήσας, τὰ συνεκτεθέντα κατεῖχον, τοῦ

earliest infancy; her mother, for reasons which you shall learn later, abandoned her to the mercy of Fortune. I found her and adopted her; for it was not permitted me to abandon without assistance a soul which had once formed part of a human body; this is one of the precepts of us Gymnosophists,[1] whose lessons I have for some time been privileged to hear. Besides, it seemed to me that divine light beamed from the eyes of the child, which were fixed upon me with a keen and, at the same time, winning glance. With her was exposed a necklace of precious stones, which I showed you just now; and, upon a silken fillet, the story of the child was traced, in the language and characters of her country; it was no doubt her mother who, in her anxiety, had deposited with her these tokens whereby she might be recognised. What was written told me who she was and the name of her parents. I took her to a country house at some distance from the city, and gave her to my shepherds to bring up, with strict instructions to tell no one. I myself kept the

[1] The naked philosophers of India.

μὴ τινα ἐπιβουλὴν γενέσθαι αὐτὰ τῇ κόρῃ. Τὰ μὲν οὖν πρῶτα οὕτως ἐλάνθανεν. Ἐπεὶ δὲ τοῦ χρόνου προϊόντος ἡ τῆς κόρης ἀκμὴ μείζων, ὡς ὁρᾷς, ἐφαντάζετο τοῦ εἰωθότος, (τὸ κάλλος δ' οὐδ' ἂν ὑπὸ γῆν κρυπτόμενον ἔλαθεν, ἀλλά μοι δοκεῖ κἂν ἐκεῖθεν διαλάμψαι) δείσας μὴ φωτισθείη τὰ κατ' αὐτὴν καὶ ἀπόλοιτο μὲν αὕτη, παραπολαύσω δέ τινος καὶ αὐτὸς ἀηδοῦς, ἐκπεμφθῆναι πρεσβευτὴς παρὰ τὸν Αἰγύπτου σατράπην ἐπραγματευσάμην καὶ ἥκω ταύτην συνεπαγόμενος, διαθέσθαι τὰ κατ' αὐτὴν ἐνθυμούμενος. Καὶ τῷ μὲν ὅσον οὐδέπω περὶ ὧν ἥκω διαλεχθήσομαι, χρηματίσαι γὰρ ἡμῖν τήμερον ἐπηγγείλατο, σοὶ δὲ καὶ θεοῖς τοῖς οὕτως ἐπιτρέψασιν ἐγχειρίζω τὴν κόρην ἐπὶ συνθήκαις ταῖς ἐνωμότως ἡμῖν γενομέναις, ἦ μὴν ἐλευθέραν ταύτην ἔξειν καὶ ἐλευθέρῳ πρὸς

things which had been exposed with her,
for fear they might lead to attempts upon
her life. Thus, at the commencement,
she lived in concealment; but, in the
course of time, as she grew up, and in-
creased in stature and beauty—to such
an extent that, even if she had been
hidden beneath the earth, her charms
could not long have remained concealed—
being afraid that the secret of her life
might become noised abroad, and that,
if any misfortune happened to her, the
result would be disastrous for myself, I
contrived to secure the appointment of
ambassador to the satrap of Egypt. When
I came here, I brought the girl with me,
in order to make all necessary arrange-
ments for her safety. I shall soon dis-
cuss my mission with the satrap, who has
given me an audience for to-day. Mean-
while, I intrust this young girl to your
care and that of the gods who have thus
decided; I place her in your hands on
the conditions agreed upon between us;
namely, that you will always keep her
free as you have received her from my

γάμον ἐκδώσειν ταύτην, ἢν δὴ καὶ αὐτὸς κομίξῃ παρ' ἡμῶν, μᾶλλον δὲ τῆς ἐκθεμένης μητρός. Πιστεύω δέ σε πάντα ἐμπεδώσειν τὰ ὡμολογημένα, τοῖς θ' ὅρκοις ἀποθαρσῶν καὶ τὸν σὸν τρόπον ἐκ πολλῶν τῶν ἡμερῶν ὧν ἐνθάδε διάγεις Ἑλληνικὸν ὄντα τῷ ὄντι περιειργασμένος.

ΛΒ'. Ταῦτά σοι νῦν εἶχον λέγειν ἐπιτετμημένως, καλούσης με τῆς κατὰ τὴν πρεσβείαν χρείας. Τὰ σαφέστερα δὲ καὶ ἀκριβέστερα τῶν κατὰ τὴν κόρην, εἰς αὔριον μυηθήσῃ περὶ τὸν νεὼν τῆς Ἴσιδος ἐντυχών. Ἐποίουν οὕτως καὶ παραλαβὼν τὴν κόρην, ἦγον ἐπικαλύψας ὡς ἐμαυτόν. Κἀκείνην μὲν τὴν ἡμέραν εἶχον ἐν θεραπείᾳ, πολλὰ φιλοφρονούμενος καὶ πολλὴν τοῖς θεοῖς ὁμολογῶν χάριν, αὐτόθεν τ' ἐμαυτοῦ θυγατέρα καὶ ἐνόμιζον καὶ ὠνόμαζον· εἰς δὲ τὴν ὑστεραίαν ἅμα ἡμέρᾳ, λίαν ἐσπουδασμένος ἐπὶ τὸν νεὼν τῆς Ἴσιδος, οὗπερ συνετέτακτό μοι πρὸς τὸν ξένον, ὥρμησα καὶ πλεῖστα ἐμπεριπατήσας, ἐπειδήπερ ἐφαίνετο

hands, or rather, from the hands of the mother who exposed her; and that you will never marry her to anyone but a free man. I believe that you will faithfully carry out our agreement; I put my faith, not only in your oath, but also in your character, which I have carefully studied during the time that you have been in the city, and which I see is truly that of a Greek.

XXXII. "'To-day I ought to have limited myself to this rapid outline, for the affairs of my embassy claim my attention; but if you will meet me at the temple of Isis to-morrow, I will give you full and accurate details concerning the young girl."

"'According to his wishes, I took the young girl, closely veiled, to my house. I spent the day in lavishing affection and caresses upon her; I offered thanks to God; already I looked upon her as a daughter, and called her such. The following morning, at daybreak, I hurried eagerly to the temple of Isis, where I had arranged to meet the stranger. I walked about for some time, waiting for

οὐδαμοῦ, παραγενόμενος εἰς τὰ σατραπεῖα, τῶν Αἰθιόπων τὸν πρεσβευτὴν, εἴ τις ἑώρα, ἐπυνθανόμην. Καί μοί τις ἀπήγγειλεν, ὡς ἐξώρμησε μᾶλλον δὲ ἐξελήλαται, πρὸ ἡλίου δυσμῶν, εἰ μὴ τῶν ὅρων ἐκτὸς γένοιτο θάνατον αὐτῷ τοῦ σατράπου διαπειλήσαντος. Ἐμοῦ δ᾽ ἐρομένου τὴν αἰτίαν, Ὅτι, ἔφη, ὁ ἀπαγγέλλων ἐπέταττεν ἀπέχεσθαι τῶν σμαραγδείων μετάλλων ὡς Αἰθιοπίᾳ προσηκόντων. Ὑπέστρεφον ἀνιαρῶς ἄγαν διατεθεὶς καὶ ὥσπερ οἱ βαρεῖάν τινα πληγὴν εἰληφότες ὅτι δή μοι γνῶναι μὴ ἐξεγένετο τὰ κατὰ τὴν κόρην, τίς καὶ πόθεν καὶ τίνων. Μὴ θαυμάσῃς, εἶπεν ὁ Κνήμων, ἀσχάλλω γὰρ καὶ αὐτὸς οὐκ ἀκούσας, ἀλλ᾽ ἴσως ἀκούσομαι. Ἀκούσῃ, ἔφη ὁ Καλάσιρις.

ΛΓ΄. Νυνὶ δ᾽ ἅπερ ἑξῆς ἐπέραινεν ὁ Χαρικλῆς, εἰρήσεται. Ἐπειδὴ γὰρ, φησὶν, εἰς τὸ δωμάτιον ἦλθον ὑπαντᾷ τέ μοι ἡ παῖς καὶ ἔλεγε μὲν οὐδὲν οὔπω τῆς Ἑλλάδος συνεῖσα

him; and at length, seeing nothing of him,
I went to the satrap's palace and asked
whether anyone had seen the Aethiopian
ambassador. They told me that he had
left, or rather, had been driven out of
the city, the satrap having threatened to
put him to death if he had not crossed
the frontiers by sunset. When I asked
the reason, I was told that his mission
had been to forbid the satrap from work-
ing the emerald mines, which he claimed
as the property of Aethiopia. I went away
deeply grieved, as if someone had dealt
me a violent blow; I was also greatly
disappointed at being thus prevented from
learning who the young girl was, and
the name of her native country and her
parents.' " " Do not feel surprised," said
Cnemon; "I myself am greatly vexed at
not hearing; but perhaps I shall know
later." "You shall," said Calasiris; "in
the meantime, I will continue Charicles's
story.

XXXIII. " ' When I reached my house,
the child came out to meet me. She could
not talk to me, since she did not know

φωνῆς, ἀπὸ δὲ τῆς χειρὸς ἠσπάζετο κἀμὲ πρὸς
τὸ φαιδρότερον ὀφθεῖσα μόνον ἀνίησιν· ἐθαύ-
μαζόν τε, ὅτι καθάπερ οἱ ἀγαθοὶ καὶ εὐγενεῖς
τῶν σκυλάκων, πάντα τινὰ καὶ ἐπ᾽ ὀλίγον
ἐγνωσμένον σαίνουσιν, οὕτω κἀκείνη τῆς ἐμῆς
περὶ αὐτὴν εὐνοίας ὀξέως ᾔσθετο καὶ ὡς πατέρα
περιεῖπεν. Ἔγνων οὖν μὴ ἐνδιατρίβειν τοῖς
Καταδούποις μὴ δή τις καὶ δαίμονος βασκανία
τῆς δευτέρας θυγατρός με στερήσειε· καὶ διὰ
τοῦ Νείλου κατάρας ἐπὶ θάλατταν ἐπιτυχών
τε νεὼς, ἀνηγόμην τὴν ἐπ᾽ οἴκου. Καὶ ἔστι
νῦν ἡ ταῖς ἐνταῦθα σὺν ἐμοὶ, ταῖς μὲν οὖσα
ἐμὴ καὶ ὄνομα τοὐμὸν ὀνομαζομένη, σαλεύω
γὰρ ἐπ᾽ αὐτῇ τὸν βίον καὶ ἔστι τὰ μὲν ἄλλα
καὶ εὐχῆς κρείττων, οὕτω τάχιστα μὲν τὴν
Ἑλλάδα γλῶτταν εἵλκυσε, τάχιστα δὲ εἰς
ἀκμὴν καθάπερ ἔρνος τι τῶν εὐθαλῶν ἀνέδρα-
μεν, ὡραιότητι δὲ σώματος οὕτω δὴ τὰς πάσας
ὑπερβέβληκεν, ὥστε πᾶς ὀφθαλμὸς Ἑλληνικός
τε καὶ ξένος ἐπ᾽ αὐτὴν φέρεται καὶ ὅπου δὴ
φαινομένη ναῶν, ἢ δρόμων, ἢ ἀγορῶν, καθάπερ
ἀρχέτυπον ἄγαλμα πᾶσαν ὄψιν καὶ διάνοιαν

Greek; but she took my hand by way of welcome, and the sight of her cheered my soul. I beheld with astonishment how, like young dogs of good breed which fawn even upon those of whom they have but little knowledge, she had from the very first understood my kindly feelings towards her, and regarded me as her father. I resolved not to stop at Catadupi, for fear some envious spirit might rob me of my second daughter. I accordingly went down the Nile until I reached the sea, where I found a ship to take me back to my native land. The child is now with me; she is my daughter, she bears my name; she is my only support. She has in every respect surpassed my wishes, when I consider how rapidly she has learnt Greek, and her beauty has reached perfection, like a thriving plant. She so surpasses all other girls in beauty, that she attracts the admiration of all, both Greeks and strangers. Wherever she appears, in the temples, in the walks, in the public places, like a perfectly-finished statue, she draws upon herself the eyes and attention of all.

ἐφ' αὑτὴν ἐπιστρέφει. Ἀλλ' αὕτη τοιαύτη τις οὖσα, λυπεῖ με λύπην ἀνίατον. Ἀπηγόρευται παρ' αὐτῇ γάμος· καὶ παρθενεύειν τὸν πάντα μοι βίον διατείνεται καὶ τῇ Ἀρτέμιδι ζάκορον αὐτὴν ἐπιδοῦσα, θήραις τὰ πολλὰ σχολάζει καὶ ἀσκεῖ τοξείαν. Ἐμοὶ δ' ἐστὶν ὁ βίος ἀφόρητος ἐλπίσαντι μὲν ἀδελφῆς ἐμαυτοῦ παιδὶ ταύτην ἐκδώσειν καὶ μάλα γ' ἀστείῳ καὶ χαρίεντι λόγον τε καὶ ἦθος νεανίσκῳ, ἀποτυγχάνοντι δὲ διὰ τὴν ταύτης ἀπηνῆ κρίσιν. Οὔτε γὰρ θεραπεύων, οὔτ' ἐπαγγελλόμενος, οὔτε λογισμοὺς ἀνακινῶν, πεῖσαι δεδύνημαι· ἀλλὰ, τὸ χαλεπώτατον, τοῖς ἐμοῖς (τὸ τοῦ λόγου) κατ' ἐμοῦ κέχρηται πτεροῖς καὶ τὴν ἐκ λόγων πολυπειρίαν, ἣν ποικίλην ἐδιδαξάμην, πρὸς κατασκευὴν τοῦ τὸν ἄριστον ᾑρῆσθαι βίον ἐπανατείνεται, ἐκθειάζουσα μὲν παρθενίαν καὶ ἐγγὺς ἀθανάτων ἀποφαίνουσα, ἄχραντον καὶ ἀκήρατον καὶ ἀδιάφθορον ὀνομάζουσα, Ἔρωτα δὲ καὶ Ἀφροδίτην καὶ πάντα γαμήλιον θίασον ἀποσκορακίζουσα. Πρὸς ταῦτα δὴ σὲ βοηθὸν ἐπικαλοῦμαι καὶ διὰ τοῦτο καιροῦ λαβόμενος

And yet, in spite of all these perfections, she causes me incurable sorrow; she rejects all ideas of marriage, and declares that she will remain a maiden all her life; devoting herself entirely to the service of Diana,[1] she does nothing but hunt and shoot, while my life has become an unbearable burden. I had hoped to marry her to my nephew, an agreeable young man, distinguished by his character and abilities; but her cruel decision has frustrated my desires. Neither attention, nor exhortation, nor argument can persuade her. The most cruel thing of all is, that she turns my own weapons against me. The varied learning with which I have filled her mind is employed by her to prove that the mode of life which she has adopted is the best; she praises virginity to the skies, shows it seated by the side of the immortal gods, calls it pure, free from reproach, and uncorrupted, while she rejects with horror the idea of Love, Venus, and all the pomp and ceremonial of marriage. For this reason I appeal to you for assistance; it is for this reason that I have seized the

[1] As a ζάκορος, or attendant, in her temple.

καὶ ἀφορμῆς τῆς ἐκ ταὐτομάτου πως ἐνδοθείσης, μακροτέρου πρός σε τοῦ διηγήματος ἐδεήθην καὶ δὸς τὴν χάριν, ὦ 'γαθὲ Καλάσιρι. Σοφίαν τινὰ καὶ ἴυγγα κίνησον ἐπ' αὐτὴν Αἰγυπτίαν· πεῖσον ἢ λόγοις ἢ ἔργοις γνωρίσαι τὴν αὐτῆς φύσιν καὶ ὅτι γυνὴ γέγονεν εἰδέναι. Βουλομένῳ δέ σοι τὸ πρᾶγμα ῥᾴδιον, οὔτε γὰρ ἀπρόσμικτος ἐκείνη. πρὸς τοὺς λόγους τῶν ἀνδρῶν ἀλλὰ τὸ πλεῖστον τούτοις συνόμιλος ἐπαρθενεύθη καὶ οἴκησιν οἰκεῖ σοι τὴν αὐτὴν ἐνταῦθα, ἐντός, φημί, τοῦ περιβόλου καὶ περὶ τὸν νεών. Ἱκέτην με γιγνόμενον μὴ περιίδῃς, μηδὲ συγχωρήσῃς ἄπαιδα καὶ ἀπαραμύθητον καὶ διαδόχων ἔρημον ἐν γήρᾳ βαρεῖ διαγαγεῖν· μὴ πρὸς Ἀπόλλωνος αὐτοῦ καὶ τῶν ἐγχωρίων σοι θεῶν. Ἐδάκρυσα τούτων ἀκούων, ὦ Κνήμων, ἐπειδὴ κἀκεῖνος οὐκ ἀδάκρυτον τὴν ἱκεσίαν προσῆγε καὶ ἐπηγγελλόμην, εἴ τι δυναίμην, συλλήψεσθαι.

ΛΔ΄. Καὶ ἔτι περὶ τούτων διασκοπουμένων ἡμῶν, εἰσδραμών τις ἀπήγγειλε τὸν ἀρχιθέωρον τῶν Αἰνειάνων ἐπὶ θύραις ὄντα πάλαι διοχλεῖν

opportunity chance has given me to tell you this story, which I have been unable to make shorter. Wherefore, good Calasiris, grant me this favour: employ against her all the wisdom and enchantments of Egypt; lead her, by word and deed, to the feelings of her sex; make her understand that she is a woman. This will be easy enough for you, if you will; she is by no means averse to talking with men, she has been brought up in their company from her earliest childhood; she lives very close to you, in the sacred precincts of the temple. Do not refuse my prayer; do not let me drag out a melancholy old age, without children, without consolation, without heirs; I entreat you by Apollo himself and the gods of your country.' I shed tears at this story, my dear Cnemon; he himself mingled tears with his supplications; I promised to assist him in any way I could.

XXXIV. "We were still deliberating, when a messenger arrived in haste to announce that the chief of the sacred embassy of the Aenianians had been at the door for some time, and was impatiently asking for

καὶ παρακαλεῖν τὸν ἱερέα παρεῖναι καὶ κατάρχειν τῶν ἱερῶν. Ἐμοῦ δ' ἐρομένου τὸν Χαρικλέα, τίνες οἱ Αἰνεᾶνες, καὶ τίς ἡ θεωρία καὶ ἣν ἄγουσι θυσίαν, οἱ μὲν Αἰνεᾶνες, ἔφη, Θετταλικῆς ἐστι μοίρας τὸ εὐγενέστατον καὶ ἀκριβῶς Ἑλληνικὸν, ἀφ' Ἕλληνος τοῦ Δευκαλίωνος, τὸ μὲν ἄλλο τῷ Μαλιακῷ κόλπῳ παρατεινόμενον, μητρόπολιν δὲ σεμνυνόμενον Ὑπάταν, ὡς μὲν αὐτοὶ βούλονται, ἀπὸ τοῦ [τῶν ἄλλων] ὑπατεύειν καὶ ἄρχειν ὠνομασμένην, ὡς δ' ἑτέροις δοκεῖ, διότι περ ὑπὸ τῇ Οἴτῃ τῷ ὄρει κατώκισται. Ἡ δὲ θυσία καὶ ἡ θεωρία, τετραετηρίδα ταύτην, ὅτε περ καὶ ὁ Πυθίων ἀγὼν, (ἔστι δὲ νυνὶ ὡς οἶσθα) πέμπουσιν Αἰνεᾶνες Νεοπτολέμῳ τῷ Ἀχιλλέως· ἐνταῦθα γὰρ ἐδολοφονήθη πρὸς αὐτοῖς τοῖς τοῦ Πυθίου βωμοῖς ὑπ' Ὀρέστου τοῦ Ἀγαμέμνονος. Ἡ δὲ νυνὶ θεωρία καὶ πλεονεκτεῖ τὰς ἄλλας.

the priest to begin the religious ceremonies.
I asked Charicles who the Aenianians were,
what was the nature of their embassy, and
what sacrifice they were going to offer.
'The Aenianians,' he replied, 'are the chief
people of Thessaly; they are a genuine
Hellenic people, · since they are the de-
scendants of Hellen, the son of Deucalion.
They dwell on the shores of the Malian
gulf, and pride themselves on having
Hypata for their metropolis; this city is
so named, according to them, because it
commands[1] the other cities of the province
and rules over them, or, as others declare,
because it is built at the foot of Mount
Oeta.[2] As for the sacrifice and the sacred
embassy, the Aenianians despatch one
every four years in honour of Neoptolemus,
son of Achilles, at the time of the cele-
bration of the Pythian games, which, as
you know, are now going on. For it was
here, at the foot of the altar of Apollo,
that Neoptolemus was treacherously slain
by Orestes, son of Agamemnon. The
present embassy surpasses all preceding
ones in magnificence: for the head of it

[1] Ὑπατεύει. [2] Ὑπ' Οἴτῃ.

Ἀχιλλείδης γὰρ εἶναι σεμνύνεται ὁ τῆς θεωρίας ἐξάρχων· συνέτυχον γὰρ τῇ προτεραίᾳ τῷ νεανίσκῳ καί μοι ἀληθῶς ἔδοξε τοῖς Ἀχιλλείδαις ἐμπρέπειν, τοιοῦτός ἐστι τὴν μορφὴν καὶ τοσοῦτος ἰδεῖν τὸ μέγεθος, ὡς βεβαιοῦν τῇ θέᾳ τὸ γένος. Ἐμοῦ δὲ θαυμάσαντος καὶ πῶς Αἰνειάνων γένος τυγχάνων, Ἀχιλλείδην αὐτὸν ἀναγορεύει, φήσαντος, (ἡ γὰρ Ὁμήρου τοῦ Αἰγυπτίου ποίησις τὸν Ἀχιλλέα Φθιώτην ἐνδείκνυται), Ὁ μὲν νεανίσκος, ἔφη ὁ Χαρικλῆς, καὶ ὁλοσχερῶς Αἰνειᾶνες τὸν ἥρωα διαγωνίζεται, τὴν Θέτιν ἐκ τοῦ Μαλιακοῦ κόλπου γήμασθαι τῷ Πηλεῖ καὶ Φθίαν τὸ περὶ τὸν κόλπον τοῦτον ὀνομάζεσθαι πάλαι διατεινόμενος, τοὺς δ᾽ ἄλλους δι᾽ εὐδοξίαν τοῦ ἀνδρὸς ἐφελκομένους αὐτοῖς ἐπιψεύδεσθαι. Καὶ ἄλλως δ᾽ αὐτὸν ἐγγράφει τοῖς Αἰακίδαις, Μενέσθιον αὐτοῦ προπάτορα καταφέρων τὸν Σπερχειοῦ παῖδα καὶ Πολυδώρας τῆς ἐκ Πηλέως ὃς καὶ Ἀχιλλεῖ συνεστράτευσεν ἐν πρώτοις ἐπὶ Ἴλιον καὶ τῆς πρώτης τῶν Μυρμιδόνων διὰ τὸ συγ-

boasts that he is descended from Achilles.
I met him yesterday, and he appeared
worthy to be a member of the house of
Peleus ; his beauty, his lofty stature, clearly
show him to be descended from a goddess.'

" I asked with surprise how he, being an
Aenianian, could claim to be a descendant
of Achilles, since the Egyptian Homer,
in his poems, makes Achilles a native of
Phthia. Charicles replied: 'In this the
young man, in common with the rest of
the Aenianians, claims Achilles as his
countryman ; he declares that Thetis,
when she left the Malian gulf, married
Peleus, and that the countries washed by
this gulf formerly bore the name of Phthia ;
that others, allured by the reputation of
Achilles, have falsely claimed the honour
of having given him birth. He is also
descended from Achilles in another way:
he reckons amongst his ancestors Mnes-
theus, the son of Sperchius and Polydora,
daughter of Peleus, one of the most famous
of Achilles' companions at Troy, who, from
his close connection with him, was chief of
the commanders of the Myrmidons. Lastly,

γενὲς ἐξῆρχε μοίρας. Τῷ δ' Ἀχιλλεῖ πάντοθεν
περιφυόμενος καὶ πανταχόθεν αὐτὸν τοῖς
Αἰνείασιν οἰκειούμενος τεκμήριον λαμβάνει
πρὸς τοῖς ἄλλοις οἷς καταλέγει καὶ τὸν ἐνα-
γισμὸν τὸν Νεοπτολέμῳ πεμπόμενον, οὗ
σύμπαντες, ὥς φησίν, Αἰνείασιν ἐξεχώρησαν
Θεσσαλοί, τὸ ἐγγυτέρους εἶναι τοῦ γένους
προσμαρτυροῦντες. Ἐκείνοις μὲν οὖν οὐδεὶς
φθόνος, ἔφην, ὦ Χαρίκλεις ἢ χαρίζεσθαι ταῦτα
ἢ καὶ ἐπαληθεύειν αὐτοῖς, τὸν δ' ἀρχιθέωρον
εἰσκαλεῖσθαι πρόσταξον, ὡς ἔγωγ' αὐτοῦ
μανικῶς ἀνεπτέρωμαι πρὸς τὴν θέαν.

ΛΕʹ. Ἐπένευσεν ὁ Χαρικλῆς. Καὶ εἰσῆλθεν
ὁ νεανίσκος, Ἀχίλλειόν τι τῷ ὄντι πνέων καὶ
πρὸς ἐκεῖνον τὸ βλέμμα καὶ τὸ φρόνημα ἀνα-
φέρων, ὀρθὸς τὸν αὐχένα καὶ ἀπὸ τοῦ μετώπου
τὴν κόμην πρὸς τὸ ὄρθιον ἀναχαιτίζων, ἡ ῥὶς
ἐνεπαγγελία θυμοῦ καὶ οἱ μυκτῆρες ἐλευθέρως
τὸν ἀέρα εἰσπνέοντες, ὀφθαλμὸς οὔπω μὲν
χαροπός, χαροπώτερον δὲ μελαινόμενος,
σοβαρόν θ' ἅμα καὶ οὐκ ἀνέραστον βλέπων,
οἷον θαλάσσης ἀπὸ κύματος εἰς γαλήνην ἄρτι
λεαινομένης. Ἐπεὶ δ' ἡμᾶς τὰ εἰωθότα ἠσπά-
σατο καὶ τῶν ἀμοιβαίων ἔτυχεν, ὥραν εἶναι τοῦ
τὴν θυσία τῷ θεῷ προσάγειν ἔλεγεν, ὡς ἂν

in order to complete his connection with Achilles, whom he claims in a manner as the property of the Aenianians, he appeals, amongst other proofs, to the offering sent to Neoptolemus, an offering which the Thessalians have agreed to leave to the Aenianians, thereby admitting that they are more closely related to him.' ' I do not grudge them that,' said I, 'whether the statement be really true, or due to self-glorification; but call in the ambassador; for I am exceedingly anxious to see him.'

XXXV. "Charicles consented, and the young man came in. There was really something about him that reminded me of Achilles; his proud looks, his head erect, his hair carelessly thrown back over his forehead; his nose revealed an impetuous disposition; his open nostrils freely inhaled the air; his dark blue eyes were at the same time proud and gentle, like the surface of the sea when a storm is succeeded by a calm. He saluted us in the usual way, and we returned his salute. He then told us that the time was come to offer sacrifice to the god, in order that he might

καὶ τὸν ἐναγισμὸν τῷ ἥρωι καὶ τὴν ἐπ' αὐτῷ
πομπὴν κατὰ καιρὸν ἐν δευτέροις ἐπιτελεῖν
ἐγγένοιτο. Γιγνέσθω, ἔφη ὁ Χαρικλῆς. Καὶ
ἀνιστάμενος, Ὄψει· ἔφη πρός με, καὶ τὴν
Χαρίκλειαν τήμερον, εἰ μὴ πρότερον εἶδες.
Συμπαρεῖναι γὰρ καὶ τὴν ζάκορον τῆς Ἀρτέμι-
δος τῇ πομπῇ καὶ τοῖς ἐναγισμοῖς τοῦ Νεοπτο-
λέμου πάτριον. Ἐμοὶ δ' ἡ παῖς, ὦ Κνήμων,
ἑωρᾶτο ἤδη πολλάκις καὶ θυσιῶν συνεφῆπτο
καὶ λόγων ἱερῶν εἴ τί ποτε ἐπύθετο. Ἀλλ'
ὅμως ἐσιώπων τὸ μέλλον ἀπεκδεχόμενος. Καὶ
ἅμα τὴν ὁρμὴν ὡς ἐπὶ τὸν νεὼν ἐποιούμεθα·
πάντα γὰρ ἤδη παρεσκεύαστο τὰ πρὸς τὴν
θυσίαν τοῖς Θετταλοῖς. Ἐπεὶ δ' ἡμεῖς πρὸς
τοῖς βωμοῖς ἐγενόμεθα καὶ ὁ νεανίας ἤδη τῶν
ἱερῶν κατήρχετο, προκατευξαμένου τοῦ ἱερέως,
ἐκ τῶν ἀδύτων ἀναφθέγγεται ἡ Πυθία τοιάδε·

Τὴν χάριν ἐν πρώτοις, αὐτὰρ κλέος ὕστατ' ἔχουσαν,

afterwards have time to accomplish the expiatory sacrifice in honour of the god and to arrange the funeral procession. 'So be it,' said Charicles, getting up. 'You will see Chariclea to-day,' he added to me, 'if you do not already know her; for, according to custom, she will take part in the procession and the funeral ceremonies in honour of Neoptolemus.' I knew the young girl, my dear Cnemon, and had frequently seen her, both when we were taking part in the same sacrifices, and when she came to put some question to me concerning sacred subjects. However, I made no answer, being eager to see what was going to take place next. We immediately directed our steps towards the temple, where the Thessalians had already made all preparations for the sacrifice. When we had reached the altar, the young man commenced the sacred ceremonies, after the priest had uttered a prayer. Then the Pythian goddess, from her inmost shrine, gave forth this oracle : 'Sing, O Delphi, of her who begins with grace and ends with glory[1]; sing of the

[1] Χαρίκλεια, from χάρις and κλέος.

Φράζεσθ', ὦ Δελφοὶ, τόν τε θεᾶς γενέτην,
Οἱ νηὸν προλιπόντες ἐμὸν καὶ κῦμα τεμόντες,
Ἥξοντ' ἠελίου πρὸς χθόνα κυανέην,
Τῇπερ ἀριστοβίων μέγ' ἀέθλιον ἐξάψονται,
Λευκὴν ἐπὶ κροτάφων στέμμα μελαινομένων.

ΛϚ'. Ταῦτα μὲν ὡς ἀνεῖπεν ὁ θεὸς, ἀμηχανία πλείστη τοὺς περιεστῶτας εἰσεδύετο, τὸν χρησμὸν, ὅ τι βούλοιτο φράζειν, ἀποροῦντας. Ἄλλος γὰρ πρὸς ἄλλο τι τὸ λόγιον ἔσπα, καὶ ὡς ἕκαστος εἶχε βουλήσεως, οὕτω καὶ ὑπελάμβανεν. Οὕτω δ' οὐδεὶς τῶν ἀληθῶν ἐφήπτετο. Χρησμοὶ γὰρ καὶ ὄνειροι τὰ πολλὰ τοῖς τέλεσι κρίνονται. Καὶ ἄλλως οἱ Δελφοὶ πρὸς τὴν πομπὴν ἐπτοημένοι, μεγαλοπρεπῶς ηὐτρεπισμένην, ἠπείγοντο, τὰ χρησθέντα πρὸς τὸ ἀκριβὲς ἀνιχνεύειν ἀμελήσαντες.

son of a goddess; when they leave my
shrine, they shall cleave the waves, and
arrive at the countries darkened by the
heat of the sun. There they shall receive
the noble meed of a virtuous life, a snowy
crown on their dusky brows.'

XXXVI. " At this declaration of the
God, those who stood by were greatly
perplexed, and asked one another what
might be the meaning of the oracle; each
interpreted the words in his own way and
explained them in a manner that accorded
with his inclinations. No one, however,
saw their true purport; for oracles, like
dreams, can only be judged after the event.
Besides, the inhabitants of Delphi, struck
with admiration, and eager to see the
sacred procession, which was on a mag-
nificent scale, did not trouble about exactly
understanding the meaning of the oracle.

END OF BOOK II

ΛΟΓΟΣ ΤΡΙΤΟΣ

Δ´. Ἐπεὶ δ᾽ ἡ πομπὴ καὶ ὁ σύμπας ἐναγισμὸς ἐτελέσθη—Καὶ μὴν οὐκ ἐτελέσθη, πάτερ, ὑπολαβὼν ὁ Κνήμων, ἐμὲ γοῦν οὔπω θεατὴν ὁ σὸς ἐπέστησε λόγος, ἀλλ᾽ εἰς πᾶσαν ὑπερβολὴν ἠπειγμένον τῆς ἀκροάσεως καὶ αὐτοπτῆσαι σπεύδοντα τὴν πανήγυριν, ὥσπερ κατόπιν ἑορτῆς ἥκοντα (τὸ τοῦ λόγου) παρατρέχεις, ὁμοῦ τ᾽ ἀνοίξας καὶ κλείσας τὸ θέατρον. Ἐγὼ μὲν, ὦ Κνήμων, ἔφη ὁ Καλάσιρις, ἥκιστά σε τοῖς ἔξωθεν τούτοις βούλομαι ἀσχλεῖν, ἐπὶ τὰ καιριώτερά σε τῆς ἀφηγήσεως καὶ ὧν ἐπεζήτεις ἐξ ἀρχῆς συνελαύνων. Ἐπεὶ δ᾽ ἐκ παρόδου θεωρὸς γενέσθαι βεβούλησαι, σὺ μὲν Ἀττικὸς ὢν κἀκ τούτων οὐ λέληθας, ἐγὼ δέ σοι τὴν

BOOK III

I. "WHEN the ceremony was over, and the procession had gone by——" continued Calasiris. "But," interrupted Cnemon, "it is not yet over for me; your narrative has not yet made me a spectator of it; when I am burning with anxiety to hear the whole story, and to be a spectator of the ceremony myself, you pass me by and treat me like one who has come, in the words of the proverb, too late for the feast; as soon as you have opened the theatre, you shut the doors again." "I did not want to weary you with such details, which have nothing to do with our subject; I was in a hurry to reach the principal part of my narrative, about which you asked me at the commencement; but, since you wish to be a passing spectator of the solemnity (just like an Athenian), I will give you a brief description of the pageant,

τομπὴν ὀνομαστὴν ἐν ὀλίγαις γενομένῳ, αὐτῆς
θ' ἔνεκεν καὶ τῶν ἐξ αὐτῆς ἀποβάντων, ἐπιτεμὼν
διαθήσομαι. Ἡγεῖτο μὲν ἑκατόμβη τῶν
τελουμένων ἀνδρῶν, ἀγροικότερον βίον τε καὶ
στολὴν ἐφελκομένων. Τὸ μὲν ζῶσμα ἑκάστῳ
χιτῶνα λευκὸν εἰς ἀγκύλην ἀνέστελλε, χεὶρ δ'
ἡ δεξιὰ σὺν ὤμῳ καὶ μαζῷ παραγυμνουμένη,
πέλεκυν δίστομον ἐπεκράδαινεν. Οἱ βόες,
μέλανες πάντες, τὸν αὐχένα σφριγῶντες καὶ
πρὸς κύρτωμα μέτριον ἐγείροντες, τὸ μὲν
κέρας ἀπέριττον καὶ ἀδιάστροφον ὀξύνοντες,
ὁ μὲν ἐπίχρυσον, ὁ δ' ἀνθεινοῖς στεφάνοις
διάπλοκον, σιμοὶ τὴν κνήμην καὶ βαθεῖαν τὴν
φάρυγγα τοῖς γόνασιν ἐπαιωροῦντες. Ὁ δ'
ἀριθμὸς ἀκριβῶς ἑκατόμβη καὶ εἰς ἀλήθειαν
τοὔνομα πληροῦντες. Ἐπηκολούθει τούτοις
ἄλλων ἱερείων διάφορον πλῆθος· ἑκάστου ξῴου
γένος ἰδίᾳ καὶ εἰς κόσμον ἀγόμενον αὐλοῦ καὶ
σύριγγος τελεστικόν τι μέλος καὶ καταγ-
γελτικὸν τῆς θυσίας ὑπαρχόντων.

Β΄. Ταύτας τὰς ἀγέλας καὶ τοὺς ἄνδρας

one of the few that has become celebrated, both on its own account and because of the results which followed it.

"At the head of the procession was a hecatomb of victims, led by some of the initiated, men of rustic dress and appearance. Each of them was clad in a white tunic, tied round the waist. The right arm, bare to the shoulder and the breast, brandished a two-edged axe. The oxen, completely black, walked along majestically; their necks were proudly arched; on their foreheads were horns exactly alike, scarcely bent, some gilded, and others adorned with flowers; their feet were broad and short, their dewlaps deep and hanging down as far as the knees. A hundred in number, they formed a true hecatomb. They were followed by a number of victims of different kinds, each walking separately and in order. They proceeded to the accompaniment of flutes and pipes, playing a mystic strain, that heralded the sacrifice.

II. "After the animals and their drivers came some young Thessalian girls, with

τοὺς βοηλάτας, κόραι Θετταλαὶ διεδέχοντο
καλλίζωνοί τε καὶ βαθύζωνοι καὶ τὴν κόμην
ἄνετοι. Διήρηντο δ' εἰς δύο χορούς· καὶ αἱ
μὲν ἔφερον καλαθίσκους, ὁ πρῶτος χορὸς,
ἀνθέων τε καὶ ὡραίων πλήρεις· αἱ δὲ κανᾶ
πεμμάτων τε καὶ θυμιαμάτων κανηφοροῦσαι
τὸν τόπον εὐωδίαις κατέπνεον. Ἠσχόλουν δ'
οὐδὲν εἰς ταῦτα τὰς χεῖρας ἀλλ' ὑπὲρ τῆς
κεφαλῆς ἀχθοφοροῦσαι πρὸς χορὸν στιχήρη
καὶ ἐγκάρσιον ἀλλήλων εἴχοντο, ὡς ἂν βαδίζειν
θ' ἅμα καὶ χορεύειν αὐταῖς ἐγγίγνοιτο. Του
δὲ μέλους αὐταῖς τὸ ἐνδόσιμον ὁ ἕτερος χορὸς
ὑπεσήμαινεν, οὗτος γὰρ τὸν ὅλον ἐπετέτραπτο
μελῳδεῖν ὕμνον. Ὁ δ' ὕμνος ἦν, ἡ Θέτις ἐπῃνεῖτο
καὶ ὁ Πηλεὺς, κἀπὶ τούτοις ὁ ἐκείνων παῖς, καὶ
ὁ τούτου πάλιν. Μετὰ ταύτας, ὦ Κνήμων—
Τί Κνήμων, ἔφη ὁ Κνήμων, πάλιν γάρ με τῶν
ἡδίστων ἀποστερεῖς, ὦ πάτερ, αὐτόν μοι τὸν
ὕμνον οὐ διερχόμενος, ὥσπερ θεατήν με μόνον
τῶν κατὰ τὴν πομπὴν ἀλλ' οὐχὶ καὶ ἀκροατὴν
καθίσας. Ἀκούοις ἂν, ἔφη ὁ Καλάσιρις,
ἐπειδήπερ οὕτω σοι φίλον· εἶχε γὰρ ὦδέ πως·

Τὰν Θέτιν ἀείδω, χρυσοέθειρα Θέτι,

beautiful and deep girdles and flowing hair. They formed two bands; the first carried baskets of flowers and fruits; the second, vessels full of cakes and perfumes which scented the air around. These offerings, being carried on their heads, did not prevent them from using their hands. Arranged in long rows, some straight, the others slanting, holding each other by the hand, they advanced and joined in the dance. The first company gave the key-note of the song; its only duty was to sing the sacred hymn, the subject of which was the praises of Peleus and Thetis, then of their son, and then of Neopto-lemus. After them, my dear Cnemon——"

"No more 'dear Cnemons'; you are cheating me again of a very great pleasure, in not letting me hear the words of the hymn; it seems that you want to make me a mere spectator of the ceremony, instead of an auditor." "Very well, then," replied Calasiris, "if you so desire it, you shall hear; as far as I remember, the words of the hymn were nearly as follows: 'I sing of Thetis, Thetis with

Νηρέως ἀθανάταν εἰναλίοιο κόραν,
Τὰν Διὸς ἐννεσίῃ Πηλέι γημαμέναν,
Τὰν ἁλὸς ἀγλαΐαν, ἀμετέραν Παφίην·
Ἁ τὸν δουριμανῆ τόν τ' Ἄρεα πτολέμων,
Ἑλλάδος ἀστεροπὰν ἐξέτεκεν λαγόνων
Δῖον Ἀχιλλῆα, τοῦ κλέος οὐράνιον,
Τῷ ὑπὸ Πύρρα τέκεν παῖδα Νεοπτόλεμον,
Περσέπολιν Τρώων, ῥυσίπολιν Δαναῶν.
Ἱλήκοις ἥρως ἄμμι Νεοπτόλεμε,
Ὄλβιε Πυθιάδι νῦν χθονὶ κευθόμενε,
Δέχνυσο δ' ὑμναίων τάνδε θυηπολίην·
Πᾶν δ' ἀπέρυκε δέος ἀμετέρας πόλιος.
Τὰν Θέτιν ἀείδω, χρυσόθειρα Θέτι.

Γ΄. Ὁ μὲν οὖν ὕμνος, ὦ Κνήμων, τῇδέ πη συνέκειτο καθόσον ἔχω διαμνημονεύειν. Τοσοῦτον δέ τι ἐμμελείας περιῆν τοῖς χοροῖς καὶ οὕτω συμβαίνων ὁ κρότος τοῦ βήματος πρὸς τὸ μέλος ἐρυθμίζετο, ὡς τὸν ὀφθαλμὸν τῶν ὁρωμένων ὑπερφρονεῖν ὑπὸ τῆς ἀκοῆς ἀναπείθεσθαι καὶ συμπαρέπεσθαι μεταβαινούσαις ἀεὶ ταῖς παρθένοις τοὺς παρόντας, ὥσπερ ὑπὸ τῆς κατὰ τὴν ᾠδὴν ἠχοῦς ἐφελκομένους· ἕως

the golden hair, immortal daughter of
Nereus of the sea, wedded to Peleus by
the will of Jupiter, glory of the seas,
our Venus of Paphos. She it was who
bore the mighty, the hero of battle, the
divine Achilles, whose glory reaches the
heavens. The son of Achilles and Pyrrha
was Neoptolemus, who destroyed the city
of Troy and defended the Greeks. Be
thou propitious to us, O hero, son of
Achilles, blessed Neoptolemus, who here
reposest in the territory sacred to Apollo;
receive this sacrifice favourably and drive
away fear from our city. I sing of Thetis,
Thetis with the golden hair.'

III. "Such, my dear Cnemon, if my
memory does not deceive me, were the
words of the hymn. In the dances there
was such grace and regularity, every
movement was so happily wedded to the
melody of the song, that for a while the
spectators forgot to look, being entirely
abandoned to the pleasure of listening, and
all who were looking on followed the young
girls as they passed in front of them, irre-
sistibly carried away by the delightful

κατόπιν ἐφήβων ἱππικὸν καὶ ὁ τούτων ἵππαρχος ἐκλάμψας, ἀκοῆς κρείττονα πάσης τὴν τῶν καλῶν θέαν ἀπέδειξεν. Ὁ μὲν οὖν ἀριθμὸς τοὺς ἐφήβους εἰς πεντήκοντα συνέταττεν, ἐμέριζε δὲ πέντε καὶ εἴκοσιν ἑκατέρωθεν, μεσεύοντα τὸν ἀρχιθέωρον δορυφοροῦντας. Κρηπὶς μὲν αὐτοῖς ἱμάντι φοινικῷ διάπλοκος ὑπὲρ ἀστράγαλον ἐσφίγγετο, χλαμὶς δὲ λευκὴ περόνῃ χρυσῇ πρὸς τοῖς στέρνοις ἐσφήκωτο, τὴν εἰς ἄκρον πέζαν κυανῇ τῇ βαφῇ κεκυκλωμένη. Ἡ δ' ἵππος Θετταλικὴ μὲν πᾶσα καὶ τῶν ἐκεῖθεν πεδίων τὸ ἐλεύθερον βλέπουσα· τὸν γὰρ χαλινὸν ὅσα μὲν δεσπότην ἠρνεῖτο διαπτύουσα καὶ θαμὰ προσαφρίζουσα, ὡς δὲ τὸν νοῦν ὑφηγούμενον τοῦ ἀναβάτου φέρειν ἠνείχετο· φαλάροις δὲ καὶ προμετωπιδίοις ἀργυροῖς καὶ ἐπιχρύσοις ἐξησκημένη, καθάπερ ἀγώνισμα τῶν ἐφήβων τοῦτο πεποιημένων. Ἀλλὰ τούτους, ὦ Κνήμων, τοιούτους ὄντας

harmony. But, when a band of youths on horseback appeared behind, with a splendidly-attired commander, the magnificent spectacle soon effaced the pleasure of listening. They were only fifty in all, divided into two bodies of five-and-twenty; in their midst was the chief of the sacred embassy under their protection. Their greaves, plaited with purple leather thongs, were tied above the ankle; their white cloaks, with purple borders round the bottom, were fastened with golden clasps over their breasts. All their horses were Thessalian and recalled in their fiery looks the freedom of their native plains; they champed their bits and covered them with foam, as if scorning a master, but nevertheless obeyed the guiding hand of their riders, in whichever direction they turned them; they were adorned with trappings and frontlets, gorgeously bedecked with silver and gold, so curiously wrought that it seemed as if the youths had vied with one another in their efforts.

"But, in spite of the brilliancy and

οὕτως ὑπερεῖδε καὶ παρέδραμεν ἡ τῶν παρόντων
ὄψις καὶ πρὸς τὸν ἵππαρχον (ἦν δὲ τὸ μέλημα
ἐμόν, Θεαγένης) ἅπας ἐπέστρεψεν, ὥστ᾽ ἔδοξας
ἂν ὑπ᾽ ἀστραπῆς τὸ φαινόμενον πρότερον ἅπαν
ἠμαυρῶσθαι, τοσοῦτον ἡμᾶς ὀφθεὶς κατέλαμ-
ψεν, ἱππεὺς μὲν καὶ αὐτὸς καὶ ὁπλίτης τυγχάνων
καὶ δόρυ μελίαν χαλκόστομον ἐπισείων, τὸ δὲ
κράνος οὐχ ὑπελθὼν ἀλλ᾽ ἀπὸ γυμνῆς τῆς
κεφαλῆς πομπεύων, φοινικοβαφῆ χλαμύδα
καθειμένος, ἧς τὰ μὲν ἄλλα χρυσὸς ἐποίκιλλε
τοὺς Λαπίθας ἐπὶ τοὺς Κενταύρους ὁπλίζων,
ἡ περόνη δ᾽ Ἀθηνᾶν ἠλεκτρίνην ἔστεφε, τὴν
Γοργοῦς κεφαλὴν εἰς θώρακα προασπίζουσαν.
Προσέβαλλε δέ τι χάριτος τοῖς γιγνομένοις
καὶ ἀνέμου λιγεῖα ῥιπή· μείλιχον γὰρ ἐπέπνει
τὴν μὲν κόμην ἠρέμα κατὰ τοῦ αὐχένος διαξαί-
νουσα καὶ τοῦ μετώπου τοὺς βοστρύχους
παραστέλλουσα, τῆς δὲ χλαμύδος τὰς ἄκρας
τοῖς νώτοις τοῦ ἵππου καὶ μηροῖς ἐπιβάλλουσα.
Εἶπες ἂν καὶ τὸν ἵππον αὐτὸν συνιέναι τῆς
ὡραιότητος τοῦ δεσπότου καὶ ὡς κάλλος κάλ-
λιστον φέρει τὸν ἡνίοχον αἰσθάνεσθαι· οὕτω
τὸν αὐχένα κυμαίνων καὶ εἰς ὀρθὸν οὓς τὴν
κεφαλὴν ἐγείρων καὶ σοβαρὰν τὴν ὀφρὺν κατὰ
τῶν ὀφθαλμῶν ἐπιδινεύων, ἔφερέ τε καὶ ἐφέρετο

magnificence of this procession, the eyes
of the spectators passed it by in contempt,
and fixed themselves upon the commander,
my charge Theagenes, who seemed to
eclipse all who had hitherto appeared, as
a bright lightning flash eclipses the lesser
fires of heaven, so brilliant was the show
he made. Horseman and foot-soldier at
once, heavily armed, he brandished an
ashen spear with a point of brass, his
beaver up, with face exposed, clad in a cloak
of purple, upon which was embroidered in
gold the combat between the Lapithae and
Centaurs; on the amber buckle that fastened
it was represented the image of Pallas,
holding before her the Gorgon's head on
her shield. A gentle breeze added to his
charms; sweetly breathing, it softly played
with the curls upon his neck, parted his
hair upon his forehead, and made the
borders of his robe float over his charger's
back and legs. It seemed, to look at his
neck arched like the waves, his head erect,
his pricked-up ears, and his fiery, swiftly
glancing eyes, as if the animal himself
were conscious of his master's beauty,

γαυρούμενος, εὐήνιά τε προποδίζων καὶ ἐφ'
ἑκάτερον ὦμον αὐτὸν ἐν μέρει ταλαντεύων,
ἄκραν τε τὴν ὁπλὴν τῇ γῇ λεπτὸν ἐπικροτῶν,
εἰς γαληνὸν κίνημα τὸ βῆμα μετερρύθμιζεν.
Ἐξέπληττε μὲν δὴ καὶ πάντας τὰ ὁρώμενα
καὶ τὴν νικητήριον ἀνδρείας τε καὶ κάλλους
ψῆφον τῷ νεανίᾳ πάντες ἀπένεμον. Ἤδη δ'
ὅσαι δημώδεις γυναῖκες καὶ τὸ τῆς ψυχῆς
πάθος ἐγκρατείᾳ κρύπτειν ἀδύνατοι, μήλοις τε
καὶ ἄνθεσιν ἔβαλλον, εὐμένειαν ἀπ' αὐτοῦ τινα,
ὡς ἐδόκουν, ἐφελκόμεναι. Κρίσις γὰρ αὕτη
μία παρὰ πᾶσιν ἐκρατύνετο, μὴ ἂν φανῆναί τι
κατ' ἀνθρώπους ὃ τὸ Θεαγένους ὑπερβάλλοι
τὸ κάλλος·

Δ΄. Ἦμος δ' ἠριγένεια φάνη ῥοδοδάκτυλος ἠώς,
Ὅμηρος ἂν εἶπεν, ἐπεὶ τοῦ νεὼ τῆς Ἀρτέμιδος
ἐξήλασεν ἡ καλὴ καὶ σοφὴ Χαρίκλεια, τότε,
ὅτι καὶ Θεαγένην ἡττηθῆναί ποτε δυνατὸν,
ἐγνώκαμεν, ἀλλ' ἡττηθῆναι τοσοῦτον ὅσον
ἀκραιφνὲς γυναικεῖον κάλλος τοῦ πρώτου παρ'
ἀνδράσιν ἐπαγωγότερον. Ἤγετο μὲν γὰρ

and, proud of his noble form, felt that he carried the noblest rider of all. Proud of the burden which he bore and of the hand which guided him, he moved along freely with reins 'loosely held, balancing himself alternately on either side, lightly skimming the surface of the ground with the extremity of his hoofs, rocking his rider by a regular and gentle motion. All gazed with admiration upon the sight; the masculine features and beauty of the young man conquered all hearts. The women, unable to disguise their feelings, flung him fruits and flowers, in the hope of obtaining a favour from him; in short, all were agreed that Theagenes was the handsomest man who had ever been seen.

IV. " But, when rosy-fingered morn appeared (to use the words of Homer), when the beautiful and accomplished Chariclea left the temple of Diana, then we saw that even Theagenes might be surpassed, but only in the sense that the most perfect beauty is always less graceful and attractive in men than in women. She rode in a chariot drawn by two per-

ἐφ' ἁρμαμάξης ἀπὸ συνωρίδος λευκῆς βοῶν
ὀχουμένη, χιτῶνα δ' ἁλουργῆ ποδήρη χρυσαῖς
ἀκτίσι κατάπαστον ἠμφίεστο. Ζώνῃ δ' ἐπε-
βέβλητο τοῖς στέρνοις, (εἰς) ἣν ὁ τεχνησάμενος
[εἰς ἐκείνην] τὸ πᾶν τῆς αὑτοῦ τέχνης κατέ-
κλεισεν, οὔτε πρότερόν τι τοιοῦτον χαλκευσά-
μενος, οὔτ' αὖθις δυνησόμενος. Δυοῖν γὰρ
δρακόντοιν τὰ μὲν οὐραῖα κατὰ τῶν μεταφρένων
ἐδέσμευε, τοὺς δ' αὐχένας ὑπὸ τοὺς μαζοὺς
παραμείψας καὶ εἰς βρόχον σκολιὸν διαπλέξας
καὶ τὰς κεφαλὰς διολισθῆσαι τοῦ βρόχου
συγχωρήσας, ὡς περίττωμα τοῦ δεσμοῦ κατὰ
πλευρὰν ἑκατέραν ἀπῃώρησεν. Εἶπες ἂν τοὺς
ὄφεις οὐ δοκεῖν ἕρπειν ἀλλ' ἕρπειν, οὐχ ὑπὸ
βλοσυρῷ καὶ ἀπηνεῖ τῷ βλέμματι φοβεροὺς
ἀλλ' ὑγρῷ κώματι διαρρεομένους, ὥσπερ ἀπὸ
τοῦ κατὰ τὰ στέρνα τῆς κόρης ἱμέρου κατευνα-
ζομένους. Οἱ δ' ἦσαν τὴν μὲν ὕλην χρυσοῖ, τὴν
δὲ χροιὰν κυάνεοι. Ὁ γὰρ χρυσὸς ὑπὸ τῆς
τέχνης ἐμελαίνετο ἵνα τὸ τραχὺ καὶ μεταβάλ-
λον τῆς φολίδος τῷ ξανθῷ τὸ μέλαν συγκραθὲν
ἐπιδείξηται. Τοιαύτη μὲν (οὖν) ἡ ζώνη τῆς
κόρης. Ἡ κόμη δὲ, οὔτε πάντῃ διάπλοκος,

fectly white oxen; a purple cloak, embroidered with gold, enveloped her down to her feet. Round her waist was a girdle, a masterpiece of work, the like of which never had been, and never would be seen. It represented two serpents, the tails of which were intertwined over her back; their necks, brought beneath her bosom, formed by their interlacing a graceful knot, from the midst of which their heads hung down on one side and the other as an appendage; you would have said that the serpents not only appeared to climb, but really did so; so life-like were they. Their aspect was neither frightful nor alarming; they rather seemed to be buried in a languid sleep and lulled by the pleasure of reposing upon the young girl's bosom. They were wrought in dark-coloured gold, which had been artificially blackened, in order to represent, by this mixture of black and gold colour, the roughness and changing appearance of the scales. Such was the maiden's girdle. Her hair was not completely tressed up, nor quite unconfined;

οὔτ' ἀσύνδετος, ἀλλ' ἡ μὲν πολλὴ καὶ ὑπαυχένιος, ὤμοις τε καὶ νώτοις ἐπεκύμαινε, τὴν δ' ἀπὸ κορυφῆς καὶ τοῦ μετώπου δάφνης ἁπαλοὶ κλῶνες ἔστεφον, ῥοδοειδῆ τε καὶ ἡλιῶσαν διαδέοντες καὶ σοβεῖν ταῖς αὔραις ἔξω τοῦ πρέποντος οὐκ ἐφιέντες. Ἔφερε δὲ τῇ λαιᾷ μὲν τόξον ἐπίχρυσον, ὑπὲρ ὦμον τὸν δεξιὸν τῆς φαρέτρας ἀπηρτημένης, θατέρᾳ δὲ λαμπάδιον ἡμμένον καὶ οὕτως ἔχουσα πλέον ἀπὸ τῶν ὀφθαλμῶν σέλας ἢ τῶν δάδων ἀπηύγαζεν. Οὗτοι ἐκεῖνοι Χαρίκλεια καὶ Θεαγένης, ἀνεβόησεν ὁ Κνήμων. Καὶ ποῦ γῆς οὗτοι, δείκνυε, πρὸς θεῶν ἱκετεύων ὁ Καλάσιρις, ὁρᾶσθαι αὐτοὺς τῷ Κνήμωνι προσδοκήσας. Ὁ δὲ, Ὦ πάτερ, θεωρεῖν αὐτοὺς καὶ ἀπόντας ᾠήθην, οὕτως ἐναργῶς τε καὶ οἵους οἶδ' ἰδὼν ἡ παρὰ σοῦ διήγησις ὑπέδειξεν. Οὐκ οἶδα, εἶπεν, εἰ τοιούτους εἶδες, οἵους αὐτοὺς κατ' ἐκείνην τὴν ἡμέραν ἡ Ἑλλάς τε καὶ ὁ ἥλιος ἐθεάσαντο,

the greater part of it, flowing down her neck, waved luxuriantly over her back and shoulders; tender branches of laurel, intertwined with the locks on her forehead and crown, formed a kind of garland, in which the freshness of the rose mingled with the dazzling reflection of the sun, and prevented her tresses from floating too freely in the breeze. In her left hand she held a bow; a quiver hung over her right shoulder; in her right hand she carried a lighted torch, the brightness of which paled before the brilliancy of her eyes." "It is certainly they, Theagenes and Chariclea," cried Cnemon. "And where are they? Show them to me, in Heaven's name, I implore you," said Calasiris, believing that Cnemon saw them at that moment. "My father," replied Cnemon, "I only thought that I saw them, although in their absence; so faithfully have you described them as I knew them." "I do not know," continued Calasiris, "whether you have seen them such as Greece and the sun beheld them on that day, in all their splendour,

ὅτι μὲν περιβλέπται, ὅτε δ᾽ οὐδαμου
ζεμένας, καὶ τὴν μὲν ἀνδράσι, τὰς δὲ γυναιξὶ
ἀχρὶ γηραιάσι. Τῷ γὰρ πρὸς θάτερα
αὐτῶν συζυγίαν ἴσα καὶ ἰδιωσίαν ἔχει, πλὴν
ὅσα τὰ μὲν νεανίαι εἰ ἐγχύρσαι, τὴν ὥραν
δ᾽ αἱ θετταλαὶ πλέον ἐδαίμαξα, ὁ τρῖτον
ἔβλετον ἑκάτερα, μᾶλλον ἐγάρσαι. Ἐδὴ
γὰρ ὄψις τῆς συνήθας ἐταιμότερα ὡς
ἀπλήξω. Ἀλλ᾽ ὁ τῆς ἡλίας ἀκέτης, ὁ τῆς
γλυκείας οὔσας, ὅτας με ἀνεττέρωσε, ὁρῶ
τοὺς φιλτάτους καὶ δειπνέσαι προσδεσθεὶς
ὁ Κνήμων. Σὺ δέ με καὶ τοῦτέτοιον ἕνεκα
ἐξαπατᾷς. Ἥξειν γὰρ αὐτοὺς ὅσω οὐδέπω
καὶ φανήσεσθαι παρὰ τὴν ἀρχὴν τοῦ λόγου
διεγγυώμενος ἐπὶ τούτοις καὶ μισθὸν τὴν
κατ᾽ αὐτοὺς ὑφήγησιν αἰτήσας, ἑσπέρας οὔσης
ἤδη καὶ νυκτὸς, οὐδαμοῦ δεικνύσαι παρόντας
ἔχεις. Καὶ ὃς, Θάρσει, ἔφη, καὶ θυμὸν ἔχε
ἀγαθὸν, ὡς ἐκείνων ἀληθῶς ἡξόντων. Νῦν δ᾽

amidst universal applause—she the object of all men's, he of all women's desires; for there was no one who would not have considered it immortality to be united to one or the other. But, while the inhabitants more particularly admired the young man, the Thessalians favoured the maiden, each being most struck with the one whom he saw for the first time. For that which is novel strikes the eyes with greater effect than that with which we are familiar. But, what a sweet illusion, what a delightful anticipation! how you made my heart flutter with hope, when I thought that you saw, and intended to show me those beloved children! And now it seems that you have completely deceived me! You assured me, at the commencement of our conversation, that they would be here directly; it was for this that you demanded my story as a reward; already evening and night are come upon us, and they are not here; you are unable to show them to me." "Do not be uneasy," he replied, "be of good cheer, they will certainly come; no doubt something has

ἴσως τι κώλυμα γέγονε καὶ βράδιον ἢ κατὰ τὰ
συγκείμενα ἀφικνοῦνται. Καὶ ἄλλως οὐδ' ἂν
παρόντας ἔδειξα, μὴ τὸ πᾶν τοῦ μισθοῦ κομισά-
μενος· ὥστ' εἰ σπεύδεις τὴν θέαν, πλήρου τὴν
ἐπαγγελίαν καὶ εἰς τέλος ἄγε τὴν διήγησιν.
Ἐγὼ μὲν, εἶπεν, ἄλλως τ' ὀκνῶ τὸ πρᾶγμα
πρὸς ὑπόμνησίν με τῶν λυπούντων ἄγον καὶ
σὲ ἀποκναίειν ᾠήθην, ἀδολεσχίᾳ τοσαύτῃ
προσκορῆ γεγενημένον. Ἐπεὶ δὲ φιλήκοός τις
εἶναί μοι φαίνῃ καὶ καλῶν ἀκουσμάτων ἀκόρεσ-
τος, φέρε, ὅθεν ἐξέβην, τὸν λόγον εἰσβάλλωμεν,
ἁψάμενοί τε λύχνον πρότερον καὶ τὰ κοιταῖα
τοῖς νυχίοις θεοῖς ἐπισπείσαντες ὡς ἂν, τῶν
εἰωθότων τετελεσμένων, ἐννυκτερεύειν ἡμῖν ἐπ'
ἀδείας τοῖς διηγήμασιν ἐγγίγνοιτο.

Ε'. Ταῦτ' εἶπε καὶ λύχνος θ' ἡμμένος
εἰσεφέρετο θεραπαινίδι, τοῦτο τοῦ πρεσβύτου
προστάξαντος, καὶ τὴν σπονδὴν ἀπέχειν,
ἄλλους τε τῶν θεῶν, καὶ τὸν Ἑρμῆν ἐπὶ πᾶσιν

detained them and prevented them from arriving as soon as we had agreed. Besides, even if I have not yet shown them to you, neither have I received my reward in full; if, then, you are in a hurry to see them, carry out your promise and finish your story." "I rather shrink from the last part of it," said Calasiris, "both on my own account, by reason of the melancholy recollections which it awakens, and also on yours, because I am afraid of wearying you by my interminable story. But, since you seem a patient listener, and eager to hear stories that are worth telling, I will resume my narrative at the place where I left off. But first let us light a lamp, and offer the evening libations to the gods of night,[1] in order that, having performed this sacred duty, we may continue our narrative with perfect safety through the night."

V. With these words, the old man gave orders to a servant, who brought a lighted lamp; and he immediately proceeded to pour libations, to invoke the gods, and, before all, Mercury, whom he begged to

[1] *Literally*, "take the last cup before going to bed."

ἐπικαλούμενος, εὐόνειρόν τ' ᾔτει τὴν νύκτα καὶ
φανῆναι αὐτῷ τοὺς φιλτάτους κατὰ γοῦν τὸν
ὕπνον ἱκέτευε. Καὶ τούτων τετελεσμένων,
Ἐπειδὴ τοίνυν ἔφη, Ὦ Κνήμων, τὸ μνῆμα τοῦ
Νεοπτολέμου περιεστοιχίσατο ἡ πομπὴ καὶ
τρίτον οἱ ἔφηβοι τὴν ἵππον περιήλασαν,
ὠλόλυξαν μὲν αἱ γυναῖκες, ἠλάλαξαν δ' οἱ
ἄνδρες, τόθ' ὥσπερ ὑφ' ἑνὶ συνθήματι, βόες,
ἄρνες, αἶγες, ἱερεύοντο, καθάπερ μιᾷ χειρὶ
πᾶσι τῆς σφαγῆς ἐπενεχθείσης· βωμόν τε
παμμεγέθη σχίζαις μυρίαις φορτώσαντες καὶ
τὰ νενομισμένα τῶν ἱερείων ἄκρα πάντα ἐπι-
θέντες, κατάρχειν τῆς σπονδῆς τὸν ἱερέα τοῦ
Πυθίου καὶ τὸν βωμὸν ἀνάπτειν ἠξίουν. Ὁ δὲ
Χαρικλῆς τὴν μὲν σπονδὴν αὐτῷ προσήκειν
ἔλεγε, τὸν δὲ βωμὸν ὁ τῆς θεωρίας ἄρχων
ἁπτέτω παρὰ τῆς ζακόρου τὴν δᾷδα κομισά-
μενος· τοῦτο γὰρ ἔθος ὁ πάτριος γιγνώσκει
νόμος. Ταῦτ' εἶπε καὶ ὁ μὲν ἔσπενδε, τὸ πῦρ
δὲ Θεαγένης ἐλάμβανεν. Ὅτε, ὦ φίλε Κνήμων,

keep away from him unpleasant dreams, and to let him see, at least in sleep, those whom he so dearly loved. After this, he continued his story as follows: "After the procession had compassed the tomb of Neoptolemus and the young men had thrice ridden round it, the women uttered mournful cries, and the men raised war-like shouts. Immediately, as at a given signal, oxen, rams and goats were slaughtered; it seemed as if they had all been put to death by a single hand. An enormous altar was covered with a heap of fragments of wood, and, after the consecrated portions of the victims had been placed on the top, they begged the priest of Apollo to begin the libations and set light to the fire beneath the altar. Charicles replied that it was really his duty to pour the libations; but that the chief of the sacred embassy ought to light the fire with the torch which the priestess should hand to him, according to custom. With these words, he poured the libation, and Theagenes received the torch from Chariclea. Then, my dear Cnemon, what took

καὶ ὅτι θεῖον ἡ ψυχὴ καὶ συγγενὲς ἄνωθεν τοῖς ἔργοις ἐπιστούμεθα. Ὁμοῦ τε γὰρ ἀλλήλους ἑώρων οἱ νέοι καὶ ἥρων, ὥσπερ τῆς ψυχῆς ἐκ πρώτης ἐντεύξεως τὸ ὅμοιον ἐπιγνούσης καὶ πρὸς τὸ κατ᾽ ἀξίαν οἰκεῖον προσδραμούσης. Πρῶτον μὲν γὰρ ἀθρόον τι καὶ ἐπτοημένον ἔστησαν καὶ τὴν δᾷδα σχολαίτερον ἡ μὲν ἐνεχείριζεν, ὁ δ᾽ ὑπεδέχετο καὶ τοὺς ὀφθαλμοὺς ἀτενεῖς ἐπὶ πολὺ κατ᾽ ἀλλήλων πήξαντες, ὥσπερ ἤ που γνωρίζοντες ἢ ἰδόντες πρότερον, ταῖς μνήμαις ἀναπεμπάζοντες, εἶτ᾽ ἐμειδίασαν βραχύ τι καὶ κλεπτόμενον καὶ μόνῃ τῇ διαχύσει τοῦ βλέμματος ἐλεγχόμενον· ἔπειθ᾽ ὥσπερ καταιδεσθέντες τὸ γεγονός, ἐπυρρίασαν· καὶ αὖθις, τοῦ πάθους οἶμαι καὶ τὴν καρδίαν ἐπιδραμόντος, ὠχρίασαν· καὶ ἁπλῶς, μυρίον εἶδος ἐν ὀλίγῳ [τῷ χρόνῳ] τὰς ὄψεις ἀμφοῖν ἐπεπλανήθη καὶ μεταβολὴ παντοία χροιᾶς τε καὶ βλέμματος, τῆς ψυχῆς τὸν σάλον κατηγοροῦσα. Ταῦτα δὲ τοὺς μὲν πολλούς, ὡς

place convinced us that there is in our
souls something divine, and that they are in
a manner allied to some higher nature. For,
as soon as they beheld each other, they
loved; it seemed as if their souls had recog-
nised that they were akin, as if, conscious
that they were related by nobility, they
hastened with a bound each towards its
affinity.

"At first they remained dumbfounded and
motionless; she, still holding out the torch,
and he, extending his hand to take it. For
a long time they continued thus, their eyes
fixed upon each other, as if, instead of having
now met for the first time, they had met be-
fore, and were trying to remember where.
Then they smiled, gently and almost imper-
ceptibly, which was only betrayed by the
movement of their eyes; soon, as if ashamed,
they both blushed; and, a moment later,
when passion had reached their hearts, they
grew pale. In a word, a thousand changes
overspread their faces in a moment, a
thousand changes of colour and features
betrayed the agitation of their soul. All
this, as may be imagined, escaped the

εἰκὸς, ἐλάνθανεν, ἄλλον πρὸς ἄλλην χρείαν τε καὶ διάνοιαν ὄντας, ἐλάνθανε δὲ καὶ τὸν Χαρικλέα τὴν πάτριον εὐχὴν καὶ ἐπίκλησιν καταγγέλλοντα. Ἐγὼ δὲ πρὸς μίαν τὴν παρατήρησιν τῶν νέων ἠσχολούμην, ἐξ ἐκείνου, Κνήμων, ἐξ οὗπερ ὁ χρησμὸς ἐπὶ Θεαγένει θυομένῳ κατὰ τὸν νεὼν ᾔδετο, πρὸς ὑπόνοιαν τῶν ἐσομένων ἀπὸ τῶν ὀνομάτων κεκινημένος. Ἀλλ᾿ οὐδ᾿ ἀκριβῶς οὐδὲν ἔτι τῶν ἑξῆς χρησθέντων συνέβαλον.

ς΄. Ἐπεὶ δ᾿ ὀψέ ποτε καὶ ὥσπερ βιαίως τῆς κόρης ἀποσπώμενος ὁ Θεαγένης ὑπέθηκε τὸ λαμπάδιον καὶ τὸν βωμὸν ἀνῆψεν, λέλυτο μὲν ἡ πομπὴ, πρὸς εὐωχίαν τῶν Θετταλῶν τραπέντων, ὁ δ᾿ ἄλλος δῆμος ἐπ᾿ οἶκον τὸν ἴδιον ἕκαστος ἀνεχώρησεν. Ἡ Χαρίκλεια δ᾿ ἐφεστρίδα λευκὴν ἐπιβαλομένη, σὺν ὀλίγοις τοῖς συνήθεσιν ἐπὶ τὴν ἐν τῷ περιβόλῳ τοῦ νεὼ καταγωγὴν ὥρμησεν· οὐδὲ γὰρ ᾤκει σὺν τῷ νομιζομένῳ πατρὶ, τῆς ἀγιστείας ἕνεκα παντοίως

notice of the multitude, whose thoughts and attention were devoted to other matters. Charicles himself, busy in reciting the customary prayer and invocation, saw nothing of it either; but as for me, my whole attention was devoted to watching the young people; for, after I had heard the oracle that had been given to Theagenes, at the time when he was offering sacrifice in the temple, their names awakened in me some suspicion of what was going to happen, although I could not clearly make out the meaning of that part of the prophecy that related to the future.

VI. "At last, Theagenes tore himself away from the maiden, as if under compulsion, placed the torch beneath the altar, and lighted the pile. The procession broke up; the Thessalians repaired to a banquet, and the rest dispersed to their own houses. Chariclea threw a white robe over her shoulders, and retired with some of her companions to her abode in the precincts of the temple; for she did not live with her supposed father, but apart, in order that she might devote herself

αὐτὴν χωρίζουσα. Περιεργότερος τοίνυν, ἐξ ὧν ἠκηκόειν τε καὶ ἑωράκειν, γεγονὼς, ἐντυγχάνω τῷ Χαρικλεῖ τοῦτο σπουδάσας Καὶ ὃς, Εἶδες, ἠρώτα, τὸ ἀγλάϊσμα τοὐμόν τε καὶ Δελφῶν Χαρίκλειαν; Οὐ νῦν πρῶτον, ἔφην, ἀλλὰ καὶ πρότερον πολλάκις [ὁσάκις] δή μοι κατὰ τὸν νεὼν ἐνέτυχεν, οὐχ ὡς ἄν τις ἐκ παρόδου, τοῦτο δὴ τὸ λεγόμενον, ἀλλὰ καὶ συνέθυσεν [οὐκ ὀλιγάκις] καὶ περὶ θείων τε καὶ ἀνθρωπίνων εἴ τί ποτε διαπορήσειεν, ἠρώτησέ τε καὶ ἔμαθε. Τί οὖν δή σοι τὰ νῦν ἔδοξεν, ὦ 'γαθὲ, ἆρά τινα τῇ πομπῇ κόσμον ἤνεγκεν; Εὐφήμησον, εἶπον, ὦ Χαρίκλεις, ὥσπερ καὶ τὴν σελήνην εἰ διαπρέπει τῶν ἄλλων ἀστέρων ἠρώτας. Καὶ μὴν ἐπήνουν τινὲς, εἶπε, καὶ τὸν Θετταλὸν νεανίσκον. Τὰ δεύτερα, ἦν δ' ἐγὼ, καὶ τρίτα νέμοντες, τὴν δὲ κορωνίδα τῆς πομπῆς καὶ ὀφθαλμὸν ἀληθῶς τὴν σὴν θυγατέρα γνωρίζοντες. Ἥδετο τούτοις ὁ Χαρικλῆς, (καί μοι ὁ σκοπὸς ἐκ τῶν ἀληθῶν ἠνύετο, θαρσεῖν μοι τὸν ἄνδρα βουλομένῳ παν-

entirely to the service of the temple. Filled with curiosity by what I had seen and heard, I purposely went to meet Chariles. 'Well,' said he, 'have you seen Chariclea, my pride and the pride of Delphi?' 'Yes, and not for the first time,' I replied; 'I had already frequently met her before in the temple; not merely in passing by, as the phrase goes; she has frequently offered sacrifice with me; she has often questioned me concerning things human and divine, when she came across anything that puzzled her, and I was pleased to assist her.' 'And what did you think of her to-day? Did she add any ornament to the procession?' 'Hush, Chariles; you might as well ask me whether the moon outshines the stars.' 'But some praise was given to the Thessalian youth.' 'Yes, to him was given the second or third place, but all were agreed that your daughter was the pride and crown of the procession.' Chariles was evidently pleased at my words, and, while I told the truth, I attained my object, which was to inspire him with perfect confidence in me. He

τούς) καὶ μαθόντας. Πορεύομαι τὸν ὡς αὐτήν,
ἔλεγον· εἰ δέ σοι φίλον, συμπαρείθητι καὶ μή
τι πρὸς τῆς ὀχλικῆς ἀηδίας ἐπιτέτραπται,
σκετίσαψαι. Χαίρω μὲν ἐπάκσιο, ἀσθανό-
μην δ ὡς ἀσχολίας ἄλλης τραγικώτερον
τίθεμαι τὸ κατ' αὐτόν.

Ζ΄. Ἐπεὶ δὲ παρεγενόμεθα οὗ κατήγετο,
καταλαμβάνομεν εἰσελθόντες ἐπὶ τῆς εὐνῆς
ἀλύουσαν καὶ τοὺς ὀφθαλμοὺς τῷ ἔρωτι δια-
βρόχους. Κἀπειδὴ τὸν πατέρα τὰ εἰωθότα
περιεπτύξατο, πυθανομένῳ τί πεπόνθοι, τῆς
κεφαλῆς ἄλγημα διοχλεῖν ἔλεγεν, ἡδέως τ' ἂν
ἠρεμεῖν, εἴ τις ἐπιτρέποι. Πρὸς ταῦτα δια-
ταραχθεὶς ὁ Χαρικλῆς, ὑπεξῆει τε τοῦ θαλάμου
σὺν ἡμῖν, ἡσυχίαν ταῖς θεραπαίναις ἐπιτάξας,
προελθών τε τῆς οἰκίας, Τί ἄρα τοῦτο, ἔλεγον,
ὦ 'γαθὲ Καλάσιρι; τίς ἡ προσπεσοῦσα τῷ
θυγατρίῳ μαλακία; Μὴ θαύμαζε, εἶπον, εἰ
τοσούτοις ἐμπομπεύσασα δήμοις, ὀφθαλμόν
τινα βάσκανον ἐπεσπάσατο. Γελάσας οὖν
εἰρωνικὸν, Καὶ σὺ γὰρ, εἶπεν, ὡς ὁ πολὺς
ὄχλος, εἶναί τινα βασκανίαν ἐπίστευσας; Εἴπερ

smiled and said to me: 'I am now going to her; if you would like it, do not hesitate to come with me and see whether the crowd and the disturbance have fatigued her.' I gladly consented, giving him to understand that I had nothing more at heart than the wish to oblige him.

VII. "When we reached her room, we found her lying on her couch, in a state of languor and depression, her eyes moist with the tears of love. Her father, having embraced her as usual, asked her what ailed her. She complained of a violent headache, and said that she would like to rest. Then Charicles left the room with me, ordered the servants to keep quiet, and, going out into the front of the house, said: 'What does this mean, my dear Calasiris? What is this languor which has come over my daughter?' 'Do not be surprised,' I replied, 'if, while walking in procession amidst so large a crowd, she has drawn upon her some evil eye.' At these words he smiled ironically: 'And do you also, like the vulgar, believe in the influence of the evil eye?' 'I be-

τι καὶ ἄλλο τῶν ἀληθῶν, ἔφην· ἔχει γὰρ οὕτως.
Ὁ περικεχυμένος ἡμῖν οὗτος ἀὴρ δι' ὀφθαλμῶν
τε καὶ ῥινῶν καὶ ἄσθματος καὶ τῶν ἄλλων
πόρων εἰς τὰ βάθη διικνούμενος καὶ τῶν ἔξωθεν
ποιοτήτων συνεισφερόμενος, οἷος ἂν εἰσρεύσῃ
τοιοῦτο καὶ τοῖς δεξαμένοις πάθος ἐγκατέσπει-
ρεν, ὥσθ' ὁπότ' ἂν σὺν φθόνῳ τις ἴδοι τὰ καλὰ,
τὸ περιέχον τε δυσμενοῦς ποιότητος ἐνέπλησε
καὶ τὸ παρ' αὐτοῦ πνεῦμα πικρίας ἀνάμεστον
εἰς τὸν πλησίον διερρίπισε. Τὸ δὲ, ἅτε λεπτο-
μερὲς, ἄχρις ἐπ' ὀστέα καὶ μυελοὺς αὐτοὺς
εἰσδύεται καὶ νόσος ἐγένετο πολλοῖς ὁ φθόνος,
οἰκεῖον ὄνομα, βασκανίαν, ἐπιδεξάμενος. Ἤδη
δὲ κἀκεῖνα σκόπησον, ὦ Χαρίκλεις, ὅσοι μὲν
ὀφθαλμίας, ὅσοι δὲ τῆς ἐκ λοιμῶν καταστάσεως
ἀνεπλήσθησαν, θιγόντες μὲν οὐδαμῶς τῶν
καμνόντων, ἀλλ' οὐδ' εὐνῆς, οὐδὲ τραπέζης τῆς
αὐτῆς μετασχόντες, ἀέρος δὲ μόνου ταὐτοῦ
κοινωνήσαντες. Τεκμηριούτω δέ σοι τὸν λόγον

lieve in it implicitly, and the following is my explanation of the matter. The air which surrounds us and penetrates into our bodies through the eyes, nose, respiration, and other passages, reaches us charged with external qualities, and, according to the different nature of these qualities, we are variously affected. After that, it is enough for anyone to look at a beautiful object with an envious eye to communicate pernicious qualities to the surrounding air; his breath spreads, full of bitterness, over his neighbour, and, thanks to its subtilty, penetrates to the bones, even to the very marrow. Thus it is that, frequently, this species of envy which has been called by the name of "fascination," affects the health of those whom it attacks. To convince you of this, Charicles, I would ask you to remember that we are frequently attacked by ophthalmia or some contagious disease, without having touched persons afflicted by them, without having been near their bed or sat at the same table with them, but simply because we have breathed the same air. Remember again—

εἴπερ ἄλλο τι καὶ ἡ τῶν ἐρώτων γένεσις, οἷς τὰ ὁρώμενα τὴν ἀρχὴν δίδωσι καὶ οἷον ὑπήνεμα διὰ τῶν ὀφθαλμῶν τὰ πάθη ταῖς ψυχαῖς εἰστοξεύονται. Καὶ μάλα γ᾽ εἰκότως. Τῶν γὰρ ἐν ἡμῖν πόρων τε καὶ αἰσθήσεων πολυκίνητόν τι καὶ θερμότατον οὖσα ἡ ὄψις δεκτικωτέρα πρὸς τὰς ἀπορροίας γίγνεται, τῷ κατ᾽ αὐτὴν ἐμπύρῳ πνεύματι τὰς μεταβάσεις τῶν ἐρώτων ἐπισπωμένη.

Η΄. Εἰ δὲ χρή σοι καὶ παραδείγματος ἕνεκα λόγον τινὰ φυσικώτερον παραθέσθαι, βίβλοις δ᾽ ἱεραῖς ταῖς περὶ ζῴων ἀνάγραπτον· ὁ χαραδριὸς τοὺς ἰκτεριῶντας ἰᾶται καὶ ὁ τοῦτο πάσχων, εἰ τῷ ὀρνέῳ προσβλέποι, τὸ δὲ φεύγει καὶ ἀποστρέφεται τοὺς ὀφθαλμοὺς ἐπιμῦσαν, οὐ φθονοῦν, ὡς οἴονταί τινες, τῆς ὠφελείας, ἀλλ᾽ ὅτι θεώμενος ἕλκειν καὶ μετα-

and there is not a more evident proof—the manner of the birth of love; objects perceived by the sight produce it; they spread around themselves a kind of light mist, and cause the passion, which is to have its abode in the soul, to penetrate through the channel of the eyes. And it is not difficult to see the reason of this: the sight, being the most fiery and mobile of all our senses, is for that very reason most susceptible to the influences around it; and, by reason of its burning spirit, attracts the emanations of love.

VIII. " ' But, if you wish for an example out of natural history, I will give you one out of the sacred books on animals: the Charadrius[1] possesses the property of curing the jaundice; when anyone afflicted with this complaint looks at it, it turns aside, shuts its eyes, and runs away; not, as is sometimes said, because it is unwilling to bestow its assistance, but because, from the moment that an afflicted person looks upon it, it naturally attracts, as it were, a

[1] Supposed to be the "stone-curlew"; so called from dwelling in " clefts" (χάραδραι).

σπᾶν εἰς αὐτὸν ὥσπερ ῥεῦμα πέφυκε τὸ πάθος·
καὶ διὰ τοῦτο ἐκκλίνει καθάπερ τρῶσιν τὴν
ὅρασιν. Καὶ ὄφεων δ' ὁ καλούμενος βασιλίσκος,
ὅτι καὶ πνεύματι μόνῳ καὶ βλέμματι πᾶν
ἀφαναίνει καὶ λυμαίνεται τὸ ὑποπῖπτον, ἴσως
ἀκήκοας. Εἰ δέ τινες καὶ τοὺς φιλτάτους καὶ
οἷς εὖνοι τυγχάνουσι καταβασκαίνουσιν, οὐ
χρὴ θαυμάζειν. Φύσει γὰρ φθονερῶς ἔχοντες,
οὐχ ὃ βούλονται δρῶσιν, ἀλλ' ὃ πεφύκασι.

Θ'. Πρὸς ταῦτα μικρὸν ἐπιστήσας, Τὸ μὲν
ἀπόρημα, ἔφη, σοφώτατα καὶ πιστικώτατα
διέλυσας. Εἴτε δὲ καὶ αὐτὴ πόθου ποτὲ καὶ
ἔρωτος αἴσθοιτο, τότ' ἂν ὑγιαίνειν αὐτὴν, οὐ
νοσεῖν ὑπέλαβον. Οἶσθα, ὡς ἐπὶ τοῦτό σε
καὶ παρεκάλεσα. Νῦν δ' οὐδὲν δέος [εἰ] μὴ
τοῦτο πέπονθεν ἡ μισόλεκτρος καὶ ἀνέραστος,
ἀλλὰ βασκανίαν ἔοικε τῷ ὄντι νοσεῖν καὶ δῆλον
ὡς καὶ ταύτην διαλῦσαι βουλήσῃ, φίλος τ' ὢν

current of the disease; for this reason it avoids the person's eyes, like a dart. It is the same with the serpent called basilisk[1]; you have no doubt heard that its breath and look alone dry up and infect everything that it touches. Nor must we be astonished if some persons fascinate even their dearest friends, those to whom they wish every happiness; for, being naturally envious, they do not do what they wish, but what their nature compels them to do.'

IX. "After a moment's silence, Charicles rejoined: 'You have solved the question in a reasonable and convincing manner; pray Heaven that the fascination which influences her may be that of love; far from considering that a malady, I should think that she was cured. You know that I have already begged your assistance in this. But, for the moment, there seems no reason to suspect this; she is the declared enemy of love and marriage. We must therefore believe that her malady is really due to the evil eye. I do not doubt that you will consent to cure her of it; for you are my friend, and your

[1] Perhaps the Cobra Capello.

καὶ τὰ πάντα σοφός. Ἐπηγγελλόμην
πάσχουσαν αἰσθοίμην εἰς δύναμιν βοηθήσ

Ι'. Καὶ περὶ τούτων ἔτι διασκοπου
ἡμῖν, ἐφίσταταί τις ἐσπουδασμένος κ
'γαθοὶ, φησὶν, ὑμεῖς δ' ὥσπερ ἐπὶ μά,
πόλεμον ἀλλ' οὐκ εὐωχίαν κληθέντες,
μέλλετε, ἣν παρασκευάζει μὲν ὁ κάλλ
Θεαγένης, ἐποπτεύει δ' ὁ μέγιστος ἡρώων
πτόλεμος. Δεῦρ' ἴτε, μηδ' εἰς ἑσπέρ
συμπόσιον παρέλκετε, μόνοι τῶν π
ἀπολειπόμενοι. Προκύψας οὖν μοι πρ
οὖς ὁ Χαρικλῆς, Οὗτος, ἔφη, τὴν ἀπὸ
κλῆσιν ἥκει φέρων· ὡς λίαν ἀπροσδιόνυσ
ταῦτα ὑποβεβρεγμένος. Ἀλλ' ἴωμεν, ὡ
μὴ καὶ πληγὰς ἡμῖν ἐμφορήσῃ τελευτῶν
μὲν παίζεις, ἴωμεν δ' οὖν, ἔφην. Ἐπ
ἐπέστημεν, αὐτοῦ πλησίον τὸν Χαρ
κατέκλινεν ὁ Θεαγένης, ἔνεμε δ' ἄρα τι

learning is vast.' I promised that I would do all that lay in my power to help her, if I found that there was anything the matter with her.

X. "We were still discussing the matter, when a messenger arrived in great haste: 'My good friends,' said he, 'one would think you were invited to a fray instead of a feast, you are so slow in coming. Have you forgotten that it is the handsome Theagenes who has prepared it, and that the greatest of heroes, Neoptolemus, presides at it? Come, then; do not make us wait until evening; we are only waiting for you.' Charicles whispered to me: 'This man's invitation is somewhat rude[1]; he shows no signs of the good manners of Bacchus, although he has imbibed pretty freely. But, let us go, for I am afraid that he may in the end proceed to violence.' 'You are joking,' I said; 'however, let us go.' As soon as we had arrived, Theagenes placed Charicles next to himself, and also treated me with

[1] *Literally*, "he has brought the invitation of the stick."

τιμῆς τοῦ Χαρικλέους ἕνεκα. Τὰ μὲν οὖν ἄλλα τῆς εὐωχίας τί ἂν λέγων ἐνοχλοίην, τοὺς παρθενικοὺς χοροὺς, τὰς αὐλητρίδας, τὴν ἐνόπλιον τῶν ἐφήβων καὶ πυρρίχιον ὄρχησιν, τἄλλα οἷς τὸ πολυτελὲς τῶν ἐδεσμάτων ὁ Θεαγένης διῄτησεν, εὐόμιλόν τε καὶ ποτιμώτερον τὸ συμπόσιον ἀπεργαζόμενος; ἀλλ' ἃ δὴ μάλιστα σοί τ' ἀκούειν ἀναγκαῖον, ἐμοί τε λέγειν ἥδιον, ἐκεῖν' ἦν. Ὁ Θεαγένης ἀνεδείκνυτο μὲν ἱλαρὸς εἶναι, καὶ φιλοφρονεῖσθαι τοὺς παρόντας ἐβιάζετο, ἡλίσκετο δὲ πρὸς ἐμοῦ τὴν διάνοιαν ὅποι φέροιτο· νῦν μὲν τὸ ὄμμα ἠνεμωμένος, νῦν δὲ βύθιόν τι καὶ ἀπροφάσιστον ὑποστένων καὶ ἄρτι μὲν κατηφής τε καὶ ὥσπερ ἐπ' ἐννοίας, ἄρτι δ' ἀθρόον ἐπὶ τὸ φαιδρότερον αὑτὸν μεταπλάττων, ὥσπερ ἐν συναισθήσει γιγνόμενος καὶ αὑτὸν ἀνακαλούμενος καὶ πρὸς πᾶσαν μεταβολὴν ῥᾳδίως ὑποφερόμενος. Διάνοια γὰρ ἐρῶντος, ὅμοιόν τι καὶ μεθύοντος, εὔτρεπτόν τε καὶ οὐδεμίαν ἕδραν ἀνεχόμενον, ἅτε τῆς ψυχῆς ἀμφοτέροις ἐφ' ὑγροῦ τοῦ πάθους σαλευούσης. Διὸ καὶ πρὸς μέθην ὁ

respect for his sake. But why need I weary you with lengthy details of the feast, the dances of maidens, the music, the Pyrrhic dance of the youths in armour, and other entertainments with which Theagenes graced his magnificent banquet, and the exquisite dishes which rendered the repast more agreeable and conduced to conviviality? I will, however, tell you things which it is necessary you should know, and which it will give me pleasure to relate. Theagenes assumed a look of cheerfulness, and forced himself to entertain the company, but I saw in what direction his thoughts were tending. He kept rolling his eyes; from time to time he heaved a deep sigh without any apparent reason; at one time dejected and deep in thought, he suddenly became more cheerful, as if he were conscious of his manner and wished to recover himself; in short, he passed rapidly from one extreme to the other. The mind of a lover, like that of a drunken man, is changeable and inconstant; both seem to be tossed upon the waves of passion; wherefore a lover is

ἐρῶ καὶ πρὸς τὸ ἐρῶ ὁ μῦθος ἐπίφορος.

ΙΔ'. Ὡς δὲ καὶ χύσεως ἐφαπτομένης ἀπέτλεως ἐφαίνετο, τότε δὴ καὶ τοῖς ἄλλοις τῶν παρόντων κατάδηλος ἦν οὐχ ὑγιαίνων· ὥστε καὶ τὸν Χαρικλέα, καθορᾶτότε ἀλλ᾿ ἦ τὸ ἀνώμαλον, ἰσυχῇ πρός με εἰπεῖν, Καὶ τοῦτον βάσκανος εἶδεν ὀφθαλμός· καὶ ταὐτόν μοι δοκεῖ πεπονθέναι τῇ Χαρικλείᾳ. Ταὐτὸν, ἔφην ἐγώ, νὴ τὴν Ἶσιν· ὀρθῶς μὲν καὶ οὐκ ἀπεικότως, εἴπερ καὶ ὁ τῇ πομπῇ μετ᾿ αὐτῶν διέτρετε. Ταῦτα μὲν ἡμεῖς. Ἐπεὶ δὲ τὰς κύλικας ἔδει περιάγεσθαι, προύπινεν ὁ Θεαγένης καὶ ἄκων ἑκάστῳ φιλοτησίαν. Ὡς δ᾿ εἰς ἐμὲ περιῆλθεν, ἔχω τὴν φιλοφρόνησιν, εἰπόντος, ὑποδεξάμενος δ᾿ οὐδαμῶς, ὀξύ τε καὶ διάπυρον ἐνεῖδεν, ὑστερᾶσθαι προσδοκήσας. Συνεὶς οὖν ὁ Χαρικλῆς, Οἴνου καὶ ἐδεσμάτων, εἶπε, τῶν ἐμψυχομένων ἀπέχεται. Τοῦ δὲ τὴν αἰτίαν ἐρομένου, Μεμφίτης ἐστὶν, εἶπεν, Αἰγύπτιος καὶ προφήτης τῆς Ἴσιδος. Ὁ δὲ Θεαγένης ἐς τὸν

prone to intoxication, and a drunken man to love.

XI. "At last, when he appeared overcome by languor and ill at ease, all the guests were convinced that he was unwell. Then Charicles, who had observed nothing but his changes of humour, whispered to me: 'Some evil eye has also looked upon him; he seems to me in the same state as Chariclea.' 'The very same, by Isis!' I replied; 'and not without reason; for, next after her, he was the most observed in all the procession.' When the time came for the cup to be handed round, Theagenes, although against his will, drank first to the health of all his guests. When it came to me, I thanked him for the compliment, but said I would not drink; whereupon he darted at me a look of rage, considering himself slighted. Charicles, perceiving this, said: 'This man drinks no wine and does not eat the flesh of any creature that has lived.' When Theagenes enquired the reason of this, he said: 'He is an Egyptian from Memphis, and a priest of Isis.' When Theagenes

Αἰγύπτιον καὶ τὸν προφήτην ἤκουσεν, ἡδονῆς
τ' ἀθρόον ἐνεπλήσθη καὶ, ὥσπερ οἱ θησαυρῷ
τινι προστυχόντες, ὀρθώσας αὐτὸν, ὕδωρ τ'
αἰτήσας καὶ προπιών, Ὦ σοφώτατε, εἶπεν,
ἀλλὰ σύ γε ταύτην δέχου τὴν φιλοτησίαν, ἣν
ἀπὸ τῶν ἡδίστων σοι προὔπιον· καὶ φιλίαν
ἥδ' ἡμῖν ἡ τράπεζα σπενδέσθω. Ἐσπείσθω,
ἔφην, καλὲ Θεάγενες, ἐμοὶ καὶ πάλαι οὖσαν
πρὸς σὲ καὶ ὑποδεξάμενος ἔπινον. Καὶ τότε
μὲν εἰς ταῦτ' ἔληξε τὸ συμπόσιον καὶ ἀπηλ-
λαττόμεθα ἐπ' οἶκον τὸν ἴδιον ἕκαστος, πολλά
με τοῦ Θεαγένους καὶ θερμότερα ἢ κατὰ
τὴν προϋπάρχουσαν γνῶσιν κατασπασαμένου.
Ἐπεὶ δ' ἦλθον οὗ κατηγόμην, ἄϋπνος τὰ
πρῶτα διῆγον ἐπὶ τῆς εὐνῆς, ἄνω τε καὶ κάτω
τὴν περὶ τῶν νέων φροντίδα στρέφων καὶ τοῦ
χρησμοῦ τὰ τελευταῖα τί ἄρα βούλοιτο
ἀνιχνεύων. Ἤδη δὲ μεσούσης τῆς νυκτὸς ὁρῶ
τὸν Ἀπόλλω καὶ τὴν Ἄρτεμιν, ὡς ᾤμην, (εἴγ'
ᾤμην ἀλλὰ μὴ ἀληθῶς ἑώρων) καὶ ὁ μὲν τὸν
Θεαγένην, ἡ δὲ τὴν Χαρίκλειαν ἐνεχείριζεν,
ὀνομαστί τέ με προσκαλοῦντες, Ὥρα σοι,
ἔλεγον, εἰς τὴν ἐνεγκοῦσαν ἐπανήκειν. Οὕτω

heard these words, he was suddenly filled
with a great joy, and, rising upright, like
one who has lighted upon a treasure, he
asked for water, and, having pledged me,
said: 'O wisest of men, at least take
this cup from me; it contains the liquor
that you love best, and let this table con-
clude a league of friendship between us.'
'So be it, noble Theagenes,' I answered;
'I have long been well disposed towards
you.' With these words, I took the cup
and drank.

"Then the banquet came to an end,
and each of us prepared to retire; I also
withdrew, after Theagenes had taken a
warmer farewell of me than our existing
acquaintance justified. When I reached
my lodging, I could not sleep; I could
think of nothing but Theagenes and
Chariclea and the meaning of the last
part of the oracle. When it was midnight,
I thought I saw Apollo and Diana (if
indeed I did not really see them). They
handed over to me Theagenes and Chari-
clea, and, addressing me by name, said:
'It is time for you to return to your native

γὰρ ὁ μοιρῶν ὑπαγορεύει θεσμός. Αὐτός τ'
οὖν ἔξιθι καὶ τούσδ' ὑποδεξάμενος ἄγε συνεμπό-
ρους, ἴσα καὶ παισὶ ποιούμενος καὶ παράπεμπε
ἀπὸ τῆς Αἰγυπτίων ὅποι τε καὶ ὅπως τοῖς
θεοῖς φίλον.

ΙΒ'. Ταῦτ' εἰπόντες, οἱ μὲν ἀπεχώρησαν,
ὅτι μὴ ὄναρ ἦν ἡ ὄψις ἀλλ' ὕπαρ ἐνδειξάμενοι.
Ἐγὼ δὲ τὰ μὲν ἄλλα συνίην ὡς ἑωράκειν, εἰς
τίνας δ' ἀνθρώπους ἢ εἰς τίνα γῆν παραπέμ-
πεσθαι τοὺς νέους τοῖς θεοῖς φίλον ἠπόρουν.
Καὶ ὁ Κνήμων, Ταῦτα μὲν, ἔφη, ὦ πάτερ, ἐς
ὕστερον αὐτός γ' ἐγνωκὼς ἐρεῖς πρὸς ἡμᾶς·
ἀλλὰ τίνα δὴ τρόπον ἔφασκες ἐνδεδεῖχθαί σοι
τοὺς θεοὺς, ὅτι μὴ ἐνύπνιον ἦλθον ἀλλ' ἐναργῶς
ἐφάνησαν; Ὃν τρόπον, εἶπεν, ὦ τέκνον, καὶ ὁ
σοφὸς Ὅμηρος αἰνίττεται· οἱ πολλοὶ δὲ τὸ
αἴνιγμα παρατρέχουσιν·

> Ἴχνια γὰρ μετόπισθε (ὡς ἐκεῖνός που λέγει)
> ποδῶν ἠδὲ κνημάων
> Ῥεῖ' ἔγνων ἀπιόντος. Ἀρίγνωτοί τε θεοί περ.

Ἀλλ' ἦ καὶ αὐτὸς ἔοικα τῶν πολλῶν εἶναι καὶ
τοῦτ' ἴσως ἐλέγχειν, ὦ Καλάσιρι, βουλόμενος,
τῶν ἐπῶν ἐμνημόνευσας, ὧν ἔχω τὴν μὲν ἐπιπολῆς
διάνοιαν, ὅτε περ καὶ τὴν λέξιν οἶδα ἐκδιδαχθεὶς,

land; such is the decree of Fate. Leave this country; take with you these two young people; treat them as your children, and lead them out of the land of Egypt, where and how the gods shall please.'

XII. "Having thus spoken, they disappeared, leaving me convinced that it was not a vision, but a reality. I did not doubt that what I had seen was a reality, but I did not know to what country or people I was to lead them." "This you will be able to tell me afterwards," said Cnemon; "but how can you assert that the gods really appeared to you in person, and that it was not a dream?" "In the same manner as Homer the sage, tells us in a riddle, which has passed unheeded by many. He says somewhere: 'I recognised the traces of his feet and legs, as he departed; the Gods are easily known.'" "I confess," said Cnemon, "that I myself am one of the many; perhaps you have only quoted this passage to convince me; I have never attached any deeper meaning to it than the ordinary one, which I found in it when I heard it for the first

τὴν δὲ συγκατεσπαρμένην αὐτοῖς θεολογίαν
ἠγνόηκα.

ΙΓ'. Μικρὸν οὖν ἐπιστήσας ὁ Καλάσιρις
καὶ τὸν νοῦν πρὸς τὸ μυστικώτερον ἀνακινήσας,
Θεοὶ καὶ δαίμονες, εἶπεν, ὦ Κνήμων, ἐπιφοιτῶν-
τές τ' εἰς ἡμᾶς καὶ ἀποφοιτῶντες, εἰς ἄλλο
μὲν ζῷον ἐπ' ἐλάχιστον, εἰς ἀνθρώπους δ'
ἐπιπλεῖστον αὑτοὺς εἰδοποιοῦσι, τῷ ὁμοίῳ
πλέον ἡμᾶς εἰς τὴν φαντασίαν ὑπαγόμενοι.
Τοὺς μὲν δὴ βεβήλους κἂν διαλάθοιεν, τὴν δὲ
σοφοῦ γνῶσιν οὐκ ἂν διαφύγοιεν, ἀλλὰ τοῖς
τ' ὀφθαλμοῖς ἂν γνωσθεῖεν ἀτενὲς διόλου
βλέποντες καὶ τὸ βλέφαρον οὔ ποτ' ἐπιμύοντες
καὶ τῷ βαδίσματι πλέον, οὐ κατὰ διάστησιν
τοῖν ποδοῖν οὐδὲ μετάθεσιν ἀνυομένῳ ἀλλὰ
κατά τινα ῥύμην ἀέριον καὶ ὁρμὴν ἀπαραπόδισ-
τον τεμνόντων μᾶλλον τὸ περιέχον ἢ διαπορευο-
μένων. Διὸ δὴ καὶ τὰ ἀγάλματα τῶν θεῶν
Αἰγύπτιοι τὼ πόδε ζευγνύντες καὶ ὥσπερ
ἑνοῦντες ἱστᾶσιν. Ἃ δὴ καὶ Ὅμηρος εἰδὼς, ἅτε
Αἰγύπτιος καὶ τὴν ἱερὰν παίδευσιν ἐκδιδαχθεὶς,
συμβολικῶς τοῖς ἔπεσιν ἐναπέθετο, τοῖς δυνα-
μένοις συνιέναι γνωρίζειν καταλιπών· ἐπὶ μὲν
τῆς Ἀθηνᾶς, "δεινὼ δέ οἱ ὄσσε φάανθεν" εἰπὼν,

time; I did not know what theological principles were contained in it."

XIII. After a few moments' silence and reflection, during which he seemed to be meditating upon some holy mystery, Calasiris went on to say: "The gods and spirits come to us and leave us most frequently in human form, rarely in the shape of other animals, that they may be known to our fancy in the likeness of ourselves. Although the profane do not recognise them, they cannot escape the eyes of the wise; they may be easily distinguished by their fixed eyes and eyelids, which never move, but even more readily by their walk, which does not consist, like ours, in the alternate movement of the feet; they seem to glide and fly rapidly through the air, which they cleave rather than traverse. For this reason, the Egyptian statues of the gods have the feet joined; Homer, being an Egyptian and skilled in sacred lore, also knew this, and expressed it symbolically, leaving it for those to understand him who were able. Thus, of Pallas he says, 'her terrible eyes flashed

fire'; of Neptune, 'I recognised the traces of his feet and legs, as he departed,' where the word ῥεῖ refers to his 'flowing motion,' and does not mean 'easily,' as some have wrongly interpreted it."

XIV. "O most divine Calasiris," said Cnemon, "you have initiated me into a holy mystery. But I notice that you have two or three times called Homer an Egyptian, which perhaps no one has ever heard; I do not indeed disbelieve it, but, as your statement greatly surprises me, I beg you will not leave it unexplained." "Although it is foreign to my subject, I will endeavour to satisfy you in a few words. I am quite willing that other countries should claim the honour of being the birthplace of Homer; the wise man's country is the world; but he was in fact an Egyptian, born at 'hundred-gated Thebes,' as he himself calls it; his father was Mercury, although commonly supposed to be one of the priests of that god. The truth is that, when the wife of this priest, having performed certain purificatory rites, went to sleep in the

κατὰ τὸ ἱερὸν καθευδούσῃ, συνῆλθεν ὁ δαίμων καὶ ποιεῖ τὸν Ὅμηρον, φέροντά τι τῆς ἀνομοίου μίξεως σύμβολον. Θατέρῳ γὰρ τοῖν μηροῖν αὐτόθεν ἐξ ὠδίνων, πολύ τι μῆκος τριχῶν ἐπεπόλαζεν· ὅθεν παρ' ἄλλοις τε καὶ οὐχ ἥκιστα παρ' Ἕλλησιν ἀλητεύων καὶ τὴν ποίησιν ᾄδων, τοῦ ὀνόματος ἔτυχεν, αὐτὸς μὲν τὸ ἴδιον οὐ λέγων ἀλλ' οὐδὲ πόλιν ἢ γένος ὀνομάζων, τῶν δ' ἐγνωκότων τὸ περὶ τὸ σῶμα πάθος εἰς ὄνομα καταστησάντων. Τί δὲ σκοπῶν, ὦ πάτερ, ἐσιώπα τὴν ἐνεγκοῦσαν; Ἤτοι τὸ φυγὰς εἶναι καταιδούμενος, ἐδιώχθη γὰρ ὑπὸ τοῦ πατρός, ὅτ' ἐξ ἐφήβων εἰς τοὺς ἱερωμένους ἐνεκρίνετο, ἀπὸ τοῦ κηλίδα φέρειν ἐπὶ τοῦ σώματος, νόθος εἶναι γνωρισθείς, ἢ καὶ τοῦτο σοφίᾳ κατεργαζόμενος, κἀκ τοῦ τὴν οὖσαν ἀποκρύπτειν, πᾶσαν αὐτῷ πόλιν πατρίδα μνώμενος.

ΙΕʹ. Ταῦτα μὲν εὖ τε καὶ ἀληθῶς μοι λέγειν ἔδοξας, τεκμαιρομένῳ τῆς τε ποιήσεως τοῦ

temple, the god lay with her and begat Homer, who at his birth bore traces of his illegitimate origin. When he came into the world, one of his thighs was covered with long hair. He was called Homer, because he wandered from one country to another, chiefly in Greece, singing his poems. He himself did not mention his own name, nor that of his native place, nor of his family; but those who knew of the mark on his body, gave him this name."[1] "But why, my father, did he say nothing about his native country?" "Perhaps he was ashamed of having been driven from it; for he had been banished by his father, when he presented himself for initiation on arriving at man's estate, because the mark on his body betrayed his bastard origin; or perhaps he in his shrewdness refrained from giving the name, so that, by concealing it, he might claim every city in the world as his birthplace."

XV. "What you say seems probable," said Cnemon. "When I think of his poems, which contain a mixture of the

[1] Apparently deriving it from μηρὸς, a thigh.

ἀνδρὸς τὸ ἀνειμένον τε καὶ ἡδονῇ πάσῃ σύγκρα-
τον ὡς Αἰγύπτιον, καὶ τὸ τῆς φύσεως ὑπερέχον,
ὡς οὐκ ἂν οὕτω τοὺς πάντας ὑπερβαλλόμενον,
εἰ μή τινος θείας καὶ δαιμονίας ὡς ἀληθῶς
μετέσχε καταβολῆς. Ἀλλ' ἐπεὶ τοὺς θεοὺς
Ὁμηρικῶς ἐφώρασας, ὦ Καλάσιρι, τίνα τὰ
μετὰ ταῦτα εἰπέ μοι. Τοῖς προτέροις, ὦ
Κνήμων, ὅμοια· πάλιν ἀγρυπνίαι καὶ βουλεύ-
ματα καὶ νυκτῶν φίλαι φροντίδες. Ἔχαιρον,
εὑρηκέναι τι τῶν οὐ προσδοκωμένων ἐλπίζων
καὶ εἰς τὴν ἐνεγκοῦσαν ἐπανήξειν προσδοκῶ,
ἠνιώμην δέ, ὅτι ὁ Χαρικλῆς στερήσεται τῆς
θυγατρὸς ἐννοῶν. Ἠπόρουν ὅτῳ δεήσει τρόπῳ
τοὺς νέους συναγαγεῖν καὶ κατασκευάσαι τὴν
ἔξοδον συμφρονεῖν. Τὸν δρασμὸν ἠγωνίων
ὅπως μὲν λήσομεν, ὅποι δὲ τραπῶμεν καὶ
πότερον διὰ γῆς ἢ θαλαττεύοντες καὶ ἁπλῶς
κλύδων μέ τις εἶχε φροντισμάτων, ἄϋπνός τε
τὸ λειπόμενον ἐταλαιπώρουν τῆς νυκτός.

ΙϚ'. Οὔπω δ' ἡμέρας ἀκριβῶς ὑποφαινούσης,
ἐψόφει θ' ἡ μέταυλος καί τινος ᾐσθόμην καλοῦν-

sublimity and charm of Egypt, and are transcendent in style, they would assuredly never have so excelled all others, had they not been built upon a divine foundation." "But, after you had detected the gods according to the indications given by Homer, tell me what you did next." "I remained awake as before, reflecting amid the silence of the night, so favourable to meditation. I rejoiced that I had succeeded beyond my hopes, and at the thought that I should soon return to my country; but I was deeply grieved at the idea that Charicles would be deprived of his daughter. I did not know how I should take the young people away and prepare them for their departure. I was at a loss how I was to keep our flight a secret and which way I should direct my course; whether we should travel by land or sea; I was tossed by a storm of anxious thoughts, and could not close my eyes.

XVI. "It was hardly daylight, when I heard a knocking at the door of the hall, and the voice of a young man calling.

τος παιδίου. Ἐρομένου δὲ τοῦ ὑπηρέτου τίς
ὁ κόπτων τὴν θύραν, καὶ κατὰ ποίαν τὴν χρείαν,
Ἀπάγγελλε, εἶπεν ὁ καλῶν, ὅτι Θεαγένης ὁ
Θετταλός. Ἥσθην ἀπαγγελθέντα μοι τὸν
νεανίαν καὶ εἰσκαλεῖν ἐκέλευον, ἐνδιδόναι μοι
ταὐτόματον ἀρχὴν τῶν ἐν χερσὶ βουλῶν ἡγη-
σάμενος· ἐτεκμαιρόμην γὰρ ὅτι με παρὰ τὸ
συμπόσιον Αἰγύπτιον καὶ προφήτην ἀκηκοὼς,
ἧκει συνεργὸν πρὸς τὸν ἔρωτα ληψόμενος,
πάσχων, οἶμαι, τὸ τῶν πολλῶν πάθος, οἳ τὴν
Αἰγυπτίων σοφίαν, μίαν καὶ τὴν αὐτὴν ἠπά-
τηνται, κακῶς εἰδότες. Ἡ μὲν γάρ τις ἐστὶ
δημώδης, καὶ, ὡς ἄν τις εἴποι, χαμαὶ ἐρχομένη,
εἰδώλων θεράπαινα καὶ περὶ σώματα νεκρῶν
εἰλουμένη, βοτάναις προστετηκυῖα καὶ ἐπφδαῖς
ἐπανέχουσα, πρὸς οὐδὲν ἀγαθὸν τέλος οὔτε
αὐτὴ προϊοῦσα, οὔτε τοὺς χρωμένους φέρουσα
ἀλλ᾽ αὐτὴ τὰ περὶ αὐτὴν ταπολλὰ πταίουσα,
λυπρὰ δέ τινα καὶ γλίσχρα ἔστιν ὅτε κατορ-
θοῦσα, φαντασίας τῶν μὴ ὄντων ὡς ὄντων καὶ
ἀποτυχίας τῶν ἐλπιζομένων, πράξεων ἀθεμίτων
εὑρέτις καὶ ἡδονῶν ἀκολάστων ὑπηρέτις. Ἡ
δ᾽ ἑτέρα, τέκνον, ἡ ἀληθῶς σοφία, ἧς αὐτὴ

When my servant asked who it was that knocked and what he wanted, he replied: 'Say that it is Theagenes the Thessalian.' I was delighted when I heard that it was the young man, and ordered him to be admitted, thinking that Fortune herself offered me the opportunity of carrying out my plans. I thought that, having learnt during the banquet that I was an Egyptian and a priest, he had come to ask my assistance in his love - affair, being, I imagine, of the same opinion of the majority of mankind, who erroneously believe that all Egyptians are equally learned. There is one kind of knowledge which is vulgar, and, so to speak, crawls upon the ground, the handmaid of idols ever busied with dead bodies, engrossed in the study of herbs and devoted to incantations, as useless to itself as to those who consult it, and in many ways self-contradictory; its successes are mean and sordid, chimeras in place of realities and frustrated hopes; in short, it is the inventor of abominable practices and the minister of infamous pleasures. The other kind, my son, which is truly

παρωνύμως ἐνοθεύθη, ἣν ἱερεῖς καὶ προφητικὸν
γένος ἐκ νέων ἀσκοῦμεν, ἄνω πρὸς τὰ οὐράνια
βλέπει, θεῶν συνόμιλος καὶ φύσεως κρειττόνων
μέτοχος, ἄστρων κίνησιν ἐρευνῶσα καὶ μελλόν-
των πρόγνωσιν κερδαίνουσα· τῶν μὲν γηΐνων
τούτων κακῶν ἀποστατοῦσα, πάντα δὲ πρὸς
τὸ καλὸν καὶ τὸ ὠφέλιμον ἀνθρώποις ἐπιτη-
δεύουσα, δι' ἣν κἀγὼ τῆς ἐνεγκούσης εἰς καιρὸν
ἐξέστην, εἴ πῃ καθὼς καὶ πρότερόν σοι διῆλθον
τὰ προρρηθέντα μοι παρ' αὐτῆς καὶ τὸν τῶν
ἐμῶν παίδων κατ' ἀλλήλων πόλεμον περιγρά-
ψαιμι. Ταῦτα μὲν οὖν θεοῖς τε τοῖς ἄλλοις
καὶ μοίραις ἐπιτετράφθω οἳ τοῦ ποιεῖν τε καὶ
μὴ τὸ κράτος ἔχουσιν, οἳ καὶ τὴν φυγήν μοι
τὴν ἐκ τῆς ἐνεγκούσης οὐ διὰ ταῦτα πλέον ὡς
ἔοικεν ἢ τὴν Χαρικλείας εὕρεσιν ἐπέβαλον.
Καὶ τοῦτο μὲν ὅπως, εἴσῃ τοῖς ἑξῆς.

ΙΖ'. Τὸν δὲ Θεαγένην ἐπειδήπερ εἰσῆλθεν
ἀσπασάμενον ἀμειψάμενος, ἐμαυτοῦ τε πλησίον
ἐπὶ τῆς εὐνῆς ἐκάθιζον καὶ Τί χρέος ὄρθριόν σε

wisdom, of which the former is the bastard daughter, is practised by us priests and ministers of religion from our earliest days. It lifts its gaze aloft to heavenly things, holds converse with the gods, and participates in the higher nature, investigating the movements of the heavenly bodies, and thence acquiring a knowledge of the future; far removed from all the ills which afflict humanity, it studies to arrange everything with a view to what is good and profitable for mankind. It was this wisdom that exiled me from my country for a time, to avoid, if possible, the evils which it foretold to me and the fratricidal quarrel of my sons. But let the Gods and the Fates decide; the issue rests with them. It was not so much, I believe, in order to spare my eyes this dreadful sight, as to make me discover Chariclea, that they have banished me from my native land, as you will learn from the sequel.

XVII. "When Theagenes had entered my room, after mutual salutations, I made him sit down upon my bed, and asked him what pressing business had brought him to

ἄγει παρ' ἡμᾶς ἠρώτων. Ὁ δὲ τὸ πρόσωπον ἐπιπολὺ καταψήσας, Ἀγωνιῶ μὲν, ἔφη, περὶ τοῦ παντὸς, ἐρυθριῶ δ' ἐκφαίνειν· καὶ ἐσιώπησεν. Ἔγνων οὖν καιρὸν εἶναι τερατεύεσθαι πρὸς αὐτὸν καὶ μαντεύεσθαι δῆθεν, ἅπερ ἐγίγνωσκον. Ἱλαρώτερον οὖν αὐτῷ προσβλέψας, Εἰ καὶ αὐτὸς λέγειν ὀκνεῖς, ἔφην, ἀλλὰ τῇ γ' ἡμετέρᾳ σοφίᾳ καὶ θεοῖς οὐδὲν ἄγνωστον. Καὶ ἐπιστήσας ὀλίγον καὶ ψήφους τινὰς οὐδὲν καταριθμούσας ἐπὶ δακτύλων συνθεὶς, τήν τε κόμην διασείσας καὶ τοὺς κατόχους μιμούμενος, Ἐρᾷς, εἶπον, ὦ τέκνον. Ἀνήλατο πρὸς τὴν μαντείαν. Ὡς δ' ὅτι καὶ Χαρικλείας προσέθηκα, τοῦτ' ἐκεῖνο θεοκλυτεῖν με νομίσας μικροῦ μὲν καὶ προσεκύνει πεσὼν, ἐμοῦ δ' ἐπέχοντος, ἐφίλει πολλὰ τὴν κεφαλὴν προσελθὼν, τοῖς τε θεοῖς ὡμολόγει χάριν, οὐκ ἐσφαλμένος, ὡς ἔλεγεν, ὧν προσεδόκησε, σωτῆρά τέ με γενέσθαι παρεκάλει· μὴ γὰρ ἂν περισωθῆναι, βοηθείας καὶ ταύτης ταχείας ἀποτυχόντα· τοσοῦτον αὐτῷ τὸ κακὸν

me so early. Having passed his hand
several times over his face, he replied:
'My happiness is at stake, but I am
ashamed to tell you the reason,' and then
he was silent. I perceived that it was
time for me to act the wizard, and to
pretend to divine what I already knew.
I looked at him kindly and said: 'Although
you are afraid to speak, nothing can be
concealed from the Gods and our wisdom.'
Then, after a few moments' silence, arrang-
ing some little pebbles in my hand, as if
counting, although I had nothing to count,
I shook my locks, like those possessed by
prophetic frenzy, and said: 'My son, you
are in love.' At these prophetic words,
he started; and, when I added the name
of Chariclea, thinking that my knowledge
was divinely inspired, he was ready to
throw himself at my feet and worship
me. When I restrained him, he embraced
me several times, and thanked Heaven
that he had not been deceived in his
hopes, and entreated me to save him,
declaring that he could not live without
speedy assistance; that the violence of

ἐνσκῆψαι καὶ οὕτως ὑπὸ τοῦ πόθου φλέγεσθαι, πρῶτον καὶ ταῦτα πειρώμενον ἔρωτος. Ὁμιλίας γὰρ ἔτι γυναικὸς ἀπείρατος εἶναι διετείνετο, πολλὰ διομνύμενος· ἀεὶ γὰρ διαπτῦσαι πάσης καὶ γάμον αὐτὸν καὶ ἔρωτας, εἴ τινος ἀκούσειεν, ἕως τὸ Χαρικλείας αὐτὸν ἤλεγξε κάλλος ὅτι μὴ φύσει καρτερικὸς ἦν, ἀλλ' ἀξιεράστου γυναικὸς εἰς τὴν παρελθοῦσαν ἀθέατος. Καὶ ταῦτα λέγων ἐδάκρυεν, ὥσπερ ὅτι πρὸς βίαν ἥττηται κόρης ἐνδεικνύμενος. Ἀνελάμβανον οὖν αὐτὸν καὶ Θάρσει, ἔλεγον, ἐπειδήπερ ἅπαξ καταπέφευγας ἐφ' ἡμᾶς. Οὐχ οὕτως ἐκείνη κρείττων ἔσται τῆς ἡμετέρας σοφίας. Ἔστι μὲν αὐστηροτέρα καὶ κατενεχθῆναι πρὸς ἔρωτα δύσμαχος, Ἀφροδίτην καὶ γάμον ἀτιμάζουσα καὶ μέχρις ὀνόματος· ἀλλὰ διὰ σὲ πάντα κινητέον· τέχνη καὶ φύσιν οἶδε βιάζεσθαι. Μόνον εὔθυμον εἶναι καὶ ὑφηγουμένῳ τὰ δέοντα πείθεσθαι πράττειν. Ἐπηγγείλατο ἅπαντα ποιήσειν, ὡς ἂν ἐγὼ προστάττω, κἂν εἰ ξιφῶν ἐπιβαίνειν κελεύοιμι.

his affliction and the ardour of the passion by which his heart, which had never felt the fire of love, was consumed, required prompt treatment. He swore that he had never known a woman, that he had always spurned them and despised the idea of love and marriage, until Chariclea's beauty had proved to him that he was naturally weak, but that he had never until then beheld a woman worthy of his love. At the same time he shed tears, to show that he had been overcome by a woman against his will. I tried to comfort and console him, saying: 'Do not despair, since you have had recourse to me; she will not be able to prevail against my wisdom. It is true that her morals are austere, and that it may be a hard task to bring her to love, since she hates even the very name of Venus and marriage; but for your sake I will do all I can; art can conquer nature; only do not lose courage, and be ready to obey my commands implicitly.' He promised to follow my instructions, even though I should bid him walk over naked swords.

ΙΗ΄. Λιπαροῦντος δὴ περὶ τούτων καὶ μισθὸν ἄπασαν ὑπισχνουμένου τὴν οὐσίαν, ἥκων τις παρὰ τοῦ Χαρικλέους, Δεῖταί σου Χαρικλῆς, ἔλεγεν, ἀφικέσθαι παρ' αὐτόν· ἔστι δὲ πλησίον ἐνταῦθ' ἐν τῷ Ἀπολλωνίῳ καὶ ὕμνον ἀποθύει τῷ θεῷ, τεταραγμένος τι κατὰ τοὺς ὕπνους. Ἐξανίσταμαι παραχρῆμα καὶ τὸν Θεαγένην ἀποπέμψας ἐπὶ τὸν νεὼν ἀφικόμενος, ἐπὶ θώκου τινὸς καταλαμβάνω τὸν Χαρικλέα καθήμενον, ἄγαν περίλυπον καὶ συνεχῶς ὑποστένοντα. Προσελθὼν οὖν, Τί σύννους καὶ σκυθρωπὸς εἶ, ἠρώτων. Ὁ δέ, Τί γὰρ οὐ μέλλω, φησίν, ὀνειράτων τέ με διαταραξάντων καὶ τῆς θυγατρὸς, ὡς ἐπυθόμην, ἀηδέστερον διατεθείσης καὶ τὴν νύκτα πᾶσαν ἄϋπνον διαγαγούσης; ἐμὲ δὲ λυπεῖ μὲν καὶ ἄλλως οὐχ ὑγιαίνουσα, πλέον δ' ὅτι τῆς κυρίας τοῦ ἀγῶνος εἰς τὴν ἑξῆς ἐνεστηκυίας, εἰς ἣν τοῖς ὁπλίταις δρομεῦσι δᾷδας ἀναφαίνειν καὶ βραβεύειν τὴν ζάκορον νόμιμον, δυοῖν θάτερον ἀνάγκη ἢ ταύτην ἀπολειπομένην λυμαίνεσθαι τὸ πάτριον, ἢ καὶ ἄκουσαν ἀφικνουμένην, ἐπιτρίβεσθαι χαλεπώ-

XVIII. "While he thus entreated me and promised me his whole fortune as a reward, a messenger came from Charicles. 'Charicles begs you will go to him,' said he; 'he is here, hard by, in the temple of Apollo, where he is chanting a hymn to appease the god, having been alarmed by a dream.' I immediately got up, dismissed Theagenes, and hurried to the temple, where I found Charicles sitting in a chair, overwhelmed with grief, and sighing. I went up to him and asked him why he was so gloomy and sorrowful. He replied: 'How could I be otherwise? I have had a fearful dream; and I have heard that my daughter is ill, and that she has not closed her eyes all night. Her sickness is the more grievous to me, since to-morrow is the day on which the priestess of Diana, in accordance with the laws, ought to present a torch to the armed runners and bestow upon them the prize of victory. Thus, one of two things must happen; either Chariclea will violate established custom by absenting herself, or, if she takes part in the ceremony against

τερον. Ὥστ᾽, εἰ καὶ μὴ πρότερον, ἀλλὰ νῦν γ᾽ ἐπαρκῶν καί τινα προσάγων ἴασιν, δικαίως μὲν ἂν πρὸς ἡμᾶς καὶ φιλίαν τὴν ἡμετέραν, εὐσεβῶς δὲ πρὸς τὸ θεῖον ποιοίης. Οἶδα ὡς οὐδὲν ἐργῶδες βουλομένῳ σοι τὸ πρᾶγμα, βασκανίαν, ὡς αὐτὸς ἔφης, ἰάσασθαι· προφήταις μὲν γὰρ καὶ τὰ μέγιστα κατορθοῦν οὐκ ἀδύνατον. Ὡμολόγουν ἠμεληκέναι, σοφιστεύων καὶ πρὸς ἐκεῖνον καὶ τὴν παροῦσαν ἐνδοῦναι παρεκάλουν, ἔχειν γάρ τι συνθεῖναι πρὸς τὴν ἴασιν. Τὸ δὲ νυνὶ παρὰ τὴν κόρην ἴωμεν, ἔφην, ἐπισκεψόμενοί τ᾽ ἀκριβέστερον καὶ παραμυθησόμενοι πρὸς ὅσον δυνατόν. Ἅμα δὲ, ὦ Χαρίκλεις, βούλομαί σε καὶ λόγους τινὰς ὑπὲρ ἐμοῦ κινῆσαι πρὸς τὴν παῖδα καὶ γνωριμώτερον ἀποφῆναι παρακαταθέμενον, ὅπως ἂν οἰκειότερον ἔχουσα πρός με θαρραλεώτερον ἰώμενον προσίηται. Γιγνέσθω ταῦτα, ἔφη, καὶ ἀπίωμεν.

ΙΘ΄. Ἐπειδὴ οὖν ἐπέστημεν τῇ Χαρικλείᾳ τὰ μὲν πολλὰ τί ἄν τις λέγοι. Δεδούλωτο μὲν γὰρ ὁλοσχερῶς τῷ πάθει καὶ τὴν παρειὰν ἤδη τὸ ἄνθος ἔφευγε καὶ τὸ φλέγον τοῦ βλέμ-

her wish, she will aggravate her malady. Wherefore, even if it could not be done before, assist her and apply some remedy; justice, friendship, and the respect due to the gods demand this from you. I know that it is easy for you, as you say yourself, to cure the charm of an evil eye, if you will; nothing is too difficult for the priests of your country to perform.' I confessed that I had been somewhat remiss, in order to mislead him, and asked him to give me a day to prepare some medicine for her. 'For the present,' I said, 'let us go and see your daughter, examine her condition, and comfort her as best we can. At the same time, I wish you would say something about me to the girl, and make her better acquainted with me; so that, becoming more familiar, she may have greater confidence in my power to cure her.' 'Be it so,' he replied; 'let us go.'

XIX. "I need not describe the condition in which we found Chariclea. Her affliction had overwhelmed her; the roses had faded from her cheeks, and the fire

ματος καθάπερ ὕδασιν ἔφκει τοῖς δάκρυσιν
ἀποσβεννυμένῳ. Κατέστελλε δ᾽ οὖν ὅμως
αὐτὴν, ἐπειδήπερ ἡμᾶς ἐθεάσατο καὶ πρὸς τὸ
σύνηθες βλέμμα καὶ φθέγμα παντοίως ἐπα-
νάγειν ἐβιάζετο. Περιβαλὼν δ᾽ αὐτὴν ὁ Χαρι-
κλῆς καὶ μυρία καταφιλήσας καὶ θεραπείας
οὐδὲν ἀπολιπὼν, Ὦ θυγάτριον, ὦ τέκνον,
ἔλεγεν, ἐμὲ τὸν πατέρα κρύπτεις ὃ πάσχεις;
καὶ βασκανίαν ὑποστᾶσα σιωπᾷς ὥσπερ ἀδι-
κοῦσα καὶ οὐκ ἠδικημένη παρὰ τῶν κακῶς
ἰδόντων σε ὀφθαλμῶν; Ἀλλὰ θάρσει. Παρα-
κέκληται Καλάσιρις ὁ σοφος, ἴασίν τινά σοι
πορίσασθαι. Δινατὸς δ᾽ ἀνὴρ, ἄριστος [ὢν]
εἴπερ τις ἄλλος τὴν θείαν τέχνην, ἅτε προφητι-
κὸς τὸν βίον καὶ ἱεροῖς ἐκ παίδων ἀνακείμενος
καὶ τὸ μεῖζον εἰς προσθήκην ἡμῖν ἐς τὰ μάλιστα
φίλος. Ὥστ᾽ εἰκότα ἂν ποιοίης, εἰ προσδέχοιό
τ᾽ ἀκωλύτως, ἐπάδειν τ᾽ ἢ καὶ ἄλλως ἰᾶσθαι
βουλομένῳ σαυτὴν παρέχοις, οὐδ᾽ ἄλλως οὖσα
πρὸς τὸ λόγιον γένος ἀπρόσμικτος. Ἐσιώπα
μὲν, ἐπένευσε δ᾽ οὖν ἡ Χαρίκλεια, καθάπερ
ἀσμένη τὴν ἀπ᾽ ἐμοῦ συμβουλὴν προσιεμένη.
Καὶ τότε μὲν ἐπὶ τούτοις ἀπηλλάγημεν,
ὑπομνήσαντός με τοῦ Χαρικλέους καὶ ὧν πρό-

of her eyes had been quenched by the constant flow of tears. However, when she saw us, she composed herself, and endeavoured to assume her ordinary voice and expression. Charicles, having kissed and fondled her, said: 'O my daughter, will you not tell your father what ails, you? Now that an evil eye has fascinated you, do you keep silence, as if you had done wrong, and had not received an injury from the eyes that have looked upon you so balefully? But, be of good cheer. I have entreated the wise Calasiris to find some means of curing you; he can do so, for he excels all other men in divine knowledge, being a priest, and, what is more, our especial friend. Wherefore you will do well to receive him with confidence; put yourself in his hands, whether he wishes to employ incantations or any other means of healing you. Besides, you are not averse to the society of the learned.' Chariclea made no reply, but nodded her head, in token that she would be glad to listen to my advice. We then left her. Charicles reminded me of my promise that I would

23

τερον παρεκάλεσεν ἐπιμεληθῆναι καὶ φροντίζειν,
εἴ πῃ τῇ Χαρικλείᾳ δυναίμην ἔφεσίν τινα γάμων
καὶ ἀνδρῶν ἐμποιῆσαι. Ἀπέπεμπον οὖν εὔθυ-
μον, οὐκ εἰς μακρὰν ἀνυσθήσεσθαι αὐτῷ τὴν
βούλησιν ἐπαγγειλάμενος.

do my best to find a way to arouse in Chariclea an inclination to men and marriage. I gave him my word that his wish would soon be satisfied, and sent him on his way rejoicing.

BIBLIOGRAPHY

1 ʻΗλιοδώρου Αἰθιοπικῆς ἱστορίας βιβλία δέκα,
edited by V. Obsopaeus. In officina J.
Hervagii. Basileae, 1534, 4to.

2 ʻΗλιοδώρου Αἰθιοπικῶν βιβλία δέκα, cum
animadversionibus J. Bourdelotii, ad vett.
edd. recensuit J. P. Schmidius. Lipsiae,
1772.

3 ʻΗλιοδώρου Αἰθιοπικῶν βιβλία δέκα, edited by
Δ. Κοραῆς (Coray). ʼΕν Παρισίοις, 1804.

4 Παράφρασις τῶν κατὰ Θεαγένην καὶ Χαρίκλειαν
Αἰθιοπικῶν. Σμύρνῃ, 1843.

5 ʻΗλιοδώρου Αἰθιοπικῶν βιβλία δέκα. Colla-
tione MSS. Bibliothecae Palatinae et aliorum,
emendati et multis in locis aucti, H. Com-
melini Opera (S. Warschewiczki interprete),
Gr. et Lat. Apud H. Commelinum (Heidel-
berg), 1596, 8vo.

6 Ib. Ad fidem MSS. ab H. Commelino
emendati, multis in locis aucti, ejusdemque
notis illustrati, Gr. et Lat. Lugduni, 1611.

7 Ib. (S. Warschewiczki interprete) J. Bourde-
lotius emendavit, supplevit, ac libros decem
animadversionum adjecit, Gr. et Lat. Apud
P. L. Febvrier. Lutetiae Parisiorum, 1619,
8vo.

8 Ib. Collatione MSS. Bibliothecae Palatinae
et aliorum emendati et aucti cura D. Parei,
Gr. et Lat. Francofurti, 1631.

9 C. W. Mitscherlich. Scriptores Erotici Graeci,
1792, 8vo.

10 G. A. Hirschig, Ἐρωτικῶν Λόγων Συγγραφεῖς:
Erotici Scriptores Graeci. Paris (Didot),
1856.

11 Heliodori Aethiopicae historiae libri decem,
nunc primum e Graeco sermone in Latinum
translati, S. Warschewiczki interprete. Adjec-
tum P. Melancthonis de ipso autore et hac
ejusdem conversione judicium. Basileae,
1552.

12 Heliodorus, translated from the Greek by S.
Warschewiczki, Lugduni Batavorum, 1637.

13 Heliodori Aethiopicorum libri decem ab I.
Bekkero recogniti. Lipsiae, 1855. (Part of
the Bibliotheca Scriptorum Graecorum et
Romanorum Teubneriana.)

14 Martini Crusii Aethiopicae Heliodori historiae
epitome, cum observationibus ejusdem.
Francofurti, 1584.

15 An Aethiopian Historie, written in Greek by Heliodorus, no less wittie than pleasaunt. Englished by T. Underdowne, and newly corrected and augmented with divers and sundry additions by the said Authour. *Black Letter*. Imprinted for F. Coldocke. London, 1587, 4to.

16 Ib. Printed for W. Cotton. London, 1606, 4to.

17 Another edition. Heliodorus, his Aethiopian History, done out of Greeke by T. Underdowne and compared by the editor, W. Barret, with other translations in divers languages for W. Barret. London, 1622, 4to.

18 The beginning of Heliodorus, his Aethiopical History in Hexameters. 1591, 4to.

19 The famous Historie of Heliodorus, amplified, augmented, and delivered paraphrastically in verse, by W. Lisle. London, 1638.

20 The Triumphs of Love and Constancy, a romance, containing the heroic amours of Theagenes and Chariclea. The first five books rendered by a person of quality, the last five by N. Tate. London, 1687.

21 The Adventures of Theagenes and Chariclea, 2 vols. London, 1717.

22 The Adventures of Theagenes and Chariclea, a romance translated from the Greek, 2 vols. London, 1789.

23 The Ethiopics, or Adventures of Theagenes and Chariclea, translated from the Greek, with notes by R. Smith. (Bohn's Classical Library.)

24 De Wonderlyke Liefde gefallen van Theagenes en Chariclea . . . In zuyver Nederduytsch overgebracht door J. Gentil, s' Gravenhaage, 1726.

25 M. v. Velden Calasires Sterfdagh. Ghenomen uyt de Historie van Heliodorus belaughende de kuysche Vryagie van Theagenes ende Chariclea (in 6 acts and in verse). Amstelredam, 1631.

26 L'Histoire Aethiopique de Heliodorus contenant dix livres traitant des loyales et pudiques amours de Theagenes Thessalien et Chariclea Aethiopienne. Nouvellement traduite de Grec en Français by J. Amyot, Bishop of Auxerre. Paris, 1547, fol. E. Groulleau.

27 Ib., ff. 296, Catherine Fontanel. Lyon, 1559.

28 Ib., Lyon, 1559, 16mo.

29 Ib., Paris, 1559, fol.

30 Ib., Paris, ff. 320; 1560, 12mo.

31 Ib., Lyon, 1579, 16mo.

32 Ib., Rouen, 1596, 16mo, T. Mallard.

33 An Aethiopian History written in Greek, Englished by Thomas Underdowne, anno

1587, with introduction by Charles Whibley. The series of Tudor Translations, Vol. V., 1892.

34 Histoire Éthiopique d'Heliodore . . . traduction d'Amyot, revue et corrigée par M. Trognon, avec des notes de MM. Coray, etc., Paris, 1822. (Vol. II. of the Collection des Romanciers Grecs et Latins.)

35 Amours de Théagenes et Chariclée, traduction de J. Amyot, 1822. (Collection des Romans Grecs, Vols. II.-V.)

36 Les Adventures Amoureuse [*sic*] de Théagenes et Chariclée sommairement descrite (in verse) et representée par figures. Dedié Pierre Vallet, 1613, 4to.

37 Les chastes et loyales Amours de Théagène et Chariclée, reduites du Grec de l'histoire d'Heliodore en huict poëmes dragmatiques ou théâtres consécutifs, par A. Hardy, Paris, 1623.

38 Les Amours de Théagène et Chariclée. Historie Éthiopique d'Heliodore. Traduction nouvelle (by J. de Montlyard). S. Thiboust, Paris, 1623.

39 Ib. Seconde édition, Paris, 1626.

40 Amours de Théagènes et Chariclée, historie Éthiopique, translated from the Greek by L. F. de Fontenu. Coustelier, Paris, 1743.

41 Ib., 1782.

42 Ib., Bibliothèque universelle des dames, 1785 : Romans, tom. 1-3.

43 Les Éthiopiennes d'Heliodore, ou, Théagène et Chariclée, traduction de Quenneville, revue par L. Humbert, 1880.

44 Théagène et Chariclée, translated by C. Zevort, 1856.

45 Heliodorus, oder eine sehr schöne liebliche nützliche Historie von Theagene und Chariclia, erstlich griechisch beschriben nachmahlen in Latin und Frantzösisch, und jetzo auff das neuw in Teutsche Spraach mit fleiss übersetzt (by T. sub Cruce), Strassburg, 1624.

46 Aethiopische Liebes und Helden-Geschichte aus dem Griechischen übersetzt durch M. C[hristian] W[ilhelm] A[gricola], Jena, 1750.

47 Theagenes und Chariclea, eine Aethiopische Geschichte in zehn Büchern, aus den Griechischen des Heliodorus übersetzt (by J. N. Meinhard), Leipzig, 1767.

48 Historia Etiopica de los amores de Teagenes y Cariclea. Añadida la vida del autor, y una tabla de sentencias, etc. (edited by P. P. Bogia). A. Martin, Madrid, 1615.

49 Historia de Heliodoro delle cose Ethiopiche. Nella quale fra diversi, compassionevoli avenimenti di due amanti, si contengono abbattimenti, descrittioni de paesi e molte altre cose,

tradotta dalla lingua Greca nella Thoscana da L. Ghini, Vinegia, 1556.

50 Ib., Gioliti, Venezia, 1587.

51 Ib., Vinegia, 1611.

52 Historia Ethiopica . . . trasladada de Frances en vulgar Castellano por un segreto amigo de su patria [F. de Mena] y corrigida segun el Griego por el mismo, Anvers, 1554.

53 La nueva Cariclea, ó nueva traduccion de la novela de Theagenes y Chariclea, que con titulo de Historia Etiopia escrivió . . . Heliodoro [translated by] F. M. de Castillejo, Madrid, 1722.

54 La historia de los dos leales amantes Theagenes y Chariclea. Trasladada agora de nuevo de Latin en Romance por Ferñado de Mena, Alcala de Henares, 1587.

Printed in Great Britain
by Amazon